The Catacomb

Also by Brian Glanville

Novels
The Reluctant Dictator
Henry Sows the Wind
Along the Arno
The Bankrupts
After Rome, Africa
Diamond
The Rise of Gerry Logan
A Second Home
A Roman Marriage
The Artist Type
The Olympian
A Cry of Crickets
The Financiers
The Comic
The Dying of the Light
Never Look Back
Kissing America

Story Collections
A Bad Streak
The Director's Wife
The King of Hackney Marshes
The Thing He Loves
Love Is Not Love

Juvenile Novels
Goalkeepers Are Different
Target Man

Sports books
The Footballer's Companion
Soccer Nemesis
Soccer: A Panorama
History of the World Cup
People In Sport
The Joy of Football

The Catacomb

Brian Glanville

Hodder & Stoughton
LONDON SYDNEY AUCKLAND TORONTO

British Library Cataloguing in Publication Data
Glanville, Brian
  The catacomb.
  I. Title
  823'.914[F]   PR6057.L28

  ISBN 0 340 42327 7

Hodder and Stoughton Editorial Office: 47 Bedford Square, London WC1B 3DP.

For Pam

I

In the mornings, now, I wake up, reach out – and touch nothing. Then I am awake with the pain. I may even have been dreaming of her, but in the dream, however strange, however distressing, there is no direct awareness that she is dead, though I suppose a Freudian would find indications, symbols. So I do not dream about her dying. I do not dream about the bomb going off, the exploding train, the carriage blown to pieces as it speeds through Tuscany, beneath those ghost-green, olive-covered hills.

Of all places for it to happen; a place where she and I would feel least at risk, most at home. Her country; almost my adopted country. And Hawkwood's country, I suppose, for what it's worth; but then, in Italy, what wasn't? My country, though, in a way that Oxford had never quite become her city. She was too vivid for it and too vital. It amused her. 'All those odd, obsessional men. Ma che capiscono? What do they understand? Books, libraries, manuscripts. They're old before they're even middle-aged. And you! What would happen to you, if it weren't for me?'

Ah, yes, what? And what will happen to me now, without her? Where will I go? Back into the book stacks? Hiding in reading rooms, buried in biblioteche? She had come to lectures, and she had laughed. Not my lectures, the older specialists'. The professors. The acknowledged experts on the Renaissance, the Medici, the Middle Ages, the Crusades, the condottieri. Ma che capiscono? And what do *I* understand, come to that? 'Oh, much more, much more!' she would exclaim. 'While you write about your Hawkwood, I'll write my book. *Il Dramma dello Storico*, The Historian's Predicament.'

Just a joke, of course, and she will never write it, now. Usually when I woke, when I touched her, we would make love. She loved making love. She was so sensuous; yet so humorous. Even in love; there was an irony to it. The sudden smiles, the looks. As if love might be a joke, as well, a

7

marvellous joke shared between us. We had so many of them. Oxford was a joke. Hawkwood was a joke. My monograph on Hawkwood. The picture of Hawkwood that hangs over my desk, if it *is* Hawkwood. The one in the Duomo that Uccello rushed off, all those years after Hawkwood had died, poor old man, when people had forgotten what he looked like and there was nothing to remind Uccello but that perfunctory sculpture, just as there is nothing left, now, in the little church in Essex, where he came from. No tomb, no effigy, no trace.

How she would laugh, Simonetta, at me, at the painting, at the motto I had put above it, picked out in gold lettering, painted for me in Florence: L'INGLESE ITALIANATO È IL DIAVOLO INCARNATO. The Italianised Englishman is the devil incarnate.

'Ma davvero?' she would laugh. 'Are *you* the devil incarnate? You're English, you're Italianised . . .' and then she'd look at me, pretending to assess me. 'No, I don't think so. Non mi pare.' The implication being that I would like to be, like to be like Hawkwood, that I was living his life, fighting his campaigns. 'How brave you are in the library!' And I would laugh. I knew it was not so. What *was* true was that he fascinated me, he obsessed me, he tantalised and baffled me. There were so many mysteries in his life, so many enigmas; how could one make the leap across the past, the whole six hundred years, and *be* a mediaeval man, even if one wanted to? Especially when there were so many gaps, obscurities, ambiguities? Il dramma dello storico.

But now she was dead, now she had died for nothing, I knew that I *must* change, or go under. It was more than just anger and hatred and revenge. I felt these too, unbearably at times, above all when I stood there at her funeral, out in the sunshine, in that ugly little churchyard on the edge of Florence, looking at her coffin, in which there was next to nothing of her, the merest relics; she had been blown to pieces with the rest of them. Trying not to weep, wanting to come out with a great, shuddering cry of rage and agony. L'inglese italianato. I wanted to sob like an Italian, but my damned English restraint bottled it all up inside. Pressure against pressure, one blocking the other, so that they cancelled out. I stood dumb, immobilised. The priest's mouth moved, but I could scarcely hear him, there might have been plate glass between us.

Her mother wept, under her black veil. Her father stood

like stone. There was nothing to be done, and so much that I wanted to do. But above all, as the days dragged past, the rage diminished, yet my pain and loss remained, I wanted to *know*. All my aggression, I could see now, had gone into my knowing, my discovering. Or trying to. Trying to discover what made Hawkwood 'tick', so much so that at times silly titles for my monograph swam into my head, like headlines from cheap newspapers. 'Hawkwood: the Mind of a Mercenary.' 'John Hawkwood: Gentleman Gangster.' Or, sillier still, 'Hawkwood: The Mercenary is the Message.' I had to do something; something radical. I could not live with the random savagery of what had happened.

Simonetta used to say that I was romantic about Italy, 'like all the English', but I do not think that was right. How can you study mediaeval Italy, the plotting and the poisoning, the cruelty and the conspiracy, how – coming to modern times – can you consider Mussolini, Fascism, the squadristi, Abyssinia, and still see Italy as paradise, a kind of chimerical un-England? Yet what had happened seemed quite new to me, a new sort of nihilism, a horrible impersonal force, de-humanised, quite ready to destroy the innocent, not even bothering to blackguard them: provided its purpose was served. If I could comprehend that force, if I could isolate it and identify it, maybe I could bear to live again.

It was an inchoate idea. I never spoke of it to anybody. But I saw it as my solitary hope, something I *could* do, an extension of me, whereas revenge was just illusory, would eat away at me. I could not bring her back, nothing could bring her back. Revenge was sterile, a relic of the Middle Ages, something preserved by people like the Mafia; anachronisms. Something . . . un-English. Even Hawkwood, l'inglese italianato, had seemed to have no taste for revenge. Today's enemy might be tomorrow's friend; he was a good mercenary. Studying his life, poring through his letters, I had found no sign of vendetta, at a time when revenge was endemic.

So when the Master sent for me and said that I could have time off, could go away – three months, six months, more if necessary – I told him I was grateful to him, but I did not want it. He answered that he understood, standing there in his beautiful study with its oak panelling, its leaded windows, its glorious green view across the quad, but he did not understand. He thought I meant I would lose myself in work; or try to. But what I intended was a different kind of work. Not a sitting in libraries, even if they were Italian libraries, not a burrowing through records, but something contemporary and dynamic. It was too personal and private to explain. I knew he would have smiled his bland smile, fluted his comprehension and approval, but I did not need them. Any more, kind though they were, than I had needed his condolences. He was a diplomat, a careerist – he had *been* a diplomat – I did not dislike him for that, like some of the more radical dons, but it made me unwilling to disclose myself.

'Italy soothes, Italy heals,' he intoned, smooth words from his smooth, round face, the product of years of good eating, 'I know it so well, myself.' Then, suddenly remembering what had happened, he changed quickly, almost imperceptibly, to 'despite your horrifying loss'.

No, I thought, *because* of my horrifying loss; that is why I am going. But again, there was no use trying to explain to him.

'And your Hawkstone?' he asked. 'You will go on? I *hope* you will go on.'

'Hawkwood,' I said, and he gave me a neat little nod, the ghost of an apology. 'I've lived with him too long to give him up.'

'Good, good,' he said. 'We're all anxious for the finished product. I think it's going to be a notable contribution.'

To what, I wondered. To Italian scholarship, the reputation of the college, to my bank account? But heads of colleges are like ambassadors; they float above the conflict, doing the best for their institution, wheeling and dealing, tacking and trimming, cutting and pruning when they have to. I suppose I envied the Master his Italy; all sunshine and culture and staying with the great and the good. A weekend with Harold Acton, a gilded tour for the British Council, a sojourn in the embassy in Rome, perhaps, who knows, even a private audience with the Pope?

'No wonder so many of us love Italy,' he was intoning. Do I love Italy? I loved my wife, who was killed in Italy, by Italians. I presume they were Italians.

When I left the Master, and his synthetic sympathy, I went back to our cottage. *My* cottage, I suppose I must call it now.

My incredibly English cottage in its utterly English village. What a privileged life we had had, I tell myself; commuting from utter England to utter Italy, having the best of both. Now I do not want to live here, here in Ransley, not just because of the memories, but because of the beauty and the peace, the lacerating, idyllic, rural tranquillity. The beams, the snug, low ceilings, the polished floors, the cosy little rooms, the hearth, the chintz, the rickety wooden window frames. It would be a haven and a prison. Too much silence and solitude. Too much time to think myself to death.

The cottage was so English, yet it was full of her. Her clothes, her pictures, her ornaments, her presence. There was no escape from her, and the awareness of her. No escape from the sense of loss. There had been something so wonderfully piquant about the very contrast between her and the house. To see her coming down the narrow, rustic wooden stairs. To see her sitting opposite me in a deep, chintzed armchair by the fire, while the flames gave radiance to her face. Such an Italian face. Such a Florentine face. With those blue eyes, that smooth, olive skin, that small, straight, narrow nose. A Primavera: how she hated to be told that!

'Macchè Primavera! Sei cretino! English romanticism! Every Florentine woman has to be a Botticelli! A prototype!'

In the village, she had been an exotic curiosity. People stood at their gates to look at her, whispered to each other as she went past; past the thick green vegetable gardens and the dogs barking through the palings, past the white-washed walls and the platoons of sunflowers. The village had not been gentrified yet, though Oxford was moving in. Academic Oxford. There was a philosophy don from Keble and his wife just down the road from us, and an economist from Balliol in the little High Street. We nodded when we met, but did not see each other much. Simonetta frightened them, I think; she was too vital and vibrant. Their wives were overwhelmed by her. Academics' wives, discreet and strangulated. 'Public mice,' she used to call them. 'You should have married one,' she told me once. 'They would have been better; for your career. Not me. I'll be a disadvantage to you.'

'That's fair enough,' I said. 'You've given your career up for me. I'll ruin mine for you!'

She was a journalist; that was how we met, at a conference

11

in Florence on Renaissance scholarship. She had been writing about it for a newspaper. I was sitting in the auditorium, a few rows behind, looking and looking at her, unable to take my eyes off her, wondering who she was, watching her take notes, till at last she noticed me, just with a glance at first, cold and aloof, but later that day, she looked at me again, just long enough to seem interested. At lunch time, I managed to talk to her, that night we had dinner in Camillo's near the Ponte Santa Trinità, and I was in love with her. She had a car. She did not let me see her home, to San Domenico, just below Fiesole.

Next day, I couldn't concentrate on any lectures, only on her, just staring at her, which amused her. Now and again, she would turn round and smile. Rewards. That night she would not dine with me. Next morning I was due to go back to England, but I cancelled my flight, called the college with some weak excuse, and stayed on to see her. Or try to.

We went to lunch that day in Fiesole. It was October, and the weather was still good. We sat outside a trattoria where you could look down into the bowl of the city, a view I had seen a hundred times but always loved to see again, the tiles climbing across the roofs like brick tortoises, the towers standing up like spears, the green copper dome of the old synagogue catching the sun, the Duomo swelling in its symmetry. Even here, though, there was no escape from thoughts of Hawkwood. It was in Fiesole, I remembered, gazing down, that he had camped and himself gazed down on the city in 1364, when fighting for Pisa in one of his earliest Italian campaigns; from Fiesole that his troops had moved down to attack the city, storming its approaches, stopped only by its massive defences, plundering and burning till the Florentines bought them off, then going back again up the hill to a night of wild celebration; music, drink and dancing, forays with drums to pretend that they would attack again.

On this occasion, however, I gave the city scarcely a glance. I was transfixed by her. She wore a white, sleeveless summer dress with a purple pattern. Her arms were slim and very brown, as if she had just got back from the beach. Her breasts were firm and full without being heavy, surprisingly large on such a slim body, and all the more alluring for that. She laughed at me, and pointed at my plate with her fork. '*That's* what you're meant to be eating.'

12

'I'm in love with you,' I said. 'I can't stop looking at you.'

'No, no,' she said. 'You're in love with the view. I'm part of the panorama.'

'Why do you think I stayed?' I asked her.

'I've no idea,' she said, and smiled into my eyes.

'You, you,' I said. 'Because of you.'

'I don't believe it.' But she was smiling, still, giving me hope. She was not mocking me, now.

The first time we made love was in Oxford. I had never even kissed her till then. Suddenly she phoned me from London; she was on an assignment. It was different in Oxford. She had never been there before, it enchanted her, there was a role reversal. Now *she* was the tourist, *I* was on home ground. Still the supplicant, but I had reached a kind of spurious equality. In Florence, she had everything in her favour. Later on I used to tell her, 'Oxford seduced you, not me'.

'Oh, yes,' she said, 'I married Oxford.'

I asked her back to my rooms in college, after we had been walking through Christchurch meadow. It was a winter day, but with a wintry sun, enough to form pale patterns on the stone and play across the grass. 'Che bello, che bello,' she kept saying, 'che caratteristico,' and she said it again, how beautiful, how quaint, when she walked into my study, with its alcoves and bookshelves and fire irons and carved wooden fireplace. Then she looked at me with a sort of resigned smile, almost the equivalent of a shrug, as if to say, I know why you've brought me here, but I'm not going to resist you, when I had brought her there with no ulterior motive at all. But when I saw the smile, I kissed her.

Later, when we were lying side by side in bed, I said, 'I want to marry you.'

'A true English gentleman. There's no need to marry me.' She laughed again, she ran her hand down my body and began to stroke me. 'To do this,' she said, 'you don't have to be married.'

'Not only this,' I said. 'It's wonderful, but more than this.'

We were married in Florence; it seemed sensible. Her parents lived there. My mother was dead, my father had retired to Wiltshire. It was a civic wedding, in the Palazzo Vecchio. I felt depressed by it all, a kind of impostor, but Simonetta looked superb, and perfectly in place, rinascimentale, a

13

Florentine face in that sublimely Florentine setting, serene and beautiful. But I: what was I doing there? Where Lorenzo had bullied the Signoria. Where the wicked old bishop had tried to trick his way in after Giuliano's murder in the Duomo. Where they had hanged him and the other Pazzi conspirators from the walls. Where Savonarola had burned in the square outside. I was an interloper. Then I wondered about Hawkwood, who might have seen it being built, might have been made a freeman of the city here, and in some strange, perverse way, this reassured me. I had a tenuous claim on the place, however secondary, as one immersed in Hawkwood's life.

He could console me even now, not just as an escape, but as a kind of example. Of endless resilience, unbounded stoicism. Wounds, disease, defeats, disappointments; he had shrugged them all off and soldiered on, into old age. *He* had lost a wife, or I supposed so, as I still ploughed through the records, failed to find her, wondered who she was. The chroniclers seemed all agreed; his wedding to Bernabò Visconti's daughter, worth ten thousand florins and the brittle friendship of Milan, was not his first. There had been an English wife, and there were children. People – though not he – died young then, carried away by plague or childbirth, slaughtered by soldiers like his own, who were always more ready to savage the defenceless than to fight one another. And he had condoned it, had looked on at it, bluff old Hawkwood, good Sir John. Hacking and ransacking his way from Crécy, right down to Pisa, anyone's hired sword, loyal only to his King; last refuge of a scoundrel. Or a mercenary.

No, I still could not understand him, still did not even know what I felt about him, knew only what I wanted to feel, but stubbed my toe, time and again, on the perfunctory ruthlessness of the man, which of course was no more than the casual ruthlessness of his times. He had been fighting for Florence, fighting against Florence, before the Palazzo Vecchio was even built. How tantalising it was to grope through libraries and record offices and to scour his old battlefields. Sometimes he seemed almost within reach, the truth about him in my grasp, then the trail would go cold. Where was the document that made things plain, cleared things up, told me about his first wife, proved he had never split the nun in two in Faenza, never run away from the Battle of Asti, never been captured

14

at the Battle of Arezzo, never worked as a young tailor in London?

Through the great, long, violent sweep of his life, which led him from his Essex village to the wars in France, from France to Tuscany, from Tuscany all over Italy, I could believe he had been callous and rapacious, but not bloody or vicious. Never a sadist. If the Florentines, in the end, made a hero of him, it must have been because, in his last years, in the final analysis, they found something to be honoured and admired. A residual sense of honour, which somehow survived and ran parallel with the ruthlessness and the brutalities. L'inglese italianato. Had Italy corrupted him? Had it made him worse than he was? After all, he was no saint when he got there with his White Company, fighting his way through France, seizing and ransoming rich clerics. No laymen; only clergy. There, too, one could surmise an odd, twisted sense of honour. If that *was* what he had done. If this *was* what he had been.

Sometimes I feel like a palaeontologist, putting dinosaurs together from scattered bits of bone, guessing at what I cannot find, endlessly painstaking, endlessly frustrated, pitifully grateful for scraps and trifles, from which I hope to construct great designs. How I cling to my favourite anecdote, trusting it as true, believing it anyway, with all its implications of a caustic humour, an implacable purpose. Riding through Tuscany, at the head of his troops, he had been met by a group of monks, who greeted him warily with a cry of, 'Peace!'

'May the Lord take away your alms!' he had responded.

'We want only to be kind,' said the monks, in alarm.

'Do you not know,' he had asked them, 'that I live by war, and peace would be my undoing?'

From this, I felt I learned so much about him, and liked what I learned. He was sardonic, funny and realistic, a hard man, inevitably, but not a brute. Those were not the words of a brute. And even if the story was not true, I would console myself, it must have had some basis, some root in the real. If only there were a bust, a painting, one could look at and learn from, though from what I had read, I could conjure him up. Tall for his times, robustly built, blue-eyed, fair-haired and bearded, gone grey in his old age; when he was still in the saddle. Because he knew no other life. Because he was poor, or never rich enough, always wanting more money as his last,

15

sad dealings with the Signoria showed. Pawned jewellery, begging letters, need.

'A Man on Horseback'; that was another facile title which swam into my mind at times, for I imagined him at home only on horseback, booted and armoured, as a sailor is at home only on a ship, even if his troops, his ferocious English soldiers, were wont to fight on foot, two men to a massive lance, advancing slowly and inexorably 'with terrible outcry'. I need never give up hope, however hopeless the quest might seem at times. There were annals to be found everywhere in Italy, for he had fought everywhere; Milan, Pisa, Florence, Rome, Naples.

The monograph might never be finished, might become a myth, like the life work of old, doddering Oxford fellows, mouldering and crumbling in their grace and favour rooms, having begun their definitive study of bee-keeping in the work of Virgil, the true identity of Homer, when they were still bright-eyed young post-graduates. For my part, I am happy for the work to stretch on indefinitely, to keep Hawkwood as my quest and my companion, an antidote to pain, a raison d'être. Good Sir John, I shall pursue you down the years. Somewhere, in some church, some library, some annal, some museum, I shall find the Philosopher's Stone, locate the Holy Grail, see you at last as you really were.

After all, I've no ambitions. I'm happy as a college fellow. I don't want a post at Harvard, a professorship at Leeds. My monograph is not a stepping stone, a bargaining counter. Now that Simonetta is dead, I am less interested than ever in advancement, especially if it means leaving Oxford. Dear old Tom Cunningham, they'll say, thirty years from now, as my spoon shakes in my hand at High Table, 'still working on that mercenary, that What's His Name! Still looking for some document or other, he says. Never find it now, of course, whatever it is.'

Now, there were other things I wanted to know, but I couldn't find them out from Cooper. Cooper and I used rooms on the same staircase. His subject was modern Italian history, the rise of Fascism and all that. We seldom had much to say to one another, but now I felt the need to talk to him, I hoped he could point me in the proper direction, even provide me with clues. No one yet seemed to know who had

16

planted the bomb; the Red Brigades, the neo-Fascists. Publicly, each had blamed the other. The police were still meant to be investigating, but one heard nothing from them but evasions.

Cooper could tell me about Fascists, I thought. Fascism was indivisible; a mentality which might change in minor aspects, but was essentially the same.

'Not *really* the same,' he said, standing with his back to his fireplace. He seemed always to be standing with his back to something; like a gaunt obelisk. He was extremely tall and very thin, with a pale, skinned kind of face, receding blond, curly hair, horn-rimmed glasses, and he always spoke slowly in a high, pedantic, public-school voice. He was in his middle forties, I suppose, he was meant to have a private income, and he had published a couple of books that I just could not read. I saw him as the quintessential don, a warning to me.

Soon after Simonetta died, we met on the staircase; he looked as if he would scurry past like a rabbit, but suddenly he stopped and turned and said, 'I'm sorry. Very sorry.' Now, he did not so much speak to me as address me, looking somewhere above my head. 'I think one must be very careful of drawing false analogies. Fifty years ago, the world was a very different place. Italy itself was essentially an agricultural society. The economic 'miracle' was still a very long way off. Communism was perceived as a threat, where today the Communists are almost part of the democratic process.'

'But the Fascist mentality,' I said. 'The nihilism. The commitment to violence. The authoritarianism.'

'*Is* there a specific Fascist mentality?' he asked. 'I *wonder* if there is?' He put his hands in the pockets of his velvet jacket, as if he were on a platform or a podium. 'Nihilism, after all, was initially a Russian phenomenon, though one *finds* it in Fascism, of course, especially in the Nazi party. As for violence, that's surely an integral part of *any* revolutionary movement.'

'But violence as an end in itself . . .' I said.

'Was it *ever* an end in itself? Even with the squadristi; their terrorism served a purpose. They cowed the peasants. They frightened the intellectuals.'

'And they enjoyed it,' I said.

'Yes, yes, no doubt they did. There are always what might

17

be called . . . fringe benefits. But their violence always had defined objectives.'

'You don't think it might have *been* the objective?'

His gaze rose higher still, almost to the ceiling, as he contemplated what I'd said as if he were seeking divine guidance. Finally he replied, 'I wonder if we're justified in employing what are still arguably *provisional* psychological concepts in an historical context.'

'If they can shed any light,' I said, though what I wanted to do was punch him. 'I accept that the appeal of Fascism has changed, but not its nature. It's been forced on to the margins, which seems to strip it bare, to show it in its most basic form.'

'I wonder whether we can *really* say that,' he said, his gaze coming down some twenty degrees or so, though he still did not look me in the eye. 'I wonder whether it isn't still a little *early*.'

And of course it was; far too early. Too early for terrorism to become history, too early for it all to be comfortably reduced to documents, to be buried in archives, to be made safe and obsolete and old. He was an historian; but then, God help me, *I* was an historian. Nothing could be touched until it had been made harmless. But Fascism was not harmless, it never had been harmless. As an *historian*, I suppose he was right to be sceptical and cautious, to touch nothing till it had been rendered remote. Irrelevant. Irrelevant as Hawkwood; if he *was* irrelevant. Looking at Cooper, listening to Cooper, I saw and heard a parody of myself. Was I any better? Was what I was doing any more germane? If anything, it must be *less* germane, far more remote.

At least he was involved with modern, if not contemporary, Italy; with his researches, notionally at least, he could cast light on the present, even if he shunned the present. What was the value, the validity, of mine?

Yet I felt my mediaeval world still had more vitality than his. His history was like himself, cerebral, all head and no body. When he wrote about Mussolini, that posturing, bullying, preening, bombastic scoundrel, it was in terms of his constitutional significance, his effect on the balance of power, his early relations with the Socialist Party. Rogue elephants tiptoed through his pages as soundless as so many cats. '. . . profound differences,' he was saying, now. 'One sees no Duce, so to speak. No rallying point, no centre. Mere fragmentation.'

'Someone must be controlling things,' I said. 'Someone gives orders.'

'Quite, quite. But no one . . .'

'No one we see,' I said, not quite sure why I had said it, and knowing it was not what he was going to say. Yet it did seem to me that if modern Fascism, contemporary Communism, had evolved to the stage where they did not need Führer figures, where the philosophy had somehow become its own justification, Fascists still took orders. It was part of the package.

'One must beware of labels,' Cooper was burbling on. 'What people call themselves and what they really are are not always the same thing. Our own neo-Nazis are scarcely what Hitler would have recognised as National Socialists.'

'There must be constants,' I said, 'something we can isolate, something the Fascists and the neo-Fascists have in common. Even if it's only believing that the end justifies the means and the means are violent.'

'Constants, yes, but even constants may be misleading. Constants can be . . . inconstant.' It was the nearest I had ever heard him come to a joke. He could tell me nothing because he knew nothing, or rather, everything he did know was abstract and intangible. He could dazzle you with facts, cocoon you in theory, baffle you with detail, but beyond that, he was impotent. The world outside, the life of the streets and squares, was something he had never entered.

'Thanks, anyway,' I said, to which he answered vaguely, 'Yes . . .' then, as I reached the door, he suddenly burst out, 'Like a sherry?' No, thanks, I did not want a sherry. Did he offer sherry to his students, I wondered; as an afterthought? Perhaps he did, especially to the public school ones, particularly to the Etonians. He, of course, was an Etonian. His tutorials would surely be *civilised*: that was the word, the quality which he would strive for, if he ever strove for anything. I sometimes gave my students beer; sometimes, when I could afford it, whisky.

By and large, I disliked teaching; it was a necessary evil, the price I had to pay for my cushioned existence. Disliked it not so much because I did not like the undergraduates, the preparation and the essay reading, but because it made me

19

feel a fraud. At lectures, and in tutorials. On a lecture platform, I find myself unbearable, I cannot understand why they don't throw eggs at me, as I hear myself rabbiting away about Guelphs and Ghibellines, the concept of chivalry, the technique of siege warfare. How persuasive I am; and how little I believe in what I am saying. Or rather, I know that it is no more than provisional, where it is not simply derivative. When I talk about Hawkwood, mercenaries, fourteenth-century Italy, then it is a bit different. I feel on firmer ground, have something of my own to say, can even get carried away by the subject, like any old academic crank.

But up there, on the dais, I am giving a performance, spouting lines, and the more often I speak them, the less they mean to me, like some actor in a long West End run. Moreover, I cannot help comparing myself with the lecturers I heard at Oxford, laughed at, mocked, been bored by, with their mannerisms, their obsessions and their eccentricities. Was I any different, any better, than they? Except that some of them obviously *liked* performing, which I did not; the exhibitionists with their pseudo-spontaneous jokes – pause for laughter – their throw-away lines, their over-rehearsed gestures; the dotards who did not care, or were beyond caring, mumbling their words so you could barely hear them, let alone understand them, like interior monologues. Which was broadly what they were.

Tutorials were a different kind of ordeal. I still felt myself a fraud, but in a more subtle way. The more respect my undergraduates showed me, the more deferentially they took my views on board, the more of an impostor I felt. On the other hand, when there were cocky students who questioned me, precocious public schoolboys, budding Union politicians, working-class malcontents – never girls, girls were more docile – I despised myself for being able to deal with them so easily, as if I had merely to pull rank.

Today, I have a tutorial with two students from quite contrasting categories; a High Flyer and a Girl Giggler. In a way I find the High Flyer the more disturbing. It is not that there is anything unpleasant or obnoxious about him. He is neat and quiet and curly-haired and quite good looking. He comes from one of those maintained schools in North London where a lot of middle-class media people send their children.

He writes excellent essays, has a very quick mind, and will certainly get a First. Then no doubt he will go on to become a don, like me. Like me, he will pass judgement on princes, Popes and potentates without ever having stuck his nose outside an academic institution. He will describe where generals have mismanaged their campaigns, where statesmen have mistaken their alliances, where kings have lost their kingdoms for their mistresses. He will do nothing and pass opinions on everything, and be rewarded with grants and fellowships and vintage ports and splendid rooms.

He has it made, I thought as I looked at him, he could breeze through on his exam technique, his fluent pen, his good intellect, to a Regius Professorship, world-wide conferences, to a richly pensioned, enviable old age. Il dramma dello storico. Like me; or like I might have been until a few weeks ago. All this, quite painlessly, without confronting anything more dangerous than an examination paper.

My Girl Giggler was a much simpler proposition. She was not interested in history, she was interested in me, or in any relatively young, relatively presentable male don. She smiled at me, she almost ogled me, she made it quite clear she was available. Mine for a glass of sherry. She was pretty and plump and dark, with large brown eyes and a big bosom, filling in these three years before she got her degree, a moderate second, went off into the world, never gave history another thought, and got married to somebody suitable. History meant nothing to her, and why should it? It was merely a means to an end, a provisional end, Oxford: a mark in her favour, inessential but gratifying. Yet perhaps her attitude was the more honest. She, after all, was not going to be immured, was simply passing through, had no illusions about history, its importance and its possibilities. Perhaps it was she who had got things right, we – the High Flyer and I – who had got things ludicrously wrong.

I am their Special Subject, his and hers: the Mercenary in Mediaeval Italy. I tell them about the economic basis of warfare in fourteenth-century Italy, the contractual obligations and financial arrangements of the condottieri, the military dispositions of the mercenary army. When Simonetta died, they were very good about it. She bought me a bunch of flowers and gave me long, understanding looks, as if to say

C1 1 44 '19 43 5 63

she wished she could make it up to me. He asked me if I would rather that they went away, but I said no, it was good of him, but I preferred to teach them.

I sometimes enjoyed teaching them. For quite selfish reasons, because I was on my own ground, doing my own thing, talking about what interested *me*. In this case, the make-up of the mercenary army. Hawkwood's army, which had come down with him through France, when King Edward did not need it any more, pilfering and pillaging. With its literally shining armour, polished and burnished by the pages, so that it shone in splendour, to the awe of the enemy. 'How *good* were they?' I demanded. 'How good were they *really*? How much of it was simply thanks to the feebleness of the opposition?'

'You make them sound like a football team,' said Giles, the High Flyer.

'More like football hooligans,' I said. 'Remember what Villani wrote about them: "Warm, eager and practised in slaughter and rapine, with very little care for their personal safety." But better for night fighting and plundering villages than for keeping the field. They were careless in camp, as well. Sprawling about without a care in the world.'

' "And their success was more owing to the cowardice of our own men than their valour and military virtue," ' Giles quoted.

'Bravissimo,' I said. 'Rather like World War Two, in the Western Desert.'

'Have the Italians always been cowards?' asked Helen, the Giggler.

'I don't think so,' I said, 'any more than the English have always been heroes. The Italians ran away in Cyrenaica because they knew there was nothing worth fighting for. But when the Germans turned on them in 1943, the partisans in Italy fought with great courage. Especially in places like Genoa, where they virtually liberated the city on their own.'

'But the Germans fought bravely all the time,' said Giles, 'and *they* hadn't anything worth fighting for, either.'

'They thought they had,' I said. 'That was the difference. Germans accept authority. Italians tend to reject it.'

'But even *he* says they were cowards then,' Helen said. 'Villani.'

'Maybe they were,' I said. 'Specific soldiers in specific circumstances. And do not forget that after Hawkwood, there was a long, long line of Italian condottieri. The Sforzas, Colleoni, Gattamelata, Federigo of Urbino, in the fifteenth century.'

'Garibaldi,' said Helen, looking very pleased with herself.

'Garibaldi was an idealist, hardly a mercenary,' I said, 'but I take your point.' She beamed at me.

'Caporetto?' asked Giles, who enjoyed this kind of intellectual badinage.

'Yes, yes, yes,' I said, 'to which I could reply: Vittorio Veneto. They ran away at one, they redeemed themselves at the other. History, my dear Giles, is rather more than a search for stereotypes. And fourteenth-century Italy, whatever certain popular American historians may say, is not a mirror of the twentieth.'

'It *is* fun, though, isn't it?' said Giles. I raised my eyebrows at him and brought the discussion back to Hawkwood. I talked about his archers, with their yew-wood bows, the chain mail and cuirasses that his knights and soldiers wore, the massive, two-man lances, the siege-ladders which were fitted together, piece by piece. 'A good metaphor for the historian's art,' I said.

'Do you think we should all be Namiers, then?' asked Giles.

'I do,' I said, 'in the sense of winkling things out, piecing things together, evolving our theories from the evidence, rather than choosing our facts to fit the theories. The best historians today are often archaeologists; they literally dig things up which can completely alter our view of civilisations.'

Then I spoke to them about one of Hawkwood's most notable Italian battles, at Cascina in 1369, when he pretended to retreat, sent his pages and horses down to the river, lured eight hundred Florentine cavalry into the soft sand, surrounded them and beat them. I went to the little blackboard that I have, and drew diagrams. I grew more and more involved, as I tend to do when I describe his battles, losing myself, thinking I am there, almost thinking I am him, so that I speak faster, move my chalk quicker and quicker, quite forgetting that there's anybody with me in the room. I turned round once and caught the two of them smiling at one another, which restrained me a little, but soon I was caught

23

up in it again, seeing the soldiers by the river, the flash of sunshine on their armour, the jingling and clanking of the cavalry as their horses sank into the sand, while Hawkwood himself moved about among his own troops, marshalling and manoeuvring.

'What you must remember,' I said, turning round to them again, 'is that for men like Hawkwood and his mercenaries, war was a business. They weren't just a bloodthirsty rabble, though of course they could be ruthless.'

'Rape and pillage,' said Giles. 'They were like business perks, were they?'

'If you wish,' I said. 'If you wish to be anachronistic. The mercenary forces travelled with treasurers and administrators who totted up accounts and negotiated with the cities who wished to hire them. They would haggle and bargain; the letters are there to show it. There was a substantial infrastructure, as we would say today. And if, in the middle of a campaign, the enemy made the condottiere a better offer, he was perfectly capable of changing sides, or of "going slow", as Hawkwood himself was known to do.'

'So much for chivalry,' said Giles.

'They had their own code of honour!' I told him, feeling myself being drawn into an argument I had had so many times before, aware that I was going beyond the call of duty, even objectivity, defending what might seem indefensible, but what had to be seen in its context. 'They were loyal to their King. They were loyal to one another.'

'And they looked on the Italians as just a bunch of dagoes, I suppose,' said Giles.

'There are more felicitous ways of putting it, perhaps,' I replied. 'All armies tend to despise civilians, and to look down on the inhabitants of a foreign territory. Just as the Americans called the Vietnamese gooks.'

'What about Hawkwood himself?' asked Helen, and I left the blackboard to sit down again, wondering how to answer her. L'inglese italianato. The Englishman who married an Italian bride. Who lived for thirty years in Italy, and died there. I knew how I thought he would feel; or perhaps it was merely how I hoped he would feel. But where was the chapter and verse, the detail, the pieces from which to put together a scaling ladder?

'We can't be sure,' I said, at last. 'We can only deduce. There's so little that he said or wrote himself. Italy must have changed him. Some obviously thought that it corrupted him and made him cruel; or worse. Il diavolo incarnato. When he arrived in Tuscany in 1363, I don't suppose he felt anything about Italians, one way or the other.'

'*Suppose*?' said Giles, and gave me a mock reproachful look.

'One sometimes must proceed on theory,' I said. 'Even scientists do that, in some of their experiments. But he stayed many years. He married there. He died there. Reluctantly. And as we know, when he was an old man, Florence took him in and made him their hero. He went back to England only when Richard II asked for his body.'

At which suddenly and horribly I thought of my poor, dear Simonetta's body, and how little had been left of it, so that for a moment I could not speak at all, and when I could, had lost any desire to do so. This time, Hawkwood had not distracted me or carried me away; he had brought me back to the horrors of the real.

They sensed my change of mood, and changed mood themselves, becoming suddenly grave rather than gay. Probably they sensed why I *had* changed, at least to the extent that it concerned Simonetta. So I filled out the hour, rambled on about the structure of a mercenary army, suggested a few books to read, and sent them away at last subdued and puzzled.

Now I must go to Italy. I had been due to go, anyway, I had research to do in Florence and Bologna, but this had become no more than my excuse, a front for what I really meant to do, yet had so little notion of how even to begin. In fact the more I thought about it, the more frustrated and dissatisfied I grew. My earlier hope, that my whole training as a historian might fit me for such investigations, was fading every day, as I stumbled over the rocks and shoals of all the difficulties. Why, any journalist, any provincial penny-a-liner, provided only that he had the language, was better prepared for things like this than I. Any hack, certainly, on an Italian provincial paper would know where to go first, whom to speak to, what to ask, where things and people might be found.

And I? I knew where things could be looked up, dead things about dead people, in deadening places. But there was no use going to the Biblioteca Nazionale by the Arno and

25

asking for the manuscript which told you who was planting bombs, no use scouring the municipal archive in Bologna for clues to the identity of who had decreed it. Besides, where, in what city, should I begin? In Bologna, which was where the investigation had its centre? In Florence, less than two hours down the line, from which the train had been coming? In Rome, where all roads still, indubitably, lead, where Parliament and the Papacy were to be found, where all the old corruption seethed and festered? Or even in Padua, where the Red Brigades were said to have their fulcrum. I saw myself being buffeted from one to the other, prey to a plethora of false trails, false leads, at last driven to distraction by the endless alternating stimuli. Perhaps a private detective could help me, but which? Perhaps there might be a sympathetic policeman, a crusading journalist; or did such people exist only in *films noirs*?

That I had at least to try was mandatory, that if I did not try I could never live with the burden of it all was axiomatic too. I was lucky, I told myself, that at least the college paid for me to go to Italy and stay there, which was at least a basic, a beginning. To console myself, I thought of other academics, historians, who had straddled the two worlds: Trevor-Roper, and his *The Last Days of Hitler*, the great investigation of the Berlin Bunker; Masterman, who had been head of a college and a spymaster as well. If they had done it, it was surely not impossible for me. I could learn, I could grow, I could take wing. Passion and energy must count for something.

Term ended. I temporised, stayed on in summer Oxford, for reasons that were merely excuses.

I flew to Italy only in August, booking a cheap flight, as I always did, that left from Gatwick. It allowed me to stay in Italy for two weeks.

II

It was the first time I could remember that I had gone back to Italy in a state of apprehension, rather than with the usual jolt of joy. I sat on the aeroplane trying to read a novel by Cesare

26

Pavese, not the most cheerful experience at any time, and intermittently jotting notes on what I might do, what I ought to do, without finding any illumination. I had the window seat, and I did not talk at all to the man beside me, a large, taciturn Italian businessman who had still less desire to talk to me. A man with an Imperial head and a ring with a huge diamond on his finger, the very archetype, I thought, of all that the Red Brigades believed they were fighting.

I realised, gradually, that I had already entered a paranoid world, in which there could be no neutrals, only allies and adversaries, in which a man like this could be a target or a threat, simply for what he represented. I could not see him as an ally. In his plump, self-sufficient silence, he embodied an Italy that I detested, an Italy which had made Mussolini its own, cut off, dehumanised, indifferent to poverty and misery. I saw him as a symbol of right-wing reaction, concerned only to keep what he had, no matter the cost, then told myself that *I* was turning paranoid, that I knew nothing about him, other than what I could deduce. My natural instinct, I knew, was to blame the Right for what had happened, however illogically, since the atrocities of the Left, the extra-parlamentari, had so often been just as bad: the cruel murder of Moro, shot dead and dumped in a car boot, then left in the middle of Rome; the callous shooting in the legs of Fiat executives in Turin, or magistrates in Genoa. There was no monopoly of violence.

The man on my left disdainfully waved away his meal, the hideous assortment of cold snacks on a plastic tray; dry, tasteless meat, soapy cheese, limp lettuce, a glutinous pudding. Doubtless something much better was waiting for him at the other end.

When we came through plump, cumulus cloud to land at Linate, I felt a shock, not of recognition, but of alarm. I was back, I was here, I was committed. As the bus took me through the grey, functional, bourgeois outskirts of Milan, the money city, as it went down neat, narrow, busy streets, through compact, anonymous squares, I tried to distract myself by conjuring up the old, mediaeval Milan that Hawkwood would have known, with all its pomp and treachery, Bernabò and Galeazzo, Hawkwood's wedding, the ceremony in the streets. It worked only for a little while;

27

modern Milan did not cater for romantic fancy. It imposed its own dull rationality on life, and its own life was one of frenetic pursuit.

It was too late to take the train to Bologna. I went to a small, good, second-class hotel in the Via Manzoni, where I usually stayed. Here there was more sense of the city and its being, the buildings were handsome and solid, the shop fronts exuded a sleek prosperity. Yet there was hardly anyone about. At night, Milan was not a bit like Rome. The crowds seemed to be sucked out of the city, on to the periphery, to take refuge there behind diligently locked doors. There was a hint of fear about these empty streets, of harsh things that had happened. To come out, even to eat in a restaurant, was to risk robbery, eruptions by armed gangsters. Such were the times.

When I woke up next morning, it was with the same, uneasy sense of dislocation. But once in the now lively street, once in the hot sunshine, once in a now bright and crowded bar, with the hiss of its espresso machine, I began to feel happier and easier.

The train journey soothed me too. Train journeys through Italy always do; I can even find some pleasure in the vast, grey, Fascist bulk of Milan's Central Station, simply because of its associations and its promises, the infinite journeys I had made from it through Lombardy and Emilia, down to Tuscany, on to Rome; or up to the lakes. If it were England, and I entered such a station, no doubt my heart would sink, as it does when I go to almost any London terminus but Paddington, which, in its shabby, formiculating way, at least means Oxford. So even now, on a mission so dark and difficult, I trotted up that grim, bleak stone stairway, shutting out the sun, down the crowded platform, into my second-class carriage, with that strange sense of release that one can get only in someone else's country; and I can get only in Italy.

On trains, as opposed to aeroplanes, I quite enjoy talking, so long as I am talking to Italians. There's no golden rule; you can go on a four-hour journey in a full compartment without so much as a word being exchanged, or you can find yourself in one where conversation takes off, after elaborate formalities, into a whirl of words, a proliferating exchange of confidences, inconceivable in England. Mothers speak of their daughters, students of their ambitions, soldiers of their homes and families, young girls of their fiancés. Photographs are shown in abundance.

This time, there was little converse for the first hour or so. The other passengers, two elderly couples, a demure dark girl, two grave young men with briefcases and documents, maintained a silence broken, if at all, only by the couples whispering over crosswords. We were out of Lombardy into Emilia with its rich red soil and its deep green fields when the man sitting opposite me clicked shut his briefcase, leaned across, and asked me if he might borrow my *Corriere della Sera*.

'*Come no?*' I said, and handed it to him, whereupon a plump woman sitting by him, in the corner, exclaimed, 'But excuse me, are you Italian or a foreigner?'

'English,' I said, and we were off.

'But you speak such good Italian.'

How often had I heard that, even before I spoke Italian at all? How often, in the last couple of years, have I replied, 'I have an Italian wife' at which the women went, 'Aaah!' their eyes dilating, while everybody in the carriage melted suddenly into a smile, as if they had received some marvellous reassurance.

My wife. I have no wife.

So all I can say this time is, 'I work in Italy a lot,' to which the response, though pleased and friendly, is more muted. 'Per quello, si, per quello.' Then some talk about where I go in Italy, and which places I like best, and I am very careful, since I don't know where any of them comes from. The housewives, the donne casalinghe, supply their usual chorus of comfortable banalities. 'Si, certo, si; grande Milano, troppo movimentato. Milan's too big and busy.'

The men with the briefcases are more self-contained and pungent. 'I live in Rome but I'm from Milan,' said the one who had borrowed my paper. 'I like to live in Rome, but I'd prefer to *work* in Milan.'

'Si, si, bella la vita romana,' said the other donna casalinga, 'it's a lovely life in Rome.'

'È difficile il lavoro,' said the briefcase man, 'and the work is hard.'

In its kind, silly, amiable way, the conversation cheered me

29

up, giving me that splendid, transient feeling of warmth which Italy, Italians, can give, only for everything to pop like a soap bubble and leave you feeling colder than before. The moment would come, sooner or later, when they nerved themselves to ask me what I did. They were manifestly longing to ask; the plump cheeks of the donne casalinghe were swelling with curiosity.

The question came from the younger of them, shyly, haltingly, 'E Lei, Signore, and you, sir . . . With all these journeys . . . Would you be a businessman?'

'I teach history,' I replied reluctantly, inuring myself to the customary sighs of admiration and congenial envy. 'Ma che bello, che bella vita!' *Was* it a wonderful life? Or just a life not lived in the nasty modern world, where no one really wanted to be? So, on our way to Bologna, we prattled amicably of this and that. A man with a briefcase confessed he worked in the Ministry of the Interior. One of the husbands said he was a pensioner, but he had been a policeman.

'Difficult life,' said a briefcase man.

'You've no idea,' said the policeman.

We must have been a mile outside Bologna when we heard the explosion. The carriage was a-babble with chatter, but it stopped dead, while we looked at one another in our shock and alarm. The train stopped almost immediately with a jolt that sent us lurching and toppling about the compartment like rag dolls. I found myself sprawled across the laps of one of the briefcase men and the policeman's wife, but it was neither funny nor embarrassing; I simply heaved myself up without an apology. Something quite horrible had happened; we all seemed to know that. Something brutal and devastating. An atrocity. It must be an atrocity; we were not, after all, at war.

'A bomb,' said the policeman, at last. And a huge bomb, I thought. 'Meno male che non c'eravamo,' said the second briefcase man, gravely. 'Thank goodness we weren't there.'

'In the station,' said the other one. 'It must have been in the station.'

'Meno male,' I echoed, but I was drawn to that station, I knew I had to be there, not as a voyeur, as one who supped on horrors, but because I somehow knew that whatever had just happened there was central to my search, a manifestation of that cruel, blind force which had murdered Simonetta.

'Con permesso,' I said, standing up, thinking how incongruous I must sound. I got my bag down from the rack, wished them 'Buon giorno', as they gaped at me, and went out into the corridor, where a crowd of people was chattering, gazing out of the windows, calling to one another: 'Look at the smoke!' I glanced over the shoulders of the passengers leaning out of a window and saw the smoke for myself; a huge, fearful black pall. Then I shouldered my way through to the end of the carriage, through the people standing in the doorway, heaved at the handle of the door, and to a chorus of, 'Ma cosa fa? What are you up to?' pushed it open, letting in the August heat, spilling out down the steps.

Down these, with difficulty, I made my burdened way, while the passengers still chattered at me. I hopped from the last step the several feet down on to the side of the track, and then began to walk, sure that the train was not going to move, so *I* must move. Walking was warm; the case was quite heavy. I was aware of cicadas buzzing in the grass, thought how incongruous it was, with the noise, the hubbub, how still more incongruous was the sunlit beauty of the day. Then there came into my mind that poem by Auden, on how the Old Masters knew pain, knew how life went on despite it, knew how the sun could still shine on a casement window.

As I came closer to the station, I became aware of a repugnant, acrid smell, and I knew it must be the smell of death. I knew that many people must have died. Just as Simonetta had died. I'd like to say that I wanted to help, that this was what drew me to the station, my pity, my humanity, but it would not be true. When I got there I would help, if they wanted me to, but this wasn't my real motive for walking. As I walked, I felt there was something inexorable in what I was doing, that I was consciously moving towards something from which there would be no escape, that I'd committed myself to a course I'd have to follow to its end. And as I walked, an image, perversely, floated into my mind, of Hawkwood on horseback following the same trail, more than six hundred years ago, Hawkwood at the head of two thousand troops, coming from Milan, as I had done, ready to commit 'their usual ravages'. Except that I came peaceably, and the ravages had plainly been committed.

There was not only the bitter smell, now, as I approached

31

the station, but the noise. It sounded like the noise of hell; of pain and panic and torment. There were shouts, there were screams, there was a thumping and a banging. For the first time I slowed my steps, alarmed by the prospect of what I was going to find. The closer I came, the less I could see. The smoke came swirling towards me, and out of the smoke there suddenly emerged two carabinieri in their red and blue uniforms, one with a gun in his hand, each almost hysterically tense.

'Lei chi è?' shouted the one with the gun, 'Who are you?' And he pointed it at me; it was petrifying. I had never had a gun pointed at me in my life, and I suddenly found I was saying to myself, 'Hawkwood, Hawkwood, Hawkwood!' illogically, absurdly, as though it were a kind of charm.

'What are you doing? What's in the case?'

'I'm a passenger,' I said. 'I got out of the train.'

'Why? *Why* did you get out of the train? Open the case!'

I put the case down, sweat breaking on my body, then bent over to unstrap it and unlock it, while the two of them stood over me, rigid with apprehension, one of them still pointing the gun. Hawkwood, Hawkwood. My fingers shook as I hauled at the buckle, then fiddled with the tiny key, to unlock the case.

'Open it, open it!' shouted the carabiniere with the gun, and as I did so, throwing back the lid, both of them jumped backwards, for fear of what might happen.

'Just clothes,' I said. 'Just books. Just personal effects.'

One of them pushed me aside, and they clawed at the case, scattering my clothes, books, washing gear over the ground.

'I'm a university teacher,' I said, ineptly. 'You'll find nothing there.' At length they seemed convinced of this, and started hurling my things back into the case. I joined them, doing what I could to limit the damage, pushing and prodding things, when they had finished, till I could close the case again.

'Passport!' they now demanded, and I showed it to them. 'Are you English? Why do you speak Italian?'

'It's my subject,' I said. 'Italian history.'

Now, no longer frightened of me, and whatever I might be carrying, their aggression turned to curiosity. What was I coming to Bologna for? What kind of history did I teach? The

32

carabiniere with the pistol put it away, then suddenly snapped at me, 'Why didn't you wait on the train?'

It was hard to answer that. 'I heard the explosion,' I said. 'I wanted to know what had happened.'

'But why? That's hardly history!'

'I wanted to see if I could help,' I told them, though I knew it wasn't true.

'If you were a medical doctor maybe you *could* help,' said the second carabiniere. 'There's dozens dead, and hundreds wounded.'

'Then it was a bomb.'

He looked at me suspiciously. 'How did you know?'

'I didn't, but what else could it be?'

Now they looked at one another. 'Come with us,' said the first carabiniere, and, one on either side of me, we walked towards the station. As we approached, the noise grew louder still, and loudest of all, quite recognisable now, the dreadful cries of pain. Beneath the smoke pall, the analogy with Hell, a Dantean Hell, was more apposite than ever.

Oppressed by it, like myself, the two carabinieri made less and less pretence of escorting me. I had never seen dead bodies before, but here, in the rubble of the platform, men, women, children seemed to be sprawled everywhere, like limp, abandoned dummies. I slipped and almost fell, then realised I had stepped into a rivulet of blood; I saw that it was running from the shattered head of a poor, plump, middle-aged woman who lay on her back, her eyes wide open, her skirt rucked above her knees, taking away from her even the dignity of death. Over another body bent a priest in his cassock, a bald, elderly man in spectacles, a cross in his hand, while his other hand held that of a dying child, a handsome, fair-haired boy, whose mouth very slowly opened and closed, like that of a fish. Moving among this carnage, I found myself invaded by a bitter anger, the more unbearable for its impotence. Why had it happened? Who could have done it? What horrible, perverse purpose were they trying to achieve? Whoever they were – and however irrationally – I knew that they must be the same people who had killed Simonetta.

Amidst the chaos, the smoke, the rubble of masonry, there was an antheap activity. Police and railwaymen were carrying the injured away, or hauling and heaving at the timber and stone that buried them. Doctors, I assumed they were doctors, leaned over casualties, trying to give first aid. I found an old man lying on his back, with blood welling from his side. He did not move, but his lips kept moving, moving, and as I bent over him I heard him saying, again and again, 'Oh, Dio; oh, Dio.'

My feeling of impotence was increased by my inability to help him, or to know how to help. I must stop the bleeding, I thought, I must stop the bleeding. I began to take off my jacket, preparatory to taking off my shirt, to make a bandage of it, but as I began to do so, a woman bundled me aside and said, 'Ci penso io, I'll see to it.' Obviously a nurse, she pulled bandages out of her bag, and began to tend the wound. As she did so, suddenly the old man's lips ceased to move, his eyes gently closed, and he was still. The woman put her fingers round his pulse, then turned to me with bleak resignation. 'È morto, poverino.'

My case still in my hand, I wandered bemused through the chaos, asking people – soldiers, policemen, doctors, railway-men – as they brushed past me, 'How can I help? What can I do?' But I might have been a ghost, for all the notice that they took of me.

'Leave!' said a police officer, in his crisp grey braided uniform, at last. 'If you've no relations here, if you're not injured, leave!'

He was right, but I didn't want to leave, however useless I might be. I felt some strange obligation to remain, simply to bear witness to the horror, convinced that the horror itself was in some way an initiation. One heard bells, now, sirens, frantic shouting, as police cars, ambulances and trucks arrived outside the station, as more and more nurses, firemen, policemen ran on to the platform and began desperately to work among the ruins.

As I stood by the blasted, splintered remnants of a kiosk, its newspapers, magazines, confectionery, sprinkled with shattered glass, fanned in a lurid kaleidoscope across the ground, a helmeted policeman strode up and demanded my 'documents'. Again, I showed my passport.

'Tourist?' he asked.

It was easiest to say, 'Yes.'

'You'd better go,' he told me, and this time I did,

reluctantly, realising that to stay would be only to attract more suspicion. I had meant to stop, anyway, in Bologna, to begin my mission here, to fill in the intervening time searching, again, through Bolognese archives. Now there could be nowhere else to start.

In the station square, police had formed a cordon. A line of taxis lay crushed, like mere toy cars, beneath a mass of rubble. Stretchers were being carried to ambulances. A man came out of the station, a nurse on either side supporting him. His head was grotesquely swathed in crimsoned bandages, like Wells' Invisible Man; he crossed the square with the slow steps of a sleepwalker. Again, I felt the urge to help, even as a stretcher bearer, and I made towards one of the ambulances, where a young, blond doctor was supervising the loading of a casualty. When I offered to assist, he waved me brusquely away. 'There's no need.' And so I left the square, step by unwilling step, feeling each to be a kind of abdication.

Usually I found Bologna a kind of refuge, a plump, red-bricked, colonnaded city of good livers, bustling geniality, people with none of the Roman sullenness or the Florentine acerbity, however ardent they had once been as Fascists, then as Communists. But now, as I made, like some zombie, for the hotel where I had booked, I knew all that had gone for good, that Bologna would always be the city of the bomb, the brutal outrage.

The streets, as I went through them, were full of people gathered into little, anxious groups, questioning rather than protesting. Again and again one heard, 'What's happened? But what's happened?' I longed to let them know, but then thought it futile. What *did* I really know, and how could I tell all Bologna, one group rather than another?

When at last I reached my hotel, in a neat, narrow street off the Piazza del Nettuno, its foyer seemed stricken like a scene from Pompei. Behind the counter, the grey-uniformed concierge and the girl receptionist confronted one another in silence. For several minutes they did not notice me, even when I had crossed the hall and stood in front of them. At last the concierge became aware I was there and started, turning to me. 'Scusi, Signore.'

'I've just come from the station,' I said.

Now they both looked at me in wide-eyed shock. 'A bomb?' asked the concierge. 'Was it a bomb? How many do they think have died?'

'Yes, it was a bomb,' I answered. 'I don't know how many died. I saw thirty or forty, and many, many injured.'

'How horrible,' the girl said, 'how inhuman. Who can have done it?'

'No one knows, yet.'

'They may never know,' said the concierge. 'The Left blame the Right. The Right blame the Left. And then, we're never told the truth. We are told what *they* want us to know.'

'They?' I asked. 'You mean the government?'

'The government, the police, the Secret Services, maybe the Mafia. Who knows? There are so many interests.'

'Perhaps we must find out for ourselves,' I said distractedly.

'How? What chance has any individual? Any poor devil? Against a conspiracy like this?'

I did not argue with him. Chance, in turn, would depend on luck, and luck might depend on diligence. For once, conspiracy theory seemed to be the only theory that was plausible. Nothing was what it seemed. Masks concealed masks with mediaeval guile and treachery, but the means were modern, the possibilities of devastation so much greater. When Hawkwood was given bombards by the Pope, it had frightened the Florentines and threatened their thick bastions. Now, a few pounds of plastic could blow buildings into the air. Perhaps, to live in this cruel new world, to survive and to succeed, you had to be like Hawkwood, keeping always, more or less, to his contracts, yet always ready to be ruthless; revealing plots to his employers, but only at a price. L'inglese italianato. *I will* find out, I wanted to say to them, the girl and the concierge, but it would have sounded no more than a futile boast.

I had meant originally to go out to eat, one of the lasting pleasures of Bologna, and its buongustai, where a restaurant can become a religion, where rich food came as from a cornucopia; but it was impossible to eat now, or even go out again, while the city, like the two people downstairs, remained in its state of shock. By the same token, I did not want to telephone my friends; they must be left alone to work through their grief. As I was still working through mine.

36

Lying on the bed, looking out of the window at an ancient campanile and its silent bell, I felt my own grief now to be somehow subsumed in that of the whole city. To that extent, at least, I was not an intruder. I could understand and share in their pain. From my case, I had taken out a file, stained now with dirt, where the carabinieri had pitched it out beside the rails. Suddenly, the telephone rang beside my bed. There was one thing, now, about telephones ringing in a foreign room. They could alarm me no longer. I had nothing to lose. Perhaps the police, I thought, checking again to make sure who I was. But no; it was Aldo Magnoni, my friend and colleague from the University, a mediaeval historian himself who had surveyed my studies with amused sympathy, helping where he could, plainly convinced that mine was not much more than an antic obsession, an attempt to turn a marauding brute into a hero.

'Carissimo Tom! Allora, sei arrivato!'

Then he couldn't know. 'How's that old rogue Giovanni Acuto?'

'Still Hawkwood to me,' I said. It was difficult to spoil his happy mood, to break the news.

'You're all the same, you English! You'll never change, any more than Giovanni Acuto did, however many years you spend in Italy.'

'Aldo,' I said, 'haven't you heard?' and the tone of my voice subdued him.

'Heard what?' he asked.

'The bomb. The station. All the deaths.'

'Good God! Sul serio?'

'I've just come from there. A terrible explosion. Dead and dying. I'm sorry, Aldo. I'm sorry I'm the one to tell you.'

There was a silence then, until he said, 'I understand. I understand. Poor people. Poor Bologna. Poor Italy.'

'I'm so sorry,' I said.

'But I'm sorry for *you*. All this, just after your poor wife . . .'

We had not seen each other since then.

'I suppose I'm lucky it wasn't me,' I said. It was the first time that the thought had occurred to me.

'Yes, yes,' he echoed. 'At least thank God for that. I must turn on the radio. I must try to find out just what happened.

37

Caro mio, quest'Italia. This Italy. But you know that better than anyone.'

What was I doing now, he asked me. Would I come out to dine?

'You're sure?'

'Of course I'm sure. My dear Tom; life goes on. It must perforce go on. Otherwise the bombers win. The terrorists achieve their intention; they terrorise us. They break up the fabric of our lives, and so they prepare the way to break up democracy.'

This filled me with a sudden and surprising good cheer. He was entirely right. It was one's duty, after such an atrocity, to go out and do exactly what one would have done, to go on doing it.

When I entered the restaurant, there was no one there but the proprietor and the waiters. Despite the atmosphere of abundance, the sloping, multi-coloured trays of fruit and vegetables, the platoons of sausages hanging from the ceiling, the bright hued napkins on the white table cloths, the trolley loads of rich cakes, there was the same aura of suspended animation as there had been in the foyer of the hotel; as if the people were under a spell. My entrance broke it, though not immediately. After an hiatus, a waiter came forward, asking for my coat, the proprietor, recognising me, bowed, and took me to a table, but there was no spontaneity to their behaviour. They might, with difficulty, have been performing a part.

The waiter asked me if I wanted an aperitif, hesitated, then enquired, 'Have you heard?'

'The bomb?' I asked. 'I was at the station,' and he instantly called the others, 'He was at the station!', and they flocked around me, the remaining waiters, the proprietor; the chef himself came out of the kitchen in his tall, white hat. 'You were there, you saw it, what happened?' as if to hear about it from an eye-witness could bring some kind of release. I did not know what to tell them; nor what I wanted to tell them.

'It had happened before I got there.' I said. 'I heard it from my train, I walked down to the station. Twisted iron, chunks of masonry. People wounded, people dying. Dozens of them.'

'But a bomb; it was definitely a bomb?'

'Of some kind, yes. No one knew what; or why, or who.'

'The Red Brigades,' one of the waiters said. 'It had to be the Red Brigades. Those murderers; they don't care about anybody. They'd blow up their own mothers. They even killed the Prime Minister.'

'Who knows?' asked the proprietor, a tall, sleek man, pale-skinned, his black hair brushed back from his scalp. 'Who can be sure? The Fascists, too; they don't care about people. They blew up that bank in Milan and blamed the Reds for that.'

I stayed silent while they argued. There was no real contribution I could make. Besides, whatever my own loss, I was still a foreigner, and the grief was theirs.

Aldo arrived, to come to my rescue, smiling, once he saw me, as he always smiled, as if his smile were the final product of a bottomless well of good humour. He was seven years older than me, I knew, but that geniality made him look younger than he was; round-cheeked, blue-eyed, broad-shouldered, with a wiry terracing of light brown hair. I stood up; we embraced each other. 'Carissimo mio: mi fai un gran piacere!' The proprietor and the waiters greeted him with a respectful solicitude.

'Caro professore! What do you think? Who could have done such a thing? What's going to happen?'

'Who did it?' asked Aldo, beaming at them. 'Lunatics did it; that's who. Left or Right. Fascists or revolutionists. Whatever they call themselves, they're two sides of the same false coin. What's going to happen? We're going to have dinner, that's what's going to happen!'

As he spoke, the door of the restaurant opened and a family of five people came hesitantly through it, as if to enter a restaurant at all, in such circumstances, constituted a kind of heresy. This time, a waiter moved towards them quickly, seemingly afraid that they might change their minds and leave.

'There you are!' said Aldo. 'We are not going to be the only ones; and there'll be others. You'll see, there'll be others.'

We ordered food and wine; he put his hand over my own. 'Poor Simonetta,' he said. 'What a marvellous woman. How sorry I am. How much I shall always miss her.' He poured wine into my glass, then into his. 'Alla memoria di una gran bella donna. To the memory of a fine, beautiful woman.' We touched glasses and I drank. Why not? Nobody could bring her back. Nothing could do her any more harm.

'They're saying it's the Fascists again,' said Aldo. 'Commemorating the Italicus bomb.'

'And you?' I asked.

He shrugged. 'As I said before, what does it matter? All that matters is what happened, not whatever bunch of lunatics did it.'

'It might help to know, so that they could be caught.'

'When are they ever caught?'

'*I* want to know anyway,' I said.

'But why? What purpose would it serve?'

'Knowing that,' I said, 'I might eventually find out who murdered Simonetta.'

'And then?'

'And then, not necessarily anything. I'd know; that's all. That would be enough. Then perhaps I could begin to make some sense of it.'

'There's no sense in it, that's the whole point. That's what I've been trying to tell you. These people want to reduce the world to chaos. Irrationality. Then they see their chance.'

'Then if we can make some sense of it, so much the less chance for them.'

'Dear Tom,' he said, 'I understand you. I know how it must feel. The rage. Not being able to do anything. The anguish. But I beg you; don't bother with it. Stick to Giovanni Acuto.'

'I shall stick to both,' I said. 'One helps the other.'

'A mediaeval brigand helps you to understand a twentieth-century terrorist? You make me laugh, dear Tom.'

It was hard to explain what I mean, even to myself, let alone to an Italian who was himself a mediaevalist. I was still, so to speak, flying on instruments; what I sensed rather than knew was that the harsh realities of John Hawkwood's world might be a means of entry into one's own, a way of transcending all my articles of faith in justice, mercy, kindness and forbearance. Something that might have no real conceptual validity, but would work for *me*.

No, no, of course mediaevalism was not a mirror, of course there was no correspondence at all to our abstract, automated, mechanised, post-Marxian, post-Freudian, post-Christian world. A terrorist of our time and Hawkwood would look on each other with a wild surmise. And yet . . .

'Cesena,' I said.

'What do you mean, Cesena?' Aldo asked.

'Just that at Cesena, many more died than died here today,' I said. 'Those who were slaughtered. Those who fell into the moat. Those whose bodies were stuffed into cisterns.'

Aldo laughed aloud. 'You're incorrigible. Now you're comparing the sack of a mediaeval town with a bomb left on a railway station! Each is a crime that perfectly reflects its period. Giovanni Acuto and his English thugs slaughter the citizens because they're paid to do it. Persons unknown, *i soliti ignoti*, slaughter persons unknown to them, because they think it might promote their cause.'

'I know,' I said. I couldn't argue with him. Yet somewhere beneath the line of logic and reason, his argument meant nothing to *me*. Cesena was the great stumbling block, the cruellest episode in Hawkwood's career, an ultimate text, if one were drawing unhistoric parallels of the exculpatory, 'I was only obeying orders.' The Papal delegate, Robert of Geneva, had first duped and betrayed the people of Cesena, then told Hawkwood that he wanted their blood. Hawkwood had demurred, had sent a thousand of them to safety, then told his soldiers to begin the massacre. Nothing his apologists have written can excuse that. Nothing I have found in my researches so far can contradict or mitigate it. Nothing can reconcile it with his reputation for a bluff if rough-hewn decency. It was the bone on which one choked, the *ne plus ultra*. All the talk of the risk he ran, had he refused his men their prey, all the efforts to set it in the 'context' of a mercenary leader's *Weltanschauung*, were futile. My whole, soft, liberal spirit jibbed at it; till now. Now I could vaguely see a way in which the present could illuminate the past, and the past might make the present bearable.

'You're a romantic,' said Aldo, spinning great forkfuls of spaghetti. 'That's the trouble with you; and with all you English who fall in love with Italy. You can never accept that we're as bad as we are.'

I knew in my bones that this was true, and that in some strange way the bomb, exploding, had exploded in my consciousness destroying this as well. I had always resisted the idea, both that Hawkwood had been Italianised, and thus debased, and the idea that, in Italians themselves, there was something treacherous and malevolent. Simonetta's death, alone, had not been enough to teach me differently; rather, it had traumatised me, the shock of her murder compounded by the fact that it had occurred in a country which I loved, and thought I knew.

Oh, yes, I had told myself so many times. *I* know Italy. I am no tourist, to be seduced by sun and stones and panoramas, to be fooled by the surface attractions of the café life, the drama of the streets, the outward show of amiability. I know Italy as it *is*: the chicanery that lies behind the smile, the squalor that lies behind the bella figura, the calculation that lurks behind the beauty. Yet Aldo was right. In the last analysis I had been deceiving myself. There was a limit to what I would accept and give credence. The dark side of Italy was something to which I paid lip service, but accepted only intellectually.

'For you,' said Aldo, as he had remarked before, 'for English like you, Italy is one big beach.'

I didn't argue with him; till a few months ago, he might have been right. 'L'inglese italianato,' he said, 'è un romantico incarnato. The Italianised Englishman is a romantic incarnate.'

'Do you think Hawkwood was a romantic?' I asked.

'Caro mio, romantics weren't invented then; or barely. There was no such thing as tourism. The English came to Italy to trade, or to plunder.'

'And the Italians corrupted them.'

'They were already corrupt. We Italians simply made them more devious. We put a polish on their barbarism.'

And the refined Hawkwood, I thought, committed that horrific atrocity. Could he have conceived or comprehended an atrocity like today's? Idiot question; crass anachronism. Guilty as my own students, as the popular American history-fakers, of drawing cheap parallels, finding analogies where none existed. Yet there *was* a totality in any nation's history; you didn't have to forsake Namier and his minutiae, you didn't have to turn into a Toynbee, to pursue it and perceive it.

'Don't stay in Bologna!' Aldo told me, pouring more red wine into my glass. 'Don't be a detective! It's too dangerous.'

42

'I've no fear,' I said. 'What's left to lose?'

'Ma no, I'm sure you're not afraid; physically. The danger's metaphysical. To your soul, to your innocence, to your integrity as a romantic Englishman.'

'Perhaps it's time I lost it.'

'No; you must never lose it. That's something else the terrorists all want to destroy; people's innocence. Cynicism serves their purpose. If you don't believe in anything, you'll believe in everything. Then it won't matter who rules. Fascism, again. Trotskyists. Stalinists. One's as good or as bad as another.'

'You can't persuade me,' I said, and our eyes met. This time, he gave me a long, appraising look. 'Very well,' he said, with resignation. 'Then I suppose I'll have to help you. But I warn you; you will achieve nothing. Italy is a hydra. Cut off one head, and another grows. Solve one mystery, and another appears. If you follow the corruption, you will find it goes on and on, probably until you reach the very top, if you're allowed to reach it. You'll find that, if it isn't the Red Brigades, it's the neo-Fascists, if it isn't the neo-Fascists, it's the Vatican, if it isn't the Vatican, it's the Mafia, and there are other powers we may not even know of.'

'I never realised you subscribed to the conspiracy theory of history,' I told him.

'It's not a theory; it's an established phenomenon. It's modern Italy. One great conspiracy in which people and functions change places, accuse one another, work for one another, like so many chameleons. You think it's hard to reconstruct mediaeval history, hard to find out about Hawkwood? Caro mio, it's easy by comparison with this; at least some of the documents are there, and you can guess at the gaps. Here, you're dealing with a million mysteries, and with people who'll deliberately maintain them. I beg you again, stick to Hawkwood! Stick with your nice, simple, savage Giovanni Acuto!'

'As I've told you before, I can't,' I said. 'Not with Hawkwood and Hawkwood alone!'

He shrugged his shoulders. 'E va bene. I'll talk to Lucetti.' He got up from the table, made his rolling, rapid way to the restaurant's telephone, and dialled a number. He seemed to find whoever he was seeking. From our table, I could not hear

43

what he was saying, but he was back to his familiar, jolly volubility, his large, free hand cutting the air in a series of vivid gestures. When at length he returned he said, 'He's coming now. He was at his newspaper, but he's coming.'

'That's good of him.'

'It's a sports paper, but he's more than a sports journalist. Much more. Mind you, sports journalists here are a special breed. They have their noses in everything. They often know more than the political journalists. All the Presidents of the football clubs are rich, influential men. Or crooks. Some of them are even senators.'

Lucetti arrived within a quarter of an hour, by which time the restaurant was almost half-full, the earlier depression had lifted, and a growing animation had scattered the silence. Lucetti was a man in late middle-age, balding, dark and ruddy, with deeply set brown eyes and an irrepressible air of mischief. Mischief, rather than malice, surrounded him like a nimbus. Even at a moment like this, he was completely unsubdued, as though the enormity of what had happened merely proved what he had suspected all along. He seemed to be bursting with information, gossip, scandal, secrets as he embraced Aldo with great flamboyance, then took my hand in both of his, smiling at me with a goblin goodwill.

'You've chosen well,' he said, 'you've picked the right day to come. To see us as we are. What has become of us.'

'I hope that isn't true,' I answered.

Lucetti sat down, but refused to eat. 'I've dined, but I'll have a whisky. To celebrate the arrival of an Englishman.'

'Tom is a mediaeval historian, like me,' Aldo said.

'You told me, you told me. Most appropriate. Italy's a mediaeval country. No modern historian can understand us. Even your Denis Mack Smith. He's too polite about us.'

The proprietor and the waiters now swarmed around Lucetti, who was plainly a star; the new oracle. 'Who did it, dottore?'

'Dopodomani,' said Lucetti. 'The day after tomorrow, I shall explain everything.'

'A promise, dottore?'

'Yes, a promise. Dopodomani.' After which they started questioning him passionately about football, and Bologna's chances in the League. When they dispersed, he grew suddenly grave and said to me, 'Aldo told me about your wife. It must have been a horrible experience for you today. I'm sorry, really sorry. È un brutto momento davvero. It's truly a nasty time.' At which I thought suddenly of that hoary description of life in the Middle Ages: nasty, brutish and short. Now, it was nasty, convenient and . . . short? Short, if you were Simonetta. Short, if you were one of those poor, crumpled people on the railway station.

'There are seventy dead at least,' said Lucetti. 'A fine Fascist victory.'

'For which no one will be charged,' said Aldo.

'They never are, are they?' I said, and Lucetti raised his eyes from his glass to give me an approving smile. 'They prefer to charge the Left,' he said. 'They're already talking about evidence. Something they found; or which the Secret Services found. Something that implicates the Red Brigades.'

'So soon,' said Aldo.

'Exactly. And they'd show the evidence all right, don't worry about that. Whether they found it at the railway station. Whether they found it in the police station. It doesn't make much difference. What you have to understand, Signor Tom, is that here in Italy, we're not dealing with what happens. We're dealing with what *ought* to have happened. Or what certain people *wanted* to have happened. Like a town that's been built on top of another town, and another town on top of that, stratum after stratum, until no one can be sure which was the original.'

What was plain to me was that he revelled in it all; he seemed to live, eat and breathe conspiracy. As he spoke, he smiled, there was a glint in his eye, and he seemed to be adumbrating something much larger than the day's atrocity, something in which this atrocity was merely subsumed. '*I* don't think it was the Red Brigades,' he said. 'That's not their style. The Red Brigades kill people, they shoot poor devils in the legs, they kidnap Prime Ministers and execute them, but they don't usually blow people up. Especially people they don't know. That's a Fascist trick. That's a right-wing thing. The Red Brigades are the best thing that ever happened to the Fascists. They can always be blamed, they can always be used, they're always an excuse. And they're no real danger.'

'Why?' I asked him.

45

'Because the Red Brigades aren't interested in power; only in destroying power. They have no programme. Not a real one. Every outrage is no more than a dramatic gesture. Just a protest. Fundamentally, they're anarchists. Creating chaos. And that's the Fascists' game; they play it for them. Chaos. Out of chaos comes fear. Out of fear comes a desire for order.'

Aldo was smiling, now, with the tolerance of a parent for a precocious child, reciting a party piece which he has often heard before. 'For Giancarlo,' he said, 'the whole world is a conspiracy, and the ultimate conspirator is God.'

'No, no,' Lucetti demurred, 'not the whole world. Just Italy. And not God. Not even the Pope. After all, they may have killed the Pope.'

At this, Aldo laughed. 'Listen to him!'

'The last Pope,' Lucetti said. 'Poor, good John Paul I. Died in his bed. A healthy man. Died of what? A heart attack? Nobody knows. Nobody wanted to. A cardinal got into his bedroom and voilà! Nothing left. No diary, papers, glasses, medicine. Why did he die? He'd discovered too much.'

It seemed the wildest flight of fantasy. Aldo grinned at me. 'Journalists!' he said. 'They're far worse than historians.'

'We *are* historians!' cried Lucetti. 'Contemporary historians. We find the truth out while things are going on. Not a hundred, two hundred, five hundred years later. We print the things historians will use; when we are allowed to. Bella, la vita di uno storico! A great life, an historian's is! I envy you all. You sit in comfort and safety, there in the warm, and pass judgement when there's no more risk. When the corpse is cold.'

'While you,' said Aldo, 'guess at what you cannot know.'

Lucetti put his forefinger to the side of his nose. His eyes gleamed more wildly than ever. 'We know more than we can ever print,' he said. 'More than we dare ever say.'

'What did the last Pope know?' I asked him.

'Ah!' he said, raising his eyebrows at me. 'No one's quite sure, but it will all emerge. There's strange things happening in the Vatican.'

'They always have,' said Aldo.

'But not as strange as now; in the computer age. The age of international finance. Of buttons pressed and billions made.

46

The Vatican's so shrewd, you know. It changes with the times. Under those robes. Beneath those red skull-caps and those mitres.'

'There's computers,' said Aldo.

'You might say that. These are modern minds. Minds that can exploit the modern world, with the cunning and wisdom of the past. And woe to those who try to stop them.'

'What are you saying?' I asked. 'That this cardinal killed the Pope?'

'Who knows?' Lucetti said. 'Perhaps he did. Somebody got to him. Somebody poisoned him. Poisoned his medicine, poisoned his drops, who can tell, now? By the time the police got there, everything was gone. There was nothing to examine, nothing to analyse.'

'And the post-mortem?' I asked.

Lucetti threw back his head in disdain. 'Ma che post-mortem!' He swallowed what was left of his whisky, and called the waiter to bring him another. 'Thank God for the Scots,' he said. 'They make life bearable. You ask, was it the cardinal? It's immaterial. If it wasn't the cardinal, it was someone else. These people can always find somebody.'

'These people? What people?'

'Ah!' he winked at me. 'There's the mystery. There's the problem. At the bottom of it all, at the bottom of everything: those people.'

'And you call *me* a conspiracy theorist!' Aldo laughed at me.

'Then how does the present Pope fit into all this?' I asked Lucetti.

'He doesn't. He's the perfect Pope for them. A simple Polish peasant. An outsider. Who cares for things that don't concern them like divorce, abortion, birth control. Who'll never stick his nose in their affairs because he's too naïve and ignorant. The perfect Pope. They'd like always to have a Pole.'

'Do you think the same people who did this today, who killed all those poor devils at the station, also blew up the train my wife was on, between Florence and Bologna?' I asked Lucetti.

'It's possible,' he said. 'Even probable. But here in Italy, today, anything is possible. As I've told you, people take on

47

protective colouring. Terrorists ape one another, and try to blame one another. We don't know who did this, we don't know who did that. We can only guess. We cannot even deduce. On the one hand, this crime resembles the other, so it might have been the same people. On the other hand, it might *not* be the same people, just because the first atrocity gives someone else the chance to strike, and project the blame.'

I was beginning to feel uneasy. He was right I supposed, but it was hardly what I wanted to hear. I could not share his fascination with the whole, horrible imbroglio.

'Tell him, Giancarlo,' Aldo said, 'tell him not to become involved. This is a mad Englishman. He wants to be a detective.'

Lucetti looked at me with approval. 'Why not?' he asked. 'Who ever knows? The real detectives find out nothing. Either because they're stupid, which is giving them the best of it, or more likely because they don't want to. An amateur couldn't find out any less. He might even find out more. He might just blunder into something. That's how the police usually find things out themselves; when they do. Look at that bank bombing in Milan. The vital tapes turned up years later in Trieste; in a police station.'

'Ma scherziamo!' cried Aldo. 'We're joking. People who find things out get killed. You know that. Journalists get shot.'

'Quite right,' said Lucetti. 'That's why it's safer to be a sports journalist. You find things out, but you don't have to publish them. And everybody's a football fan; even the terrorists.'

'Mi raccomando,' said Aldo. 'I implore you. You know your way around. You're an Italian. A Bolognese. A journalist. What does Tom know of Italy? He knows the Middle Ages!'

'And very useful too,' Lucetti replied. 'The perfect preparation.' Then he turned to me. 'But what do you want to find out? And what use would it be if you did?'

'No use, I suppose,' I said. 'No practical use. Only to me; and to my peace of mind. It's difficult to explain.'

'No, no, I understand,' he said, and, curiously, I felt he did; on that intuitive level which was perhaps the only valid one. 'Vuol vendicarsi,' he said, regarding me. 'He wants to vindicate himself.'

'He's mad,' said Aldo.

'There are times when madness has its uses,' said Lucetti. 'After all, we are dealing with a kind of madness, In those who commit the atrocities. But not with those who plan them.'

And I felt myself being drawn again, into the whole, great, paranoiac fantasy, in which I too would now play a part, I too would be crazily categorised.

'Vecchio brontolone!' Aldo smiled at Lucetti, 'You old rumbler! Leave him alone! Don't include him in these daft inventions of yours!'

'They're not mine,' Lucetti said, 'and they are real. They're Italy's. They're yours, as much as mine, they're his, they're everybody's. If I can help you, come to me,' he told me. 'I might be useful. I can introduce you to people; people who would put you in touch with other people.'

'Who would put him in touch with other people who would shoot him in the head,' said Aldo.

'Not necessarily,' said Lucetti. 'You're a mediaevalist. Okay. I'm an existentialist. I understand your friend, which you can't. He's interested in the search, not in the solution. He isn't looking for revenge. *He's* a mediaevalist; but he isn't mediaeval. He wants to make a protest. A protest against the mania of the world.'

'Is that right?' Aldo asked me quietly.

'There's something in it,' I said. More in it than I cared to concede. In his strange obsession with plot and counter plot, Lucetti could enter my private world in a way that a more rational man like Aldo could not.

'I must get back to the office,' said Lucetti, downing his whisky and rising from his chair. 'I've still the last edition to get out. We'll put the news of the bombing on the front page; in black borders. We may be a sports paper, but we try to live in the world. Beyond the stadium. Come to me tomorrow, Tom. I'll be in my office at twelve. I'll send you to see an honest policeman.' And, embracing Aldo again, with solicitude, he was off.

I spent the following morning in the archives. My head was awhirl; I had hardly slept all night. I needed the brief peace of a quiet room, the distraction of documents and the distant past. By now I had been again and again through those papers which bore directly on Hawkwood's life, which told me how the Bolognese had feared him, how once, in 1377, they had held his two small sons to ransom, a guarantee for good behaviour. Those elusive sons of a mysterious mother, brothers, perhaps, of a sister supposedly called Fiorentina, figures who still lurked in shadow, waiting for documents to authenticate, identify them.

Now I looked at them again, knowing I would eventually succumb and ask once more for the chronicles of what had happened thirteen years later, when Hawkwood was an old man, an astonishing old man, fighting for Bologna, as well as Florence, against Milan and the invading mercenaries of Dal Verme. Zuzzo, Hawkwood's trumpeter, sent with a ritually blood-stained glove to challenge Dal Verme as he camped outside the city; sent a second time, then a third, till Dal Verme, still unwilling to fight, detained him there. Hawkwood with the buongustai of Bologna at his back, even then rich in good things to eat and drink, plying him and his army with provisions, while Dal Verme and his men went hungry. What, in the end, had won the war on that Midsummer's Night; swords or cutlery?

But to read of the glove, now, disconcerted me. I had seen too many bloodstains the day before; blood-stained shirts, blood-stained blouses, blood-stained dresses, blood-stained bandages. And none of them on the body of a soldier.

I knew, anyway, that I was gambling, taking shots in the dark, reduced to sifting through manuscripts and records which had no direct bearing on Hawkwood, but might just throw a glancing light, or in themselves lead to somewhere more solid. At my desk in the quiet room, where a handful of sedentary men bent over books in utter silence, I achieved a transient calm. And yet, as I read and meditated, the work seemed less and less of a distraction, more and more relevant to what I was doing, what I had seen the day before.

The Italy that rose again before my eyes was one in which sheer self-preservation demanded Hawkwood's attitude of rugged self-sufficiency, in which to manifest the slightest weakness, give any ground or purchase, was to risk obliteration. What I seemed gradually to be finding was a new perspective on him, one from which I needed no longer to excuse or justify him, from which the bleak realities of his time precluded any such need.

This was not to condone Cesena; an abdication of morality, albeit twentieth-century morality, which was no more imaginable than condoning yesterday's bomb. Yet I realised, as I read through the Latin of the city annals, that I was seeking, more than ever, that glimpse of exculpation. Somewhere, perhaps, buried and forgotten, there was a despatch from Hawkwood himself, expressing dismay, disclaiming responsibility, insisting that his orders had been disobeyed. Lucetti would have understood him, I thought. Lucetti would have dismissed the massacre with a smile and a shrug. 'Cosa vuoi? Altri tempi! What do you want? Different times.' Times he would probably have felt quite at home in, telling tales of the Pope, of conspiracy in Rome and Avignon, of high intrigue and poison at the court of Bernabò Visconti in Milan, of deadly plotting in the Florentine Signoria.

I felt strangely happy to be seeing him again. In his boundless cynicism, he could comfort me. 'Caro Tom!' he greeted me, arms outstretched, as I walked into his office. I had come through the dusty newsroom of the paper where men in shirtsleeves shouted into telephones, clanked at typewriters, and exchanged badinage with large, black-overalled women, who swept in and out like galleons.

Lucetti's office, marked DIRETTORE, Editor, was glassed off from the rest of the floor. He, too, was in his shirtsleeves, large, round gold links in his cuffs, a diamond pin in his blue silk tie. 'This Englishman is trying to understand modern Italy,' he told a tall, slim, grey-haired man who stood beside his desk. 'And I've told him no one can. No one does.'

'That's certain,' the grey-haired man replied.

'So if he wants to be confused,' Lucetti said, 'it's better that he come to me. Then at least he can be confused in a nice way.'

'Meno male, just as well,' said the other man. He bowed to me, and went out. Lucetti shut the door, sat down behind his desk, and motioned me to a chair.

'You've seen the papers?' he asked, gesturing at the profusion of them spread across his desk, each with its images of death, each with its headlines crying of a Fascist plot.

51

'Yes,' I said.

'Everyone's blamed the neo-Fascists. Everyone's sure who it was. Not even the Secret Services dare blame it on the Red Brigades. Not yet. They'll try in time; be sure. When they feel safe to do so. When the trail's gone cold. When the impact fades. When the public begins to lose interest. Then they'll "discover" something. Wait and see.'

'If I must,' I said.

'Now, I've a policeman who will see you. The one I mentioned to you; Inspector Roccomonte. Very young. Very honest. Very serious. Very frustrated. He's from the Veneto. He was involved in the investigation of . . . the explosion.' He paused a moment. 'Of the train on which your wife died. He would like to help you. The other man I've got for you is a journalist. Not a journalist like me. He used to be, that's how I know him. He was a sports journalist. Then he went mad, and got political. Before, he went mad about women. I'll write his name and a phone number. He won't be there. He's a Florentine; he may be there. Or in Rome. He moves about. He isn't on the run; but when you work for a paper like *Lotta Operaia*, it's best not to stay too long in one place.'

He gave me a slip of paper on which he had written, in heavy pencil, Claudio Della Martira, and a Bolognese telephone number. 'È molto donnaiolo,' he said. 'A great ladies' man. But now, every fuck has to be a revolutionary statement. Either he's screwing an upper-class woman out of revenge, or a girl comrade out of proletarian solidarity. But he's a good lad. Say that I sent you, when you find him.' I thanked him. 'Always at your disposal,' he said, rising, shaking hands, escorting me to the door. 'Whatever you need, wherever you are, whatever I can do. And my regards to Giovanni Acuto!'

Inspector Roccomonte was indeed a serious young man; he exuded seriousness in a peculiarly Italian, bureaucratic way, a kind of seriousness which presupposes humourlessness, a devotion and dedication to duty which seem to stifle feeling, condition response and promote the moral equivalent of tunnel vision. He was perhaps a year or two younger than myself, his dark hair was cut short, his pale cheeks were closely shaved, his neat grey suit eschewed any claim to elegance. He sat behind his desk, the incarnation of rectitude and formality, and I wondered what he could possibly tell me that was anything other than minimal, relentlessly official.

'Dr Lucetti informed me about your wife,' he said. 'Allow me to offer you my most sincere condolences.'

This, too, had the ring of an official pronouncement, and I thanked him with a similar formality.

'And now, in what way can I help you?'

The ball was inexorably in my court, as I sat in his bare and narrow little policeman's office, with its ugly, functional furniture, its pronouncements pinned to the walls, its solitary departure from impersonality a photograph, framed on his desk, of a pretty, dark, smiling woman, with two little girls beside her on the grass.

I was not sure how he could help me, or whether he could help me at all. In my frustration, I spoke the words that came straight into my head. 'I want to find out who killed my wife.'

This clearly startled him. His head jerked up, but then he was impassive again. 'We are trying to find that out, professore.'

'But haven't you some idea? Some clue? After all this time?'

He looked up at me with his official impassivity. 'Certainly we have our theories. We are following up our suppositions. More than that . . .'

Less than that, I thought. How could there possibly be less than that?

'These things are better left to the police, professore.'

'I don't want to arrest anybody,' I said, 'I don't want to shoot anybody. I simply want to find out what happened.'

'But that's not a simple thing,' he replied.

'Inspector,' I said, with a great fury welling up inside me, 'I know that well. I don't have to be told. I may be a foreigner, but I am not naïve.'

'Permit me. I never said you were . . .'

'But you implied as much!' I found myself crying. 'Lucetti said that you might help me. If you don't want to, well, all right, I'll go. Tolgo il disturbo. I'll remove the nuisance.' There was, besides a certain desperation, method in my outburst. So long as I stayed on his level of buttoned-down rationality, I would get nowhere. Moreover, in Italy, outbursts could be effective, while in England, where one had

53

learned restraint, they were simply counter-productive. And indeed, his tone did change, becoming suddenly apologetic. 'We in the police have many difficulties.'

'I know,' I said.

He looked down at his desk. 'Over and above the usual difficulties, the ones that any policeman has, there are . . . let us say, structural difficulties . . . internal difficulties. Perhaps I don't make myself clear.'

'Yes; very clear.'

'Dr Lucetti told me that you are a very brilliant man. A great historian. A great expert on Italian mediaeval history.'

I tried not to smile. Lucetti had been romancing again.

'Our theory,' the Inspector said, 'that is to say, the official theory, is that that train was bombed by the Red Brigades.'

'Like yesterday?' I said. 'Like the Italicus?' and again he looked uncomfortable.

'It's too early to be certain of what happened yesterday. In . . . your wife's case, in the case of that train, there was no evidence. We found only the remains of the suitcase in which we feel sure the bomb was placed. But they were so fragmentary that forensic tests were virtually useless. We think we know, however, the kind of explosive that was used, and it would implicate the Red Brigades.'

He might have been reading, without a grain of conviction, an official statement. 'But it wasn't the Red Brigades, was it?' I demanded.

He looked up at me now, looking deeply weary, and he said. 'I don't think so. That's a personal opinion. Just my own supposition.'

'And yesterday?'

'Too early,' he repeated, 'it's still too early,' which in itself seemed, by implication, an admission.

'I'd just like a name,' I said. 'Somewhere to start.'

Regarding me, he said, 'There are a thouand places to start, and nowhere to finish. Nowhere for you, and nowhere for anybody else.'

At that moment, all my irritation with him subsided, and I only felt sorry for him, a decent man in an intractably malignant world.

'This is not England,' he said. 'You realise there are dangers.'

'They don't worry me.'

He shrugged. 'There's a colleague of mine,' he went on, 'in Padua. A very honest man.' Out of a desk drawer, he took a small white square of paper, and wrote on it. 'In the questura there,' he said. 'You can tell him I sent you. There I think you might find out who didn't do it; which might possibly explain to you who did.' I took the piece of paper, thanked him, and shook hands with him. He looked irretrievably tired now, with something that went beyond mere physical exhaustion. He rose from his desk and ushered me to the door. 'I wish you luck,' he said, in the voice of a man who knew that he would never have any.

I went back to the archives. It was difficult, at first, to apply myself. The meetings had left me in a state of vibrant restlessness, physical in its effects; a persistent throbbing in the chest. This was absurd, I told myself. There was no reason for it. What had I had but a couple of conversations, neither in itself productive, each holding out merely the prospect of other conversations; provided I could even find the relevant people. In its way, it was all less rewarding than what I was doing now! At least I had in front of me records, evidence, facts on which a conclusion might be reached; or altered. This was not even their useful equivalent.

And there was danger as well, I dutifully reminded myself, though the concept of danger was merely intellectual. When had I ever been in physical danger? In a car, perhaps. Once, driving back to Oxford from London, entering that little pocket of mist some fifteen miles from the city, a vast, articulated lorry had cut in on me, forcing me in a desperate swerve on to the hard shoulder of the motorway, where I hauled the wheel round again before I crashed into the chalk hill, and stopped, shaking and sweating. Once or twice on the rugby field in school and college, fallen among the flying boots, putting my arms over my head and hoping for the best. Once in a swimming pool in Tewkesbury, where I mistimed my dive, lost all sense of place, crashed into the pool, swallowed water, choked, and thought that I was going to drown. But those were casual accidents, with no active malevolence behind them.

The idea that people might positively try to do me harm was difficult to absorb, most of all in a country which was not my own, where, however well I thought I knew it, the 'real' stayed at a distance, like a world perceived through glass. Why, even Simonetta's death, however wanton the act, had been by chance, had not involved her as herself, as an intended victim.

To be in danger. To live perpetually in danger. Now, willy nilly, I was back to Hawkwood again, to the very documents I had in front of me. Dangers were different now, but was *danger* any different? A fourteenth-century soldier was unlikely to be blown apart at random, but a longbow was as deadly as a rifle; more deadly, perhaps, than any other weapon for five hundred years. A sword could cut your head off. A dagger, worse still, could always stab you by surprise.

Living with this, would one become inured to it? Could *I* become inured to it? The question seemed academic, almost frivolous. In front of me, I now had letters sent from the Signoria to Bologna, speaking of the threat from Milan, the invasion by Dal Verme, the need to hire and pay Hawkwood: Giovanni Acuto. Somehow, I found my tension was subsiding. What was my predicament, after all, compared with a whole life of danger, of danger faced from day to day, from youth into old age? And not the anonymous danger of artillery shelling, aerial bombardment, remote riflemen, but the imminence of hand-to-hand combat, broadswords, axes, maces, a violence that was intimately personal. Yes, it could be borne, it could be done, so I, too, could surely do it if I had to, provided that it lasted long enough, that it achieved its own infernal rhythm, enabling me to bear it.

At dinner, for which I had invited him to the same restaurant, Aldo tried again to discourage me, disparaging Lucetti's notions as mere paranoid fancy. But they had excited me, there was no denying it, even if I dare not tell Aldo so. Lucetti might be wrong, but he was insidiously stimulating. His certainty that there was a pattern, a motivating force, a figure in the carpet, struck a response in me.

'Did he help you?' asked Aldo.

'He gave me two names,' I said. 'He sent me to see a policeman.'

'That would be Inspector Roccomonte. As usual. Who was the other?'

'A journalist called Della Martira.'

Aldo laughed. 'That was to be expected too. Della Martira's the only person with crazier ideas than Lucetti. The difference being that Della Martira puts them into practice. Or tries to. Della Martira's quite mad. Lucetti just pretends to believe in mad ideas.'

'Lucetti says Della Martira's a womaniser. Or used to be.'

'And how,' said Aldo. 'He should have stuck to women. But something bit him: God knows what. Probably a woman. A woman revolutionary. One moment he was a journalist, writing exposés for scandal magazines. The next, he was another Trotsky, ready to die on the barricades. He'll probably end up a Fascist. Such people do. Then he'll go back to being just a womaniser again. But how's Giovanni Acuto?'

'Fascinating,' I said. 'Still elusive. I pursue him through the archives.'

'Stick to that!'

'I wish I could.'

The restaurant, this evening, was almost back to normal. Only a couple of tables were unoccupied. Large, florid, red-cheeked men, napkins tucked into their collars, set about great piles of pasta, big bowls of soup, vast palisades of pastry. Plump, well-dressed women chattered at the tables, cheerful and relaxed, eating little less than their husbands. The waiters, too, seemed released from their anxieties of the night before, moving about now with rapid dexterity.

'You seem to have had your wish,' I told Aldo. 'Life is going on.'

He looked around. 'Effettivamente. We're like that, we Italians. We recover very quickly, thank God. But how long can it go on? There's a limit to everything.'

'You mustn't let yourself reach it. You said so, didn't you? Life must go on.'

'Yes, yes, of course it must go on. If it doesn't, we're doomed. But so much unneccessary pain, so much random suffering. The suffering you've experienced yourself.'

'I'm not Italian,' I said, 'but I'm doing my best.'

'Unquestionably you are. You're an example to us. To *me*.'

And mine, I thought, is Hawkwood, l'inglese italianato. Perhaps that was how *he* had learned to soldier on through the long years; English endurance, refined by Italian resilience. He too had lost a wife; though no one knew where.

'My God,' I said, 'you Italians survived the war. What could be worse than the war?'

'*This* is worse than the war,' he answered. 'You expect to suffer in a war. We're used to wars; a thousand years of them. In wars you have enemies, even if they are your own countrymen. But when there's no peace in peace, when the enemy's invisible, when the outrages make no sense, then the people are demoralised. The young, above all; who didn't know the war. Who don't know much about Fascism, and what it did here. Who look around and see corruption, violence, cynicism, treachery.'

I laughed. 'Aldo, we're mediaevalists.'

'We're anachronisms,' he said. 'We still have hope. We still live by illusions. Decent illusions. Not some inhuman ideology. But we were brought up in an easier world. That's how we are able to survive. I'm pessimistic.'

If I am to survive, I thought, it will only be through action and discovery, but I did not tell him this. We had touched on it before, and I knew there was no convincing him.

'Did Roccomonte help you?' he asked.

'He may have done. I don't know, yet. He gave me a name. Someone to see in Padua; another policeman. After I'd lost my temper with him, when he stalled me.'

'Policemen are good at that, even the honest ones.'

'Do you know him?'

'No, but I can imagine him. They fall into certain patterns. He'll be a good Catholic. A good family man. Eager to do the proper thing; until he finds he just isn't allowed to. Then one of three things happens. He turns sour, he turns corrupt, or he leaves the force. He knows he can never change it.'

'He's turning sour I think,' I said. 'I don't believe he'll ever be corrupt.'

'Who can blame him,' asked Aldo, 'when Italy's corrupt?'

'You sound like Lucetti.'

'Do I? We're different. He accepts it; he makes a game of it. I hate it, but I'm like that policeman, I know I can't do anything about it. So my escape is mediaeval history, where I find a worse world, or one that's just as bad; but one that's dead, that doesn't threaten me.'

'It's not entirely dead,' I told him. 'It can bring comfort too. It's more than a refuge.'

He laughed at me. 'Giovanni Acuto, again! But he wasn't alone, Tom, he had an army. Sometimes three thousand men. And many spies. Spies all over Italy. He wasn't Quixote, Tom; and even Quixote had Sancho Panza!'

'You'd have had to pay Hawkwood to tilt at a windmill,' I said.

'Ecco! Precisely. So you can still see clearly.'

'I don't identify with him, I just admire his resourcefulness.'

'But not his butchery. You'd never cut a nun in two!'

'And nor did he!' I said angrily. 'You know that's just a slander. It's been discredited!'

'Pazienza!' he said, laughing again. 'At least it made a good story. Two of his soldiers brawling over a Faenza nun, and he cuts her in two to satisfy the pair of them. Of course I know it's nonsense, but it's always amused me. "Half for each!" he said.'

'Or didn't say. A Sienese slander.'

'Certo, certo, but an inventive one.'

I wondered if he still half-believed the tale, or wanted to believe it. After all, each of us had an interest to declare; as an Italian, his received archetype of Hawkwood would be the truculent English barbarian, as mine would be the sturdy soldier.

'Tom,' said Aldo, with sudden solicitude, 'you should go home. It's much better you go home. Whatever you're looking for, you will not find it here. This Italy can't give it to you.'

'*He* never went home.' I responded. I meant it to come out light-heartedly, but instead it emerged as a kind of defiance, so that Aldo looked at me, surprised. 'And he died in old age,' I added.

'Right,' agreed Aldo, as if now he were humouring me. 'That's true, he was a very old man. Poor, but respected.'

'A bit of a Quixote,' I said, which amused him.

'Già. That might even be true. Right at the end. Only at the end.'

'Pawning his wife's jewellery,' I said.

My wife. I have no wife. I fell silent. Aldo could see my misery. He poured me some wine, then put his hand on my arm. 'I can't convince you,' he said.

Back in my hotel room, I tried to call Della Martira. A

man's voice asked from the other end, 'Where are you calling from?' and when I told him, said, 'Phone from outside.'

I went downstairs, out of the hotel, found a bar, and called the number again. The same voice answered: 'Why do you want Della Martira?'

'Dr Lucetti thought he could help me.'

'How could he help you?'

'I'm an English historian. My wife was blown up in a train.'

'Between Bologna and Florence?'

'Yes.'

'What can Della Martira do about that?'

'I don't know until I see him,' I said.

'He's not here. He isn't in Bologna.'

'Is he in Florence?'

'Who told you that?' the voice asked, sharply.

'Lucetti said he might be in Florence. Can you tell me how to find him; if he *is* in Florence?'

'What's your name?'

'Tom Cunningham.'

'Who was your wife?'

'Simonetta. She was a Florentine.'

There was a silence, then the voice said, 'Go to Florence. Ring this number at the same time next Friday. Then I'll tell you if Della Martira will see you.'

He rang off. I wondered if it had been Della Martira himself, but somehow felt it wasn't. I'd willingly go to Florence, as I always did, even though there were so many, inescapable memories there of Simonetta; at the turn of almost every corner, at the sight of almost every square. I would not stay with her family in San Domenico. They would want me to, or say that they wanted me to, but the interaction of their grief and my own would be just too much to bear. Besides, as I moved into this half-world of concealment and intrigue, I needed a free hand. I could not function if I stayed with them, could not bring them into my secret, which they would never understand, and which I never could explain. Not even, fully, to myself.

Why bother, they would ask? Why keep the pain alive, why open up the wounds? Why, indeed, except that I knew the wounds would never heal, for me at least, if I did nothing. I would go, of course, to see them. Not to do so was unthinkable, when they were bound to hear that I had been in Florence. Then I would tender some excuse; the need to be near the Biblioteca Nazionale, perhaps. They would pretend that they believed me, believing, probably, and not wrongly, that I found it too sad to be with them.

III

It was always hard; and it was hard again, the day after I arrived, when I lunched with them in San Domenico. How beautiful it was to drive up the beautiful, steep, narrow road, with its high stone walls, the overhanging canopy of green, the smell of foliage soaked by the rain. How many times had she and I walked or driven up this road, toiled up the hill, stopped, in the earlier days, in some alcove, to embrace? As for the three of us, her parents and myself, we were trapped, as in a moral air pocket, from which there could be no escape.

Out of our delicate concern for one another's feelings, we dare not talk about her, yet there was nothing else to talk about. As the butler, in his striped blue and white jacket, let me through the great, green metal gates, as the rain dripped from the branches on my head, as I crossed the short, gravel driveway to the villa, I found myself struggling to move forward, fighting not to stand still, even to turn and to go back. Go down the hill again; escape to Florence. But I was now at the villa's door, and her mother was greeting me. How poignantly like Simonetta she looked; the same fine carriage, tha same quizzical tilt of the head, the same superbly shaped eyes. Even her hair, though she must surely dye it, was close to the same fair colour.

'Ciao,' she said, 'ciao, Tom!' and her smile, too, was poignantly like Simonetta's. I embraced her, ending the illusion, for where her daughter's body would always come eagerly to meet mine, hers, quite properly, remained unrelaxed in my grasp. She had been very beautiful, Simonetta had often told me, 'Much more beautiful than me. But I'm younger. She can do nothing about that, but she can never really accept it.'

61

'Tom, Tom!' said the General, coming forward. He was a surprisingly young-looking man, of great geniality, his military aspect seldom revealed. Just now and then, talking to the servants, reacting to some opinion he considered ludicrous, one would hear the rasp of command. We embraced, in turn, and he made me sit down. The pleasant sitting-room, with its red-tiled floor, was warmed by an exquisite tall terracotta stove. There were family portraits on the walls, one of which showed a younger, undoubtedly beautiful Signora, infinite photographs of Simonetta: as a pretty child; a lovely, shy adolescent; a young woman; a bride. I could not bear to look at them.

I turned to look instead at the panoply of mementoes the General had brought back from all over the world. Carved, perfect, elongated African heads; jade elephants; red Bohemian glass; bark paintings from Mexico; parades of porcelain. What taste he had, and how eclectic he was. Now he offered me a drink. A whisky. His whiskies were always very strong, and I was glad of that. When I had drunk it, I would accept another. And perhaps another. At lunch, always a good, plain lunch, I would knock back their excellent Chianti. It made things so much easier. By the end of lunch, I would be a little drunk. Not noticeably, still less offensively. Just drunk enough to bear the memories, not to give way to the associations. Through my growing, comforting alcoholic blur, I admired the General's kindly smile, his rosy cheeks, his deep, considerate decency. He must feel the loss of her just as much, in his own way, as I, and my presence must distress him just as much as his, his wife's and their mementoes did me.

We talked about the bomb in Bologna; how could we avoid it? But there were bitter associations here as well. A railway station. An explosion. Death. As she had died. 'I was there,' I said.

'Ma no!' said Laura, my mother-in-law. 'Come mai? How was that?'

'My train was coming into Bologna just as the bomb went off.'

'So you might have been in the station!' she cried.

'Yes. There was only a few minutes in it.'

'How long afterwards did you get into the station?' asked the General.

'Oh, within a quarter-of-an-hour. I walked down by the side of the track.'

'Macchè!' exclaimed Laura. 'Why ever would you want to do that?'

'I don't quite know,' I said, and it was true. I still didn't really know.

The General looked at me enquiringly. 'You wanted to help?'

'Yes. No. That was part of it, I suppose. I wasn't much help. I was pretty useless. They wouldn't let me do anything. Not even carry a stretcher.'

'How horrible!' cried my mother-in-law. 'All those poor people!'

'Yes,' I said, 'it *was* horrible.'

'Most horrible of all in peace,' the General added. 'Or what's supposed to be peace.'

Laura started crying. 'I'm sorry,' I said. 'I wish I hadn't mentioned it.'

'*We* mentioned it,' the General responded. He rose, and put an arm round his wife's shoulders, till at last, with a convulsive movement, handkerchief to her face, she got up, and rushed out of the room.

'Cosa vuoi?' asked the General. 'What would you expect? It's always hardest for a mother.'

Hard for all of us, I thought. We sat in wretched silence. Should I tell him, I wondered, what I was doing? A military man. Perhaps he *would* understand; he might even be able to help. Alcoholic fantasies. As a military man, he was a rational man, and what I was doing was utterly illogical. A soldier responds to orders, not to impulses. So I finished my drink, he poured me another drink, and I wanted to be gone, away from their grief, which only increased my own.

'They seem to know whom they're looking for,' the General said at last. 'There's no real doubt, this time.'

'So they say.'

He looked at me. 'Don't you believe them?'

'I don't know,' I said. 'I don't know what to believe. Or whom. That's almost the worst of it.'

'That's true,' he said. 'The enemy's invisible. Anonymous. It's not a soldier's war.'

'It doesn't seem to be a policeman's either,'

'It's hard for the police,' he said. 'They're working in the dark. The newspapers get at them. The politicians bring pressure on them. The young are disaffected.'

'Are you surprised?' I asked.

He looked at me again. 'There's no discipline,' he said. 'This is a country without discipline.'

I did not argue with him. He was an honest man, quite liberal for a soldier, especially one who had grown up under Fascism. Yes, there had been discipline then, of a perverted sort. Black shirts and marches. 'Giovinezza.' That fat fraud in his fez, spouting nonsense, bombast, rhetoric from the balcony of Palazzo Venezia. The illusion of purpose. The façade of order. Things must have seemed simple, then.

'Excuse me,' he said. 'I'll go up and see Laura.'

Left alone, I wandered round the room, picking up pictures of Simonetta, looking at her lovely face, thinking of her in this room, in his house, which had gone so bleak without her. For the second time that day, I felt a great impulse to escape, even took a step towards the door, before I stopped myself, aware it was absurd. After all, I wasn't staying here. I thought of the good, kind, ultimately simple General upstairs, comforting his wife, when I was sure he needed comfort himself. How he loved her! How he had loved Simonetta! Had she loved Simonetta as much? I doubted it. She was too much involved with herself. When I took Simonetta away, I don't think she was sorry, but he, I'm sure, was devastated, however well he may have deceived even himself. And I? I had loved her deeply. I still did. He and I had that in common; it was an unspoken affinity between us. Perhaps, though never consciously, we had been rivals. Now we were simply united in our lasting love.

If I wanted the truth, I was sure that he, on some unacknowledged level, wanted revenge, though he would never admit it, or even formulate it.

Soon he and Laura would come down. He would still be consoling her, when it was he who needed consolation. And down they duly came, the General with his arm around her shoulder, she *en souffrant*, the little, lace handkerchief still dabbed to her eye. 'Mi dispiace, Tom, mi dispiace, I'm sorry.'

'Sorry for what?' I asked. 'It's only natural. One horror after another. One horror recalling another.'

'You're right, quite right, it's all horror. That's Italy today. A country of horror. Where no one's safe; even the most innocent.'

It was true, however false her tone. I could only agree with her.

The meal, as usual, was both light and good; pastina in brodo, a Milanese cutlet, and of course the Chianti, which helped me to survive it. Eating, at least, saved one to some extent from talking, while the hovering presence of the butler saved one from talking about intimate things. Yet what else was there to talk about? What else remotely mattered? To ignore what mattered, to chatter about inconsequential things, was as depressing as to talk about our misery.

I drove my little, blue, hired Fiat 127 quickly down the hill, trying to ignore the beauty of the journey, with its cruel accretion of the past. Beauty and cruelty, I thought; if you wanted a symbol for Italy, there it was. And then Hawkwood blessedly distracted me.

Had *he*, I wondered, been aware of its beauty, which must have been so much greater then, even if great domes and palaces had still to be built? Did soldiers ever care about such things? Some did, I knew; those elderly men you sometimes came across – scouts at Oxford, publicans, railway guards – whose seamed faces would suddenly light up at the mention of Italy, with all its bright associations, the transiently open, welcoming Italy made known to them in the world war. But to a military commander, land was terrain, hills were something to be stormed or occupied, mountains were mere barriers. As for cities, even the most magnificent of them, even Florence itself, they were places to be attacked or defended, sometimes – as with Cesena – destroyed.

Then I thought of Hawkwood and his men coming, perhaps, down this very hill, on their march from Fiesole to the outskirts of the city. He'd have taken Florence then, if he could, if mediaeval cities – like all cities for a hundred years – had not been so difficult to storm. And taking it, who knows what damage his uncouth forces would have done?

It seems, despite himself, that he finally succumbed to Italy, never going home, retiring at last to Tuscany itself.

Such thoughts, at least, got me unscathed down the hill, and back into the city.

That evening, I called the number in Bologna. I was staying in a hotel in the narrow Via Porta Rossa, just off the Piazza Santa Trinità, as I had often done since my undergraduate days, but I telephoned from a pay phone in a nearby bar, anticipating the inevitable question.

'Where are you calling from?'

'A bar,' I said. 'You can hear the noise.'

'Can anyone hear *you*?'

'No one's near enough.' There was an hiatus; the silence, I thought, of paranoia. Then the man said, 'Della Martira will see you. There's a bar in the Piazza Santo Spirito, the one with tables outside. Be *in*side, at ten o'clock tonight.'

The church of Santo Spirito, the piazza itself, had always been great favourites of mine, not only for the glory of the cupola, the elegant, elaborate campanile, the solid majesty of the great, grey walls, the splendour of the massive steps, but for the air of pathos and neglect. Here, in Oltrarno, just behind the river, the piazza and its church seemed somehow forgotten. Boys would kick fat, soft balls around the steps, on which sad, young derelicts would often be sitting. Tourists came, it seemed, quite rarely; it was a part of Florence which had stayed inviolate from these hordes, maintaining shabby-genteel grandeur.

I sat at a table in the cramped little bar, drinking a cappuccino; it was nearly half past ten before Della Martira appeared. I was sure it was he, as soon as I saw him come briskly in, dashingly dressed in an open leather jacket, a gold medallion round his neck, dangling within the open collar of his red silk shirt, dark glasses shielding his eyes. He had the bright, blond hair of a true Florentine; he was barely of middle height.

He saw me at once, sat down at my table, and asked the barista to bring him a cognac. 'I'm Della Martira,' he said. We shook hands; he barely let his hand rest in mine. 'What do you want from me?'

There was about him a strange amalgam of the conspiratorial and the chic. He seemed too elegant, too good-looking, too narcissistic, to be a real revolutionary. His dark glasses were disconcerting, as perhaps they were meant to be. It was difficult to see his eyes, even when they were looking at you, as now they were.

'Your wife was killed,' he said, flatly.

'Yes,' I answered. 'She was blown up on a train.'

'I know, I know,' he said impatiently. 'And you want to find out who did it.'

'Yes.'

'That's easy,' he replied. 'The Fascists did it. They do all such things.'

'And Bologna station?'

'They did that, as well.'

'The Secret Services . . .'

'Those pigs,' he said, with a contemptuous gesture, 'those cretins. They'd love to prove it was the Left. Fascists, the lot of them. They want a coup. And when there's an atrocity, it's ways the same: "The Red Brigades have done it! We've got evidence!" Till years later, it all comes out. The Red Brigades *haven't* done it. The neo-Fascists have done it. Then one of them gets caught, then perhaps extradited and there's a trial. Somewhere right down in the south, some town nobody has ever heard of, that nobody even knows how to get to, and it trails on and on till everyone forgets it. Then they acquit him. It will happen again.'

'I hope not,' I said, 'I hope not!'

'There *is* no hope! Why do you think the Red Brigades exist? You want to find out? There's no need to find out! It's quite obvious now. And if you did find out, what would you do?'

'I don't know,' I replied, aware of how inept I must sound.

'Ma!' he cried, throwing up his small, elegant, well-kept hands in contemptuous despair. 'You must want to do *something*. If you don't want to shoot them, you surely want to denounce them.'

'I'm not sure,' I said.

'Then why are you doing it? A che cosa serve? What's the use of it?'

There was now subliminal awareness, as there had somehow been with Lucetti. Della Martira had cast himself, as I could see, as a man of action, though I could also sense there was an element in it of masquerade. Still, that was how he saw himself now, and there was no place in his new world for passive, indecisive people. 'If you want to track them down,' he said, 'and finish the bastards, then I'd help you. Denouncing them would be no good. The police would laugh at you. Or else, at the very most, they'd put them on trial the way I told you. A fiasco. In Italy today, you do these things yourself, or they never get done at all.'

'The way they were done to Aldo Moro,' I found myself saying. Such indiscretions, under the pressure of events, seemed to flow from me now in a way they had not done before; least of all in England. This time, even Della Martira's dark glasses could not hide the animus of his stare.

'That,' he said, 'was a great symbolic gesture. It wasn't a case of killing a man; it was a case of destroying an image. An image of corruption. A man at the head of the political party which has debauched Italy. Which has robbed and screwed and exploited Italy for nearly forty years.'

'We shall cut off his head with the crown on it,' I said.

'What?'

'It's what the Roundheads said when they executed King Charles I.'

But that was in public, I thought. Poor Moro had been shot in the head, stuck in the boot of a car, and dumped in the middle of Rome.

'You're an historian,' said Della Martira. 'Can't you see the significance of what was done?'

'I can see what you mean,' I conceded.

'It told them none of them was safe. If we could get the President of the Council and leave his body right in the middle of Rome, with all his guards, all his escort, all his protection, we could get anybody.'

We, I thought and, as if he guessed what I was thinking, Della Martira said quickly, 'They are everywhere. They can do anything. The police arrest them. The police throw them in prison, take them to court, stick them in cages like so many animals. No matter. There are always more. There will always be others.'

'I expect there will,' I said. 'But I'm not Italian. I am not a revolutionary. If I *were* an Italian, perhaps I would be.'

'Your wife was an Italian.'

'Yes,' I said.

'How hard it is to make you English move. If it were me,

nothing would hold me back. Nothing could stop me. I'd give my whole life to it. Just to find out what happened. Just to leave it at that. How could it ever be enough? It would be like *coitus interruptus*.'

All this was said in a fierce, low, cautious tone which lent what he said a greater intensity. This was the world seen in black and white; my own chromatic view could never be reconciled with his. Yet I still wanted him to help me.

'Wouldn't *you* like to know who they were?' I asked him, disingenuously, though this was as far as I was ready to go, further than I had ever meant to. Yet to get something, I realised I would have to offer something. 'I mean, exactly who they were.'

He raised his handsome head, dismissively. 'Why would we need *you*?'

Why, indeed? 'I'm not asking you to find them,' I said. 'I'm asking you to help *me* find them. Then . . . you could do what you like.'

'We'd need something in return. Something more than just that.'

Something like what? I wondered uneasily. Into what depths could I be drawn? Would I be asked to place a bomb, lure some victim into a trap? Who could tell where such things might lead? I thought, abruptly, of Feltrinelli, the intellectual, the left-wing publisher of fashionable talent, victim of his own bizarre fantasy, found dead beside a pylon he was supposedly trying to blow up. I shuddered, and, as Della Martira looked sharply at me, turned up the collar of my jacket, pretending I felt cold. 'I could take messages,' I told him. 'Things like that.'

He shrugged. 'Better than nothing. We need couriers at times. People they don't suspect. An English professor; that might be quite useful.'

There was something of Feltrinelli in Della Martira, I thought, to the extent that he was, for all his commitment, somehow behaving out of character, overcompensating, denying the image of a peaceful non-combatant. Doing things other people should have done, and would have done more effectively, running less risk, less chance of the Nemesis which seemed not only to be waiting but in some strange way to be desired.

69

When at last he took off his dark glasses, I was suddenly given a glimpse of what he must have been, perhaps, essentially, still was. His eyes were bright blue, vividly alive with a cold animation. They did not seem astigmatic. If he was wearing glasses, I thought, it was for effect, concealment, some kind of conscious choice to disguise what he was. A slim, dark girl walked past the door of the bar almost simultaneously, and his eyes flashed towards her; a hunter's look, a womaniser's look, at once appraising and predatory. He turned quickly back to me, caught my glance, and instantly resumed his dark glasses, with a grimace of irritation; a man revealed.

'Do something for us,' he said, 'we might do something for you.'

'A test?' I enquired.

'Call it what you like. We can't afford to take chances. We can't afford to do something for nothing.'

'And if *I* do something, are you certain you can help me?'

'We can guarantee nothing. The Fascists are cunning; very cunning. They deal in lies, deceits, disguises. But we have our people too; all over Italy.'

As Hawkwood did, I thought; though spies was what they called them then. Spies everywhere in Italy, providing him with secrets he could use or sell.

'Have you heard of Sindona?' asked Della Martira.

'Vaguely,' I replied.

'We want Sindona. And he might help you, too. He'd *know*; almost certainly. He fled to America; they gaoled him there, a bank swindle; but he may be back it Italy, again. Allowed to slip out of prison. He had someone shot; in Milan. He came back and lived in Sicily, that's where he comes from. Disappeared, pretended he'd been kidnapped, got a doctor friend to shoot him in the leg. He was charged with the murder; in the end. When he'd had time to cover his tracks here. When they were sure he'd be able to escape. When they knew he'd be gaoled in the States.'

Recollection stirred. 'Wasn't he some kind of banker?' I asked.

'A very big one. A very crooked one. A very well connected one. A Mafia banker, with interests the length and breadth of Italy, a thousand different, interlocking

70

companies; and very good friends in the government. A gangster. A bastard. A murderer. We're sure he's slipped out of gaol and back into Italy. Unbelievable. He can even do it in the States. The authorities here turn a blind eye; he's got too much on them. In the States, it's the Mafia. They're meant to be extraditing him from America, but they never will.'

'And if they do,' I said, 'they'll put him on trial somewhere in Calabria.'

Della Martira laughed for the first time, and the change in his face was remarkable, even though he was wearing the dark glasses. The taut, fanatic's bitterness dissolved, and I saw him suddenly as young, feckless, funny. I could see why women would be drawn to him. He controlled his laughter quickly, as though it were a heresy, proscribed by his party's rules. 'We think he's in Rome,' he said. 'We think he flew in yesterday, on a Uruguayan passport. We want to know what he's doing, we want to know whom he's seeing. We want to find out how long he's staying.'

'Why ask me?' I said.

'He doesn't know you; and he'd be flattered by you. That's always been his weakness; un vanitoso. A vain, jumped-up Sicilian.'

The idea made me laugh. 'If I did find him, what would I ever tell him?'

'That you're an English historian. That you're writing a book about modern Italy, in which he'd be an important figure. That's enough. That should do it.'

'And how would I have recognised him? How would I have ever come across him?'

'Ma non ha fantasia? Haven't you any imagination? You know all about him. You've always wanted to talk to him. And there he is! What a wonderful coincidence!'

'You think he will accept that?'

'Yes, I do. If you flatter him. And even if he doesn't quite believe it, he'll try to.'

So it proved. I found Sindona in a small, shabby restaurant off the Piazza Vittorio, that rump of Rome built by the invading Piedmontese – Roma Umbertina, Umberto's Rome – a sullen wasteland, where ugly green market stalls, their shutters drawn, stood around the square like a regiment from Mars. It

71

was a no-man's-land, nothing to do with the real Rome, full of drab, hectic, bustling life, of ill-dressed people shuffling about on a thousand obscure errands. The last place, I thought, that a financier of Sindona's pretensions would willingly choose; which was no doubt why he had chosen it.

Once in the restaurant, there was no difficulty in recognising him. He stood out like an emperor in exile. His gestures to the shuffling waiter, in his stained white jacket, were wholly too grandiose for the scene. If he had come here to be inconspicuous, he was finding the masquerade hard. There was an air about him of subdued opulence, rather than distinction. With his short, white hair, his long, large, curving nose, his thin, wide mouth, he was certainly a striking figure. But his eyes, large too, and dark, mitigated the effect. They were alert and crafty, the eyes of a clever scallywag, constantly shifting, calculating and assessing.

Beside him sat a big, swarthy, heavy man with stubbled cheeks and chin, whose own eyes moved about the restaurant, dwelt on me at the door; but these were the wary, small, suspicious eyes of a professional bodyguard. Meeting his gaze, I felt a frisson, a spasm high up in my chest. Like Della Martira himself, like Feltrinelli, I had been miscast, but I had none of their passionate involvement to carry me through.

The gorilla's gaze was like a barrier. For a moment, I was reluctant to cross it, and what I knew about Sindona did nothing to reassure me. He had certainly had one man killed, poor Ambrosoli, the honest liquidator, the decent accountant, shot to death in a Milan street – Lucetti had cheerfully briefed me – just before he could publish Sindona's prolix accounts: and, above all, the long list of all those powerful men for whom he had been channelling money. Then there were the threats; to politicians like Ugo La Malfa, who had stood strong and firm against his machinations; against Enrico Cuccia, the banker who had first befriended him, then put a spoke in his crooked wheel. The thug who sat beside him would no doubt shoot me dead with as little compunction as William Aricò, the imported hit man, had murdered Ambrosoli.

What I needed was a table by Sindona, without which accosting him would be extremely hard; and even this would be only the beginning.

Every table was full, but no one else was waiting. 'Momento, Signore, momento, pazienza!' cried the short, plump proprietor, hurrying up to me. Almost immediately, the man and woman dining at the next table but one to Sindona's got up to go, and it was mine. Not ideal, but at least practicable. Sitting down, I darted a quick glance at Sindona and the gorilla and saw, to my relief, that they were still on their main course. Two large bottles of wine, one white, one red, stood on the table

I ordered my meal, propped up a copy of *La Repubblica* in front of me, and affected not to notice them. I was aware, however, that both of them were periodically looking at me; listening when I gave my order, assessing me as I read the newspaper. It was disconcerting but would give me, eventually, a chance to meet Sindona's eyes, and so converse with him. I wondered if the gorilla was carrying a gun. I felt sure he was. I found myself beginning to sweat. When my spaghetti alla carbonara arrived, it was heavy, and I found it hard to digest. I had to counterfeit, I realised, the shock of recognition; but at that, the bird might fly, or, if it stayed, I might meet a bleak hostility. I could well imagine how hard those dark eyes could become.

In the event, my chance came when the two men at the table next to me got up to leave. As they went, I sensed Sindona looking at me again, and glanced back as casually as I could. Our eyes met. His, as I had guessed, were hard with suspicion. I did my best to show a dawning delight, as I appreciated who it was. Would the bird fly? Sindona turned away, and now the bodyguard looked at me, a steady, brutal, affectless look. At the same time, he took a toothpick from its little, glass chimney and began to investigate his teeth, one huge hand cupped over his mouth in a parody of politeness. I looked away, but had to look back again; it was part of the pantomime. Now I knitted my brows, as though striving to be sure that it was he, Sindona.

But before I could speak, or move myself to speak, the gorilla spoke to me. 'You're not Italian.'

'No, I'm English.'

There was an instant fall in tension. He stopped picking his teeth and gave a satisfied nod. 'You're English; not American.' Sindona, too, seemed to relax, but the old man

73

was giving nothing away. He nodded in his turn, though his eyes now were opaque, rather than hard.

'But I come to Italy a lot,' I volunteered. 'I'm an historian.'

At this, as I had hoped, Sindona looked interested. 'Of English history or Italian history?' he asked.

'Of Italian history.'

The eyes quickened. 'And where do you practise your profession? In England or in Italy?'

'At Oxford University,' I said. My trump card; and he fell for it.

'Bello, Oxford,' he said. 'Bellissima cittadina. How I would like to have studied there.'

'You know England well?' I asked. There was no need to 'recognise' him, yet. We could meet on middle ground.

'Not well, unfortunately,' he said, and now the eyes changed again, they softened. He had decided to charm me. He was the man of affairs, the self-made success, too busy in the flux of life to do the things he would have wanted to do. 'I had so little time, when I was young. Earning one's living . . . Now I realise what I missed. But I have been to Oxford. Just a few times. Bello. Bella, l'Inghilterra.'

The bodyguard relaxed, and began to pick his teeth again. There was no danger here. I could be safely ignored.

'In what period of history are you interested?' Sindona asked. His charm was indisputable, but disconcerting: it was the charm of an evil man, far more frightening than the gorilla, who merely did what he was told, beat when he had to beat, shot when he had to shoot, a mindless force of nature.

'Modern history,' I lied. 'Contemporary history now, above all.'

Sindona smiled and gave a little nod, tightening his thin lips. 'I could tell you things . . . .'

'I'm sure you could,' I said, taking the plunge, regarding him now as one who knew who he was. Della Martira was right. He was already, exquisitely, flattered. He had been recognised; and by an Oxford historian. The evident pleasure of it clearly outweighed the irritation at being unmasked. His eyes, now, took on a melancholy, reflective look. 'Many things,' he said. 'Things you never would believe. Not even here. Not even in Italy.'

74

The bodyguard was finishing his *osso buco*, with noisy satisfaction; he plainly wasn't listening to Sindona. Perhaps he had heard it all before.

'I've saved this country,' said Sindona. 'You're an historian; you should write about it. I saved it from Communism; that's what they can't forgive me. That's why so many of them hate me.' Again his expression changed; now it took on a relentless, chilling ferocity, and I could see how Ambrosoli, the honest liquidator, must have died. 'The dirty Left,' said Sindona. 'The filthy, decadent Republicans and Social Democrats who whore for them. The Christian Democrats who betray their party and betray their religion.' He looked me in the face, murderous no more but principled, defiant. '*I'm* a Christian. I always have been and I always will be. I am at peace with God.'

At this, even the bodyguard looked up, but his face remained expressionless. He neither smiled nor looked surprised but merely, greedily, resumed his eating.

'Why do you find me here, in questo postaccio di merda?' asked Sindona. 'In this crappy little place? Why? Why do I have to slip into Italy like some delinquent? After all I've achieved! All the good I've done! Because they're frightened of me. They've conspired against me. They've told lies about me. When I've made billions for people. When I've created trusts and deals and structures other bankers never dreamed of. Envy! Fear! That's what's behind it. The envy of little people for a man with vision. A man who makes them feel even smaller than they are.'

He realised that his voice had grown louder, that he might easily be overheard, and beckoned me to his own table. I picked up my second course, a plate of leathery steak, poured what remained of my Chianti into my glass, and joined the pair of them. The bodyguard looked up at me from his plate with slight surprise now, rather than suspicion.

'Franco,' Sindona said, 'an English professor. An historian. From Oxford University.'

'Piacere,' mumbled the bodyguard, and briefly took my hand in his own great, threatening paw. Sindona himself shook hands with me.

'Your name?'

'Tom Cunningham,' I said.

75

'I think you know who I am.'

'I do'.

Almost as a reflex action, Sindona glanced cautiously about the room, to assure himself that no one else was privy to his secret. 'Sto qui in alberghaccio,' he said bitterly. 'Here, I'm staying in a lousy hotel. But in New York, I used to live properly. In the Hotel Pierre. You know the Pierre Hotel? You should have come to see me there. I had a suite. With seven rooms. An office in a skyscraper.' Now rage and resentment had got hold of him again; now the look in his eyes of vicious self-righteousness was back. 'I'll help you write the truth,' he said. 'I'll make you famous. You'll know things that no one else has ever known. About the most powerful men in America; the best known politicians in Italy. Even about the Pope.' He looked closely at me now, to see if I was impressed. I did my best to seem so, widening my eyes, nodding my head. 'They even pursued me in America,' he said. 'Me, who gave a million dollars to the Presidential campaign! It's inconceivable! But they won't win. They'll never beat me. You'll see. And you can write about it.'

'Thank you,' I said.

He ordered another bottle of wine, and filled my glass. 'What wine!' he said contemptuously. 'If you come to New York, I'll see you have wine. The best champagne! That's how I'm used to living.'

'Yes, of course,' I said.

'And you?' he asked. 'What brings *you* to Rome?'

'My researches,' I said.

'Researches?' and he narrowed the dark eyes, which now grew opaque with suspicion. 'What research is there to do in the Piazza Vittorio? In Roma Umbertina? How ever did you find your way to this lousy restaurant?'

Through Della Martira, was the true answer, through Della Martira, who had told me, 'We know he's living in the Piazza Vittorio, in a so-called first-class hotel; he eats usually in a grubby little restaurant nearby: you should find him there at lunchtime, or at dinner.' I had gone there the previous night at dinner time; he was not to be seen. But I had my answer ready for him.

'Nostalgia,' I said. 'When I was a student here, when I had very little money, this was where we ate.' I was aware that the bodyguard was looking at me too, monitoring my answer, but it seemed to satisfy Sindona, and the bodyguard relaxed as well, pouring himself another glass of wine.

'La vita studentesca,' said Sindona. 'The student life. One understands. By the way, do you like Rome?' Sindona asked me.

'It's very beautiful,' I answered cautiously.

He nodded, uninterested. 'Do you know what Rome is?' he enquired. I shook my head, as I assumed he wished me to. 'Rome is a city of catacombs. Do you see what I mean?'

'Not really,' I replied.

'You've been down a catacomb?'

'A long time ago.'

The bodyguard looked up and rumbled, 'A long time ago! That's when they built them! A long time ago!' and laughed with great self-satisfaction.

Sindona ignored him. 'What is a catacomb?' he asked. 'It's a secret place; and a religious place. It's a place where people hide. Where people plot. Where they conspire. Like Rome has always been. Like Rome today. Rome has never lost the mentality of the catacomb.'

'Giusto, giusto, quite right,' said the bodyguard, through a mouthful of food.

'It's amongst the great regrets of my life, la vita studentesca,' Sindona went on, 'I never really had it. Not even as a student, not at university. Always too poor. Always too busy working. A poor Sicilian; like this fellow here. Eh, Franco?'

The bodyguard looked up. 'Siamo tutti poveracci,' he said. 'We're all poor devils.'

'But there are those who stay poor and those who come out of it,' Sindona said. 'With this,' and he tapped his head. 'We're a race apart, we Sicilians. Always kept down, but always breaking out. Eh, Franco? They can't keep us down!'

'Davvero,' agreed the bodyguard, through a mouthful of cake, 'davvero! True.'

'Chi con la testa,' said Sindona, 'chi con la lupara. Some with their heads, some with a shotgun. Pirandello, Verga. You've read Pirandello and Verga?'

'I have,' I said.

'Great Sicilian writers. Great *Italian* writers. We Sicilians were like the Irish to the English. A persecuted race. A race that's always faced discrimination. But you can't keep us down. Eh, Franco?'

'Giusto, giusto,' repeated the bodyguard, but he did not raise his head from his plate.

Sindona looked at me, now, with the satisfied approval of a vain man looking in a mirror. '*I'll* tell you,' he said. '*I'll* explain to you, and you will write it. You'll become rich, thanks to me. Like so many others. It's right that an Englishman should do it. An English historian. You could never trust an Italian. Da noi, non c'è serietà. There's no trusting people here. I'm not in Rome for long; just a few days. But I'll bring you to New York; to the Hotel Pierre. You'll be my guest. You can stay there in my old suite. And I'll explain to you what's happened in Italy. What's *really* happened in Italy.' He regarded me again. 'But how well you speak Italian.'

'I have lived here a lot,' I replied. 'And I had an Italian wife.' I was pursuing my own purpose. If he knew so much, then there were surely things that he could tell *me*.

'Had?' he said, picking up on this immediately. '*Had* an Italian wife?'

'She's dead,' I told him. 'She was blown up on a train.'

Again the eyes contracted, but this time without hostility; assessing, calculating. 'When? Which train?'

'Earlier this year; between Florence and Bologna.'

'Ah, sì,' he said, and nodded. 'Ah, sì.'

'You know about it?'

'I *heard* about it,' he said warily. 'How tragic. How horrible. Poor woman. Not in the station; in the train.'

'In the train, yes,' I said. '*I* was at the station; at Bologna.'

'You were there?' he said, with a sharp glance. 'On the station? When the bomb exploded? In a train?'

'My train stopped just outside,' I explained. 'I walked there, down the line.'

'Ah! Meno male!'

'Who did it?' I asked, leaning forward to him, the automatic pilot taking over again. 'Who blew up the train?'

'Ma. The train? How should I know?'

'Who else would be so sure to know?' I asked, remembering again that I should flatter him. 'Who knows as much about what goes on in Italy as you?'

Once again, he was mollified. It was a challenge. A tug of war was clearly going on, between his claims to omniscience and his affection of innocence.

'Who do you think it was?' he asked me.

'I've no idea; that's why I'm asking *you*. The police don't seem to know; at least they say they don't.'

'Then why should I know more than the police?'

'Of course you know more than the police!' I exclaimed. 'Or more than the police admit to knowing.'

'And if I did?' he asked, the shrewd, rapacious eyes growing small, again. 'If I did tell you? What's in it for me? Where's the advantage to me? And what would *you* do?'

It was the same, stark question, and once more I avoided it. 'I'll have to decide,' I said.

'You're a strange kind of Englishman. The English are meant to be decisive. To know what they want. To do what has to be done. They don't waste time, like us Italians, philosophising and disputing. Don't you want revenge? Don't you want to kill whoever killed your wife? Excuse me. Excuse the presumptuousness: did you not love your wife?'

'Of course I did.'

'Ecco! Of course you loved your wife; as we all love our wives. And if someone kills our wives, we want to kill them. It's logical. It's natural. Perhaps even more to a Sicilian than to an Englishman. We still have the custom of vendetta. You know what that is, of course.'

'Indeed I do.'

'It's not such a bad thing, vendetta. There's a logic to it. Someone does you harm, you hurt him back. Otherwise, how can you live at peace with the world? *I* have a vendetta; I admit it. A gigantic vendetta. So many people who have done me wrong. So many people who betrayed my trust. How can I live in peace, when people like that exist and flourish, people like that make mock of me!' He seemed transported. The eyes, now, were full of murderous hate. My own request, my own predicament, were quite forgotten. Even the gorilla seemed alarmed, looking up from his plate with a wary apprehension.

'Dottore!' he said. 'Dottore!'

'Macchè dottore! I've learned to know my enemies. To know them, and to deal with them!'

79

People at nearby tables were looking round. Sindona noticed it, and lowered his voice. 'La rivincita è un piatto che si mangia freddo,' he said. 'Revenge is a dish you eat cold. If you want revenge, I understand you. Who wouldn't want revenge?'

'Then you will help me?' I asked.

'Perhaps. Perhaps not. Can you help *me*? Can you help me present the truth? Show the whole world what really happened?'

'I hope I can,' I said ambiguously.

'Then come to me tomorrow!' he said, abruptly rising. 'See me tomorrow. I'm in that big hotel across the square; that calls itself first-class. A swindle! Room 652, the sixth floor. Knock twice, then twice again; at six o'clock. And don't tell anyone. Have I your promise? As an Englishman?'

'You have,' I said. What else could I say?

He gripped my hand, and looked at me. I felt as if I had made a pact with Lucifer. The gorilla's big, cruel hand gripped mine, in its turn. Again, I felt soiled. Then they were gone.

I sat there, slightly dazed, feeling I had somehow supped with the devil, with a spoon that was too short by far. I had felt horrified, yet strangely fascinated. That Sindona could help me, I was certain. That Della Martira wanted to destroy him, or at least to seize him, was plain to me as well. I felt myself being sucked into a moral quicksand, making promises to those who would break any promise without compunction. Sindona was at once riveting and repellent, a kind of lightning conductor for all kinds of corruption, every sort of chicanery. Sometimes he talked sense, sometimes he clearly spoke nonsense. Sometimes he seemed to be telling the truth, at others he was manifestly lying. What was quite obscure was whether he even knew he was lying. But I myself had gained his acquaintance under false colours, I myself was playing a role. Yet now, increasingly, it was a role I was playing for myself. Sindona *knew*. Knew what I needed to know. I was convinced of it. Perhaps Della Martira had surmised as much. 'Six o'clock,' Sindona had said, leaving the restaurant with inappropriate grandeur, the bodyguard lumbering in his wake. 'I'll be in my room,' he had said. 'Don't go to the desk. Come straight up. And bring your notebook. You'll hear things that will amaze you.' The bodyguard loomed over him

80

like a mountain; over the repository of God knew what strange secrets.

Had no one else in the restaurant recognised him? After all, he had taken no trouble to disguise himself, and his face must have stared out of an infinity of newspapers, of television sets. Had they not noticed his limp, the product of his carefully contrived wound?

I ordered coffee, and tried to subdue the excitement that was surging in me. The meeting, the conversation, had left me in a strange state of alarm. The man in himself was plainly odious, the very symbol of all that was rank and wrong in Italy, perhaps in America as well, the quintessence of Sicily, in its most negative sense. Not the Sicily of Verga and Pirandello of which he so spuriously prattled, but the Sicily of Lucky Luciano, the Old Moustaches, the shotgun blasts in the dead of night, the multiplicity of sprawled, blood-stained bodies, rigid in the agony of death, these, too, staring day-by-day out of newspapers and newsreels.

Oh, yes, Sindona could surely help me, if he wanted to. And I? Would I be ready to help Della Martira?

IV

'Ciao!' said a girl's voice. 'Scusa se ho fatto tardi, sorry if I'm late,' and I looked up, astonished, from my reverie, to see that a dark young woman had sat down opposite me, at my table.

'Don't look surprised,' she said, in a lower, urgent voice. 'Don't say anything until I've talked to you.' And then, in normal tones, 'The traffic's terrible; I don't know what's happening to Rome. But how are you? How was your journey?' and she smiled, putting her hand on mine. 'I'm Teresa. Della Martira sent me. So you found him? You talked to him?'

'I did,' I said.

'Bravo! Bravissimo!' She was a vigorous, lively girl, with short, dark hair and a face that was animated rather than pretty, the nose short and small, the eyes very large and dark,

81

the lips full. It was, I thought, a very Roman face, one full of a kind of knowing mischief, a lambent irony. She seemed, all the time, no matter what she said, to be testing, teasing, questioning. Whatever one said, whatever one did, was weighed in the balance by this sceptical spirit.

'Are you seeing him again?' she asked.

I hesitated; he had told me after all to tell nobody, but it was hard to hold out against that mocking demeanour. 'Yes, perhaps,' I replied at last.

'In his hotel? The one across the square?'

'Yes . . . If I do see him.'

'*If* you see him,' she repeated, and she laughed. 'You're very English.'

'Obviously,' I said.

'But very, *very* English. An English gentleman! All cautious and formal and reserved.'

'L'inglese italianato è un diavolo incarnato,' I said, and this made her laugh more than ever.

'Che bello! That's beautiful! What's that from?'

'From six hundred years ago,' I told her. 'They said it about mercenaries, like Hawkwood.'

'Who?'

'An English condottiere. John Hawkwood. He fought in Italy for many years, and died in Florence.'

'Ockvard,' she said; and it reminded me of the endless difficulties Italians had had with his unfamiliar name, from Giovanni Acuto to Giovanni Aguto to the Sir John Haukkodoe which the Florentines were still calling him, to the day that he died, a freeman, in their city.

'Che lingua buffa, l'inglese,' she said, 'what a comical language English is. E tu,' she had begun at once with the familiar form, 'are you the devil incarnate?'

'I don't think so,' I said, 'but I may have just met him.'

'Bello, bellissimo,' she laughed. 'You could easily be right. You didn't care for him?'

'Not a great deal.'

'He's a disgusting man,' she said and lost, almost for the first time, her ironic smile, replacing it, unexpectedly, with a look of fierce hostility. 'Scum. The kind of person that's destroyed the whole fabric of this country.'

'So you want to kill him, as the Red Brigades killed

Moro?' I found myself asking her. Again, diplomacy had gone out of the window.

'Della Martira does,' she said, very low. 'I believe he does. But Della Martira's a little mad.'

'You think so?'

'Of course he is. And it may be my fault. Before we knew each other, I don't think he had a political idea in his head.' So it was you, I thought. 'All he cared about was screwing. That, and making money. He was obsessed with sex, now he's obsessed with revolution. The first time he ever fell in love.'

'Not with you?' I asked.

She shrugged. 'I was just part of it; part of the Revolution. Still, he's a good-looking boy, even if he did have some funny kinks.' She regarded me. 'And you? Are you married? No, of course you're not. Your wife died, didn't she? I'm very sorry. That's why you're here. That's why you are helping us.'

'It is.'

'Sindona has people killed, you know that?'

'Yes, I do.'

'Like Ambrosoli. They shot him in the street. An American killer: William Arricò. There were others as well; at least three of them. None of those others has been found. Sindona doesn't stand on his own, though; that's what's so horrible. He's still got friends here, right up to the top levels of Government. How else would he have ever got away with it so long? You know they even gave him a golden statue? The saviour of the lira. Andreotti presented it to him; one of the big Demochristian bosses. Che schifo! How disgusting! And not just here; he has friends in America too. That's how he's here.'

'So he told me.'

'Oh, he'd tell you! Powerful American politicians. They all protect him. But now he's dangerous to them if he talks. Now, a lot of people want to kill him, people who used to help him. For their own ends. So what's the point of us killing him? It's more important to keep him alive.'

'No symbolic execution this time, then,' I said. She gave me a sharp glance. 'You don't believe in revolution, do you?'

'I'm English,' I said. 'We had ours long ago. Unless you count the bloodless one, after the war.'

She smiled at me again. 'English, yes, very English.'

'Would you like some wine?' I asked. She hesitated for a moment then smiled once more, and nodded. This time, the smile was sensual and affectionate, reminding me poignantly of Simonetta's smile. I found myself looking at the curve of her breasts beneath her tight, red silk blouse. She noticed, without embarrassment or pique; it seemed to please and amuse her. Since Simonetta died, I had lived in a kind of sexual vacuum, a matter half of sustained shock, half of deference and respect. There were plenty of women at Oxford who were obviously ready to comfort me; women academics, colleagues' wives, students whom I tutored. I had no interest in them; not even as a transient way of dulling pain.

But now, beyond control and will, like the sudden breaking up of great ice floes, it was changing. I wanted her. As if she sensed all this, she asked me, 'Tell me about your wife. Was she beautiful?'

'Yes. She was a Florentine. She was called Simonetta. She'd been a journalist.'

'Ah! What kind of a journalist?'

'Third-page stuff. Interviews. Cultural affairs.'

'And you want to find out why she died.'

'Yes,' I said. I didn't want to talk about it. Not to her. Not while I was feeling as I did about her.

'In other words,' she said, 'to find out which damned Fascists did it.'

'Assuming they were Fascists.'

'Of course they were Fascists,' she said scornfully. 'Just as the bastards who put an incendiary bomb on the Italicus train six years ago were Fascists. Just as the ones who exploded the bomb on Bologna station were Fascists. Commemorating the Italicus bomb. Haven't you seen? In all the papers? They're pulling them in every day. All kinds of filthy Fascist. From petty criminals who rob flats in Rome to professors of criminology.'

'I hope they've got the right people,' I said.

'They never get the right people. They never *want* the right people. Only the small fry and the lunatics. That's why *we* have to go after the big ones.'

'And if you did get Sindona?'

'We'd make him talk,' she said, lowering her voice, and

leaning forward, so that I could smell the sharp tang of her scent. 'We'd get everything on tape, every dirty deal, every tie-up with a big politician, every swindle with a big banker, and we'd publish the lot.'

'Then kill him?'

'Then it wouldn't matter. We could let him go. Back to his American gaol.'

'I'm surprised you're telling me all this.'

'Why not? You want help, don't you, and he's the one who would most likely know something. If we had him, he could tell you.'

I felt as if I were floating in space, above the real world. Rome itself had always seemed a surreal city to me, one in which bizarre events were common currency, but this was piling Pelion on Ossa, a mere, outrageous dream. She was trying to enlist me as a decoy, an accomplice, while Sindona in turn seemed to want me as an apologist.

Teresa switched, suddenly, in her disconcerting way, from righteous contempt to sensuality, giving me her provocative, ironic smile. 'We can't keep talking here. I'll make you coffee at my house.'

I agreed, before I could even think about it, and we were in a taxi, travelling across Rome, towards Trastevere. To have her beside me and so close was more unsettling still, and she manifestly knew it, looking more amused than ever.

'You like me, don't you?' she asked, as we sped through the summer city, with its dazzling kaleidoscope of colours, deep blues, dark greens, the rich redness of the walls. It remained to me, still, a city of sublime surprises, of corners turned to disclose something superb and quite unforeseen; a fountain, a glimpse of an exquisite courtyard, a massive, sloping, mediaeval wall, vast as the side of a mountain; all of it lit, now, by the relentless brilliance of the autumn sun. So close to her, Teresa's scent distracted me still more, strong rather than subtle, like a deliberate provocation.

'I'm sure most people do,' I said.

'How English, how English! Ma sei simpatico! You're nice.' She took my arm. I thought for a moment she was going to kiss me, but with the same smile she said, 'We're here,' let go of me, and opened the door.

We were in a small, run-down square in Trastevere, not

far, I surmised, from the Piazza In Piscinula, where children played and shouted, and noisy diners were still sitting at tables outside a little restaurant.

Teresa walked briskly through the front door of one of the houses; the hallway was like a dank, stone cavern. Up the winding stairs she went, quick as a gazelle, her flat shoes tapping as she ran. She was wearing a jean-suit, and as she climbed, I was mesmerised by the sight of her neat, firm buttocks disappearing around corner after corner, as I followed her. The ice floes . . . I wanted her again, I felt strangely sure that I would make love to her now, but when at last she stopped at a landing, to knock at a scored, shabby wooden door, it was opened by Della Martira.

My reaction was part surprise, part disappointment, and as though this had been part of a prepared joke, Teresa turned round to smile at me.

'Ciao,' Della Martira greeted her, kissing her most perfunctorily on both cheeks. To me, with equal indifference, he stretched out his hand. 'Piacere,' he said, barely regarding me. He was at his most intense and conspiratorial. 'Were you followed?' he asked Teresa, at which she burst out laughing.

'Followed! You're joking! Why should we be followed?'

But Della Martira evidently was not joking.

'Ma non sia cretina!' he shouted, closing the front door. 'Don't you know Sindona's watched all the time? Don't you realise that that could bring them to us? This is meant to be a safe house!'

'But we've done nothing!' she replied.

For a moment, I thought he was going to strike her and tensed myself, prepared to intervene, but it was merely another of those furious Italian rows which subside just at the moment when they seem to have reached a point of no return, inevitable violence. Teresa seemed quite unperturbed. 'Let's go in,' she said, and walked past him, leading the way into the room, which looked more like a squat than a normal habitation.

There was an air of squalid transience about it. The boards were bare, but for a few meagre rugs; there were camp beds in two of the corners, and a couple of mattresses. On one of the camp beds there was sleeping a large, dark-headed man in jeans and a green T-shirt which revealed heavy, hairy, very white arms. He had his back to the room. On one wall hung a familiar picture of Che Guevara, in a beret, on another the famous photograph of poor Aldo Moro, in front of the insignia of the Red Brigades.

Teresa dropped into a battered armchair and lit a cigarette. I sat down on a hard wooden chair near her. 'What did Sindona tell you?' Della Martira asked.

'He spoke a lot about himself,' I replied. 'Of what he'd done for Italy. How badly he'd been treated. How he intends to take revenge.'

'No, no, no, not that,' said Della Martira. 'We know all about that. I mean how long he's staying, where he's going, whom he's seeing.'

'You know where he's staying,' I said, 'in the Hotel Vittorio.'

'Which room? We need to know which room.'

'I'm not sure,' I told him, an unwilling accessory.

'Are you meeting him again?'

'I think so, yes. Your plan seemed to work. He was flattered. He wants me to write about him.'

'That's good. You'll tell us when you're next due to see him.'

I gave a non-committal nod. If Della Martira meant to kill Sindona, then I wanted no part of it. Whatever Sindona might have done, he had not done it to me. I was a spectator, reluctant to be drawn into so dangerous a game.

'Dai, Claudio!' Teresa said, in her Roman way. 'Give him a chance. He isn't one of us. All this is new to him.'

'He wanted help,' said Della Martira. 'If he wants help, he has to *give* help.'

'But help for what?' I asked, with careful innocence. Della Martira lit a cheroot and began to smoke it with a febrile energy.

'As I've said to you, there are things we need to know. Like when he's leaving Rome. When he's leaving Italy. When he goes back to New York. Whether he's going back at all.'

'I've told you,' I said, 'I've no idea, but he's promised to invite me there. To stay in his suite in the Hotel Pierre.'

'That scum!' said Della Martira, bitterly. 'And we know where all the money came from. All the filthy tricks he pulled.

Did you ask him anything about your wife? Did you ask him about the train?'

'I did. He was evasive. He said more or less what you've said. That he might help me, if I helped him.'

Teresa laughed. 'Very Sicilian,' she said. 'One hand washes the other.'

'You've got to see him again,' said Della Martira. 'You've got to find out when and where he's going.'

'So you can kill him?' I asked. The censor was nodding again.

'*Who* told you that?' he demanded, ferociously, and turned upon Teresa. 'Did *you* tell him that? Was it *you*?'

Teresa remained calm and casual. 'Well, it's true, isn't it?' she enquired.

'What does *that* matter? This is *our* business! It's nothing at all to do with him.'

'It could have quite a lot to do with him,' she said, still sprawled in her chair.

'You know what I mean! You know perfectly well what I mean!'

The shouting woke the big, bearded man on the camp bed, who rolled over on his back, blinked, yawned, stretched and sat up. 'Ma che cazzo succede? What the fuck's going on?'

'It's her!' cried Della Martira, pointing at Teresa. 'She's an imbecile! She told this Englishman that I wanted to kill Sindona!'

'*You're* an imbecile for even wanting to,' the bearded man said, swinging his legs to the floor. He looked at me, rubbing sleep from his eyes. 'You're the English historian,' he said. 'I'm Sandro. Now you can see what we revolutionaries are like.' Almost absently, he put a hand into the pocket of his jeans, pulled out a black, automatic pistol, broke it open, examined it, closed it, and pocketed it, again. It was the very nonchalance of his action which alarmed me. He might have been handling a comb, or a bunch of keys.

'It's a disgrace!' shouted Della Martira. 'She puts all of us at risk!'

'You've never shot anyone,' said Teresa, contemptuously, 'not even in the legs,' and from her tone, her disdainful expression, I realised with a frisson what she implied. She *had* shot people. It was as though, quite inadvertently, I had let

88

myself be drawn into a vortex which now was whirling me about, increasingly helpless and impotent.

'But don't let's have these useless arguments,' said Sandro, standing up. He was well over six feet tall, heavy and powerful, with none of Della Martira's frantic disposition. 'We've discussed it, we've decided on it. We want him alive, so whether Claudio would like to kill him or not doesn't matter. Someone's going to kill him eventually, if he doesn't do away with himself. If we turn him loose when we've finished with him, if they ever put him in gaol here, how long could he last? They'll stick a mafioso in with him, or they'll poison him like they did Pisciotta in Palermo, after he'd ratted on Giuliano. That's how Sicilians die, when they've betrayed their friends.'

'There you are, then,' said Teresa to Della Martira. 'All a big fuss about nothing. Sindona isn't Moro.'

'And we're not the Red Brigades,' said Sandro, plodding bare-footed across the floor. 'We haven't got their training, we haven't got their resources, we haven't got the personnel. Which means we have to make the best of what we've got, and not waste time quarrelling about nonsense.'

'What nonsense?' muttered Della Martira, 'what nonsense?' But he subsided.

'Con permesso,' said the big man to me, with a sudden access of formality, and he shuffled out of the room, leaving Della Martira forlorn.

Teresa smiled at him. 'Don't take it so seriously,' she told him. 'You'll see that we're right. It's much the better way; however you feel about Sindona.'

'In front of *him*!' said Della Martira, head bowed, almost choking on the words. 'In front of strangers. That's what I can't accept.'

'Oh, don't exaggerate! He knows Italians. He knows how explosive we can be.' She turned, to smile at me. 'Now let's have coffee.'

'I don't want coffee,' mumbled Della Martira. 'What I cannot take is the betrayal. Mi son vergognato. I've been shamed.'

'Macchè!' she said, and stood up, putting an arm around his shoulders, smiling again at me. 'Tom is our friend. He understands, don't you?'

'Well, I think so,' I said. What I meant was that to understand was not necessarily to sympathise. But then, where did I stand myself? I seemed now to be living from moment to moment, the prisoner of circumstances, moving without moral direction, making promises to murderous charlatans, consorting with violent subversives. In this dangerous dream world, I sensed that I was changing. The perennial questions, what was I doing, what was I proposing to do, grew steadily harder to answer, because of this change. While only days ago, the answers would straightforwardly have been, I am seeking the murderers of my wife, when I find them I propose to do nothing to them, now I did not know what I would do, and in this uncertainty lay ambiguity. By the time I met them, met the murderers, what would I want? What would I be? I would not betray Sindona, if it lay in my power to do so, yet Sindona clearly deserved death, if anybody did. For all his histrionics, I could identify with Della Martira. Sindona deserved death in a way that the unhappy Moro, merely a symbol, a hate-object for embattled fanatics, had never done. Whom had Moro ever killed, or had killed?

I felt, too, that Rome itself had something to do with my state of mind. The potency of the place. Its arrogant and overwhelming beauty, always at its strongest in the sunshine. It was still, in its majesty, an imperial city, intransigent and harsh; Sindona's city of the catacomb.

'I'm sorry,' Della Martira addressed me, with sudden change of tone and demeanour. 'It wasn't the way to behave. But you've met him, now. Perhaps you can see what he is, what he represents.'

'I've got a good idea,' I said. Yet Della Martira had spoken of Aldo Moro, too, as the embodiment of evil. 'You've never met Sindona?' I asked.

'Ma! Who needs to meet him?' Hatred was abstract. He had hoped I would hate Sindona, having met him, but his own hatred had no need of intimate acquaintance, merely of objective co-relatives. A true revolutionary, who would purge the world with violence.

'You'll keep in touch with us?' he asked. 'You'll tell us what he's doing?'

'Well, I'll try,' I said, a reluctant accomplice.

'When you're seeing him, let us know. When you've seen him, tell us what he said. And we'll help *you*.' This, as an afterthought.

I wanted to get away from them. From them, from Sindona, even from the Rome that lay outside in streets and squares, hot, arrogant, exquisite Rome, where I had never felt at ease, where I found no solace even in the music of the fountains. Those very walls, the walls of Ancient Rome, were now beginning to oppress me again, with a bulk and a size which somehow were not merely physical. Whenever I passed beneath them, in the Forum, in the Via Appia Antica, in the Piazzale Ostiense, or, suddenly and starkly, in a street unknown to me before, they seemed to loom like a gigantic threat, more massive than any skyscraper.

Refuge, once more, could come only in a library. In the Vatican, quiet among the desks and documents and manuscripts, transported into a past which was not the past of Ancient Rome, I could find tranquillity, if not peace; there was no peace to be discovered in those records. I had been there that morning. It was the one place in Rome I could bear to be in.

Della Martira, unexpectedly, now left before I did. 'I've a lot of things to do,' he said, with renewed self-importance, and shook hands with me, briskly but not coldly. 'Ciao!' he said, with equal briskness, to Teresa, but she caught his hand before he could go, pulled him towards her, and kissed him affectionately on the lips. 'Stai buono!' she said, then he was gone.

She smiled at me. 'Don't take any notice of his oddities. I told you, he's a little mad. And very Florentine.'

'Do you find Florentines like that?' I asked.

'They're more impatient than us Romans. More impulsive.'

Rome, I thought, the great limbo, where no one wants to move.

'You're always so grave!' Teresa said. She came to me, stroked my cheek, then kissed me. I put her arms around her, and she jammed herself hard against my body. There was nothing I wanted to do more than make love to her, as she gyrated, but then I heard the door creak open and, looking round, saw that Sandro was back. Neither he nor Teresa was

91

perturbed. She disengaged herself from me without haste. 'Another time, then,' she said.

So out into the sunshine of the square, out into the sunshine of the streets, into the same beauty, at once so poignant and so menacing, of the incomparable city. How could the Romans ever take Rome for granted? I asked myself now, as I walked. How could they simply stroll past ruins and palaces, the breathtaking contrast of walls and overhanging leaves, past pines and cypresses and palm trees, past domes and pyramids and obelisks, past water spurting out of a hundred different orifices; shells, mouths, fish. If I did not like Rome, I at least paid tribute to it, acknowledged its sublime, refulgent pomp. Had I been born here and grown up here, would I have been scuttling about, indifferent as they?

I felt, after what had just happened, exhilarated, yet ashamed of feeling exhilarated. A girl had kissed me, a sensual, desirable Roman girl had pressed herself against me, had made me, virtually, a promise or a proposition, and here I was, reacting like some moonstruck adolescent. Besides, how much of it was even genuine, how much of it was mere manipulation, sex as carrot, a lure to make me do what they wanted me to do? I told myself this, but I didn't believe it, or didn't want to believe it. So, as I walked, the sunshine which lit the streets rendered them not stifling and oppressive, but brilliant with promise. I knew we would make love, I felt certain of it; for the first time since Simonetta died, I had found a woman whom I wanted; and who wanted me.

You are sentenced, I told myself, to three more mornings in the Vatican archives. From that refuge, from that communion with Hawkwood, I would decide what to do; or not to do.

My appointment with Sindona was for the following evening. By then, I must have clear ideas of conduct. Without them, I was at the mercy of others. Della Martira and the rest had plans for me, I knew; Sindona, plainly, used everyone and anyone. In the Vatican archives, within the shelter of the colossal walls, I was at rest – he deplored the word peace – with Hawkwood.

The papers I asked for were from Avignon. I had been through them time and again, but I still lived in hope there was something I had missed, something that might explain, or mitigate, Cesena. There could always be documents I had not seen, drawn up, or kept, by those in the Papal retinue at Avignon, a forgotten cardinal, a treasurer; one thing, notionally, leading to another, as with documents it often could, until at last something new to me, however old, was found.

This, above all, was the excitement of the chase; that you never knew quite what you were chasing, what beast would be in view, until it suddenly broke cover.

In the papers of Robert of Geneva, who became the anti-pope Clement VII, there had never been any attempt to deny responsibility for Cesena. He had ordered the massacre, he had insisted on the massacre; the citizens of Cesena, however treacherously, were to be taught a lesson. Hawkwood's protests, too, were on record, as was his ultimate participation. 'I was only obeying orders.' But Hawkwood, I was sure, would never have hidden behind that, never have felt the craven need to dodge the blame. A mercenary, after all, lived by obeying orders, even if there were times when Hawkwood, with two paymasters, had trod water in his campaign for one, to accommodate the other.

The cataclysms of the past few days left me, at first, in no real mood to sit in the quietness of this large, fine room, among the scratching pens of the other studiosi, poring through the past. I was restless and distracted; there was almost a physical resistance in me to sitting still. But as I continued to read and to compare, as the whole picture of that hot and horrible day in Cesena rose in my mind again, I found myself achieving a curious kind of synthesis, and from that synthesis, a new tranquillity. These last, few, frenzied days, which had left me so unsettled, were in some way being subsumed into what I was reading. The effect, though shocking, was also soothing.

In the documents, I read again of what had led to the massacre: the bravery of Cesena's citizens, standing up to Robert of Geneva's vicious Bretons, and defeating them; the Papal Legate's fury, his elaborate stratagem of betrayal, convincing the Cesenans all was forgiven, the brutal treachery which put them to the sword; Hawkwood's reluctance and his arguments, his final acquiescence, hardest of all to accept. Then the slaughter itself, the comparative mercy of the English, who robbed their victims but largely let them go, the pitiful attempts to escape across the narrow bridge, the people hurling themselves down, in despair, into the moat, the stuffing of bodies, later, into cisterns. If there was no excuse for Hawkwood, or none that had yet been found, might there be evidence of remorse? I did not think so, I had come across none, nor anything to suggest it might be in his make-up.

But the change in me, that change I could already feel, dictated daily by what was happening to me, helped me to understand the change in him, if change there had been. In myself, I was convinced it had occurred. L'inglese italianato. The very phrase suggested metamorphosis, a brutalising, a refinement of cunning. How else to survive in mediaeval Italy? Even taking account of the coarseness of the age, its casual violence, something had surely happened to him when he crossed the Alps, as something was happening to me. As for Robert of Geneva, though there was no way to exonerate his cruelty, to condone his perfidy, my meeting with Sindona, the first truly evil man I had ever known, helped me a little to understand him. Robert of Geneva had had thousands slaughtered; Sindona had sent the gangster, Arricò, to murder Ambrosoli, but the difference was merely quantitative. Were Sindona in a position to mow down his many, postulated, enemies, in any given place, would he not do it, or have it done, as treacherously as Robert of Geneva?

I stopped here and reproached myself; I was falling into the very trap I warned against, being unhistorical, drawing the kind of specious, spurious analogies I so often deplored to my students. But to take solace from such comparisons was no crime against history. As for Hawkwood, he had become, in his moral ambiguity, more real to me than ever. He had surely understood Italy, his Italy, in a way that I was only now beginning to understand my own, the danger always being of a violent swing from the romantic to the disenchanted; like those benighted British tourists, their eyes full of stars and sentiment, who turn from the country in disgust, after being robbed in the streets and rebuffed by the police.

Simonetta's death, I could see, had traumatised me, leaving me unable to live not only with the grief of her loss but with all its implications. It meant Sindona. It meant the bomb and the suffering at Bologna station. It meant Della Martira's murderous dilettantism, and the gun that Sandro had pulled out of his pocket. It meant the readiness of the Red Brigades to kill coldly for one cause, and the readiness of the neo-Fascists to slaughter indiscriminately for another. Once he left France, Hawkwood stopped killing for a cause. Loyal always to his king, he had no further need in his life to serve him in deed, rather than in word. But this was another, simpler kind of commitment, one to be shown on the battlefield, not in treachery, atrocity, assassination, all of which he would meet in Italy.

Out again in the sunlight, beneath the rugged slope of the Vatican walls, I felt a new energy and vigour, a confidence that I could cope and survive, and that steadily, existentially, I would discover what I meant to do.

Hawkwood would help me. The words which popped into my head, unbidden, seemed glib and absurd, then made a kind of sense. An advertising phrase. Hawkwood will help you! A decent man corrupted? A decent man dealing with corrupt men? How many Sindonas must he have met? And worse than Sindona; far worse, and far more powerful. A Robert of Geneva, who could order a massacre without a qualm, and compound it with duplicity. A Bernabò Visconti who, with equal indifference, could have any enemy assassinated – how many Ambrosolis had there been, in his Milan? – and would die in the end just as they had died. As Sindona now feared he might die. As Della Martira would like him to die.

Again, as I walked through the hot streets, I felt a certain, guilty exhilaration? Where was the logic of it, or the justification? My wife was dead. In Bologna, I had come upon a scene of carnage. I had just met a man who had swindled, murdered and deceived; and flourished. I had consorted with revolutionaries who embodied a violence born out of despair. Yet even Rome, with the sullen force of its persona, could not subdue this feeling. There in that archive, in some strange way, I had been making sense of things. I would go to see Sindona, I would string him along, and get out of him whatever I could.

Day by day now, in the newspapers, one read of a plethora of neo-Fascists who might have bombed Bologna station. A young French police inspector called Durand had been flitting between neo-Fascist groups in France and Italy. The prisons were being combed for neo-Fascists who might, in some way – God knows how – have had something to do with the atrocity. Amidst this grotesque and murky underworld lurked, I was sure, the man I hoped to find, and into its viscous depths I was sure Sindona could peer, perceive and point.

I knocked, next evening, as he had asked me to do. The hotel was large but somehow flyblown. There was space but no opulence, rather a kind of seedy splendour, a lowering décor of massive chandeliers, peach-tinted mirrors, purple wallpaper, long, spuriously Venetian sofas, a kind of parody of elegance, a de luxe hotel for those unused to staying at them. I could imagine how Sindona, quintessential upstart, would resent having to be there, in a place as gimcrack as he.

There was silence behind the white door of his room, then, finally, the heavy tread – I could tell – of the bodyguard. 'Chi è?' his thick voice called.

'It's Tom Cunningham,' I said, 'the Englishman. Il professore.'

At this, bolts shot back, a key was turned, the door narrowly opened. For a moment, the bodyguard examined me, then he opened the door sufficiently to let me in: with his left hand, I noticed. His right hand was in his jacket pocket, no doubt resting on a gun.

Sindona was sitting behind a small table in the middle of the room, a curiously innocent figure, his hands swiftly, dexterously, folding squares of coloured paper. As I entered, he finished making a paper bird and held it up, like a proud and happy child, for my admiration, whimsically pulling its tail, and agitating its wings.

'Ecco!' he exclaimed. 'Do you know origami?'

'Only by name,' I said. 'I don't know how to do it.'

'It's an art,' he explained, 'a great skill. Japanese, of course. In origin.' He picked up another piece of paper, orange, this time, and began folding and coaxing it into shape. I thought how perfect a metaphor it was for him, the trickster, the quick conjurer, making something alluring out of nothing, or nearly nothing; something insubstantial, finally worthless. This time, he had produced a paper tortoise. He handed it to me. 'Take it; a souvenir. A tortoise, to remember the old tortoise; who always finishes the race ahead of his enemies.' I took it, thanked him, and reluctantly shook hands with him. His grip was soft and dry.

'Have you brought your notebook?' he asked brusquely.

'Yes, I've bought a new one.' I took it out of my briefcase. It was square and fat, big enough to record the rise and fall of a dynasty.

'Good,' he said. 'Sit down. Would you like an ice cream? I'm going to have an ice cream.'

'I will too, then,' I said, though when the gorilla brought it, I regretted it, having forgotten how large and glutinous Italian ice creams could be. He brought the ice creams in stemmed glasses, each a white whorl, like a tiny sugar loaf. He set one before Sindona, on his table, one before me, but Sindona nodded at him sternly, and after a short hesitation, a tacit moment of mutiny, the gorilla crossed the room, picked up a small spoon from beside the huge double bed, returned, lifted Sindona's glass, took a minuscule flake of ice cream in the bowl of the spoon, and with grotesque delicacy, carried it to his thick lips. He hesitated once more, then stuck out his tongue, while Sindona watched him like a cat. It was a truly mediaeval scene, I thought, the Prince and his taster. The fat tongue withdrew, though the gorilla did not swallow; no muscle moved in his throat. No harm came to him, though, and now the throat muscles moved, he swallowed, the tiny speck of ice cream was consumed. Sindona turned his glance on me. 'That's how they'll try to kill me,' he said, and I thought of Sandro's words. 'That's how they've tried already, and they'll try again. Open your book. I'll tell you things. If they knew I was telling you such things, nothing would stop them trying. And you. Once you know. You'll have to be careful, too. To keep my secrets till the moment comes. I'll tell you when the moment comes. Then you can publish. Then you'll be famous. Then you can have any professorship you like, anywhere in the world. Oxford, Harvard, Rome, anywhere. And your book about me will make a fortune. But can I trust you?'

'Why not?' I asked.

'I can trust nobody. This has been my problem. I spoke to the FBI last month; in New York. You didn't know that, did you? But they wanted me to tell them. Of how I planned to save Sicily. Me and the Masons.'

How often I would hear that word, what labyrinthine

complications it would lead me into, what intricacies of power, ambition, plotting. But at the moment, it was a word that hardly registered, as I seemed to be hearing the ramblings of a paranoid, the romancings of a fantasist. I tried to keep pace with him as the tale came pouring out.

'I nearly saved Sicily. I can still save Sicily. I shall try again. I shall save it from the Communists. Who want the missiles. Who would use the missiles, if they got them, against the Americans. That is why Sicily must secede from Italy. Why we must take it over, and bring in the Americans. Bring in their naval bases.'

Should I believe him? Did he believe it all himself, or any of it?

'Why you?' I asked.

'Why me?' he said, and his chest puffed like a pigeon's. 'Why anybody else? They *knew* I was the man. The people who brought me there. The people who smuggled me in from New York. The Sicilian of Sicilians; that's who I am. Who else has my connections? Who else is so respected in America? I was kidnapped last year; did you know that?'

Yes, I knew that. Knew it was a fake. 'I'd heard,' I said.

He rolled up the leg of his trousers, and pointed at a raw, red scar. 'Look, that's where I was shot,' he said. 'Last year.'

'Who shot you?'

'They did,' he replied, his eyes shifting, then he looked at me, querying how much I knew. 'They did, the people who kidnapped me.'

I did not write it down. Noticing this, his tone changed. 'You're smart. I see you know things. Very well; I'll tell you what I told the FBI. I was shot with a small gun. A woman's gun. By the Masons; the people who brought me to Sicily. So I could save Sicily. To make it look as though I *had* been kidnapped.'

I made desultory notes. His world, like his financial finagling, was plainly one of Chinese boxes, complex and ultimately, I was sure, as hollow as the centre of his operations. 'Why did you tell the FBI?' I asked.

'The same reason as I'm telling *you*. I want the truth revealed. I want the truth recorded. When I'm gone, if they kill me, there it will be: to confound and condemn them.'

So I let him talk, and took down what I chose to. It was

impossible to distinguish fiction from fact, the more so after days of such turmoil and surprise, in which the unexpected seemed to be the norm, the inconceivable seemed commonplace, the fantastic became real. Now and again, I asked him questions, wanting him to explain or clarify, but I gave up challenging anything he said, however seemingly preposterous. His story was best perceived, I sensed, as half apologia, half metaphor. He was telling me not what had happened but what he would like to have happened, what he thought should have happened. Sometimes, as in his story of Sicily, it seemed the wildest fancy, yet what could be more fantastic than that attempt which had been planned, not long ago, to take over Rome for the Right, to poison – a word so dear to Sindona – the very water supply? That the Communists should ever have planned to seize the missile bases in Sicily seemed ludicrous, that Sicilian-Americans should plan to take the island and use him, Sindona, scarcely less so. But someone might have made such plans, plans he heard about, and wove in bright colours around himself.

In that exotic tale there were the Masons – not the Mafia – 'Revolutionary' Masons, who had spirited him from America, through Austria, to be their . . . leader? talisman? adviser? Revolutionary Masons, a contradiction, clearly, when Masons traditionally existed not to change the system but to manipulate it, helping and promoting one another. Again, though, as he rambled on, his face alight with his illusion of martyrdom, I guessed at something real beneath the romance. Somewhere or other, somehow or other, Masons did play a part in his Odyssey, but hardly there, hardly in Sicily, where the Americans he spoke of had names like Gambino, Mafia names, men who would have no need of antic ceremonies that were not their own, rolled up trouser legs, bizarre handshakes, to promote their brutal ends.

He had been kidnapped, he said at first, to say, in turn, that the kidnap was counterfeited, to throw people off the scent, to get him from New York to Sicily. But the kidnap, I remembered, came hard on the heels of Ambrosoli's murder, in Milan. The heat was on. The Italians wanted to extradite Sindona, for his infinite frauds. The Americans were closing in on him for the massive failure of the Franklin Bank, hoist with its own speculations. It clearly suited him to disappear.

Now and again, as the words poured out of him, as the bodyguard dozed in a chair, my attention failed, and I found myself listening only to the rough music of the words, just looking at his face, lambent with self-pity, self-justification.

'Ambrosoli . . .' I heard suddenly, and it triggered me.

'Hadn't he found a list?' I asked. 'Five hundred names?'

'He was using it!' Sindona cried, his face suffused, now, with a murderous rage. 'He was getting to the people on it! Blackmailing them! He deserved to die!'

One statement seemed as monstrous as the other. 'So you had him killed?' I was about to say, but not even my automatic pilot could allow this, and I asked, 'So someone had him killed?'

'So it seems,' he said, his eyes evading me.

The list. The five hundred. The powerful and distinguished men, bulwarks of the Establishment, whose capital Sindona had spirited abroad for them, the old conjurer. Generals, judges, statesmen, industrialists.

'They accused me!' Sindona said. 'And where was I? Was I in Milan? I was in New York! A little accountant did it. A nobody. Who thought that he was cleverer than I. Who thought that he was going to destroy me!'

The questions of truth and falsehood were of no interest to me; not even, in the exact sense, of academic interest, for there was no book to be written, unless it be a book that he would dictate, I as his 'ghost', not an historian, merely a conduit. To listen now, to take it down, to feign diligence, conviction, were merely means to an uncertain end. That he would help me.

Meanwhile, names peppered his narration. Graham Martin, the American Ambassador to Rome. He had been friendly with *him*, I knew. Nixon; now disgraced. A suitable referee. Micheli, head of the Italian Secret Service, that doubtful body, riddled, it was supposed, with Fascism; Colombo, the Christian Democrat minister who had helped him in the sixties; Andreotti, the eternal survivor, for ever assailed, for ever slipping free. 'He gave me a golden Trevi Fountain. In New York. And you know what that means? Come back! Come back to Rome! But how could I come back? Any other way than this; secretly, furtively. Just think of it! A man like me! I've told you: they'd kill me, otherwise! At the very least, throw me in gaol! An Italian gaol, not an American one, where I'd be at their mercy!'

Amidst such a plethora of names, surely, eventually, he would have a name for me. 'My wife's train,' I tried, at last, at a moment when the torrent of words had briefly subsided, and even he, for an instant, needed rest. 'Have you had time to think about it? Can you tell me anything?'

He was dealing, again. *Quid pro quo*. Again, he wore his devious, calculating look. 'There's two or three people. I have to make some inquiries. I have to talk to certain people, if I can. Before I leave Rome, I hope I'll tell you something.'

And when? When would that be?

The bodyguard had quite dozed off, now. He gave a rumbling snore. Sindona poked him furiously with a finger till he woke, then turned back to me, redolent of mystery. 'Ah! Chi lo sa? Who knows? It won't be long; I'll tell you, if I can.'

It was to be a lure. How good he must always have been at that! One phrase peppered and punctured his narration: 'Sono un perseguitato politico.' A victim. Persecuted for his politics. He had done nothing wrong. 'What small investor has ever suffered? Bring him to me; anyone who has lost money through me.' I believed that he believed it. 'My conscience is at peace with God. I remain what I have always been, a good Christian.'

Perhaps, if you accepted that all finance was ultimately fraud, there was even a case to be made for him. You did the deals, shuffled the papers, merged the companies, watered the stock, at a speed which kept you clear of trouble, while you were making billions. Stop the momentum, let some little hitch occur, while you were between deals, hopping from one log to the other, and you could plunge into the icy water. Into trouble. Into gaol. You had allowed yourself to be found out, and the financial Establishment would condemn and disown you. The very people for whom you had made money would cast the first stone.

'I lectured at universities,' he said, 'all over the United States. On economic affairs. Do you think they'd ask me to do that if I were a criminal? I'll show you letters.' And walking to an ugly chest of drawers, he indeed produced letters, from a fat leather file. American letters, from bank presidents, senators. 'How honoured we were to have your participation

101

in our debate.' 'How grateful we are for your assistance in this complicated and delicate matter.' 'How pleased we would be to have you give this important lecture on our campus.' 'How happy we are with your most generous contribution to our campaign.'

'You see? You see? Are these the letters that are written to a criminal? As I told you: sono un perseguitato politico.'

But the other side of it, the side that Della Martira, Teresa and Sandro would see, was that his whole world was rotten, everybody in it; all part of the conspiracy, all betraying trust, all with their snouts in the trough.

'I'll fix them all!' he cried. 'La Malfa, that Republican bastard, who won't let me alone! Enrico Cuccia, because he's jealous of me, because I outstripped him, I outgrew him, I became a bigger banker than he ever was! He wanted to keep me always in his shadow. As his pupil. I'll destroy them!' And the fury came back into his face. The bodyguard, disturbed by the noise, turned his heavy head to look at him, with a bovine surprise. 'You'll see!' Sindona shouted. 'One by one, I'll get them!' And he would if he could, I saw.

Here you are, then, I told myself, living as you think a historian should really live, right out of the study and the library, trying to make sense of the present. But the present was fluid and intractable, bewilderingly amorphous, in a perpetual state of flux and change. Where to take hold of it, where to authenticate it, where to pin it down? Could Cooper be right? To make sense of Sindona, it was necessary for him first to be dead, for the momentum to stop. Only then could one begin to sift, compare and judge. In fifty years' time, a historian would come along, and probably reduce him to a paragraph, a footnote, reduce him to a jumped-up, self-deluding crook, important only for the light he threw on a putrescent period and its squalid denizens.

Sindona, meanwhile, behaved as though he were showing me the treasures of the world, as though he had somehow at once penetrated and distorted my thoughts. 'How they'll envy you, the other historians! What wouldn't they give to write of history as it's made, to be told about it by a man who's making it?'

Ah, but to be told what? The names kept dancing by me. Sometimes I would reach out, grasp at them, and stop the

102

parade, at which they would be vaunted or depreciated, for his own self-aggrandisement. Nixon. 'A great man. A great President. We understood each other. A political martyr: like me.' Aldo Moro. 'A real martyr? That's what you'd call him?'

'Yes. If there are such things.'

A cunning, knowing look. 'But he sent money to Switzerland. Clandestinely. That's what people don't know. He used it to fix politicians. His cronies took it out for him. You'll see. It'll come out; sooner or later. These things always do.'

Here, as contemporary historian, was my chance. The martyr, the sainted Moro, the beloved Christian Democrat who would not play the party game, suddenly besmirched and made equivocal. I should stop Sindona there, ask him for proof, chapter and verse, a guide at least to the rabbit hole down which I should burrow. But I let him go on, unchallenged, repelled by the world he presented, reluctant to enter it. Time would give distance, and I had no distance; the recent past was too close to have lost its emotional charge.

'Write, write!' Sindona said. 'Write everything down!' He finished his ice cream with the undisguised joy of a child. He offered me more, but I refused. 'Write! These are golden words! All of them priceless! I'll tell you things about America, too; what *really* happened with Nixon. What he told me about Watergate, himself!'

How to dam the flood? Divert it for my own purposes? As he talked on and on, I started to despair. After all, I might never see him, again. He could disappear tomorrow. The invitation to New York seemed chimerical; no more than a grand gesture in the void. Besides, they might kill him before he even got there; or was I being drawn into his paranoia? I wanted to stand up and shout, 'Tell me! Tell me what *I* want to know! Who could have killed my wife?' But once again, though my censor, like his bodyguard, had been dozing, it was not as deeply asleep as that.

He seemed, at last, to sense my restlessness, never quite too self-absorbed to pick up nuances and vibrations, anything that might help him. 'I might have sent you to Professor Chiara, but they pulled him in when that magistrate got shot, last week. Right here in Rome, in the middle of the street. Just a few days before the bomb in Bologna. He was hunting down Fascists, and they killed him. Chiara's always being

103

pulled in. He's at Rome University; a professor of philosophy.'

My surprise was clearly evident. 'Oh, yes,' Sindona said, 'you can't believe that, can you? How many of them are professors. Of philosophy. Of criminology. They're not all thugs and peasants, you know.'

Then back again to his exploits, his acquaintances, the injustice he had suffered. 'I'd no need to go back to Sicily,' he said. 'It was my sense of duty. I could live in Formosa; did you know that? In Taiwan. Chiang Kai Shek himself invited me; five years ago. Stay here, he said. As an adviser to my bank. Here in Taipeh. Don't go back to America, he said, or they'll betray you as Nixon betrayed me. But I refused. I said, I'm innocent. I mean to clear my name. And in America, they gaoled me for twenty-five years!'

At last, as I was finding the show of interest harder and harder to sustain, he said that he must leave. 'There are people to see. Important people. If I told you who they were, you'd be astonished.'

No, I wouldn't, I thought. Nothing about you could astonish me, now.

'Franco,' he told the bodyguard, 'go and get the car. You have a car?' he asked me.

'No,' I said. 'I don't enjoy driving in Rome.'

'You're right, you're right. No discipline. No thought for others. I dislike it, myself. But Franco drives. Ten minutes,' he said to Franco, looking at his watch and tapping it. 'Ten minutes, precisely. Outside the hotel.'

'Certo,' said the bodyguard, and left the room, holding the door ajar and looking out, before he went. 'Shall I come up for you again?' he asked.

'No, no, I have my friend here, my English friend. He will look out for me, before I leave.'

Left together with me, he stood up, and glanced down at my notebook. 'Good, good, you've written it all down, but that's just a fraction of it. I'll tell you more; but you must come to New York to visit me!'

He walked across the room, went to a cupboard, took out a beige raincoat, put it on, then placed a black, Homburg hat on his head, carefully pulling down the brim. It gave him the air of a malevolent old gnome. 'Andiamo!' he said. 'But first,

104

please look outside the door. Along the corridor, both ways. Then turn to the right, towards the lifts. Lead the way, if you please.'

I obeyed him. There was no one to be seen in the corridor but a maid, to the left, pulling her big trolley. 'No one but a maid,' I said.

'*Where?*' he snapped, hovering in the doorway.

'To the left!' I told him.

'Let me see!' With great caution, the old tortoise poking his head out of his shell, he peeped out behind me, looked long at the maid in her pink, aproned uniform, and finally decided it was safe to emerge. 'Go first!' he urged me, and I walked down the corridor, towards the lifts. His fear was contagious; I felt a sensation in the small of my back, as though the maid, at any given moment, might draw out of her trolley not a broom but a gun and shoot at us; or shoot at Sindona and hit *me*. 'Go on!' he said, then we were at the lifts, the corner turned, the maid safely behind us. I pressed the call button. Beside me, Sindona stood tense and alert. When the lift arrived, he stepped quickly and carefully out of range of its opening doors, but when they did open, nobody was in it. I held the doors as he got in. 'One has to be careful, always careful,' he muttered.

'Will I see you again in Rome?' I asked, as he pressed the button for the ground floor, and the lift began to go down.

'That depends,' he said. 'It may not be here. As I told you, it may have to be New York. What's your hotel? The Bergamo? Right, I'll get in touch with you there. I'll leave a message for you. Maybe I'll see you tomorrow. Briefly. But no promises. Only if I'm still here.' Then we had reached the ground floor.

Again, there was a pantomime of caution. 'You first,' he said. 'If there's anything you see, anything that's strange, tell me!'

There was nothing strange but a group of Japanese tourists, camera-carrying and bespectacled, herded, docile, around the receptionist desk. 'Tutto bene,' I said.

Even so, he came out carefully, almost surreptitiously, peering into the foyer, one finger poised to press the button of the lift, should he see anything to scare him. Then we were crossing the hall together, and had reached the revolving door of the hotel. 'You first!' Sindona said.

I went in first, feeling, as the door moved, like some hapless target, and emerged to find the bodyguard waiting on the pavement, a large, black Lancia drawn up by the kerb. The vast, ugly square was illuminated, now, by great, round, milky lamps, like so many moons. Sindona came out and stood beside me.

Suddenly, in the lee of one of the shuttered green market stalls, I saw Della Martira. His right hand seemed to be moving towards the pocket of his jacket. 'Giù! Down!' I shouted to Sindona. He threw himself immediately to the pavement, and as he did so, a gun exploded, a bullet hummed over my head, and I heard it hit the wall behind us. I, too, went down on the pavement, while the gorilla pulled out his own gun and fired at Della Martira, who himself had dived to the ground. The next moments were noisily chaotic; there were more shots, the sound of running feet, of voices shouting. Sindona leaped up from the pavement, pulled at the gorilla's left arm, and cried, 'Via, via, subito!' Then they were both in the Lancia, the gorilla at the wheel. For an instant, Sindona's sly old face looked out at me from the window. 'You saved me with one word, I'll give you another,' he said. 'Gelli.'

Then the car started off, its tyres shrieking as it took the corner of the square.

Now there was the whoop of police cars' sirens, and I wanted to get right out, not to be detained, delayed, interrogated, or drawn away from what I had to do and into something that was no real affair of mine. I hurried across the pavement, trying not to run, then across the square, hoping to disappear among the market stalls, darting quickly from one to the other, feeling once more like an involuntary target. I had reached, at last, the distant other side of the square when all at once Della Martira was beside me.

'You saved me!' he said, grasping my arm.

'Saved you! You were shooting at him!' I exclaimed.

'I never shot at him. God knows who shot at him. I haven't even got a gun. I was just watching, that's all. To find out where he went. It was his bodyguard who shot at *me*. Just after you shouted. The bullet flew just above my head, as I fell. I heard it hit the stall.' He shuddered. 'I have to get out,' he said, 'they mustn't find me here. They'd make me a suspect. You'd better get out, yourself. I'd leave Rome, if I were you, as soon as possible. Go to Florence. Go back to England. Somewhere where they won't be looking for you. You're a foreigner. Someone's bound to have noticed you in the hotel.'

Suddenly I found that I was trembling too.

'*He* won't be back,' said Della Martira. 'Sindona. He can't afford to go back with the police, or whoever was out here, looking for him. We've lost him now, damn it. God knows where he'll go. Maybe I'll see you in Florence.'

Then he was away, slipping into the shadows, leaving me to move off in a different direction, between market stalls, down sidestreets, up towards Stazione Termini, the Piazza Cinquecento, with its anonymous, itinerant, continuous bustle. And I found myself, perversely but poignantly, thinking of Teresa.

V

And so I went back to Oxford. To an August Oxford, slumbering in the sunlight of the Long Vacation. Tempted to stop both in Florence and Bologna, but deciding against it – not out of fear, but out of fear of losing time, of being hauled into police stations, hauled before investigating magistrates, dragged in front of courts, while my chance of finding out what I wanted ebbed away, perhaps for ever. And Oxford now, more than Italy, seemed a foreign country, time out of war, a kind of oasis where the pace was disconcertingly slow, where there was no danger in the streets, where life seemed to be going on in a state of primal innocence, a privileged and protected frivolity. What tales I could tell them next term, the blinkered dons and the rapt students! Travellers' tales, soldiers' tales. Tales for High Table, when the port was passing, and we supped in splendour while, beneath us, the undergraduates made do, uncomplaining, with their noxious fare.

107

'Oh you were *there* when the Bologna bomb went off! How extraordinary! You must tell us about it! Actually there in the station! Good Lord! What a devastating experience!' Yes, it was.

The summer was splendid, the city beautiful, a marvellous antidote to Rome, if only I had not wanted urgently to get back to Rome, to leave the city of lost causes, dead issues, dead languages. At least there was no question of eating at High Table, where I had taken to dining often, reluctant to cook for myself and eat alone in our cottage. My cottage. I accepted, now, what invitations I got, from those people who were left 'up', hoping especially to avoid Cooper, to avoid that desiccated interest he was sure to show, his vampire ability to draw blood out of any event, even this. Contemporary crisis reduced to instant, flyblown history at the blink of a bifocal. Perhaps I should envy him, try to acquire his capacity for seeing everything as though it had happened five hundred years ago. Six hundred years ago. As Hawkwood had happened.

I should, in any case, apply myself now to history as I was meant to teach it, rather than history as experience was now presenting it to me. To the questions of plague and population, the strip system and the economics of feudalism, marriage and dynasty in Plantagenet England, the sale of indulgences and Papal finances, the growth of usury and Catholic doctrine. I should be in the Bodleian, or beneath the perfect dome of the British Museum Reading Room, seeking new insights into ancient material, rather than pursuing what was surely my obsession with a single mercenary, of no more than token, marginal significance, veteran of a hundred inconclusive campaigns aborted before they could ever be important. If the Cult of Personality had become a crime in history as in Communism, then this was double a crime, for the personality, however relevant and fascinating to me, was quite peripheral.

This was the time of year that the ease of living, the lazy afternoons on the Isis, had been so joyful when I spent them with Simonetta, and which made them the more unbearable, now she was not here. Tourists. No undergraduates. A mere sprinkling of dons.

I had left Rome the morning after they had shot at Sindona,

whoever had shot at Sindona, my plane ticket invalid, the
train journey hot, long and unbroken. On the way, I bought
newspapers in every city. The shooting had been reported in
all of them, but vaguely. No one, yet, had identified Sindona.
He had carefully pocketed his precious letters, I recalled,
before we left his room.

The homicidal attempt was made on a guest of the Hotel
Vittorio, registered as Antonio Improta. He disappeared
at once from the square in a black Lancia car, driven by
another guest, Franco Bianchini, and has not been seen
since in the hotel. Improta is described as a small,
grey-haired man, about 60 years old. Police so far have
advanced no theory as to why such an attempt should be
made on his life. No trace has been found, either, of a
fair-haired man of foreign appearance who was standing
beside him outside the hotel, at the time. Police inquiries
are continuing.

So, in my railway carriage, I kept a newspaper in front of
my face, and talked to nobody. I soliti ignoti. The usual
unknowns. And I had become one of them. But no one had
been killed, no one even hit. No one, yet, had guessed it was
Sindona.

How differently the sun played on the stones of Oxford, on
its quads, its meadows and its willows! On its little lakes, its
swans, its cloisters! A smaller, kinder city, with its own
poignancy, its own, subtly potent, character. But Rome, and
what was in it, drew me – making the weeks in Oxford no
more than a hiatus, till I could return. I attended to my duties,
dutifully performed my studies, but Hawkwood alone could
distract and occupy me as I worked at my book, sifting
through my notes, above all seeing him, now I was home, with
the new perspective that my days in Italy had given me. Only
days! It seemed as though I had been there for weeks, even
months. I looked through what I had written of my book, and
it jarred on me, seeming at once evasive and sentimental.
Anachronistic. An attempt to judge Hawkwood by the
standards of my time, not his own, when all one could
properly claim, six hundred years on, was, perhaps, a clearer
perspective. If even that. I needed him now, filling in the

lonely, waiting weeks, in which the pastel beauties of the place, far from soothing me, made me the more aware of how far I was from where I wanted to be.

One thing, above all, had been re-emphasised to me. There was no place in his philosophy for revenge. He might be called calloused, brutalised, even, at Cesena, savage, but in that era when every offence would be avenged in blood, when nothing and no one was forgiven, Hawkwood seemed to find revenge irrelevant, even a luxury. Sindona, speaking of revenge as a plate eaten cold, precisely echoed the princes of that time. But Hawkwood, l'inglese italianato, had stayed immune from this Italian trait at least. Perhaps simply because, like peace, he found it bad for business, getting in the way of the mercenary's perpetual need to keep his options open, change sides, change masters, earn whatever he could from whomever he pleased.

Did *I* want revenge? There were moments, during those days in Italy, when I thought I might. Now, at home, he seemed an example to me, but if I did not want revenge, what *did* I want? What was pulling me back to Rome? Truth, I thought, truth, in itself a kind of revenge. The rending of this whole, horrible web of conspiracy and mystery, the bringing into the light of the shadowy people who planned these outrages and atrocities. Then there was Sindona's last word to me, the word he had given me in exchange for my own word of warning: Gelli.

I telephoned Lucetti in Bologna. When he answered, I could hear the hubbub and the tapping, clanking typewriter keys of his newspaper office. 'Momento!' he said. Now I heard his footsteps, the noise of his glass office door being shut, and there was quiet. 'Who gave you his name?' he asked. 'What do you want to know about him?'

'Who he is, for a start. I can't tell you who gave me his name. I'm sorry.'

Lucetti laughed. 'I'm not surprised,' he said. 'Where are you? Oxford? I'll ring *you*. I can't talk about it, here.' There was an edge of anxiety to his voice which I had never heard before. For once, he was not enjoying the delights of secrets, gossip, scandal. 'Give me your number,' he said. 'I'll talk to you.'

'Tonight?'

'Perhaps tonight. Perhaps tomorrow. Not now. It's impossible.'

Given to me as it had been by Sindona, and chilling as it had the exuberance even of Lucetti, the name of Gelli seemed to take on an almost talismanic force. Whoever could he be? I tried to suppress my excitement. It seemed too simplistic, the stuff of cheap romance, of History as People, the old, discredited school – now partly pardoned – which made Great Individuals the movers and shakers of the world. Such things as Simonetta's death, the outrage on the Italicus train, the bombing of Bologna station, could surely not be ascribed to any one man. They were the product of impersonal forces, economic movements, the birth and currency of ideas, a myriad influences which, in complexity and confluence, met to fashion any given event. A Mussolini, a Hitler, was no more than the product of his place and time, an instrument of change produced precisely because the time itself was changing.

Futile arguments. I still had to know who Gelli was, could shelter, if I chose, behind the Poverty of Historicism. Thesis, antithesis, synthesis. The times produce the man, the man changes his times; but every man is a mystery. Who was Gelli? Cooper wouldn't care. From his Olympian height, the contemporary was barely visible.

Of course I met him on my stairs, having hoped he had gone away. 'You've been in Italy,' he said, regarding me with his expressionless blue eyes.

That's right. Been to the Bologna bombing. Met Sindona, the biggest crook in post-war Italy. Got shot at in the Piazza Vittorio. Really? he'd say, colder than a fish, passionless as a robot. These were non-events. These were un-persons. History had not yet admitted them through its portals; they must wait, amorphous, in the antechamber, till it did. But all I said to him was, 'Yes.'

Pressed against the wall, as though I had him at bay, he said, 'They appear to be volatile times.'

'You might say that,' I answered, thinking that he alone could say it.

'Bologna Station,' he said. 'Quite appalling.'

'Your Fascist friends again,' I was tempted into saying.

'My friends? Hardly my friends. Has that been proved? Or is it merely speculation?'

'It's been taken for granted,' I told him.

'Always so dangerous, to take a thing for granted. We historians surely know that.'

'Historians and policemen,' I said.

'What do you mean?'

'Aren't we like policemen? Sifting clues. Discarding theories. Piecing things together.'

'Detectives,' he replied. 'Yes, I suppose we're a little like detectives. *Ex post facto*, though.'

'All detective work is *ex post facto*, surely,' I said. 'You can't detect a crime until it's been committed.' And he smiled. Occasionally, he did. It was not what one would usually call a smile. There was something about it both private and introverted; he was smiling to himself, without warmth, amused by something he wouldn't share. 'It follows the neo-Fascist pattern exactly,' I said. 'A bomb. Random outrage. Attempted destabilisation.'

'Which is precisely why I'm sceptical,' he said, tilting his head in his familiar, maddening manner. You, *you*, I thought, what right have you to be anything at all? You weren't there. You didn't see the pain. You didn't hear the cries. And yet I knew that wasn't fair. I, myself, had been there only by chance.

'Bomb outrages have scarcely been a Fascist monopoly,' he said, or intoned. 'Not even a Fascist innovation. Anarchists. Nihilists. They, surely, were the first.' And so he sent the argument spinning up, up and away, into that stratosphere where there was no real blood, no real pain, no real life at all, just history and the impersonality of history. It was there, and only there, that he could deal with anything. There, I assumed, that he somehow projected the problems and anxieties of his own life, so that they must seem, almost, to be happening to somebody else, or to have happened long ago. I did not know whether he was to be pitied or emulated, only that I found him intolerable. Not least for his air of implicit superiority. I was a mediaevalist. He was a modernist. I was impinging on his period; even if that period had yet to come within history's domain. And that superiority, I felt, extended to history itself, his very role as a historian; what it gave him – at least as he appeared to see it – was the superiority to his material which, God-like, he judged with the advantage of hindsight.

'Fascists *are* nihilists,' I insisted, as I had said before. 'A philosophy that legitimises smashing things up. That preaches blackness.'

Again, the smile. I had committed the sin of subjectivity. 'I think Hitler and Mussolini *knew* what they were smashing up,' he said, carefully. 'And surely when you talk of destabilisation, that implies an end in view. Destruction for a *purpose.*'

'Can't it be both?' I asked. 'One sanctioning the other. After all, what's been achieved? In Italy or West Germany, for that matter. The bomb at the bank in Piazza Fontana. The Italicus bomb. The bomb on my wife's train. Now the Bologna bomb. How far has it got them? What *have* they destabilised? From what I could see, after Bologna, the neo-Fascists were detested by the whole country.'

'If it *was* them.'

'Oh, for Heaven's sake!' I cried. 'The whole country *assumed* it was them.'

'In which case, it could be a very clever strategy to inculpate them.'

I gave up. I was there, I thought, I was *there*. But I could picture the smirk on his face if I said it aloud, and knew it would be hard not to hit him. 'You want to bet on it?' I asked him, desperately. 'I'll give you any odds you like against the Red Brigades!'

He smiled once more; he could afford to. 'I'm not a betting man, I'm afraid.'

How could you be? 'Never mind,' I said, 'it'll all come out in the wash,' and hastened up the stairs, with all the fury I might otherwise have vented on him.

Lucetti did not telephone that night, but he called the following evening. His voice, though he was clearly not ringing from his office, still sounded subdued. 'You wanted to know about this man,' he said, avoiding the very name and, by his tone, warning me against using it. 'Well, then, he's a Tuscan. He lives somewhere near Arezzo. He's extremely rich; or said to be. He spends a lot of time in South America. He's said to have powerful friends there; and Fascist friends in Italy.'

'Would he be involved in atrocities?' I asked.

'I don't know,' Lucetti said, his voice fading. 'I've no idea. I've told you all I know.'

'Would he be acquainted with Sindona?'

His voice grew fainter, warier still. 'I've no idea. Perhaps. Who knows. Sindona knew everybody. But he's in America.' Then he rang off. There was enough, at least, to go on. Gelli. Again, after this stiff, short conversation, I sensed a curious kind of nimbus about the name. It made me more anxious than ever to be back in Italy.

Each day – a day late – I bought an Italian newspaper, looking to see if there was anything about the shooting in Piazza Vittorio, if Sindona had been named, if any more had been discovered about the Bologna bomb. The bullet that flew over my head had left me, then, oddly disturbed. Too much had been happening too quickly at the time; Sindona's word, the need to escape, the fleeting exchanges with Della Martira. That night, back in my small, snug hotel in Via Sistina, above the Spanish Steps, lights out, listening to the traffic that sped by below, I felt a modicum of delayed shock, a shudder or two, but by the time I was on my train, I seemed to have come to terms with what had happened. The bullet, after all, had been fired not at me but at Sindona. I was an outsider, drawn by sheer chance into someone else's turbulent world. Yet on another level, the bullet had confirmed me in that world, had served as a kind of initiation, made me one of the dubiously elect. I could have been killed. Instead, I had escaped, and in escaping, gained the gratitude of Sindona and of his enemy Della Martira; all things to all men, the saviour, with one word, of a murderous swindler and a revolutionary.

They were continuing to arrest neo-Fascists. Strange creatures, some of them: a Professor of Criminology, white-haired and venerable, absurdly inappropriate, a God the Father figure surely far above such squalid doings, privileged, it seemed, to pass in and out of Roman courtrooms at will. There was also the flotsam and jetsam associated always with right-wing extremism, young toughs with alibis, promising candidates, released as suddenly as they had been detained. The Mayor of Bologna spoke out bitterly. No one of relevance, no one of consequence, had yet been arrested. He impugned the Secret Services.

A few days later, I received a large parcel. It had been sent from Harrods, in the familiar green and gold wrapping. I signed for it, puzzled. Was it really for me, and who could possibly have sent it? But my name was on the delivery man's list, and on the label. I tore off the paper; it was a case of Mumm champagne. Half-a-dozen bottles. A small white envelope. A card inside. *Con la mia riconoscenza, affetto e stima. S.* With my gratitude, affection and esteem. Sindona. Should I keep it and drink it? Send it back to Harrods? I could scarcely send it back to him, to the state penitentiary. Pour the champagne away? Give it away? He was, after all, trying to turn me into yet another client; his classic *modus operandi*, undoubtedly, throughout the years. And yet I had saved his life. He was not asking for a favour, simply returning one, one which in fact could never be returned, unless some day he was in a position to save *my* life.

I could turn to no moral preceptor; to ask would be necessarily to reveal. I laughed to myself, thinking, what would Hawkwood have done? And I knew what he'd have done; he would have drunk the champagne with robust enjoyment, taking what was offered from whoever offered it, lands from the Pope, a dowry from Bernabò, remaining utterly his own man. Yes, I would keep it, but I would not drink Sindona's health.

The next gift, I could imagine, would be a plane ticket to New York, on Concorde no doubt, that great, superfluous, supersonic bird. Would I accept that? No, I did not think I would. I had seen and heard enough of him, enough of his distortions and fantasies. He had given me a name. Should I need him again, he was there, albeit in gaol, provided nobody killed him in the meantime. Whoever had shot at him would no doubt try again; and who had it been? He had, as he confessed, so many enemies, so many people who sought vengeance, or would like to shut his mouth for ever, as he had shut poor Ambrosoli's. Yet the list had emerged, the greedy five hundred. If Sindona died, how many more lists would come to light?

A few days later, I was dragged from sleep by the telephone. It was ten past three in the morning. 'Ti ho svegliato?' asked a man's voice at the other end, did I wake you?

'Yes,' I answered.

'It's Della Martira,' the voice said, as if this excused everything. 'When are you coming back to Italy?'

'I don't know.'

'We need to talk to you. As soon as possible. We believe we can help you. To do what you want to do.'

'Are you in Rome?'

'No, I'm not in Rome. Never mind where I am. I'll call you, again. In about a week.'

'Not at this time of the morning, please.'

'We trust you. You can trust us. What you've done won't be forgotten.'

'One more thing,' I said, in sudden haste. 'Who's Gelli?'

There was a pause, I wondered if the line had gone dead, then Della Martira's voice said, 'Questo è un altro discorso, this is another matter,' and the phone was hung up.

I could not get back to sleep. Too many images, too many possibilities, were jostling in my mind. I wanted to plunge back into the conflict where I too, I thought, now had my place. I too, had been exposed to danger, even death, and had escaped. Did I trust Della Martira? I wasn't sure; even if he believed I had saved his life. As for Sindona, whose life I *had* saved, there was clearly no trusting him, at any time. He had his rat-like instinct for survival, Della Martira his all-consuming ideology. I could be sacrificed to either.

An hour or so later, still lying awake, I thought I heard the snap of a twig, as someone stepped on it outside my bedroom window. A mere couple of weeks earlier, I would have ignored it, but not now. Propped up on my hands, I lay listening in the bed, a throbbing in my chest. The sound was not repeated. Carefully and slowly, I slipped out of the bed, on to the floor, crawled to the window sill, then raised my head, to look through the leaded panes. It was too dark to make out shapes that did not move. I waited, watching, for what must have been ten minutes, then I crossed the room, quietly closed the door, and went to a cupboard in the hall where I kept a torch. This in my hand, I went to the front door, opened it, slipped out, and began to edge around the front wall of the house.

Scarcely had I reached the corner than I heard running footsteps on the road beside the house. I ran in my turn, but whoever it was had already disappeared. The roadway was badly lit by a single, small street light, and there was no one to be seen there. As I ran, barefooted, down it, I heard a car

116

start up, and drive rapidly away. I ran on, around the corner, but by the time I had done so, the car had already vanished around a bend and into the dark. I stood there panting, suddenly aware that the night was cold. Just as in the Piazza Vittorio, it had all happened too quickly and unexpectedly for me to feel frightened and besides, this time nobody had shot at me.

I trotted back to the cottage and, inside, poured myself a strong whisky. As the adrenalin subsided, I began to ponder the implications of what had happened. Someone had been spying on the house. Someone, presumably, had wanted to get into the house. Not to do me harm. In that case, they would hardly have run away. But obviously to search and steal. To look for anything which would help their purpose, which was surely to know about Sindona, know what he planned, know what he had told me.

When I had finished the whisky, I went into my study and took the notebook, with its record of our meeting, out of a drawer. Not that there was anything there, in that farrago of self-aggrandisement and self-justification, which could be of any use to them. But I grudged them even that. Indeed, who could tell, they might take seriously claims and accusations which to me seemed palpably grotesque. There was, though, another dimension to the thing, almost a metaphysical one. The world of fantasy had invaded the world of reality or, if you chose, the other way around. For as I have said Oxford, though it was my world, was the less 'real', more of a cosy oasis than Italy, which once had seemed a land of escape. In a word, there was now no safety. The life of bomb, intrigue and gun had made its way from Italy to England, from Rome to Oxford.

This, in the small hours of the morning, after the alarm of the snapping stick, the pursuit of the vanishing car, was the true shock. I could no longer choose when and where I wished to be involved. They would break into my home, I was certain of it, or at the very least they would surely try. The police would not watch the cottage, I felt sure; or not as it would need to be watched. I could fit catches, put grilles over windows, buy burglar alarms, but these were no more than deterrents. I had saved Sindona, I had been privy, as far as they knew, to Sindona's secrets. That was more than enough.

The following morning I brought a locksmith over from Oxford. 'It's a very old cottage, sir. How much are you prepared to spend on it?'

'How much would it need to make it really safe?'

He shrugged and smiled. 'Hard to say. You can't do much with these windows, not without spoiling them. A burglar alarm might be the best idea. Make 'em think twice, anyway.' I did not believe it would make them think even once, but I thanked him.

As I walked through the porter's lodge into college an hour or so later, the porter came up to me, 'We've been trying to reach you, Mr Cunningham. Someone's broken into your room.' How stupid of me not to think of that. 'Turned everything upside down, sir. Don't know if they've taken anything. Place is in one hell of a mess, I'm afraid.'

And so it was. The lock had been skilfully forced. No damage had been done, thank goodness, to the splendid oak door. Papers lay everywhere, as though scattered by a wind. Drawers had been pulled from my desk, turned upside down, then tossed to the floor. Files, assiduously kept, had had the contents pulled out of them and scattered. I felt, at once, infuriated and depressed. God knew how long it would be before I could put things back together.

The college Dean had joined me, a lean, bald, spectacled man with a jutting chin, somewhere in his middle fifties. 'We've called the police,' he said.

'They won't find anything,' I told him.

'What makes you so sure?'

'Oh,' I said, 'just feelings.' I had already wondered whether there were any point in telling the police of my prowler, of the incipient burglary of my cottage, sure as I was that they would never believe me, and could hardly help me, if they did.

They arrived while I was still there, clearing up what I could of the chaos, a young constable and a middle-aged detective in plain clothes. 'You shouldn't have touched anything, sir,' the detective said, reproachfully.

'Shouldn't I?' I said. 'I'm sorry. I've not touched the door or the desk, if it's fingerprints you're looking for.'

'Have they stolen much, sir? Valuables? Money?'

'They forced a drawer,' I said, pointing towards it. 'The

only one in the desk that was locked. They took a cashbox out of it. It may be there somewhere, under all those papers.'

'Was there much in it, sir?'

'Five or ten pounds, perhaps. Just a float I keep for convenience. As for valuables, there's a few little statues and ornaments I've brought back from Italy. They don't seem to have taken those.'

'Fits into a pattern,' the detective said. 'There's been quite a lot of this kind of thing since the end of last term. We've advised all the colleges to put safety locks on the doors.'

'A good idea,' I said. Should I tell them about last night? Should I confound their theory? Would they help me, if I did? For a moment, I was about to do so, then I found I couldn't. It would make no sense to them. Besides, in some strange way, I felt this was a battle I had to fight on my own. They pottered about a little more, debated whether it would be worth taking fingerprints, then left. I continued clearing up, then I put the notes on Sindona I had brought with me into an envelope, walked to my bank in the High, and placed them in my deposit box.

Next, I went to a sports shop and bought an air pistol. It was a silly gesture, I knew, but I needed some symbol of defence. This was not America; real guns were not to be bought and sold across the counter. Later, with a permit, I told myself, I might buy a shotgun, but I needed something now, something for tonight, something better than a burglar alarm, even if my instinct was to leave my front door unlocked, my windows open, an invitation to get on with it, ransack my cottage, and find nothing. What did I expect to do with my neat, new, shiny little air pistol? Frighten him, or them, away? Fire it, fire a pellet at them, while they levelled their Beretta or Kalashnikov at me, and blew me away? I was probably worse off with it than without it, but I would keep it, anyway. I had ducked one bullet, I could duck another. At one level of consciousness, I seemed to believe that I was invulnerable.

But now I climbed into my car, the blue, second-hand Volvo saloon which Simonetta had driven with such carefree Italian zest, and rushed back to the village, fearful lest the break-in had happened already, taking country corners with frantic abandon, braking in front of the cottage like a police car in a *film noir*, leaping out of it, down the crazy paving of the short path, through the front door: to find only an astonished cleaning woman.

'I'm sorry, Mrs Gregg,' I told her.

'Whatever is it, Mr Cunningham?' she asked, trembling behind her broom, which she clutched strongly for comfort.

'I'm a little upset,' I told her. 'Someone broke into my room, in college.'

'Oh, I'm sorry to hear that,' she said, 'but no one's broken in here.'

No, I thought, not yet, but they will. They were bound to.

That evening, I had been invited out to dinner. I wondered whether to go, and leave the cottage to whoever wanted to get into it, but I decided that I should. It was ridiculous to allow my life to be dictated to me, reduced to an obsessive guarding of my house.

The dinner party was being given in Woodstock by Harold Collings, Professor of Mediaeval History, and his wife. His college was Corpus, he had taught me when I was an undergraduate, to some extent he had been my mentor. He was in every way what an Oxford professor was 'meant' to be, consumed and circumscribed by his subject, eccentric, unworldly; committed, indeed, to the mediaeval world which he clearly found much more authentic than the one which confronted him day by day. He was not a television professor or a newspaper professor. He did not posture in public, appear on brains trusts or discussion programmes, or write pompous letters to *The Times*. Indeed, he disdained his colleagues who did. Collings was the genuine article. He was a pure academic, where Cooper was a parody of the pure academic who exulted in the life and colour of his subject, making it, in his lectures as in his writing, vivid and immediate. It was he who, so many years ago, had first spoken to me about Hawkwood, who had encouraged me to write my monograph, who felt such natural sympathy for that bluff, crafty old Englishman, who had retained that Englishness, that fealty to Crown and country, to the end of his days. Collings's home, at once shabby and splendid, was a treasure trove of mediaeval artefacts; illuminated manuscripts hung on the walls, a knight's visored helmet stood above the fireplace of the large, untidy, uncomfortable sitting room and on its shelves and among its sprawls of books there were

120

maps, daggers, even a crossbow. So comfortable in the Middle Ages, why should he have any truck with today? It was this which at first tempted me to tell him what had happened, and prevented me from doing so. He would be fascinated, robustly sympathetic, but quite uncomprehending.

His wife Jean, slender, handsome, white-haired and impeccably gracious, said very little, regarding him, in his enthusiasms and his rhodomontades, with what seemed a kind of loving amusement, the merest vestige of a smile. She, perhaps, more than anyone in Oxford, had done something to console me after Simonetta died. Simonetta had both admired and adored her. 'How serene she is, how beautiful, how patient with that naughty old rascal!' For the professor had liked her too, very evidently, giving her roguish glances, kissing her often on both cheeks, losing no chance to squeeze her hand or her arm, to pay her jocular attentions. At all of which his wife looked on with that composed, vestigial smile.

Another don and his wife had been invited, Joe Silverstone from Wolfson College, a specialist in mediaeval Russian history. He was dressed with his usual, costly carelessness, in a cashmere jacket, an open-necked silk shirt offset by a red foulard, while his rich wife, May, wore her usual, sensible suit, a white blouse, fastened by a cameo brooch, quite happy, so it seemed, with her secondary role, eyes always mild behind her spectacles.

'Tom!' cried Joe Silverstone. 'I hear you've been in Italy again. How was it?' though he did not really want to know, for which, as things were, I was grateful.

'Turbulent,' I replied.

'It always has been,' said Collings. 'Always will be. When has that country ever been at peace? Real peace?'

'They've not done so badly since 1945,' I remarked.

'And now look at it!' said Collings. 'Murders, bombings, terroism. It's virtual civil war.'

'Not quite,' I said.

'It will be, soon. You mark my words.'

'It's still not a country, is it?' asked Silverstone. 'Still really just a collection of city states. I notice that, every time I go there.'

'It's not the cities that are fighting one another,' I said.

121

'No, but they probably would, if they could. The North hates the South. The South resents the North.'

'Florence hates Pisa!' exclaimed the professor. 'Rome detests Milan.'

It was all partly true, but all irrelevant. I sat, with my generous gin and tonic, on one of the comfortable, chintz-covered armchairs, and let them enjoy themselves.

'How's old Hawkwood?' Collings asked me, at length. 'He'd have understood it, wouldn't he? Meat and drink to him!'

'I wonder if he would,' I said.

'Of course he would! Violence. Assassination. Kidnap. Power struggles. Be in his element.'

'Yes and no,' I replied, still reluctant to be drawn.

'No? Why no?'

'It's ideological, now,' I said.

'Oh, rubbish, rubbish!' said the professor. 'Different labels, that's all. Used to be Guelphs and Ghibellines, now it's Communists and Fascists. Still just the same old battle for power, I'll be bound.'

'Battle,' I said. 'But there *are* no battles. No open battles. No more wars out in the open. Everything's surreptitious now, underhand.'

'Treachery!' cried the professor, with glee. 'When was Italian politics not treacherous? Daggers in the back! Poison in the wine! *Plus ça change,* my dear Tom! *You* should know that, better than anybody!'

I did know that better than anybody, or better, at least, than anybody in the room, but I was not going to talk about it. Sitting there, I wondered what was happening in my own house. Had they prised open a window, jemmied a door, broken in there as they broke into my college room, leaving me to find a snowstorm of paper?

'What's this I hear about a burglary in your rooms?' asked Silverstone.

'Oh, yes,' I said, unwillingly. 'In college. It was broken into. Nothing stolen. It's been happening quite a lot, I understand.'

'That's awful,' said Mrs Silverstone. 'Did you call the police?'

'They came, but I don't think they're very hopeful of arresting anyone.'

'They never are,' said Silverstone. 'I'll put an extra lock on my door. Why you, though? Were you the only one?'

'In *our* college,' I said. 'So far as I know.'

'Battles!' said Collings, staring at space. 'Oh, there'll be battles! You'll see. It isn't Italy, without battles.'

I laughed, almost despite myself. 'There'll never be another Castagnaro,' I said.

The professor's eyes shone. ' "Hawkwood's great battle, a triumph of his old age." '

'Sir Charles Oman,' I said.

'Yes, yes; and he was right! A magnificent battle! A magnificent victory! Hawkwood fighting for Padua.'

And in Padua, I remembered, there was a policeman who might tell me things.

Battles were the professor's passion, old battlefields his favourite haunts. 'Of old, far off, forgotten things, and battles long ago,' he would intone, during his lectures, his fine head thrown back, savouring the carnage of the past. Battles he examined as a modern literary critic might examine texts. There was always something new to be gleaned, however long ago the battle, some gloss to put on a famous victory, some topographical or tactical insight to be found. I had heard him before on the subject of Castagnaro. So, infinite times, had his wife, whose eyebrows rose frantically in a moment of weary resignation. 'I must see to the joint,' she said, and disappeared from the room.

The professor was not deterred. 'Five hundred men-at-arms, six hundred mounted bowmen!' he cried. 'English bowmen, with their yew bows; the deadliest weapons of the Middle Ages! Split a man at two hundred yards!'

The professor had fought in the last war, he had soldiered through Italy, he had been fascinated, he always said, by the fact that he was so often crossing ancient battlefields. 'But in tanks!' he would say. 'The view from a tank is very limited. I'd rather have been on a horse.'

Now, he spoke of Hawkwood's calm, carefully planned retreat from the siege of Verona, down the River Adige. 'No one could retreat like Hawkwood! No commander in mediaeval history! He made a retreat look like a triumphant advance! Kept up morale! Kept his troops together!'

Before the crackling fire he stood, his eyes alight, his large hands gesturing, as though we, his tiny audience, were his lecture class. I knew the battle by heart, and was always a little bored by battles, except Hawkwood's; what interested me was the professor himself, his delivery and his gestures, though even these, by now, had become almost stylised.

'Moving south-east. Young Francesco Novello riding by his side. Poor devil would get strangled in a Venetian prison, in the end. On the way to his supply dump' – he occasionally enjoyed such anachronisms – 'at Castelbaldo. They stopped at Castangaro. The Veronesi on their heels. Nine thousand men-at-arms. Two thousand six hundred pikemen and archers. Crossbowmen; they couldn't hold a candle to the English archers. God knows how many citizens and peasants. What happened then, eh, Tom?'

'Hawkwood stood firm,' I said. 'He didn't withdraw to Castelbaldo.'

'Quite right. He looked at the terrain; damned soggy. Perfect for English infantry. All wrong for the Italian horses. Struck camp. Stayed where he was.'

At this, an image rose which had always fascinated me. Hawkwood before the battle. The brave old man, now well into his sixties. Moving about on a Thessalian charger, chatting with his men, asking if they had had their breakfast, bestowing knighthoods, golden spurs, here and there. Shrewd old devil. Diavolo incarnato.

The professor moved to a small table, pushing aside books and papers. 'Canal on his right flank. Swamp on his left flank. No worries, there. River behind him. Couldn't run away if he wanted. Lined up his men like this, in six "battles". Three here, three there. Another in reserve.'

His wife slipped back into the room, and watched him with her tolerant and affectionate smile.

'He'd use that last group when the right moment came; had his own company beside it. Hadn't enough English archers; kept them at the rear.'

We would not eat until the battle was over. No doubt his wife, aware of this, had turned down the oven. She sat, smiling still, a paragon of patience.

'Took the whole damn day for Ordelaffi to get his Veronesi ready. Got 'em off their horses, marshalled them in two long ranks, then it began!' He moved back, beaming, to the fireplace. 'The Veronesi shouting, "Scala, Scala!" Filling the ditch with faggots. The Paduans retorting, "Carro, Carro!" Hawkwood galloping into the front line. The Veronesi fighting their way across, against the lances; making little dents in the line. Shoved the Paduans back, step by step. Not too many casualties. And *then!* What happened then, Tom?'

'The old Poitiers trick.'

'That's right! The flank and rear attack he'd modelled on Captal de Buch, the old Gascon. Took all his own men down to the right, raising his baton.'

And for a moment he *was* Hawkwood, Hawkwood on horseback, his own right arm raised, brandishing the baton, bringing them all hurrying in his wake. 'How did he get across the water? No one knows. Must have planned it all. Ordelaffi never knew what hit him. Arrows, crossbow bolts.'

Now came the peak of his performance. It had always been worth waiting for, and I happily prepared myself for it.

'And Hawkwood *flung* away his baton!' He flung the invisible baton away. 'Flung it at the foe! Knew he'd get it back! Drew his sword.' He drew and raised his imaginary sword. 'Galloped into the fray. Carne! he shouted. Carne! Carne! That means flesh,' he explained to Silverstone and his wife.

'Yes, I know,' said Silverstone, with a smile.

'And that was that!' the professor said. 'The Veronesi retreated. Hawkwood destroyed their left wing. Ordelaffi tried to counter-attack. No use. He was swept back by his own, retreating forces. Then Hawkwood captured the caroccio! The magic ox-wagon! Ordellafi was taken; put up a damn good fight. And one group of poor damn peasants fought to the death. Didn't know the rules; took the whole thing seriously. And Hawkwood only lost a hundred men.' He subsided.

'Carne, carne!' said his wife. 'It should be ready, now. Let's go and have dinner.'

'Carne, carne,' I thought, as we passed into the dining-room, to take our places round the polished, oval table, each place so perfectly arrayed with glass and cutlery, all manifestly old, all plainly inherited. Carne, carne. I wondered that the words had not come into my mind while I had been in Italy; it might have been easier for me to reconcile myself to them, then. For I had never quite succeeded; indeed, had shoved them into the back of my mind. The old man baying not for blood, but for flesh. 'Sangue, sangue!' might even have been more acceptable. The picture of him, in his old age, hurling his baton at the enemy, drawing his sword and thundering in among them, was exhilarating to Collings, but ambivalent to me. For it meant that he exulted in battle, that it was more to him than just a means to a living, that he needed the charge and the challenge of it, almost to the end of his life, as much as he needed the money; or more. Carne, carne! And it was here that Castagnaro threw light upon Cesena, light that I had wanted to avoid. Eager for carnage as he had been at Castagnaro, could he not have been as eager at Cesena, might he not have taken part in all the slaughter, there?

I noticed Mrs Collings glancing at me with sympathy. If I was quiet and withdrawn, she doubtless put it down to thoughts of Simonetta. But there was carne and carne, I told myself, as I had often done before. A soldier's flesh, an armed enemy's flesh, was not the same as the flesh of a defenceless civilian. Hawkwood enjoyed battle, not murder. The story of the nun he split in two at Faenza still seemed the grossest libel, quite out of character with the man, the warrior. I would like to have talked about it to Collings, but then I thought it would be useless. Collings would simply sweep such doubts aside. For him, not least when he was *being* Hawkwood, re-living his battles, galloping along the Adige, Hawkwood was quintessentially the good soldier, courageous and true, with nothing in him of blood lust or sadism; merely the military virtues. Of which love of battle was surely one. Hot battle. Close-quarter battle. What soldier like that would enjoy the dropping of a bomb, the laying down of an artillery barrage?

We both, in our ways, were fascinated by Hawkwood, but where I sought to excuse him, Collings identified with him. 'Carne!' he cried, at the sideboard, cutting meat from the joint. 'Read a damn good essay in an American historical review the other day. "Poison and Politics in the Middle Ages." Come across it, have you, Tom? Or you, Silverstone?' We said we had not. 'It analyses all the different poisons that were used, especially in Italy. Didn't get as far as the Borgias, of course. Talks about antidotes, precautions.'

'One man's meat, another man's poison,' said Silverstone, with a pleased smile.

And I thought of Sindona, afraid he would go the way of Gaspare Pisciotta, squirming out his life in a cell. I thought of Lucetti and his theory on the poisoning of the Pope.

'It may still be going on,' I said. 'I met someone who thought the last Pope had been poisoned.'

'They're not accusing the poor Poles, I hope,' said Silverstone. 'Poles have never been very good with poison.'

'John Paul I,' mused the professor.

'Sheer fantasy, surely?' Mrs Silverstone said.

'No, no,' said Collings, 'well within the bounds of possibility. A mysterious death; comes back to me, now. Thought it was odd at the time. Found him in bed one morning, didn't they? Hadn't been a thing the matter with him.'

'We mediaevalists!' cried Silverstone. 'We project our era on to the modern world.'

'And why not?' Collings asked. 'It's highly relevant. Just that the poisons now are getting more sophisticated. Like that poor Bulgarian they killed on Waterloo Bridge with a pellet from an umbrella. Something to do with the castor oil plant.'

'Would you like wine?' his wife asked us. 'I promise you it's not poisoned.'

'After all your husband has said,' Silverstone answered, 'perhaps I really ought to employ a taster!'

I drove home, afterwards, with increasing anxiety. How was I going to find the cottage? Broken into? Ransacked? The intruder still inside? Or lurking in the garden? Would he come again when I was in bed? I had the air pistol, the ridiculous air pistol, in the glove pocket of the car. As I drove into my narrow road, I turned the headlights full on, illuminating the garden and the cottage. There was no one to be seen, no overt sign of disturbance. I turned into our little drive, my heart beating shamefully hard, opened the glove compartment, and took out the gun. Leaving the headlights switched on, I darted out of the car, ran to the front door, unlocked it, and threw it open. Once again, perfect tranquillity. No sign of entry or disturbance. I heard myself, ashamed again, give a great sigh, and was turning back to switch off the lights of the car when the telephone rang. Anxious again, I dashed into the sitting-room and snatched up the receiver.

A man's voice with a heavy Italian accent asked, 'Meester Cunningham?'

'Yes,' I said, cautiously.

'Ma sono Sindona!'

'Sindona!' I repeated, breathless still. 'You're in . . . New York State.'

'Yes; I'm in New York State in gaol again. Have I disturbed you?'

'No, no,' I said. 'I've just got in.'

'Did you receive my gift?'

'Yes, thank you very much. Gentilissimo.'

'A small token. When can you come to New York?'

'I don't know,' I said. 'Not in the immediate future.'

'It's important. I have things to tell you. Our book.'

'Listen,' I said, 'my room in college has been burgled. And I think someone was snooping round my cottage, last night.'

Instantly his tone changed, and he said brusquely, 'Then they may have tapped your telephone.'

It had never occurred to me. 'I don't think anyone's got in here yet,' I said.

'How can you tell? How can you be sure? Without examining your telephone? Seeing if there's a bug.'

'I'll have it checked,' I said.

'Ring me. From somewhere outside; a public phone. Call collect: my contact in New York. Then I'll call back. I'll give you the number.' As soon as he had done so, he rang off.

A bug! How did you detect a bug? By taking your telephone to pieces, identifying the tiny tell-tale object which was relaying all your conversations to a listening ear? Again, it was as though my safety, my privacy, were being taken away, as though stout walls were being removed around me, leaving me alone, exposed and vulnerable. Come, come, I thought, I must not share Sindona's paranoia, or let myself be infected by his delusions of martyrdom and persecution. Tomorrow, I would have the phone looked at. But by whom, I thought, by whom? What did one tell the Post Office: I think there's a bug in my phone? 'Oh, yes, sir, any particular kind? A Mafia bug? An MI5 bug? An industrial spying bug?' Should I, instead, go to the police, or hire a private detective? And if the telephone, then, proved 'clean', what guarantee was there that it would not be bugged in the future? None. And I could scarcely bring the telephone engineers in once a week.

'Giù!' One word had done it. 'Giù!' and I was intimately involved. No amount of protests – and to whom, anyway, could they be made? – could exculpate me, obliterate the moment when Sindona had ducked, when the bullet had whizzed above my head. Still, Sindona apart – and he would no longer be ringing me – what did it matter if my phone *was* tapped? What, of incriminating consequence, could they possibly hear; whoever they were? And even if Sindona did ring me, did I care? I had no intention of going to New York, or of ever writing his fatuous book, his apologia.

And yet, next day, I found myself calling his contact number from college, partly from a lingering sense of *comme il faut*, absurd in context, partly because there was just the chance that he had something else to tell me; something beside his own, Munchhausen story.

He called back an hour later. 'Where are you phoning from?' he asked me, instantly. 'From your home?'

'No, from my college. There's a switchboard here.'

'That's no guarantee. Call me from another room.'

Unwillingly, I did; from the telephone in the Senior Common Room.

'Did they find anything in your room?' he asked immediately. 'Anything to do with me? Things I told you?'

'Nothing,' I said. 'It was all in my house. And now it's in the bank.'

'Meno male,' he said, 'just as well. But make sure there's nothing else. Nothing you've forgotten. There are names mentioned, things I wouldn't want to get out, until I say they should.'

'Don't worry,' I told him.

'Come to New York! Come next week! Come by Concorde; it takes a few hours, that's all. I'll send you a ticket. You'd be back in a day.'

'I must first go back to Italy. I had to leave before I meant to. Like you.'

'Yes, like me,' he said, his voice quickening. 'You saw what those bastards tried to do? How they tried to kill me? I still had people to see. Important things to be done. That name I gave you. Have you found him, yet?'

129

'I've had no time.'

'*He* can help me; as he can help *you*. When you go back, when you find him, I have messages for him. I send them, but I never know if he gets them. That's why I wanted to be there. Life's difficult for me here, now. My enemies in Italy are stirring things up. I'm persecuted. They won't rest till they've destroyed me.'

'Where will I find him, then?' I asked.

'Who knows? Who ever knows where he is? He may be in Tuscany. He may be in Buenos Aires. Or Montevideo. He's often in Montevideo. As soon as you're going back to Italy, tell me. Then I'll tell *you*: where you might find him. What I want him to know.'

'Is it safe to go back to Italy yet?' I asked him.

'For me or for you? For me, it's never safe. You've seen that for yourself. For you, it ought to be all right, by now. They're not looking for you.'

'Someone is,' I said.

'Be on your guard,' he warned me. 'Always on your guard. They're everywhere. There's no escaping them.'

'Who *are* they?' I demanded, but the phone went dead.

He had set me off once more. What was happening in the cottage? How long would it be inviolate? Had they tampered with my telephone? I would definitely call the engineers.

I did so at once, and stayed home the following morning till the man came.

'Don't seem much wrong with it to me,' he said, after taking the telephone to pieces. 'You say you was having trouble with the incoming calls?'

'Well, sometimes, yes,' I lied. 'I can hear them, but they can't hear me.' It had happened once in the past. How could I ask him, 'Have you found a bug there?' Instead I asked, 'There's nothing there that's . . . untoward?'

'Untoward?' he echoed, giving me a quizzical look. 'What d'you mean? Something there what shouldn't be there?'

'Well . . . yes.'

He gazed again at the innards of the telephone, as if he were humouring me, and slowly shook his head. I looked over his shoulder, trying to memorise what was there, so that if a bug, whatever that was, should appear, I would be able to recognise it. He put the phone together, made a couple of test

130

calls, told me, 'Nothing wrong that I can see, sir,' and left, in an aura of perplexity.

How the hell did I put an end to all this? Come, come, come, you bastards, I thought. Come when I'm here, come when I'm not, come by day, come in the night, but get the damned thing over.

And they did come. That night, while I lay in bed, asleep, my door deliberately left open. I was deep in a dream. I was in Florence, in the Duomo, looking at the pictures of Hawkwood, by Uccello. Sindona was beside me, dressed in mediaeval costume, a pink and blue doublet, bright red hose. 'Look at him!' he said. 'Look how aggressively he sits there! Can't you just imagine him shouting, "Carne!"?' There was a muffled footstep beside us, which woke me at once, becoming, as I woke, a footstep in the room.

I snatched the air pistol from under my pillow and shouted, 'Carne!' A figure slipped from the room, through my open door, out into the shadows of the hall, across which footsteps now thudded. I jumped out of bed, the pistol in my hand, shouting, 'Stop! Stop, there! I'll shoot!' Then the front door had been thrown open, I raced through the hall and out of the door in my turn, saw a man running, running down the drive, leaping the low garden wall, rushing along the road.

'Stop!' I shouted again, at which the man turned, he was wearing a balaclava, and pointed a gun at me. Now, suddenly remembering my vulnerability, I threw myself down – for the second time in my life. This time, though, there was no explosion, just a plop and a hiss, then the sound of a bullet hitting the cottage wall. I stayed down, shaking, while the running footsteps sounded again, grew fainter, died away. Then came the inevitable noise of a starting car.

I stood up, still trembling. 'Bastard, *bastard*,' I heard myself saying. In the cottage nearest mine, some thirty yards down the road, lights went on, the front door opened, and the voice of its owner called, 'Is everything all right?'

'Yes, quite all right, thank you, Dr Atkins,' I called, trying to keep my voice steady. He was a retired doctor who had moved here from Birmingham. 'There was someone in my cottage,' I told him. 'An intruder. I just chased them away.' I realised the air pistol was still in my hand and quickly hid it behind my back.

'My goodness! Will you call the police?'

'I shall,' I said, 'but maybe I'll wait until tomorrow. There's no chance of catching anybody, now.'

Before he could question me I thanked him, said good night, and trotted back into the cottage. I had not stopped trembling, so I poured myself a strong whisky. You fool, you bloody fool, I told myself. Do you want to get killed? Do you really want to get killed?

The lock of the front door had clearly been forced back, but it was still functioning. A door had been opened in a bureau in the hall, but obviously he had not had time to look elsewhere. Irritably I threw the pistol on to a chair, aware of how foolish I had been. But at least it had frightened him away. For good; I was sure of that. Having shot at me, he would hardly return. The air pistol had achieved that, at least. But the experience had left me far more shaken than what had happened in the Piazza Vittorio. This, for a start, had been alarmingly more personal. The first bullet, however close it had come to me, had after all been fired at Sindona. This one had been meant for myself. Moreover it was an intrusion, if not a bullet, which I had been expecting and fearing. It had come out of the dark, but not out of the blue. There had been abundant time to feel threatened.

I would have to go to the police, I supposed, but again, I would not tell them what I suspected. Even if they believed me, there was little they could do to help. They were English police, and this was not an English crime. I would certainly not tell them I had been shot at. Again, what was the point? It had been a silenced gun, thank goodness. I did not think my neighbour had heard what noise it made, or he would surely have remarked on it. Once more, the worst of it all was my feeling of isolation. No one to talk to, no one to tell. No one, anyway, in England. In Italy, there was Aldo Magnoni. There was even Lucetti, who would fasten on it like a fox hound. There were Sindona and Della Martira, who, in their different ways, would at least take it seriously, and understand what had gone on. But here in Oxford, here in England, I was on my own.

Collings, if told, would mediaevalise it, fit it, quite uselessly, into a great, persisting pattern. Cooper would pigeonhole it, till it had happened long enough ago to be taken out and examined. I drank another whisky, then I went to bed.

Surprisingly, I slept, perhaps the consequence of nervous exhaustion. I dreamed again, though this time Sindona did not figure in the dream. Collings was there, riding on a charger, dressed in chain mail, though without a helmet, trotting down the bank of some unknown river. 'No sword, no lance, no dagger!' he was shouting. 'Do it with poison; so much easier!' Then he turned to look at me, and it was Hawkwood's face, or how I imagined Hawkwood's face to be, in his late years, the face of a healthy old man, ruddy and weathered. He looked straight at me and shouted in a hearty voice, like the professor's, 'Where's your air pistol? Brought your air pistol with you?' and he laughed, a swelling, booming, terrifying laugh, that seemed to fill the sky. It woke me up.

When I had made breakfast, I telephoned the police. 'Why didn't you let us know last night, sir?'

'There didn't seem much point. He'd gone, whoever he was.'

'That's for us to decide, sir.'

Before they came, I looked for the bullet, first raking the grass in front of the wall which I had heard it strike, then on my hands and knees beside the flower bed. Finally I found it, beneath a rose bush, a grey, flattened lump of lead. Which was meant to hit me, I thought, as I held it in my hand, and I shuddered. I slipped it into my pocket, wondering what kind of gun it had been fired from, telling myself that some day, I would find out.

The police came over for the usual pantomime. This time, they dusted for fingerprints; to compare, no doubt, with the ones they didn't get in college. It was not the same detective, though both those who came knew about the other break-in. 'Think they're connected?' I asked them, innocently.

'Two break-ins in a few days. Seems too close to be coincidence. Any idea what they might be looking for, sir? Documents, valuables?'

'I've no idea,' I said. 'I'm as puzzled as you are.'

He regarded me with a policeman's steady, sceptical gaze. 'No one with a grudge against you?'

'No one I can think of. The students I ploughed are all gone; or on vacation.'

He did not laugh. 'Well, if you think of anything, or anybody, let us know.'

133

'Of course,' I said.

Opening a drawer, he found the air pistol. 'What's this, sir?'

'Oh, that. We had a lot of trouble in the garden. Sparrows, rooks and things. I use it to scare them.'

He looked from it to me. He didn't believe me, but who cared? 'Sure that was all, sir?'

'Yes, positive,' I said. 'It's not illegal, is it? I don't need a permit, or anything?'

'No, sir,' he said, 'you don't need a permit.'

VI

Oxford, now, was as unrestful as Italy. I needed peace, a parenthesis. I would go back to Sible Hedingham, where Hawkwood had been born, had grown up, where he had wanted to die, and where finally they had brought back his body. Peace – the word he so detested – peace, in a place that had produced such a warrior. Yet always, when I'd been there before, on a strange sort of pilgrimage, I had found some kind of solace, some curious kind of inspiration.

So I drove across from west to east, from Oxfordshire into rural Essex, through the narrow lanes, past timbered mansions, past fields full of black and white cows, munching and ruminating, fields full of wheat, fields full of cabbages in dark green abundance, till at last I was in Sible Hedingham.

Cars, single-decker buses, lorries roared past Hawkwood Manor, on the main road; peace was relative. The pink, two storeyed, gabled house itself, with three great chimneys in the middle of its roof, had nothing to do with Hawkwood. It had been built in early Tudor days, the façade was two hundred years and more younger, but I liked to think that Hawkwood, perhaps, had lived there in some other, earlier house, with his father, the tanner.

It was the church I wanted, though, the church with the magic alcove, the church with the hawks and the boars, the church without a tomb. The church to which they had shipped him back from Florence, at Richard II's behest, had placed him, it was said, within the south wall, with effigies of both his wives beside his own. All long gone, now; only the splendid alcove remained, with its tomb-chest. Even Pevsner, slightly disdainful about the unexceptional nature of the church, built early in the fourteenth century, had to concede this, at least, to be remarkable. Let him dismiss the West Tower, which had been added. Let him ignore the fine, stone font, the dark, carved, wooden remnants of the first ceiling, nearby, with their De Vere star; even if they were crudely set off by orange cables. The place had its permanent romance for me.

I drove, in bright, August sunshine, past the old alms-houses and the decaying, abandoned house beside them, turned the corner, left, down the little canal, tried to ignore the discordant, recent, council houses on the right, then stopped at the foot of the green hill, looking up at the church, before I climbed to it, admiring the plump, deep green fullness of the yew bush, the infinite small stones of the grey, church wall. I was relieved to see, as I climbed, that the church door was open, revealing the green baize door behind it.

Passing through it, I saw the vicar, in his cassock, talking amiably to a little group of fair-haired children. He smiled and waved to me, well used to my sporadic visits. Then I went to the tomb; or where the body had been. Just bare stone, tantalising space now, beneath the white-washed wall, beneath the line of shields which Pevsner had approved, beneath the roundel with a flower; a boar, the snouted sign of the De Veres, on one side, a Hawkwood hawk on the other. L'inglese italianato. But never truly italianato; why, other-wise, would he long to come back here, to somewhere so uniquely English; still more so in those remote days?

Here, even now, Italy seemed a hemisphere away. Inside was English stone, outside was thick green English grass, the kind of green one never sees in Italy, green for which English expatriates, Hawkwood surely among them, have so often been known to yearn and pine. Here, contemplating the hawk, the boar, the flower, the tomb-chest, the six shields, I was aware above all of the paradox of it, the profound contrast. How had he ever grown so used to Italy? How could he be anything but a country Englishman? Had they been proud of him, here? Had he been a hero of the village? Had they talked about his exploits? Or had they known nothing of

135

him; thought of him, if at all, as someone lost and gone, more so even than a sailor or explorer who at least might come back from time to time, bringing his traveller's tales?

Hawkwood never came back; only his dead body would come back, and even that was not there any more. God knows where it had gone, and why. He had had his grand funeral in Florence, but he would rather have died here, had his funeral here, not in splendour but in intimacy, just relatives, friends, villagers to bury him. Just that – a muted end to the great Odyssey, the huge sweep south, through all of France, across the Alps, down into Tuscany; and back here, again, in the end.

Did he really go from Sible Hedingham to London, really become apprentice to a tailor, really get snatched and press-ganged into the French wars? No, I had never quite believed it. He had been a soldier, I was sure, by choice, not accident. He would have longed to fight in France, to serve, as he did, under the Black Prince, in those villainous wars. 'Exchanged his needle for a sword.' No, nonsense. I could imagine him tanning, never sewing.

Leaving the church, I strolled a little while among the graves outside, the eighteenth-century tombstones, and the rest, grown deep into the grass; none, of course, as old as Hawkwood and his vanished tomb. I walked beneath the cedar, thinking that he would have grown familiar with these, of all trees, in Italy. In some way, I felt curiously peaceful and calm, refreshed, just as the very memory of the place, the feeling he could one day come back, must have been a solace to Hawkwood in his Italian episodes. A place to grow up in, and a place to die. But if he had, during his long Italian years, been able to visit it from time to time, if travelling had been the easier thing that it became, would he have been content? Would he not have grown restless in the prettiness and peace, the rustic backwater? After so many cities, sieges, skirmishes? After so much blood and battle? After the pomp of his second wedding, in Milan? After the intrigues, the deaths, the great and small betrayals? After France and the Black Prince? After Crécy and Captal de Buch? After the burnished armour of the White Company, the furs and gowns and jewels of luxurious Florence? No; this was a place to yearn for and regret, just as Italy, had he ever come back home to die, would have been a land to yearn for. Not for the green that he had found again in England, but for the sharp, clear, summer light, the massive, sculptured, pompous clouds, the skies of a translucent blue. L'inglese italianato. He would never have got Italy out of his soul.

As for me, I thought, driving back along the narrow, tree-hooded lanes, past the gently sloping fields, I was besieged in Oxford. I was at risk in Italy, but I had to go back there; the country drew me like a lodestone. It was where I knew I should be, where duty and a kind of reality lay, however bizarre. At least for the present.

Had anyone, I wondered, ever tried to assassinate Hawk-wood, as opposed to trying merely to kill him? There was no record of it that I had ever seen. Mercenaries were ransomed more often than they were assassinated; Hawkwood himself had been ransomed, once or twice. No, the stab in the back or chest, the sudden dagger, were largely reserved for princes, potentates, or those whom they considered their rivals. Still, there might, at some time or another, have been a disaffected soldier, a jealous, fellow condottiere. With his wonderful ability to survive, he would clearly have survived that as well.

And I myself, I thought, with a sudden access of good cheer, driving past green hedges, catching a glimpse of a black and white timbered mansion behind a five-barred gate, had twice survived. Within barely a week, two bullets had missed me, one shot directly at me. Surely that indicated something; if it were only luck, the luck my dear Simonetta did not have, the ability at least to stay alive.

And as day succeeded day, escape followed escape, surely I must be growing and learning, subjected as I was to a truncated, almost Darwinian, process of selection. I would go to Italy again, and I would look for Gelli, whoever he might be. I would fear no evil. Bullets, I knew now, did not hit me; they flew over my head. Visiting Sible Hedingham always revived me and inspired me, but today, it seemed to have given me something more; a confidence with which to face violence. Hawkwood's world was one of violence, it was the element in which he swam, though he was not – save in battle – a noticeably violent man, himself. My world was one of sedentary peace, of violence recollected in tranquillity, until

137

now, when I had been confronted by violence, and lived through it.

I had been given a reprieve, I knew. The intruder would not come back again; not in the forseeable future. He had tried to kill me, and he had failed; for all he knew, the police were looking for him. Probably, too, he thought that I had tried to kill *him*; in the dark, who could distinguish an air pistol from one more lethal? I would go to Italy next week, take another cheap flight, land anywhere I could, then make for Tuscany. In Florence, I would find Della Martira, or someone from his band. Then, picaresque, I would go where things might take me. If not immediately to Gelli, then to Padua, where there were other things I might discover. There was Sindona, too. I could call his contact number collect at any time, from anywhere, doubtful repository though it was of useful information. I would use him, he would try to use me; but he could never pay off his debt. His life.

The following day, I phoned the bucket shop I used in London and booked a flight to Bologna; the earliest they had was one that suited me perfectly; I could talk to Aldo Magnoni and to Lucetti. But that night, the phone rang again, before I went to bed; it was Della Martira.

'Don't come to Italy,' he said.

'But why?' I asked.

'They tried to kill you, didn't they? We know all about it. Don't come, you'd be in danger. We'll tell you when it's safe. We'll tell you when to come.'

No more than that, and then the click. It caused me a frustration which was worse than fear; the kind a runner must feel when, rising from his blocks, leaping on to the track, he hears the starting pistol fire again, and knows that somebody has jumped the gun; he must go back. Was I safe even in England, then? I had not had time to ask Della Martira that, but I supposed I would be, or he would have told me. The implication was that I must simply keep out of Italy.

Then who was looking for me? Who had shot at Sindona in Rome? Who had shot at me, here, in Oxford? Did Sindona himself now know? To know would be a start. Della Martira must know, of course; how else could he have warned me? But Della Martira came and went, a remote voice on a telephone, with no point of contact. How long would I have to stay here, champing at the bit, like one of Hawkwood's horses on the verge of battle? Soon, in only a few weeks, it would be term time, and Oxford would close in on me till almost the end of the year. The beautiful Oxford autumn, with its spinning, browning leaves, carpeting the rich, green lawns of parks and quadrangles; Oxford winter, murky light, grey stone buildings against stone grey skies, the rain beating bleakly into the worn old faces outside the Ashmolean. Usually, I loved Oxford colours, Oxford watercolours, Oxford weather, but now, the place was going to be a prison. I would long for Italy. I cancelled my flight.

Each time my phone rang now, in college or in my cottage, I hoped the call would be from Italy, or from the penitentiary. I even hoped that Della Martira would come, as he always did, as a thief in the night. At last, after a few fraught days, I myself phoned Aldo Magnoni, in Bologna. Phoned him from the cottage, confident, for the moment at least, that no one had bugged my telephone. I did not talk to him about the shootings. It was something, instinctively, I wanted to keep to myself, or with that small circle of people who were somehow involved with it.

'Tom!' he replied. 'Che piacere! You're in England; but I thought you were coming back to Bologna.'

'It's a long story,' I said. 'But I need to know something. About a man called Gelli.'

'Never heard of him. What is he?'

'I'm not sure. Somebody powerful. Somebody who makes things happen. Someone with Fascist friends, a home in Tuscany. Connections in South America.'

'You ought to ask Lucetti,' he said.

'I did,' I told him, 'but he wouldn't say very much. He seemed afraid to.'

'Not like him. I'll talk to him. I'll see what I can do.'

'He may not tell you,' I said.

'Then I'll ask someone else. It shouldn't take too long, if he's a Tuscan.'

But how long would it be before I went back to Italy? Marooned in Oxford, waiting for the term, the interminable term, I played guessing games. If Della Martira had warned me to stay away, the people who had tried to shoot Sindona, then shoot me, were presumably from the Left, rather than the Right. They could hardly be Della Martira's own group, or they would not have shot at him. And if they were from the Left, they must want to kill Sindona for ideological reasons, for his infamy and villainy, his swindles and malefactions, rather than simply to shut him up. Knowing he had talked to me, they no doubt wanted to find out what he had said, to use it for their own purposes. There was no certainty to this; nothing was what it seemed, that was the mandatory rule, but as a working hypothesis, it was acceptable.

I filled the time as best I could, spent hours in the Bodleian, visiting the British Museum Reading Room and the Public Record Office, thought endlessly about Hawkwood, in the light of the Italy I had been discovering, and of my own continuing sea change, played tennis for hours on the college courts with a small, blond English don called Andrew Mountain, slept uneasily at nights, and threw my air pistol into the coal shed, reluctant quite to let it go. I had decided against buying a shotgun.

I took the notebook, into which I had transcribed Sindona's rantings, out of the bank, secreting it in the college safe whenever I wasn't reading it. It still seemed little more than a self-aggrandising tirade, an exercise in name dropping and self-justification, yet there were things in it that made me wonder. The Sicilian Masons, for example, his 'revolutionary' Masons. Again, why Masons, instead of Mafia? Why revolutionary at all, rather than conservative? The questions came back to me. Why Masons at all, for that matter, save that they, with the Jews, had eternally been the symbols of conspiracy; scapegoats and whipping boys? Sindona, I was sure, had Mafia connections; what Sicilian arriviste hadn't? Without them, there, it was impossible to move. And he had mentioned New York Mafia names. Had he Masonic connections, too?

There was little I could do but speculate, till I heard again from Della Martira, Magnoni, or perhaps Sindona himself. Who was Gelli? I could ask Sindona whenever I wanted, but he clearly would not give me a straight answer, unless perhaps I went to New York, and saw him face to face. It was a time in which, more achingly than ever, I missed Simonetta. It was she, I realised, whom I truly wanted to talk to, and there was no one, no woman, who could take her place. Yet it was she on whose account I had become embroiled in all this, or rather – for I could see her laughing at me, saying, 'For *me*? For *me*?' – for myself, in my attempt somehow to come to terms with the fact that she was gone.

I wrote and re-wrote my monograph on Hawkwood. I searched, with little hope, through still more documents, trying to trace the missing years between his living in Sible Hedingham and fighting in France, the years when he was so improbably meant to be an apprentice tailor, years which had never made good sense to me, years when he was supposed to be in London.

One hot day in early September, I sat at a green desk in the British Museum Reading Room, a bearded student in spectacles and blue jeans on my left, on my right a girl who looked as if, from her books and demeanour, she might be a medical student. Each, in absorbed silence, was staring at their books, while I made notes, notes on Hawkwood's battles, relishing that day in 1387 when Venni, his opponent, sent him a fox in a cage and Hawkwood – a hawk in a cage – answered him, 'the fox knows how to find its way out.' Which he did, after Venni broke down the banks of the Adige, and nearly swept him away.

I got up from my place, eventually, to go out for some sort of lunch at the pub across the road, leaving my books, my briefcase behind, with the confidence engendered by that great, round, handsome room. I walked through the narrow channel, past the security guards, through the great entrance hall, with its milling parties of schoolchildren from France and Germany, Japanese tourists, parents and their offspring. In the pub, I stood at the counter, drinking a pint of bitter and eating a ham sandwich. Back in the Reading Room, taking the student and the girl as landmarks, I at first lost my bearings, as it is easy to do. Student and girl had gone, but I remembered the number of my seat. At last, with relief, I spotted my briefcase, and walked quickly down the desks towards it. I got there. My notes had disappeared. I had left them on the desk, I was sure of it. I looked inside the briefcase. The two books it had contained were still there, but not the green file which held some lecture notes I had been reading on the train. Nor the notes which I had left on the desk. I looked underneath the briefcase; nothing. Under the

141

desk: there was nothing there, either. To my right, three or four places away, an elderly man with an aureole of white hair and thick-lensed spectacles was crouching over his books. He would have noticed nothing. Down on my left, an Indian in a blue turban was diligently studying. What could I ask him? If the girl, the bearded student, someone else, had stolen my notes and file, he could hardly have seen it happen; unless the student and the girl had gone and someone, that someone else, had suddenly appeared.

I walked over to him. 'Excuse me.' He looked up at me, eyes apprehensive behind his spectacles. 'I . . . wondered if you'd seen anybody come along within the last half-hour. Just there. To my place. I seem to be missing some notes.'

'I have seen nothing at all,' he answered, in a sing-song, plaintive voice. 'I have seen nothing. I have touched nothing at your place.'

'No, no, I'm sure you haven't,' I said.

'Nothing! Nothing at all!'

'Of course, of course!' I walked away from him. I felt both angry and impotent. I soliti ignoti. Again, I was the victim. My cottage was not safe. My college room was not safe. Now even the sacrosanct British Museum Reading Room was unsafe. Was it the girl? Was it the student? Could they have been in collusion? Was it worth checking in the admissions office, where everyone was photographed? But what would one check? If only he or she had still been there! I was angry at the loss of my notes, still angrier about the loss of my file, and all the work that was in it, but the feeling of dislocation was worse. Where would it end? How much more must I put up with? What the hell did they expect to find?

Word of Sindona, I thought, giving back my books, leaving the library, too distressed to carry on. That, and only that, must be what they were still after. I walked briskly and angrily past the fine, high railings of the Museum, to the car park where I had left my Volvo, thinking, at last, well, it is better than being shot at. But in fact, I reflected, driving up the motorway to Oxford, it was neither better nor worse, merely different, another aspect of the same persecution. That word! I was beginning to think like Sindona.

What would they make of the notes, I wondered. The notes on Hawkwood, the notes on usury, and the attrition of the feudal system? Would they think they were in code? Would they subject them to computer analysis? I was tired of being a sitting duck, an easy target. If I did go back to Italy, what could be much worse? People here in England, in Oxford and in London, were shooting at me, stealing from me. And I could take no initiative, could only wait until the next thing happened. 'I soliti ignoti' were mere shadows, faceless people who emerged from the dark to burgle my cottage, who slipped somehow into the British Museum, to steal my notes. Besides, they were Sindona's enemies, not mine. If they were to the Left, it would not be they who killed Simonetta. Or most probably not. God knows there was no certainty.

It was tempting to ring Aldo again, to ask him what he had discovered, but I restrained myself. Here, too, I had to be passive, waiting for the calls to come, from Italy or from New York. In the event, Aldo did not telephone, he wrote. A fat envelope, Italian stamped, was waiting for me one morning when I came into college. I took it out of my pigeon hole with growing excitement. It had been registered. It was superfluously marked, PERSONAL. I hurried to my room, and opened it.

'You have asked me about our friend,' it began. 'I have gleaned what I can, but it is difficult. People are frightened of him, though it is hard to say why. He lives in a villa near Arezzo. Ostensibly, he has a small factory which manufactures clothing. I don't think this is something which would usually frighten people. He is unquestionably a Fascist, and has been one for a long time. Since schooldays, as far as I can tell. His origins are humble. His father was a factory worker. Powerful Fascists seem to have taken him up, and furthered his career.

'In the war, he was in Yugoslavia, where something happened, I am not sure what; something very strange, involving gold and treasure. Possibly even the State treasure. He got hold of it, with some Italian general. It seems that even the Germans didn't know about it. He returned to Italy, and somehow got involved with the partisans. Just as a cover, I surmise, but it seemed to take the heat off when he needed it. Afterwards, he was discredited, again.

'He goes to South America a lot, to Uruguay and Argentina. He knows the military dictators there. He seems to have been a close friend of Peron. There's something else, as well, but I don't know what it is. People clam up. Something important. So important and so secret that they do not dare to speak about it. He seems a frightening man, with fingers in a thousand pies. An evil man. You know I don't often use the word. I have been warned not to get too close to him, or I'll be burned. I gather he has friends in the Vatican, and others in the Mafia. Friends everywhere. A dangerous man to cross.

'Have you heard of somebody called Calvi? That is another name which has come up. A banker in Milan, who has been involved in shady deals, from what I understand. A bit of a Sindona. But the man you want to find is bigger than either of them. He has some curious kind of power which I have been unable to fathom. If I were you, I would keep away from him. I've told you so many times, Italy is not England. We are not a modern country. Things you take for granted in England aren't even acknowledged here.

'What are you trying to achieve, Tom? I understand your impatience, I understand your pain, but what is the point of immolating yourself? Whatever you do, you can never bring dear Simonetta back, and if you do not want revenge, what *do* you want? Leave Italy alone, come here for holidays, come here to work on good old Giovanni Acuto, but leave sordid intrigue to the sordid intriguers. Of whom our friend seems to be the most sordid.'

The effect of all this on me was precisely the reverse of what Aldo wanted. Gelli was my man, as I had sensed before, perhaps *the* man, the fixer, the manipulator, the very fount of all malice. I could not wait to get to Tuscany and find him, beard him, demand that he tell me who had blown up Simonetta's train and who had told them to. He would know, I felt more sure of it than ever.

The months in Oxford would be still less bearable now. This was someone who made Sindona seem a petty, paltry villain, for all his massive swindles, his boasts of consorting with principalities and powers. If all that Aldo wrote was true, then Gelli, by implication, *was* power, the very essence of power, Black Eminence, twitching the strings which made his puppets dance and gyrate. My mind was racing. What villainies had he encompassed? Could he have poisoned the Pope? Blown up Bologna station? In South America, certainly, he consorted with vicious men. But he seemed always to have done so. Greedy, evil men had plainly made him. They had worked with him in the war. They manifestly worked with him now.

I could not be still. On an impulse, I picked up the telephone and made a collect call to the contact number. When he eventually called back we went through the usual charade. Where was I calling from? Was I sure my telephone was 'clean'? When was I coming to New York? I told him how my notes had been stolen, in the British Museum.

'Nothing about *me*?'

'No, nothing about you.'

'It will happened again,' he said. 'They never rest. Once they think you know things about *me*.'

'Tell me about Gelli,' I said. 'Is it true he was taken up by Fascists? Is it true he stole gold in Yugoslavia? Is it true he has links with the Vatican and the Mafia?'

There was a sustained hiatus. Finally, Sindona asked, 'Who told you all this?'

'I asked my friends to find out. My friends in Itlay.'

Another pause. 'All these things are true. But only part of the truth. I can't tell you the whole truth. You'll have to find it out for yourself. You'll have to find *him* for yourself.'

'But where? In Tuscany? I can't very well go to South America.'

'He'll be back in Italy, eventually. He has to come back to Italy. That is the basis of his power.'

'But I've been told not to go back to Italy. That it is dangerous for me.'

'By whom?'

'By people I know. Left-wingers.'

His voice grew cold. 'They never tell the truth. They say what suits them. They may not want you back in Italy. They'd have their reasons.'

'This is somebody I trust,' I said. 'At least in this.'

'You can't trust any of them.'

And you? I thought. Can anyone trust *you*? Why had I telephoned him, save on an impulse? I knew he would never give me a straight answer about Gelli; not until it suited him.

'Do you know who shot at you in Rome?' I asked him.

'Those who would deliver Italy to Communism,' he

intoned. 'Those who hate me because I have opposed their schemes.'

I recognised that voice all too well, from our colloquy in his hotel, the sonorous protestations of altruism, innocence, victimisation. 'They know that I stand in their way,' he went on. 'You saved me, therefore you are in their way as well.'

I was no better off than before I rang him, I thought, unless his grudging confirmation served to bear out what Aldo had written. I could only stay in England and make the best of it, feed on the scraps provided by occasional telephone calls, intermittent letters. Lucetti could tell me more, I was certain, might even have told Aldo something of what he had given me, but Lucetti would not talk on the telephone. Somewhere near Arezzo, somewhere in that region where Hawkwood had made so many of his marches – marches by day, and those marches by night for which his troops were famed – was the spider at the centre of the web. I felt sure of it, even though it might seem conspiracy theory at its wildest, history reduced to personality, the level of a trashy spy film: 'Mr Big', the malign individual who controlled the grand strategy, with tentacles that spread across the world.

What did Sindona want from Gelli? What were the messages he wished to send him? Again, there was no way I could find out until I went to Italy. It was tempting to say to hell with risk, defy Della Martira, fly to Bologna, as I had planned. But if it was Gelli I wanted – and now it surely was – what guarantee was there that he would even be there, that in the little time left to me before the start of term I had any hope of finding him?

So the days dragged slowly by, until the undergraduates began to arrive, the city was transformed by their fleets of bicycles, their dangling scarves, their fresh faces, their young and eager voices, their *dégagement*. My colleagues came back, too, my fellow dons and learned professors, deep-tanned from their protracted holidays. Term at last began, and I could find some distraction in my duties. Some, but not enough. What the summer and its maelstrom of events had done was to make me question, more than ever, what I was doing, what my students were doing; indeed, what the whole business of academia, let alone history, was doing.

As I sat at High Table and listened to the droning voices,

the gossip and the backbiting, the cloistered trivia of smug and selfish men, as I sat in my room, listening to my students' essays – clever and ignorant, vapid and ignorant – listening to myself aridly discussing their essays, my impatience grew almost unbearable. It all seemed an exercise in the void, a feeling exacerbated by my urgent wish to be somewhere else.

Helen, the Giggler, continued to simper at me, Giles, the High Flyer, continued to make his precociously donnish observations. Out of their deep inexperience, I was asking them, and others like them, to pass judgement on lives lived in circumstances we could scarcely comprehend. Was I, with my endlessly uncompleted monograph on Hawkwood, any better? I thought I had come to understand him more, through those days in Italy, but was that even now sufficient? Could the leap ever be made?

VII

I found myself thinking more than ever of Simonetta, and sometimes, slightly to my shame, of Teresa. I was glad, now, that I had not made love to her, but caught myself wondering, every now and then, whether I would ever see her again, aware that I wanted to. One night, to my surprise, as though I had conjured her out of nowhere, she telephoned me. It was midnight, I was lying in bed, half absently reading the paper on mediaeval poisons which Collings had recommended to me.

'Ciao!' said a woman's voice, with great warmth, as I picked up the phone. 'Sono Teresa. Do you remember me?'

'Of course, of course!' I said. 'How good to hear from you! How are you? Where are you?'

Instantly, her voice became guarded. 'I can't tell you where I am. I'm in Italy. But Carlo told me to call you. He said the people you are looking for may be in London. Young neo-Fascists. One of them is living with a girl Carlo used to know. Her name is Annabel Carlton. He says she's very tall and blonde and rather stupid. They all go drinking in a pub called the Coldstream. He says you'd know where it is.

147

They're on the run from the police here. English Fascists give them money. One of them's only just arrived from Italy; his name is Guido. Carlo says, be careful.'

'Yes, I will,' I said. 'But when can I come back to Italy? When will it be safe? By the end of the year?'

'We'll tell you when,' she said. 'Not yet. Pazienza. Soon, I hope. I want to see you.'

'I want to see you, too,' I said. Oh, yes; I did want to see her.

I had been brought to life again, out of limbo, out of lethargy. There were things to be done without going back to Italy, and there was Teresa, too, when I did go back there; I would see her, again.

I had been in the Coldstream now and then, but it was not my kind of pub. It stood in a mews in Belgravia. It was narrow, snug and small, what the Italians would call caratter- istico, with an abundance of dark, polished wood, brasses above the bar, like a country pub, old military prints on the walls, a low ceiling; a conscious attempt at anachronism. But it was the haunt of the jeunesse dorée, the Rahs, with their booming and fluting, their pretty, silly, dressed-up women. Just the place for a pretty, silly woman such as Annabel Carlton, whom I was sure I recognised as soon as I walked into the pub, on the next visit I made to London, two days after Teresa's call. I had been working all afternoon at the British Museum. This time, nothing had been stolen.

It was almost half past eight when I arrived, hoping to find her, and them; and there, almost certainly, she was. She was a tall woman of about my own age, with long, streaked, blonde hair falling to her shoulders, large, drop earrings, black corduroys tucked into boots, beautiful but bovine blue eyes, a full, heavily crimsoned mouth, and the demeanour of a highly strung racehorse; a nervous, twitching self-consciousness, her head for ever moving to one side or the other, her hair time and again tossed back, her laugh frequent, loud and facti- tious. A blue cloak was flung casually over her shoulders.

The two men with her were obviously Italian, though one was fair and one was dark. They showed none of her exuberance. Though they responded to her, there was a wariness about them; they would smile, they would even laugh, but then they would subside into a sullen watchfulness, throwing her own, febrile behaviour into relief. Both men were in their late or middle twenties. The dark one was the taller; heavy set, with wavy, carefully styled hair, he wore rings on the fingers of both hands. Like the girl he had a light coat thrown over his shoulders.

The blond man had a rough, pock-marked skin, and a small zigzag scar on his right cheek; he wore a gold chain with a medallion round his solid neck. His eyes were narrow and grey, his hands curiously thick and stubby. As the girl talked, she often touched, pushed or stroked them, but her eyes nonetheless moved about the pub, focusing once on me, for that fraction of a second too long, that transient intensity, denoting interest.

I had armed myself with a copy of that day's *Corriere della Sera* as means of possible introduction, a kind of earnest of Italian associations. I pushed my way through to the bar, as close as I could come to them, and ordered a pint of bitter. All three of them were drinking shorts, and they were talking Italian. The girl spoke it with the excruciating accent of the upper-class Englishwoman, a kind of filleted, parodic Italian which never sounds anything but a burlesque, even when the grammar is good, which in her case it was not. Indeed, it was very bad. She spoke in spurts and snatches, amplified by helpless, appealing gestures. From time to time, the dark man lapsed into an English far worse than her Italian, to make himself understood. I caught her eye, again; this time she smiled at me. I held my newspaper up still more prominently.

'Are *you* Italian?' she asked me, cordially, in English.

'I'm English, but I speak Italian,' I said.

'Oh, how *super*! I wish *I* spoke really good Italian, but I don't, do I, boys?'

The two men now stared at me, with no goodwill in their glance. 'Ma! Si capisce,' said the dark one, we can understand.

'I'm Tom Cunningham,' I said, and held out my hand. She took it instantly, saying, 'Annabel Carlton'.

'Molto lieto,' I said, and extended my hand in turn to the two men. There was a moment's hiatus before the dark one finally took it, then the blond man, too. Both continued to look hard at me; the air was thick with their suspicion.

'Enzo,' the dark man said.

'Guido,' said the blond one.

'I've never seen you in here before,' said Enzo.

'I don't live in London,' I said, 'I live in Oxford. I come here when I'm around Belgravia.'

'What do you do?'

'I teach mediaeval history.'

'How come you speak Italian?'

'Italian history is my speciality.'

They seemed to relax a little at this, but they were still manifestly on their guard. There was an aura of suppressed violence about them. Unlike Della Martira, unlike Teresa, it was easy to imagine them as terrorists. They stood at the bar, drinks in hand, like two cornered animals, ready to spring. By contrast, Annabel Carlton was supremely unconcerned. She linked her arm through Enzo's, she smiled at me, she flung back her long hair, she prattled on about the beauties of Italy, the difficulties of learning Italian, how marvellous it must be to be a don at Oxford.

'I *adore* Oxford! Do you remember when we went there, Enzo? When I drove you there, and we went on the river? My father was at Oxford. I forget what college. One with a lake in it.'

Guido clearly could not understand her. He was the one, presumably, who had just arrived from Italy. Had he anything to do with Bologna? I found myself detesting both of them, and tried to subdue my antipathy, sensing that they were as alert to such vibrations as a couple of cats, that they would pick up hostility in an instant. They did not want to talk to me; that was quite plain. Their concern was wholly with survival. Even she picked up their uneasiness.

'Ma che cos'hai?' she cooed at Enzo, putting her cheek close to his.

'Niente, niente,' he answered, without looking at her. Around us, the Hooray voices brayed and squawked. Annabel was in her element; the Italians could scarcely have been more out of place. I offered them a drink. She accepted cheerfully, 'How *nice* of you!' They, surly, received their drinks as though they might be poisoned. From time to time, they would look towards the door, and at last a man came in, heavy-shouldered, crop-haired, dressed in a blue raincoat. He saw us, and shouldered his way through the crowd. 'Hallo,

Annabel,' he said, in a Cockney accent. 'All right, Enzo? You're Guido, right?' He shook hands with them. 'Don't know you, do I?' he said to me.

'Oh, this is Tom,' said Annabel. 'We've just met him. He's a don at Oxford.'

He gave me a hard, cold look. 'What's that? A teacher?'

'More or less,' I said.

'What you teach?'

'History.'

He nodded, half contemptuously. About him, too, there was a kind of contained violence. There was a difference, though, between him and the Italians. He struck me as a bar-room bully, a National Front thug, probably; a brawler, a beater-up of Asians, a pourer of petrol through letter boxes, at the very worst. The Italians came across not as bullies but as true terrorists. Where *his* aggression, so to speak, was personal, theirs could be quite impersonal, ideological killings in the abstract. And while he looked implacably at me, the Cockney regarded the Italians with a kind of respect, verging on deference. 'Have you brought it?' Enzo asked him.

The Cockney glanced quickly at me, then he said, 'Yeah, I brought it.' I offered him a drink. 'Guinness,' he said, 'I'll 'ave a pint,' and turned back to Enzo. 'A grand,' he said, lowering his voice. 'That's what you wanted, wasn't it?'

'Che dice?' said Enzo.

Annabel laughed. 'I'm afraid he doesn't understand,' she said. 'Mille,' she whispered to Enzo, and he nodded, without gratitude. Ted took the pint of Guinness from the barmaid and tipped about half of it down his throat. He put the beer glass down on the counter and jerked his head, beckoning Enzo to follow him. When they had gone, Annabel asked me, 'When were you last in Italy?'

'Quite recently,' I said.

'I'm *longing* to go back. I just *adore* it there. But at the moment, I can't. There are . . . *reasons*.'

'I see,' I said, as vaguely as I could.

'You're one of the reasons, aren't you, darling?' she asked, smiling at Guido, who did not understand her but merely grunted, and looked into his glass. 'I suppose you know a lot about Italian politics, being so clever,' she said to me. 'I honestly don't understand the half of it.'

No, I thought, of course you don't, you silly bitch. You don't even want to understand. You like the frisson of it. The kicks from violence. From being on the edge of violence. From mixing with your Italian rough trade. And I found myself detesting her even more than I did them, the three thugs, the three Fascists. Indeed, it was the first time in the whole saga that I had caught myself hating anybody. Including Sindona, though he was unquestionably hateful, and though not violent in himself, had promoted violence, even murder, at second hand, and surely would not hesitate to do so again. You could not hate Della Martira and the rest of his group, or even dislike them. Sandro, with his gun in his jeans pocket, was no doubt the equivalent of these two neo-Fascist toughs, but he had aroused no antipathy in me.

These men, by contrast, the two Italians and the Englishman, were deeply alien to me, natural antagonists. It was people like Guido and Enzo, I was sure, who had killed Simonetta; it might even have been Guido and Enzo themselves. Or did I merely *want* to be sure, believe that only hateful people could do such a hateful thing? What if it had in fact been Della Martira, or someone like him?

'Enzo and Guido are *so* committed,' said Annabel, 'they're so *passionate* about things, they're such idealists.'

'Is that what you'd call them?' I could not help myself asking.

'Well, yes, I think they *are*. One gets quite carried away. I see their point; I mean, Italy *is* terribly corrupt, isn't it? It's not a bit like England.'

'No, not a bit,' I said.

Enzo and Ted came back from the lavatories; Enzo's expression seemed marginally less dour. This time it was Annabel who bought a round of drinks. I was finding it hard to dissimulate my antipathy, but it had to be done. Somehow or other, I must break down their mistrust, or there was nothing to be done, nothing to be discovered.

We spoke Italian, which at least froze out the surly Ted, who simply stood glowering, his Fascism at odds with his xenophobia, beer mug in hand, from time to time trying to talk to Annabel. But she was quite absorbed in Enzo, listening to him, laughing at him, talking her bad Italian to him and to

152

Guido, giving Ted, when he spoke to me, only the solace of a dazzling, dismissive smile.

I knew what I wanted to ask Guido and Enzo, however absurd it might seem. The $64,000 question: did you kill my wife? They could easily have done so, I felt it in my bones, just as I felt that, however I might deprecate revenge, if it transpired that they had, I would gladly kill them, too. But now I had to play this role, one I must make up as I went along. I was the historian, the Italian-speaking innocent, unversed in the political actualities of the day, mired inexorably in the Middle Ages.

'You go to Italy a lot,' Enzo challenged me. 'What do you think of it?'

'It's hard to say,' I told him. 'I don't have much contact with modern Italy.'

'Then you're lucky,' said Guido.

'Possibly,' I replied. 'I'm a mediaevalist. I work in libraries. I look at documents. I'm interested in dead people. People like Hawkwood.'

'Like who?' asked Enzo.

'John Hawkwood. Giovanni Acuto. He was an English mercenary, a condottiere of the fourteenth century.' With a mirthless smile, I quoted, 'L'inglese italianato è il diavolo incarnato'.

For the first time since I had joined them, the Italians laughed. 'Bello, bello!' said Enzo. I translated, for the benefit of Ted and Annabel. 'Goodness!' she said. 'I hope that won't apply to me.'

'Scarcely. He fought in Italy for thirty years, and died in Florence, as a freeman of the city.'

'Brava gente,' said Guido, 'good people,' and Enzo nodded.

'We're talking about an English mercenary,' I told Ted, thinking it was something which might gain a response. 'He fought in France, at the Battle of Crécy. Then he fought all over Italy, for the next thirty odd years.'

'Make any money, did he?' Ted asked.

'He made it and he lost it,' I said. 'Lots of it. It never seemed to stick to his hands.'

'Mate of mine was a mercenary,' said Ted. 'Fought in Angola; made bugger all out of it. Them niggers made him all kinds of promises; never kept none of them.'

'Hawkwood used to have the same trouble,' I said. 'Particularly with the Pope.'

'What's he to you, then?'

'I'm writing about him.'

'What, a book?'

'I hope so.'

'*You* make any money out of that, will you?'

'I doubt it,' I said.

He shook his head, incredulously. 'Don't know why you bother.'

'*I* do,' said Annabel Carlton. 'I think history's fascinating. I'd *love* to read your book. Ti piace la storia? Do you like history?' she asked Enzo.

'I don't trust history,' Enzo said. 'I don't believe in history. Not the history that's written in Italy, let alone in England. The Italian history that's been written since 1944. Liberals' lies. Communist lies. Christian Democrat lies. Jewish lies. Never the truth.'

'Now come on, Enzo!' she reproached him, in English. 'You're being very rude to our friend. After all, he *is* an English Professor of History!'

'He's writing about the Middle Ages,' said Enzo. 'That doesn't come into it.'

Ted bought a round of drinks. When these had been finished, I noticed Annabel pushing money into Enzo's hand, and whispering quickly and discreetly in his ear. Then Enzo bought a round. As we drank, Annabel Carlton's laugh became still louder and more frequent, Ted told stories of assaults on Asians in the East End – 'Three of us got hold of this fucking Paki' – to which Enzo listened with a faintly disdainful smile. Both he and Guido were no longer tense, and now they turned their backs on Annabel, talking to me. 'Italy has to be changed. Italy has to be purified. In blood, in violence. That's the only way. You wouldn't understand that. You're not Italian.'

'Do all Italians understand that?' I asked.

Enzo fixed me with a challenging stare. 'Siamo fascisti,' he said, 'we're Fascists,' as if this would suffice. 'He's a Fascist, too,' he said, nodding towards Ted, 'but an English one. They're not serious. They understand nothing, even if they're helpful to us.'

154

'He's talking about Italian politics,' I told Ted.

'Said something about me, though, didn't he?'

'Just that you're *different*, Ted,' gushed Annabel. 'Didn't he, Tom?' We were on first name terms, by now. 'That English Fascists and Italian Fascists aren't the same.'

'That's right,' I said.

We drank till closing time, when Annabel cried, 'It's been such fun! Let's all go back to my place, and carry on!'

'Not me,' said Ted, to my relief. 'I got to get home.'

I feigned hesitation. 'I should really be driving back to Oxford. I've an early tutorial.'

'Oh, *do* come!' she urged, clutching my arm.

'Well, yes,' I said, 'thanks. I suppose I could stay for an hour.'

She lived nearby, in a block of flats in Lowndes Square. We passed across a thickly carpeted foyer, lined with mirrors. 'I do hope Rosie's not awake,' she said, as we waited together for the lift. 'She *will* try not to go to sleep until I'm home.'

'Your daughter?' I asked, as the lift arrived.

'Yes, she's five. She's absolutely *gorgeous*, but I think I've spoiled her.'

Spoiled her and neglected her might be more like it, I thought. Going up in the lift with her and the Italians, I wondered whether I could sustain the masquerade; the English ingénu, the Italian history teacher, who knew all about the past, but nothing at all about the present. At some point, I feared, the disguise was going to slip. It was so hard to smile at the two young Fascists. Arrogance came off them like a scent. Ted was a brutal lout, I was glad to see the back of him, but in some sense he had acted as a lightning conductor. Now I must face the pair of them without mediation; save for the brittle presence of Annabel.

Her flat was large and opulent, furnished with a kind of careless good taste, full of old furniture which she must have inherited, with gestures towards the fashionable in the shape of a few, framed posters by Miró, a Chagall reproduction, another of a David Hockney. A stereo stood in a corner, with long playing pop records scattered on the floor in front of it. The sole surprise, the one discordant note, was provided by a large photograph of Mussolini, speaking from the balcony of

155

Palazzo Venezia, black fez on his head, his great chin raised above the multitude.

A small, dark, melancholy girl appeared at the door of the living room and said, in a strong foreign accent, 'I think maybe she is now asleep.'

'Oh, super, Consuela!' said Annabel. 'You go to bed, now; I'll just take a peek at her. Our au pair,' she explained to me. 'She's absolutely marvellous, so reliable.' She followed the au pair girl out of the room, leaving the three of us alone. Enzo and Guido ignored me, talking to one another in low, intense, inaudible voices.

When Annabel returned she said, 'She *is* sleeping, bless her.' She gestured us to chairs and sofas, then offered us drinks. Enzo took his with characteristic gracelessness, sitting, legs apart, on a large, leather covered sofa. Now Annabel went to the stereo and put on a rock record, a male singer, repeating, over and over again, some two or three lines, above a strident background of electric guitars and percussion.

'Ma no!' protested Enzo. 'Quello fa schifo! That's disgusting!'

'I thought you liked him,' she said.

'You know I don't like any of them.'

'Very well, I'll put on something else. Something Italian, if you like.'

'Don't put on anything,' he said. 'Your Italian records are dreadful, too.' Worse than the way in which he sat there like the lord of the manor, the contemptuous way in which he ordered her about, was the way she passively submitted to it, tacking and trimming to every foul wind that blew. She was, I thought, like a kind of high grade gangster's moll, an accessory after the fact. What he was, what he and his friends were doing, somehow thrilled her, gave her the kind of 'high' that so many of her kind got from drugs. Now, I thought, she was high on masochism. I did not dare mention Della Martira to her, in such company, but I was convinced he must have been her lover; doubtless she would have got her kicks just as readily from such a group as his, or from the Red Brigades. I felt as if I were walking on eggshells. Whatever I wanted to know had to be attained by nuance and indirection. I had written my own part, and it contained no room for knowledge

156

of things as they were, of Italy now; no hint of the Bologna bomb, Sindona, least of all Gelli. As it was, it was they who raised the subject of Bologna station. They were still talking largely to one another, ignoring me as well as Annabel, dealing in unfamiliar names, allusions, though from time to time, I could pick up a reference.

One, unquestionably, was to the Roman magistrate who had been shot. Enzo mentioned his name and then laughed. 'Quello stronzo,' he said, 'that turd. He won't be doing any more investigating.' He looked quickly at me, then, but I made my face completely blank, while Annabel, if she had heard, probably did not know what he meant. Failing Enzo and Guido, she made the best of it by talking to me. It was a great temptation to mention Della Martira, but I subdued it. Instead, we spoke of holidays she had taken in Italy, courses and classes she had sporadically attended, such problems as driving in Rome, the maddening vagaries of Italian trains.

At this, I finally drew a bow at a venture. 'But nothing could be worse than what happened at Bologna.'

Her response to this was strange but significant. Her fulsome tone changed, her eyes fell, and she murmured uneasily, 'No, I suppose it couldn't.'

I took another chance then, calling to Enzo and Guido, 'We were saying what a shocking atrocity that was, at Bologna station.'

Both looked at me silently for a moment, then Enzo said, 'As I said before, you have to understand Italy.'

Now I modified my role, becoming the well-intentioned simpleton. 'I don't understand why it was *done*,' I said, 'if that's what you mean.'

'That isn't what I mean. You call it an atrocity. Other people might call it something else.'

'Such as what?' I asked, though now my dissimulation had grown more difficult, my anger threatened to subvert it.

'There can be necessary crimes,' said Enzo, 'except I wouldn't call them crimes, because they have as their objective something so much larger, something positive, something truly grandiose.'

'What kind of thing?' I asked.

'The destruction of a corrupt and evil organism, and its replacement by something morally clean.'

157

'You're saying that the end justifies the means.'

'If the end is important enough, yes.'

Guido spoke suddenly, with great passion. 'One purifies with fire,' he said. 'One burns democracy away.'

'And do *you* believe in that philosophy?' I could not resist asking Annabel.

'Well,' she answered hesitantly, 'Italy's so different, isn't it?'

'Of course it's different,' said Enzo, scornfully. 'That's what I've been telling you. How could the English perceive that? You haven't been invaded for nine hundred years. You've had your Empire and you've lost it. You've prevented us from having ours. You've overthrown the only government that ever offered us any hope. How can the English know?'

'How indeed?' I answered mildly, but my natural animus was now exacerbated by all I'd drunk, and I realised I must be careful, must stop drinking, or disguise would disappear, I would say the things I dearly wanted to say, and undo everything I'd worked for.

'But they *are* letting you stay in England, darling,' Annabel said.

'Exactly. Because they don't *know*. They don't understand. Any more than they ever understood Mussolini. They think that's it's all gone away, that Fascism's dead, that what we're doing now is of no consequence. All the better! They won't let us be extradited. We can stay here, we can get help from English Fascists. Like that one in the pub. He's an idiot, he doesn't know the first thing about Fascism or the first thing about Italy, but at least he believes in what we're doing. What he can grasp of it.'

'English Fascism tends to be a little basic,' I said. 'It's never really got beyond street fighting.'

'Street fighting can be useful, too,' said Enzo, 'when it's a means to an end. Mussolini used it early on, with the squadristi. Hitler had the storm troopers. But when they're all street fighters, nothing but street fighters, people like Ted, cretins, then there's nothing to be done.' Thank God, I thought. 'The English have been lucky!' cried Enzo, whose Roman accent grew thicker by the moment. Guido, so far as I could tell, came from the Veneto. 'They never suffer.

Nobody invades them. No one conquers them. Because they are an island. That's what saved them in 1940. But today, there *are* no islands. They're as vulnerable as everyone else. And they won't escape next time.'

'If there *is* a next time,' I said.

'Of course there'll be a next time! There's always war! There has to be war!'

'There must be!' said Guido.

'That's how man grows,' said Enzo. 'And without war, he rots. As the Duce said, "molti nemici, molto onore", many enemies, much honour. In 1944, he was betrayed. Betrayed and killed by Italians; that's the shame of it! The Italians were unworthy of him. Just as in the end, the Germans were unworthy of Hitler. He wanted to exterminate the lot of them, and he was right.'

'Enzo!' cried Annabel, but her protest was that of a mother, rebuking a beloving child.

'You shut up!' he shouted. 'What the hell do *you* understand? You're English! You're a woman! You understand *this*!' and he patted his cock. At that, even Annabel looked distraught. Guido, slumped in his chair, regarded them with a malevolent grin.

'That's too much, Enzo,' I said.

'Too much? You're like her; you know nothing!' He switched into a malevolent parody of English, and of Annabel. 'Oh, I *lurv* Fascists, I *lurv* Italy, I *lurv* being fucked by Italians.'

'Enzo . . .' she began.

'You do!' he shouted, now in Italian. 'Of course you do! And it doesn't have to be a Fascist. Who did you have before me? What Italian was getting up you before I did? And who was up you before he was?'

She broke into tears. 'You're cruel, you're horrible, I won't put up with it!'

For all her fatuity, her silly voyeurism, she did not deserve such brutality. She stood up, sobbing, and rushed out of the room. What should I do now? Walk out myself, in sympathy and disgust? Stay, and implicitly condone what he had done?

'Ma che cretina,' muttered Enzo, and he lit a cigarette. Guido was grinning. The most humane thing to do was to go

159

after the girl and try to comfort her, but that would disqualify me for good, so far as the Fascists were concerned.

Enzo stood up, shuffled to the drinks table, and poured himself another whisky. When he sat down again, the three of us were silent for a few minutes, until Enzo said, 'She'll be back.'

'You're sure?' asked Guido, with another grin.

'She always comes back,' said Enzo. 'She cries, she walks out, then she comes back. She's an imbecile.'

'Perhaps she's in love,' Guido said.

Enzo shrugged. 'Who cares?' He looked at me and asked. 'Don't you believe me? Don't you think she'll be back?'

'How would I know?' I said, hoping that she wouldn't, fearing that she would, that this was a foul, masochistic pattern. I wondered how she had been treated by Della Martira; or any other Italian man.

Twenty minutes later, she was back. She had brushed her hair, she had made up her face again, she was smiling.

'Come here!' Enzo smiled at her, patting the arm of the sofa, and she came to him, perching beside him, putting an arm around his shoulders, while he rested his hand on her thigh. The sight of them together, her happy smile, his preening self-satisfaction, was worse to me than the way he had insulted her. He was right, she would always come back to him, not in spite of what he did, but because of it. Did he regale her with tales of his atrocities, make her flesh creep with his vicious exploits? And if he did, I thought, suddenly, perhaps it was she whom I should talk to, she who would know; and might tell. At least there was no need now to take sides, or moral attitudes, no need to stand up and be counted. Enzo looked at me disdainfully and said, 'You'll see how well we Italians understand English women.'

'So it seems,' I said.

'And you? Do you understand Italian women?'

'I was married to one.' Both men gave me sharp, sudden looks; Annabel regarded me with new interest and sympathy. 'Did you . . . split up?' she asked.

'No,' I said, 'she died.'

'Oh, I'm so sorry.'

'Where was she from?' asked Enzo.

'She was a Florentine.' And she died on a train. And for all

I know, you bastards blew her up. And if you did, and if I find out that you did, God help you.

'Was it long ago?' asked Annabel, finally.

'This year,' I said.

'How awful!'

Yes, quite awful. And murdered by people like your friends. Who would approve of her murder. The small sacrifice for the greater cause. The means that could never be justified by the ends, because both are wholly poisonous. What would I answer if any of them asked me, how did she die? But Annabel would not because she still, in her brainless way, had traces of humanity; the others would not, because they did not care.

I thought suddenly of Italy as a vast killing ground, a place of random death, far worse than Hawkwood's mediaeval Italy, worse in its way even than the Second World War, because a plethora of fanatics, all ideologically programmed, made war on one another and the public. Civilians suffered in any war, from the poor old Tuscan, Sardi, who complained that Hawkwood's men ('The Lord destroy them all') had stolen even his cupboards and his wardrobes, to the peasants shot and burned by the Nazis in the last war, but in the new dispensation, civilians were not merely booty or hostages, they were fair game, their lives forfeit to a higher end.

'Are you sure that it helps?' I asked. 'Blowing up trains? Blowing up Bologna station?'

'Trains?' repeated Enzo. 'Stations?' and he looked at me with abrupt askance, while I looked back at him with all the ingenuousness I could command. Guido, I noticed, was staring at me, too.

'Haven't trains been bombed as well?' I asked. 'Didn't I read that, somewhere?'

'Oh, yes,' said Annabel. 'Wasn't there an Italic something or other?'

'You shut up!' Enzo bellowed at her. 'That's just the filthy, scandal-mongering newspapers! The Italicus bombing was six years ago. Now they're trying to link it with Bologna. They blamed us for that, but they never proved a thing. They throw Fascists in gaol for months, for years, but they can't make anything stick. Now they're saying Bologna was meant to commemorate the Italicus bombing! Liars! Sons of whores!'

161

'So the Fascists didn't do either of them?' I asked.

Guido shrugged. 'Who knows who it was?' he replied.

A strange double standard seemed to be at work. They at once rejoiced in what had been done, and were incensed that they should be accused of doing it.

'That's why we're here,' said Guido. 'Do you think we want to be here? In Italy, they'd sling us into gaol. There's an explosion; blame the neo-Fascists. There's an atrocity; blame the neo-Fascists.'

'Exactly,' said Enzo. 'Now all this crap about extraditing us, the ones in England. Look at what happened with the bomb in the bank; Piazza Fontana. If they can't get us one way, they'll get us another. First they blamed the Reds. Then it was all eventually turned upside down, and it was us who'd done it, the neo-Fascists.'

'Didn't they find proof?' I asked. 'Didn't they find tapes, or something?'

'Proof!' said Enzo. 'What proof? They manufactured it, they always do! Who killed Aldo Moro? Was it the Fascists? No, it was the Red Brigades. They'd have blamed us for that as well, if they could, but the Red Brigades had claimed it, they even put the photo out with their filthy flag.'

'But if the Fascists *had* bombed Bologna station,' I said, 'you wouldn't blame them for it?'

'That's another matter,' Enzo said.

In their paranoiac world, it seemed, the great injustice was to be accused of a crime they had committed. Yet somewhere, between the stirrup and the ground, between atrocity and alibi, I sensed there might be space for me to work.

Annabel, now, was lovingly running her fingers through Enzo's hair. He gave no sign of even noticing it, suffering it, at best, without complaint. Emptying his glass, he jerked it towards her, without a word. Obediently, she took it and crossed the room to the drinks table, asking both Guido and me whether we wanted another, but we both refused.

Guido was becoming increasingly morose. 'Ma cosa faccio qui?' he was muttering to himself. 'Cosa faccio qui? What am I doing here?'

'It's better than gaol,' said Enzo, taking his drink from Annabel without thanks.

'Who are you telling?' Guido asked. 'I've been in gaol. Che schifo!'

'Think of being in for life,' said Enzo. 'That's what they've been doing to people, the bastards.'

'They won't do it to me,' said Guido.

'They'd do it to any of us, if they could,' Enzo said.

'Then I'd go to South America,' said Guido. '*He'll* help me. He's helped other people.'

'Zito!' Enzo yelled at him. 'Shut up!' while I did my best, in my excitement, to seem unaware. I had, in any case, reached a perfect moment to leave. I had had enough of them. The more he drank, the more aggressive and provocative Enzo was becoming. The last thing I could afford was to meet him head on, the last thing I could stand was passively to take his digs and jeers.

'I must go,' I said, standing up. 'It's been most interesting.'

Enzo cocked an eye at me, drunkenly. 'Arrivederci, professore. L'inglese italianato, eh? Bello, bello! He's not like you, Annabel. You're stupid. He's not stupid. We've Italianised him. He understands things. But sometimes he pretends he doesn't.'

Reluctantly, I shook hands with him, then with Guido. Annabel saw me to the front door. Opening it, she looked at me almost pleadingly. 'Come and see us again,' she said, 'promise you will! My name's in the phone book.'

'I will.'

'Oh will you, will you? Please see you do!' She kissed me suddenly on the mouth, then, as though frightened by what she had done, quickly closed the door.

Gelli was looking after them, I felt sure of that, Gelli was the mysterious 'he' to whom Guido had alluded, to Enzo's fury. I was convinced of it, however illogically. I felt the need to move fast, before they could find out too much about me. Their antennae bristled, Enzo's especially, and he had already shown me that my facsimile of innocence had not taken him in. It should not take them very long, if they so chose, to check up on me, to discover how Simonetta had died, to surmise from this that I had not been in the pub by accident, and even to discover that I had saved Sindona.

VIII

I met Annabel on an October afternoon; in Kensington Gardens, at her own suggestion. 'Oh, how super to hear from you!' she exclaimed when I telephoned, then, more cautiously, 'I *do* want to see you, I *do* want to talk to you. There are difficulties . . . Perhaps you can guess. I'll call you back . . . I'll call you later on.'

She had done so, eventually, from a pay phone, and made the rendezvous with me. 'By the Round Pond. Tomorrow afternoon. Say three o'clock. They won't suspect. I often take Rosie for a walk on Thursday, when Consuela has her day off. I hope it doesn't sound silly to you . . .'

No, it did not sound silly. By now, I was more likely to be surprised by anything straightforward, anything devoid of subterfuge and camouflage. I had no idea what she wanted, but I knew, more or less, what I wanted from her.

It was a sharp, clear, sunny afternoon. Nannies in blue and brown uniforms were slowly, ritually, walking their charges up and down the Broad Walk. The trees, but for the evergreens, had largely shed their leaves, some of which still lay in antic patterns across the grass. On the Round Pond itself, a little motor boat buzzed in tight, noisy circles, watched by an enraptured small boy and his father. A group of young Arabs sat chattering and laughing on one of the benches. Annabel was not there when I arrived, but soon I saw her walking across the grass, from the general direction of the Bayswater Road, hand in hand with a little, dark-haired girl, who was formally dressed in a smart blue winter coat.

As Annabel approached me, she raised her hand in a pantomime of surprise. 'Oh, hello,' she said, when she reached me. 'I *thought* it looked like you. This is my daughter, Rosie. Rosie, darling, this is Tom Cunningham. He's terribly clever. He teaches history at a place called Oxford.'

The little girl lifted her pretty, pink-cheeked face to regard me sombrely, as if wary by now of the men her mother knew.

164

'Say hello, darling!' Annabel insisted, but the child turned away, burying her face in her mother's coat. Annabel raised her eyebrows at me, in apology. 'They've gone to Brighton for the day,' she said. 'They've got friends down there, if you see what I mean.'

'I think I do.'

'*Political* friends. I don't know them, actually. People like Ted, the one you met in the pub. They're all such yobs. Does that sound terribly snobbish?'

'Just accurate,' I said.

'So you can come back to tea if you like,' she said. 'The coast's clear.'

'That would be fine.'

'I want to see Peter Pan!' the little girl cried, jumping up and down, tugging at her mother's hand, 'I want to see Peter Pan!'

'Darling, we've already *seen* Peter Pan, and it's *miles* away!'

'I want to see Peter *Pan!*'

Annabel gave me an appealing look. 'Do *you* mind if we go and see Peter Pan?' she asked. 'It's rather a trek; right across the Gardens.'

'Not at all,' I said. 'I haven't seen it for years.'

The little girl skipped happily along in front of us, enabling us to talk. 'They know about your wife,' she said. 'How she died. I'm so *terribly* sorry.' Sorry that she died, I thought, or sorry merely that they know, but I thanked her, anyway. 'How horrible for you,' she said. I nodded. 'Now they're suspicious,' she said. 'They think you're after them.'

'Is that what *you* think?'

'I don't know,' she said. 'I mean, you did come to the Coldstream to find them, didn't you?'

'Yes,' I answered.

'I don't blame you,' she said. 'I mean, I'm sure I'd do the same.'

I found myself, once again, invaded by that strange throb of excitement. Did they do it? I wanted to ask her. Did they say they did it?

'You were at Bologna station, too, weren't you?' she asked. 'Just after the bomb. They know that, as well.'

'Yes, I *was* there,' I said.

'So they think you're spying on them, that you want to get revenge on them. That's one of the reasons they've gone down to Brighton. To talk to the English Fascists they know there, about what to do.'

I sighed, then gave a melancholy laugh. 'I seem to be getting it from all sides,' I said. 'I've been shot at by the Far Left, and now I'm in danger from the Far Right.'

'*Shot* at?'

I didn't mention Rome. 'Somebody broke into my cottage near Oxford, I pointed an air pistol at them, which probably wasn't a very sensible thing to do. So he shot at me. Fortunately, he missed.'

'Why was he there?'

'It's an awfully long story.'

The little girl came running back, crying, 'Carry me, Mummy, carry me!'

'Darling, you're so *heavy*! I knew this was going to happen!'

'I'll carry you,' I told the child.

'No, no, no! I want Mummy!'

'I'll carry you on my shoulders if you like,' I said. 'High, high up, so you can see the world!'

'Go on, darling!' said Annabel. She picked the child up and, despite her protesting cries, sat her on my shoulders, while I took hold of her. '*There*!' said Annabel. 'Isn't it a lovely view?'

Rosie was quiet now, but gave little cries of delight as I walked off with her on my shoulders, followed by screams of excitement and alarm when, from time to time, I broke into a run.

'You're so good with her,' said Annabel. 'Enzo's good with her, too, when he's in the mood. Nicer than he is to me, really,' she added, with a deprecating laugh. 'But Italians are marvellous with children, aren't they?'

'Yes, usually,' I said. Even Italian Fascists; when they are not blowing children up for the good of the cause.

'Enzo didn't do it,' she said, as though she sensed my thoughts, 'I'm sure he didn't do it. I know he's *done* things. That's why he's here, in England. But nothing like that. And Guido's here . . . Well, you may have guessed; the other night, when we were all talking. That . . . thing in Rome.'

'Faster, faster!' shouted Rosie.

166

'The magistrate?' I asked Annabel, before I began to gallop.

'Yes,' she said, reluctantly. Then I galloped.

When I reached the Peter Pan statue, with its bronze, attendant fairies, I put Rosie down, and she rushed to it, and embraced it. 'She just loves it,' Annabel said. 'We saw the play last year three times.'

I wondered what her Fascists would make of it. I could imagine them, lolling in the stalls, sneering at the antic sentimentality. But then, what in its way was more sentimental than Fascism, who was more spurious in his appeal than Mussolini?

Watching the child, Annabel put her arm through mine. 'I suppose you despise me,' she said.

'Not at all,' I said. 'Why should I?'

'I sometimes despise *myself*. I wish I really *could* be passionate about things, and believe in things.'

'Like Enzo and Guido?' I asked.

'But it gives them something to live for. Something to fight for. I can't help admiring them for that.'

'Even when they blow up women and children?'

'There's no proof of that, is there?' she said. 'I mean, there's lots of different terrorists in Italy.'

'It seems to be a Fascist speciality, though. Blowing up trains and stations.'

'You mean you think they killed your wife.'

'I'm pretty sure of it.'

'You must hate all of them.'

'I'm not very fond of them,' I said.

Rosie came running back from the statue, grasped my hand, and pleaded, 'Carry me, carry me!' I lifted her up again on my shoulders.

'It's so terribly hard to explain,' said Annabel, as we began to walk again, back in the direction of Kensington High Street. 'But when Enzo and the others talk about it, it seems to make sense. It's what he says, himself. You have to make the leap. You have to have faith. Then you can understand.'

It made me laugh. 'Like the Inquisition!' I said. 'But at least they knew whom they were torturing and burning, whose souls they were meant to be saving. The Fascists haven't any idea who they're blowing up.'

167

Annabel switched back her long hair in the familiar way; like an impatient horse. 'You'd have to get Enzo to tell you.'

'Gallop, gallop, gallop!' shouted Rosie, and I galloped. Annabel trotted breathlessly behind us. She was wearing a red leather coat and tight, dark green trousers, but she tottered on high heels.

We drove back to Belgravia, she and Rosie in her Mercedes, I in my old Volvo. When we got back to her flat, we had an elaborate nursery tea, with abundant sandwiches, chocolate fingers and sponge cake. Rosie, in a state of high excitement and glee, kept bringing me her dolls and books, then, tea over, insisted on sitting on my knee, while we watched children's television. 'You've really made a hit with her!' said Annabel.

At six, we left the brightly painted nursery, with its blackboard, its doll's house, its scattered games and toys, for the familiar living-room, where Annabel poured me a whisky, and a sherry for herself. Rosie, told to play on her own, insisted on accompanying us, and sent up such a caterwauling when her mother tried to put her out of the room that I said, 'Do let her stay.' Again, she sat on my knee, insisting now that I read her a story. A bargain was struck; I would do so if she then had her bath, and went to bed.

When, happily exhausted, she had at last done so, Annabel poured me another drink, and came to sit beside me on the leather sofa. 'You're *so* nice to Rosie,' she said.

'It isn't difficult.'

'I think you're probably just nice, anyway,' she said, and put her hand over mine. It was then that I found myself asking her, 'Didn't you once know Claudio Della Martira?'

She started, pulling her hand away. 'How do you know that?' she asked, in an urgent, anxious voice. 'Do you know him? Did he tell you?'

'No, he didn't.'

'Then who did? How do you know? Who else could have told you where to find us? Who else could have told you about him and me?'

'Somebody who's close to him,' I said.

'Whom he told to tell you. The little shit. That's just what I'd expect of him. The nasty little pervert. He's gone all political now, hasn't he? All left-wing. When I knew him first, he couldn't have cared less about politics. All he wanted to do was screw as many girls as possible in the sickest ways he could think of. I suppose he put himself over to you as a great idealist.'

'Not that,' I said, 'so much as a fanatic: who was over-compensating.'

'What does that mean? I'm not clever. Didn't you hear what Enzo said about me? You have to explain words like that.'

'It just means that I think he's bending over backwards to be something that he fundamentally isn't.'

'That's *perfectly* true. You should have seen how self-righteous he became. I was a class enemy. He didn't want to see me any more. The life I led was parasitic. "What about the life *you* led?" I asked him. "It's all behind me, now," he said. "I've changed, but *you'll* never change. You're rich and spoiled. You're corrupt. There's just no hope for you."

'Enzo is *quite* different. Enzo's sincere. He's doing what he believes in; whatever *you* might think about it. Claudio is just posturing. That's all he ever did. It's just a new fad, that's all.' But one that could get him killed, I thought. 'How do you know him?' she asked. 'How did you come to meet him? Where is he, now?'

'Somewhere in Italy,' I said. 'I don't know where. He moves about. I met him in Florence. Then again, in Rome.' Once more I held back from mentioning what had happened in the Piazza Vittorio.

'Please, please don't mention him to Enzo, if you see him again.'

'That doesn't seem very likely,' I said.

'Did he talk about me?' he asked. 'Claudio? What did he tell you about me?'

'Nothing,' I said. 'I never heard him mention you.'

This seemed to reassure her. 'Well, *that's* a consolation. I suppose I ought to warn Enzo that they know he's here, Claudio and his ghastly lot.'

'None of *them*'s in England, so far as I know,' I said.

'Yes, perhaps I'd better not. Enzo would only want to know how I knew. Then how I knew about Claudio. He's incredibly jealous. A typical Italian male. Goes off and screws any girl he wants to, but expects you to live like a nun.'

Suddenly she leaned across, kissing me on the lips. 'Why do I always have to fall in love with bastards?' she asked. 'Why can't I fall for someone like you?' Because you're a mess. Because you're a masochist. 'Actually, I think I have,' she said, and kissed me again, this time putting her tongue in my mouth. I drew back and looked into her great, blue, splendid, vacant eyes, suffused, now, with . . . what? Emotion? You could hardly call it love. You're giving yourself again, I thought, you're always giving yourself. Yet the effect she made on me was one of pathos. What she was looking for, I sensed, was reassurance. Della Martira had humiliated her, Enzo had humiliated her. If only I would accept her!

Or could there be more to it than that? Humiliation for Enzo! A doubly climactic moment in which he burst into the bedroom, finding us together? 'Annabel,' I said, 'let's be clear about one thing. I see these people as scum. I don't accept any of their rubbish about faith and commitment. That's crap. That's rationalisation. They're just a bunch of brutal thugs. They've lost, and they'll never win again. The best they can do, the worst they can do, is to commit atrocities; which lead nowhere, except to other atrocities. People are blown up, people are killed, like my poor Simonetta. People suffer. But it doesn't change anything. They're irrelevant now, however much pain they cause; which is probably why they cause it. History's overtaken them. Perhaps that's the worst thing about it, that my wife and all those others died for nothing. In a lost cause. Something that's forty years out of date. Fascism is dead, Annabel. It can never come back. It had its moment, and it failed. And history doesn't wait. It moves on.'

'In other words,' she said, 'I'm just a kind of groupie. You despise me.'

'Not at all. I just feel very sorry for you. People seem to exploit you. Claudio. Enzo. One's no better in his way than the other.'

'*You* are,' she said, 'you're better than either of them,' and she kissed me again. This time, I found myself responding. After all, I had made myself plain. I had told her what I thought of her friends, and what I thought about Claudio. No Right, no Left. No revenge; save whatever private revenge she might enjoy in her head. Nothing but us, now; the moment. Her need, my need. Her need to be reassured. Mine, after so many months, for physical relief, escape, transient oblivion. Her hand went to my groin, and she began to stroke me. In my turn, I put my hand on her breast, then slid the other underneath her sweater, feeling for her nipple.

'You're so nice, so nice, so nice!' she said, and pulled down the zip of my trousers. I had, for one wild instant, a fearsome picture of Enzo and Guido charging into the room, seeing us on the sofa, pulling out guns, and blasting us to pieces; another kind of oblivion. Then she had me in her hand, I had wrenched down her slacks, and I had penetrated her. But in that very moment, I saw another picture. The door opened, and it was not Enzo and Guido but little Rosie, appalled by the sight of the primal scene. With this in mind, I went faster, faster, while Annabel exclaimed, in joyful abandon, 'Oh, it's marvellous! Go on, go on, go on, darling!' Her head was thrown back, her eyes were closed, there was a smile on her face of seraphic content.

It was a smile that abruptly gave me pause. She must have smiled like this at Della Martira. She had smiled like this at Enzo. I was merely the latest lover; from the Left to the Right, from the Right to the Centre, politics as penis, politics engulfed by the vagina, the orgasm omnipotent, triumphant.

When she came, Annabel gave a great, ecstatic cry, as her long, supple body shuddered beneath mine, a cry that made me feel that I had somehow been used. Against Enzo, against Della Martira, against the whole sad, squalid compromise of her existence. She lay, then, on the leather sofa, with a smile of sated delight. Her eyes were closed. 'Darling,' she said, '*darling*,' but the words did not touch me, they went into the void. Sooner rather than later, Enzo would be back, and she would welcome him, strong in the knowledge that she could still seduce someone who was 'nice'. As I withdrew from her, it was his lowering face that I saw. She could look at him, now, when it was he who had brought her to climax, with a secretive satisfaction. She had not only betrayed him, but betrayed him with someone who did not treat her like dirt.

I wanted to leave, now, not because I was afraid of Enzo and Guido, but because I found such thoughts unbearable. But though my great impulse was to go, there were still things that I might learn from her. If she had just used me, wasn't I using her, too? Another good reason for going.

171

She bent her head forward to kiss me on the lips, then pulled her pants up above her thick, brown brush of pubic hair. She caressed my cheek. 'Are you sorry?' she asked.

'No,' I replied automatically. 'Of course I'm not.'

'I'll find things out for you,' she said. 'Just tell me what you want to know.'

'I want to know about Gelli.'

'Gelli?'

'Haven't they ever mentioned him? I thought they might be on the verge of it when I was here, last time. When Enzo jumped on Guido; because he'd said there was someone who could get him to South America.'

'Gelli?' she said. 'I'm sure I've never heard that name. Who is he?'

'Someone who calls the shots. Someone very powerful. I'm not quite sure, myself.'

'I'll listen,' she said. We were accomplices. Again she caressed me. 'If they *had* done it,' she said, 'and you found out, what would you do?'

It was the inevitable, familiar question, though never posed before in such circumstances. 'That's hypothetical,' I said. 'Besides, haven't you told me that you're sure they didn't?'

'Quite sure,' she said, kissing me. 'Quite, quite sure.'

'When they heard about my wife, how she died, did they mention anything? About who might have done it?'

'No,' she said, 'but when they do mention names, they don't usually mean anything to me. Unless of course they're people who are living in England. But I'll try to find out. It won't be easy. They're frightfully suspicious now of anything to do with you.'

'Thanks,' I said.

'I do wish you could stay. I'd really love to sleep all night with you.'

But you'll be sleeping with Enzo, I thought, and moved, instinctively, away from her.

'Oh, dear,' she said. 'I suppose you'd better go; before they get back.'

We both stood up. She flung her arms around my waist, and buried her head in my shoulder. Her hair had a sweet, strong, pleasing scent. 'You will come again?' she said.

'It won't be very easy, will it?'

172

'Then I could come to Oxford. Would you mind that? Would you mind seeing me there?'

'We'll think about it.' I kissed her cheek, detached myself, and moved out of the living-room, into the hall, where she took my coat out of a cupboard. Again, we embraced. She opened the front door, and I walked down the corridor, towards the lifts. '*Do* be careful!' she said.

I laughed. 'Don't worry about me. People are always shooting at me.'

'They haven't got guns. They carry knives. If they arrive when you're leaving, just walk past them as if you haven't noticed.'

'What about *you*?'

'Oh, I'd deal with it somehow. Make up some kind of story. Enzo would probably knock me about a bit, but it wouldn't be all that bad.'

'Then I'll stay, for God's sake.'

'No, no, you mustn't! *Promise* me!'

'I'm sure we'll be all right,' I said, and turned the corner to the lift. She had infected me with her anxiety. As the lift moved down to the ground floor, I myself began to wonder whether they would be there, what I would do if they were, what *they* might do. If they saw me, I couldn't run away from them, leaving Annabel to their mercies. I was thinking, still, when the lift reached the ground floor. The doors opened; the foyer was empty. With an involuntary sigh, I walked across to the glass front doors, pressing the button which buzzed, and opened them.

I had just stepped out on to the pavement when a taxi came round the square, and stopped in front of the flats. Out of the taxi came Enzo, followed by Guido. Enzo saw me immediately. 'Pay him!' he snapped at Guido, then rushed up to me. There was no chance to avoid him. 'Che cazzo fai qui? What the fuck are you doing here?' he snarled at me, and indeed there was now a knife in his hand, a flick knife, the blade snapping out of the handle like a silver tongue, and he pushed it point first into my stomach. I found myself trembling.

'I've had tea with Annabel, that's all,' I said.

'Stronzo! Bugiardo! You turd! You liar!' He shoved me round, and back towards the front door of the flats, keeping very close to me, removing the point of the knife from my

173

stomach and pushing it into my ribs. 'You came here to spy on us! She asked you over, didn't she? Did you have her? Did you screw her? That whore!'

He unlocked the door with a key, and hustled me through the foyer, towards the lifts. Guido came hurrying up behind us, and seized my left arm. As we waited for the lift to arrive, Enzo said, 'Don't say anything to anybody, or I'll use this!'

But there was no one in the lift, when it arrived. As it ascended, Enzo had the knife point against my ribs. 'Figlio di puttana!' he said. 'Son of a whore! We know all about you. *And* about your wife!' At this, my body ceased to tremble, and was possessed by an enormous surge of rage, a feeling worse than fear, because I could give it no release. '*She's* dead, you could be dead,' said Enzo. 'You should have stuck to your history.'

When the lift stopped and its doors opened, he pushed me out, the knife now in my back, while Guido still had tight hold of my arm. With his free hand, Enzo handed Guido the door keys, and motioned him to open the door of the flat. He did so, flinging it wide, then going in first, letting go of me for an instant, as Enzo shoved me in his wake. The door of the sitting-room now opened and Annabel came out, saw us, stopped in her tracks, and gave a cry, putting her hand to her mouth, her face suffused by horror and surprise.

'Puttana!' said Enzo. 'Come here!' She hesitated. 'Come *here!*' he shouted. She came hesitantly towards him, and when she reached him, he raised his left hand and gave her a great blow across the face. She gasped, and put her hand to her cheek.

'Ma cosa fai!' he snarled at her. 'What are you up to? Betraying us! Helping this English bastard! Screwing him, weren't you? Weren't you?' and with each repetition, he hit her again, till blood began to flow from her mouth and nose. Again, she covered her face, and began to sob. 'Get her into that room!' Enzo told Guido, and Guido took hold of Annabel, forcing her back into the living-room, while Enzo, his knife in my ribs, propelled me forward, too. 'Buttala giù! Shove her down!' he ordered Guido, and Guido pushed Annabel roughly down on to the leather sofa, where she cowered, shaking and sobbing, her hands over her face. 'Cretina!' said Guido, contemptuously.

174

'You asked him here, didn't you?' Enzo demanded of her. 'Go on, admit it! You knew we'd be in Brighton, so you asked him here. *Didn't you?*' She did not answer, but merely went on crying.

'Hit her!' Enzo commanded. 'Hit her till she tells me!' Guido drew back his right hand and struck Annabel across the face. More horrifying then the blow was the expression he wore; one of sadistic joy.

'Do you want to get hit again?' Enzo asked her. 'Tell me!' He nodded at Guido, and again Guido struck her.

'For Christ's *sake!*' I said.

'You keep your mouth shut!' shouted Enzo. 'I'm not finished with you! Come on!' He turned to Annabel. 'Answer!'

'Yes, I did,' she wept. 'Why shouldn't I? I wanted to talk to him. At least he's somebody who treats me decently.'

'Talk to him about what?' demanded Enzo, while the knife still prodded at my ribs. I hardly noticed the discomfort; it was merely one of the causes of my searing hatred, of an anger which had now become almost uncontrollable.

'What could I talk to him about?' she asked, between her sobs. 'I don't *know* anything!'

'He asked you about his wife, didn't he? He asked you about that train, who blew it up!'

'I told him that it wasn't you,' she wept. 'I told him I was *sure* it wasn't you.'

'And then you slept with him, didn't you?' Enzo shouted. 'You filthy whore! It wouldn't be you if you didn't sleep with him!'

'I didn't!' she cried, 'I didn't!'

Enzo beckoned Guido to him and handed him the knife. 'Watch him!' he said, and walked over to Annabel, while Guido pushed the knife into my stomach. Reaching the sofa, Enzo grabbed Annabel by the hair, and pulled her upright. She gave a cry. 'Go on: tell me!' he said. 'Did he screw you? Tell me, or I'll smash your face in!' She did not answer, but simply stood there, whimpering, her head pulled forward as he kept hold of her hair.

'That's what you're best at, isn't it, you Fascists?' I said to him. 'Beating up women. Murdering women.'

'Shut up!' yelled Enzo. 'You're going to get it, too!' and Guido, raising his free hand, struck me across the mouth.

175

'Are you going to tell me?' said Enzo. He pulled Annabel's head still farther forward, then drove his fist into her breast. She screamed, and from the down the corridor, one heard a door open, the pattering, panic stricken steps of a child. 'For the love of Christ, see she doesn't come in!' I said.

Enzo strode across the room and locked the door, just before the child reached it and began to beat on it in a pitiful tattoo, crying, 'Mummy, Mummy, Mummy! What is it, Mummy?'

'Tell me,' Enzo commanded Annabel, 'or I'll let your daughter in. Did you screw with him?'

'He made me, he made me!' she exclaimed, weeping, again. 'It wasn't my fault! He made me!'

'Made you!' said Enzo, scornfully. 'You tart! No one has to make you.'

'It's quite true,' I said. 'I forced her. She didn't want to.' Guido laughed. 'It's true,' I said. 'Leave her alone. You can do what you like to me.'

'Yes, we will!' said Enzo. 'We'll do what we like to both of you. You think we killed your wife, don't you? That's why you're here. That's why you screwed her. That's what you came to find out.'

'It was someone like you,' I said. 'Some fascist filth like you,' and this time Enzo came forward, driving his fist into my face, though I ducked, so that the blow glanced off the side of my head, and he swore, rubbing his hand, while Guido hit me again, but again I ducked, so it was only a glancing punch.

'What would your wife have said, if she knew you screwed somebody like Annabel?' Enzo mocked me. 'Someone who fucks with Fascists. Someone who fucks with anybody.'

Again, Rosie cried out, desperately, from behind the door. *'Please, Mummy! Mummy!'*

'Let me go to her!' pleaded Annabel. 'I'll put her to bed. I promise I'll come back.'

'You want her to see you like this?' asked Enzo. 'I know what you're up to, anyway. You'll go and you'll lock yourself in her bedroom. You've done it before.'

'I won't! I swear to you I won't!'

On the low, glass-topped, central table, almost within my reach, stood a bottle of whisky. Annabel had left it there, after replenishing my glass. I tried not to look at the bottle,

176

fearing that the two men's eyes would follow mine, as it became my compelling focus, my hope, my potential weapon.

'If you've screwed her once, you can screw her again,' Enzo said to me, and Guido laughed. 'Right here. Right in front of us. Let's see you enjoy it. Eh, Annabel! We'll let Rosie in, if you like. She can enjoy it, too.'

'*No!*' screamed Annabel, at which Rosie in turn renewed her cries, her drumming on the door.

'Go on, get your clothes off,' Enzo told Annabel.

'She's probably only just put them on,' Guido said.

Enzo let go of Annabel's hair. 'Hurry up,' he said, 'or do you want me to take them off for you?'

Whimpering, she began slowly to undo the buttons at the side of her trousers. 'Hurry up,' said Enzo.

Guido watched her lubriciously, and in his moment of distraction, I saw my chance. Shoving him away from me with both hands, I lunged for the table, grabbed up the whisky bottle, and smashed it down as hard as I could, on his skull. He dropped without a sound. The bottle did not break, but there was no need to hit him again. Now I made the second move that I had planned. As Guido fell, and before Enzo could reached me, I plunged to the floor, frantically prising open the fingers of Guido's hand, wrenching the knife, sticking the point of it against his throat. 'Get back, or I'll kill him!' I shouted at Enzo. It was as though I was possessed; as though a damned-up, frustrated violence which had been growing through all these weeks had suddenly exploded in me. In the heat and frenzy of action, I felt no fear; if there were any prevalent emotion, it was sheer hatred of the two of them.

It was no bluff; I knew I *would* kill Guido, if I had to, and in that moment, I would willingly have killed Enzo, too. 'Right back!' I told him. 'Right back across the room! Go on! Put your back against the wall!'

Slowly and sullenly, looking at me with a murderous animosity, he retreated to the far wall. 'Quanto sei bravo!' he said, sarcastically. 'How splendid you are!'

'Stay there,' I said. Guido still was not moving.

'What if you've killed him?' Enzo asked.

'Then that's one fascist bastard less,' I found myself saying, while a word kept echoing in my head, 'Carne, carne!' Annabel stood, one hand incongruously on the buttons of her trousers, in an evident state of shock. The only noise, now, was Rosie's tearful voice, raised, unbearably, outside the door. 'Go to her, Annabel, *please!*' I said, and with a manifest effort, she came to life, again, fastened the last button, and walked uncertainly towards the door. Unlocking it and opening it, she let in Rosie, who rushing at her, looking at her, cried, 'Mummy, Mummy, what's happened to you?'

'It's nothing, darling, nothing,' murmured Annabel, and she picked up the child, went out of the room, and disappeared down the corridor, till we heard the door of Rosie's nursery shut.

Guido groaned, and began to stir. He was alive, then. 'Don't move,' I told him, and jabbed the blade against his neck.

'That's a joke,' Enzo said, beginning to move infinitesimally forward. 'You'd never kill him.'

'Don't try me,' I said. Nor was that a threat. A week, a day, even an hour ago, I might not have made it. A minute ago, it would have been no more than a threat. Now, not only had I made it; I had felled Guido with a whisky bottle. I was sailing uncharted seas, and something of all this may have conveyed itself to Enzo, for he stayed where he was. 'Who killed my wife?' I asked him.

'How do *I* know who killed your wife? *I* didn't kill your wife? Guido didn't kill your wife!'

'Tell me!' I said, moving further into the unknown, 'or I'll stick this knife in him! *Tell* me!' My hatred, now, was suffused with desperation. This was my chance; certainly the best chance I had yet had, or was likely to have. These were the very people who might have killed Simonetta, or at least would know who killed her. It was imperative that in this moment, which would surely never be repeated, I find out everything I could, so I jabbed the point of the knife into Guido's neck again, making him cry out, wishing as I did so that it were Enzo's neck, that I could somehow get across the room to Enzo and make him suffer for the cruel and brutal way he had made Annabel suffer.

Coming to full consciousness, Guido began to moan, 'Non sono stato io! Non sono stato io! It wasn't me!'

'No,' I said, 'I don't suppose it was. You're more of a gunman, aren't you? You killed the judge?'

'*She* told you, didn't she?' Enzo burst out. 'I'll kill the sow, I'll kill the whore!'

'Touch her,' I said, 'and you'll suffer for it. I'll see that you're deported. I'll see you go straight into an Italian gaol. Who wants shit like you over here?' Again, I jabbed the knife into Guido, just enough to make him howl, again. 'Give me a name, you bastards!' I said. 'If it wasn't you, who was it?'

'Do what you like to him,' said Enzo, defiantly, chin tilted at a Mussolini angle. '*He* doesn't know, and *I* wouldn't tell you, if I did.'

I jabbed again. 'Tell him, you big prick!' Guido yelled. Enzo stayed silent. Again, I jabbed, but harder. '*Tell* him!' screamed Guido. 'Tell him, or I'll fix you!'

At this, finally, Enzo shrugged and said, 'It could have been Barbuti.'

'Who's Barbuti?' I demanded.

'He's an expert in explosives. He's a teacher. He lives in Padua. He may have put the incendiary bomb on the Italicus. Nobody knows for sure.'

'Except for Gelli,' I said. 'Eh? Except for Gelli!'

At this, each was suddenly silent, as though a pall had fallen over them, as though they had been instantly mesmerised. And I knew in that moment I was right, that it *was* Gelli; Gelli at the centre of the web, Gelli the puller of the strings, Gelli the caller of the shots, Gelli the paymaster. 'Gelli sent Barbuti,' I said. 'Gelli paid Barbuti. Did he tell him to blow up Bologna station? Did he poison the Pope?'

'Lies,' said Enzo. 'Fabrication. They blame him for everything. It's convenient. They blame him for things he couldn't possibly have done.' He seemed at once indignant and frightened.

'He won't be pleased you've told me,' I said.

'Told you? I told you nothing!' Enzo shouted. 'Neither of us did!'

'You've told me enough,' I said, and, looking up from the floor, I enjoyed the sight of Enzo's frightened face. If I could not stick the knife in his neck, rather than Guido's, at least I could make him squirm, exact some slight recompense for what he had done to Annabel. 'Where's Gelli now?' I asked. Neither replied. 'Where is he?' I demanded, again, and once more made play with the knife.

179

'I don't know,' moaned Guido.

'But you do, don't you?' I asked, looking up once more at Enzo.

'I know nothing,' Enzo said, gazing at the carpet.

'Well, is he in Italy? Is he in Argentina? Is he in Uruguay?' I jabbed at Guido's neck again.

'Non so, non so, non so,' he whimpered. 'I don't know.'

I believed him. 'But you know, don't you, Enzo?' I asked.

'Nothing,' said Enzo, 'I know nothing.'

I had had enough of maltreating Guido when it was Enzo I truly loathed, Enzo who had beaten and humiliated Annabel, Enzo who would have tried to force us to make love in front of him, had I not picked up and used the bottle, grabbed the knife. It was the very frustration of this that gave me the impetus to leap up suddenly from the floor, spring at Enzo, and push the knife into *his* throat, rather than Guido's. 'Tell me, you pig!' I said.

It was a moment of intense satisfaction, deep gratification, the end of that tormenting situation in which I could reach Enzo only at second-hand. But I had him now, and where I had hurt Guido as little as possible, or only as much as necessary, I realised that I was quite easily capable of cutting Enzo's throat. Quite easily, and though the notion was so strange to me, not to say shocking, I knew that all that stopped me was the probable consequences. 'Carne, carne!' Again, Hawkwood's words floated into my head. It was not so much, I was suddenly aware, what *had* been done, but what *could* be done; by him, by me. In war. In blood. In anger.

'Ma cosa fai?' Enzo whispered. 'Sei matto? What are you doing? Are you mad?'

No, I wasn't mad. It might be a form of possession, but it was not a form of madness. I was still aware and concerned about consequences. 'Where's Gelli?' I asked, again. 'Tuscany?'

'How the devil do *I* know?' Enzo said. 'I'm not even in Italy!'

'But you're in touch with him. You still get orders from him. Even money from him, perhaps. So where? Where, if not Tuscany? Buenos Aires? Montevideo?'

'Buenos Aires, I think,' he gasped, and who knew if he

180

were telling me the truth, or merely telling me the thing most convenient to himself?

'Where was he when you last heard from him?' I asked.

'Who said I ever heard from him?'

I pressed home the point of the knife.

'Uruguay!' he exclaimed. 'Montevideo.'

'When?'

'Weeks ago. I don't how many weeks ago.'

'All right,' I said. 'Now, out of this flat. Both of you. Subito!'

'Are you mad?' asked Enzo, again. 'It isn't *your* place. I live here. You can't turn me out.'

'I can,' I said, 'and I will. At least for now. At least for tonight. I'm not leaving you swine here with that poor woman and her kid. Then I'll see about keeping you away for good. Beating up a woman. The police would be interested in that. I don't suppose you'd stay very long in England. You'd be back in Italy, before you knew it.'

'She'd never testify against me,' Enzo jeered.

'No, but I would,' I said. I felt a tremendous temptation to use the knife, a violent impulse to slash him across his sneering face with it, to exact some kind of vengeance for what he had done to Annabel, and to Rosie. Once again, he seemed to sense what I was feeling, for he flinched, and was silent. 'Come on, out!' I said. 'Both of you. Get up!' I said to Guido. From the floor, Guido gave another groan then, slowly and awkwardly, he got up on all fours, put a hand on the table, and hauled himself to his feet. 'You first,' I told him. 'Through the door, then out of the flat.'

Still slowly, staggering a little, he complied, going through the door, and shuffling out into the corridor. 'Now you!' I told Enzo, and propelled him forward with my free hand on his shoulder, still keeping the knife against his ribs. 'Pagherai, pagherai,' he was muttering, as he went, 'you'll pay.'

'Keep your mouth shut,' I told him, 'or *you'll* pay.' I wanted them out of the flat, out of the block, though beyond that, I had no strategy, other than an overall desire to see that they never came back again. I was making things up as I went along, the whole situation was so deeply alien to me that I could do nothing else, moved simply by disgust and anger. I had no notion even of whether I should put them into the lift,

181

or take them down and see them out into the street. As it transpired, there was, as our slow procession turned the corner, a man and woman waiting for the lift.

'Stop!' I told Guido, and the three of us stood back until the lift had come, and the couple had disappeared in it. I waited several long minutes, during which none of us spoke. Guido supported himself, still groggy, with a hand against the wall. Enzo breathed heavily; his whole, heavy body exuded a ferocious resentment. Once, it grew tense, and I reacted instantly, prodding the knife into him. 'You're frightened, aren't you?' he sneered. 'I should have seen to you when *I* had the knife.'

'Well, you didn't,' I said. 'But *I* will, if you don't behave yourself. Just give me your keys.'

For the situation was clear to me, now. I would take the two of them downstairs, and put them into the street. Without keys, they could not come back in again; unless they prevailed on Annabel to let them in. For a moment, he did not respond. 'The *keys!*' I said, again, pushing in the knife. He put his hand in the left side pocket of his jacket, then, with an abrupt, explosive movement, pulled it out, holding the keys, whirling round towards me. As he did so, I automatically thrust the knife into his side. It went in with surprising ease, sliding through the flesh between the ribs. He gave a cry of agony, dropped the keys, and collapsed to the ground. 'You've killed me, you've killed me!' he shouted.

Blood was welling from his fingers as he clutched the wound, and for a moment, I thought perhaps I had indeed killed him. Guido turned to him, shouting, 'Ma cos'ha fatto, cos'ha fatto? What have you done?' and while I held the point of the knife towards him, to keep him at bay, dropped to his knees beside Enzo. It was then that I heard the door of Annabel's flat fly open, and suddenly she came rushing round the corner towards us, saw Enzo, screamed, and cried, 'Enzo, darling!' she, too, going down on her knees beside him. The door of a flat almost opposite our distraught group was opened cautiously; a pale, frightened, middle-aged woman with dyed red hair looked out. With horror, I realised she might call the police, and said, at once, 'It's all right, it's all right, we're going to get a doctor!' It was meaningless, the first, confused thing that swam into my head, but perhaps it worked. At least she closed her door. Then I realised I had been standing with the bloody knife in my hand, and my impulse was to drop it and to flee, for of course she would phone the police, and when the police arrived, whom would they arrest but me? I might have killed him, I had certainly stabbed him, and the bizarre circumstances, the nightmare of it all, would mean nothing to them.

Annabel suddenly looked up at me. 'Go, go, for Heaven's sake go!' and with one last look at Enzo's contorted face, I obeyed her, not waiting for the lift, but racing to the stairs, rushing down flight after flight of them, realising I still had the knife in my hand, letting the blade spring back into the handle, stuffing it into the inside pocket of my overcoat, reaching the foyer, panting, slackening my speed, trying to compose myself, emerging as slowly and calmly as possible from the door to the stairway, praying that the foyer would be empty. Which it was.

Once out of the front door of the flats, my impulse was again to run, but I fought it, walking again, though briskly, around the square, to where I had left my car. There were few people about. A young couple were getting out of a Citroën on the far side of the square. A taxi came round the corner, then turned out of the square again. I climbed into my Volvo, shut the door, put on my seat belt, and felt an enormous sensation of relief. I shuddered. Illusory though it might be, the car felt like a haven, where I was home, I was safe; and I could move. I could escape from the square, now, escape from the city. In my small, moving haven, I could leave all that had happened behind me. I started the car, drove out of the square, into Sloane Street, into Knightsbridge, into the Park, and north, up to the Bayswater Road, where I turned west.

'Carne, carne!' The words kept coming, unbidden and unwanted, into my head. For I had not wanted to stab Enzo; at least not then, not at the moment. I had stabbed him only because he had tried to hit me with the keys; a reflex action, performed in self-defence. And suddenly, emerging from the Park at Lancaster Gate, I had a moment of intense satisfaction. He had *deserved* to be stabbed, however inadvertently I had done it, deserved even to die, to be punished for his dreadful cruelty to Annabel. Driving down Holland Park

Avenue, beneath the leafless plane trees, past the Victorian bulk of the tall houses, I thought abruptly, I must get rid of the knife. My God, the knife. For all I knew, the murder weapon; the incriminating evidence. But where to conceal it? In what bottomless pit, what well, what lake, what quarry? What if the police stopped me on the way, somewhere between here and Oxford? They would search me, or the car, find the knife, and discover my fingerprints on it. The knife seemed to shriek aloud in my pocket, to give out a high pitched, keening sound, which would bring every policeman down on me for miles around. I could almost hear, as well, the whoop-whoop-whoop of their horrible new sirens, as they homed in on me. For God's sake, I admonished myself, it's only a flick knife. I don't need a reservoir; all I need is a drain.

And I found one along Westway, as the traffic cut and flashed its way three abreast through the darkness, past the endless, ugly, two-storeyed houses of the suburban road; found it when stopped at a traffic light. I darted out of the car, pretended to examine the windscreen, surreptiously bent to slip the knife down the drain, afraid for a moment it would get stuck between the bars. But it didn't, down it went, and with cars honking impatiently behind me, I jumped back in the Volvo, and drove on. They could stop me now, I thought, and at least they would find no knife on me. But if he died, I wondered, if Enzo died. Stopped at another traffic light, the urban sprawl hideous about me in the gloom, I felt a sudden palpitation in my chest. It had nothing to do with guilt, still less with sorrow. If Enzo were dead, I would be glad, provided it was not I who'd killed him. Even that was not true. I would gladly have killed him, could I only be sure that I would never be found out.

But now, if he were dead, there was no chance of escaping. Too many people knew. Too many people had seen what happened, either when it happened, or moments afterwards. Annabel, Guido, the frightened woman in the flat.

I was on the motorway at last, and being able to drive without interruption, to drive fast, achieving a rhythm, without the endless hiatus of traffic lights, roadworks, roundabouts, soothed me and began to calm me. He would surely live. I hadn't stabbed him through the heart, only through the ribs, and on his right hand side, at that. He had

184

been bleeding badly, but they would call a doctor, or drive him to hospital. One way or another, the bleeding would be stopped, and he would recover. Of course the doctor, or the hospital, would call the police; but what would Enzo tell them? That it was I? An Oxford don? Then why ever did I do it? Annabel might perjure herself; I could see the possibility of it, after the way she had bent over him in the corridor, all his sins forgiven, his cruelties forgotten. Oh, yes, back she would surely go to the perpetuation of sadism, masochism, suffering and forgiveness. I myself, as I had suspected at the start, surely stood for a kind of revenge.

But Enzo was in England on sufferance, he could not afford trouble with the police, appearances in court. That way lay extradition. With such thoughts, I comforted myself; then I comforted myself too with thoughts of Hawkwood. How petty and irrelevant he would have found all my qualms and alarms, a man immersed in a life of violence, for whom blood and death and battle were the very stuff of existence. He would have understood what happened, he would not have disapproved. Alarm giving place at last to pride, I thought I had acquitted myself well. I had escaped from God knows what horrible predicament, and saved Annabel from it, too. I had turned the tables on two thugs, both, unlike me, steeped in the world of violence. I had been driving them out of the flats, no more, and what I had done to Enzo was merely for my self-protection.

Yet that would bring vengeance, I had no doubt of that. Enzo had already threatened it; before I even stabbed him. 'Pagherai, pagherai!' And so, to whatever left-wing terrorists were spying on me, stealing my notes, breaking into my house, shooting at me in the dark, were added the neo-Fascists, who had far more reason now to wish me harm, and could, if they chose, use the bullying thugs of the National Front to implement their purpose.

I looked at my watch, saw that it was nearly nine o'clock, and turned on the radio of the car, to see if there were any news of my escapade; but there was none. I was in that long, dark stretch of the motorway now, unlit by any lamps and I revelled in the darkness. Yes, I had done quite well, and with luck I thought that I could do as well again. I had survived my baptism of violence, just as I had survived my baptism of fire, and its sequel. I had survived, I knew, partly through luck, but partly through accumulated rage, built up through all the months of misery and impotence. Next time, it would be easier; the following time, easier still. It was not so much that violence bred violence, a commonplace, but that the experience of it bred indifference to violence. Violence itself became a commonplace. Next day, I thought, when I had given my tutorial, delivered my lecture on money and the mediaeval world, I would be back in the Bodleian, grappling with Hawkwood, my companion and my solace; for what other companion had I? Whom could I go to? Who would listen to me or believe me? What other Oxford don, even Collings, though he would certainly enjoy it? Aldo was in Bologna. So was Lucetti, who would seize upon it all with glee, in his strange voyeurism. Sindona? Della Martira? They would simply turn it to their own ends. I thought, as I turned the knob of the radio until I found a station which was playing jazz, that it might be worth going to the police, simply to pre-empt what could happen, to get my own version in first. 'I see, sir. And then you stabbed him. Would you call that a reasonable use of force?'

I had been doing over ninety in the fast lane, reducing my speed each time that I became aware of it, for fear I might be picked up for the banality of speeding then, when I gave my name, be arrested for what had happened in Belgravia. 'We have reason to believe you are the Thomas Cunningham who earlier this evening . . .'

It had all, in the corridor, happened too quickly even for shock, let alone remorse, but now I lived again the moment when Enzo whipped out his keys, when I, in response, drove the knife into his ribs, felt again the sensation of the blade gliding through flesh and gristle, *human* flesh, saw again the bright crimson blood spurting horribly thick and fast through Enzo's fingers, as though from some hidden well. As if to escape from my own thoughts, as well as from some notional pursuer, I now deliberately put my foot hard on the accelerator, racing on into the night, towards an Oxford in which, if I were to be logical, there could be no escape from whatever might pursue me.

Yet as I reached the end of the motorway, as I moderated my speed, as I had to give up my illusion of escape in movement, I realised that now I was curiously unworried, strangely sure I would survive. Once again, something had happened to me, one more event in the process of change which had begun in the station at Bologna, continued through the evening in Piazza Vittorio, the night in my cottage, and now, with me as agent rather than victim, had made its longest leap yet. It was one thing to be passive, simply to endure, quite another to have been the aggressor – however inadvertently – to have felled a man, and to have drawn blood. In this euphoria, I drove through the outskirts of Oxford, through the beautiful, deep canyon beneath the iron bridge, past the little, suburban shops of Headington. I felt buoyant and free. Let them try what they wanted; neo-Fascists, Red Brigades, whoever the hell they might be. I had nothing to lose now Simonetta was dead, and I would fight my corner. I had no delusions of immunity. No doubt they might shoot me, knife me, burn me, blow me up, even poison me. Short of an armed bodyguard, an armour plated car, a house turned into a fortress, how could I stop them? But at the root of my being, I did not believe they would be able to.

IX

I drove not round Oxford but deliberately through it, soothed as I always was by the stone symmetries, the lamplit succession of ancient walls, towers, gateways, spires, unblemished now by the scourge of daytime traffic. By the time I reached the cottage, I was quite at peace.

I unlocked the front door, pushed it open, stood back, and waited an instant, as I was now accustomed to do. No sight or sound of disturbance. I switched on the lights, went into my study, and had just poured myself a whisky when the telephone rang. I picked up the receiver, then held it to my ear without speaking, fearing that it might be the police, hoping that it would be Annabel. It was neither.

'Tom?' said a man's voice. 'Sono Della Martira. Did you find them?'

'Oh, God!' I answered. 'Yes, I found them,' and I laughed.

'What happened?'

'Can I speak safely?' I asked.

'Yes, yes; quite safely. I'm in the street. In a booth.'

'Well . . . he's been stabbed,' I said enigmatically.

'Stabbed? Who's been stabbed?'

'Enzo.'

'Bravissimo! Who did it?'

I hesitated. 'I did,' I said finally.

'Ottimo! When did it happen?'

'Tonight. I couldn't help it. It's a complicated story. The man's a brute.'

'All those Fascists are,' said Della Martira. 'Is he alive?'

'I think he is,' I said. 'I hope he is. For my sake. But I couldn't really help it. It happened in London. Now I suppose they'll all be after me. They and all their British Fascist friends.'

'Don't worry,' said Della Martira, 'I'll get you a gun. Someone will bring it to you. It's always best to have a gun.'

'Thanks,' I said bitterly.

'But did they tell you anything? Who it was killed your wife?'

'They told me who might have done. I know it was the Fascists now. I think it was Gelli who planned it. I think it was Gelli who planned Bologna.'

'We think he planned it too. When are you coming back to Italy?'

'God knows,' I said. 'God knows what's going to happen to me here. I could end up in gaol.'

'In England? No, you won't end in gaol. Don't worry. If anybody ends in gaol, it'll be them. In Italy. The net is closing in. They won't involve you. They can't afford trouble.'

'That's my only hope,' I said. 'I'll come over when I can. *If* I can. It won't be before the end of my term, in December.'

'We'll wait for you,' Della Martira said. 'And I'll send you the gun.'

The gun! Not an air pistol, but a gun. I sat in the armchair by the telephone, wondering whom I would shoot with the gun, and whether I would kill him. After all, I had already stabbed somebody; this was the logical progression.

I went to bed and slept well. I dreamed, but it was not about Enzo, knives, blood, beatings, or Annabel. I was back home in Gloucestershire. I had come to tea, my father met me at the gate and said, 'But we expected you yesterday,' which filled me with a great frustration, because I knew he was wrong. But when I woke, it was with a start of foreboding. I had stabbed a man. I might have killed a man. Whatever the circumstances, whatever the provocation, I had committed a violent crime. Never had I had such need of Hawkwood! Never had I felt such longing to immerse myself in his life and ruthless times, to escape from violence into violence.

My tutorial did not start till eleven o'clock. I got up, quickly made myself breakfast, then took out my files and notes and photostats, immersing myself in the sack of Faenza. As I read I felt, for the first time, that I began to comprehend. The experience was working both ways. If I could gain some consolation from Hawkwood's imperturbably violent life, my own quite new exposure to violence gave me in turn a new perception of it. To have endured it passively had been helpful. To have actually inflicted it helped even more, as though it was a kind of initiation.

Here, in Hawkwood, was another episode to be explained away. 'Such dogs,' wrote Muratori, in his *Annals of Italy*, 'did the Pope's ministers keep in their service in Italy.' Faenza, the plump prize for an army which had not been paid by the Pope, and which had just failed in a tedious, frustrating siege of the Castle of Granaroli. Three hundred citizens imprisoned for alleged revolt. The city plundered by Hawkwood's soldiers. Three hundred children murdered. Three hundred children. And a nun cut in two? Discounting the second, should one believe the first? The Sienese chroniclers, notorious enemies of Hawkwood, had concocted the story of the nun. Could that of the three hundred children have been concocted, too? Again the enigma, the anomaly. The honest, bluff, loyal, decent soldier whose troops had indulged in savagery. 'Unhappy country where these fierce and greedy locusts settled,' wrote Muratori.

I could not countenance the death of children, yet now I was discovering a strange anomaly in myself; indeed, a still more striking one. For Hawkwood was after all a soldier, professionally involved in carnage. I was a non-combatant, an academic, and I had struck one man down, stabbed another. Now I would have a gun. What lay in store for me? What fresh excesses? But I would not kill children, nor stand by and see them killed by other people. It was Rosie, still more than Annabel, who had aroused my pity, provoked my rage, last night.

Thinking so often of Cesena, I had tended to forget Faenza, all but the cloven nun, that Sienese piece of black propaganda. 'Carne, carne.' The flesh of little children. He could never have done it, ordered it, himself. 'Thou shalt not kill but needst not strive . . .' Just as the ineffable Robert of Geneva had ordered the massacre of Cesena, so there was a third party in the background at Faenza; the supposedly 'abandoned' Count of Romagna. I must avoid, I knew, more than ever now, the role of an apologist. My new apprehension of violence and the conditioning effect of violence did not extend to atrocity. Yet if some neo-Fascist propagandist were to write an account of what had happened in Belgravia, what might he say of me? That I was a savage, who had struck down one poor Fascist with a bottle, stabbed another with a knife, after raping their hapless girlfriend? I disbelieved the story of the three hundred slaughtered children, but disbelief alone was not enough; here, too, I must keep going to primary sources, wherever I could find them, and seek endlessly for proof of the contrary: or of the charge itself.

As the hours passed, I began to feel less apprehensive of what might happen to me. My newspapers had been delivered; there was not a word of what had happened last night and none, still, on the radio news. No sirens, no policemen at the door; not even, yet, a telephone call, other than Della Martira's. I felt tempted to ring Annabel, but it was too hazardous. The police might be tapping her telephone by now, it might be answered by Enzo, if he had survived; or by Guido. Yet I needed badly to know where I stood, what had been said and done, whether I could carry on quite normally, or must prepare myself for interrogation, arrest, trial, even gaol.

There was still no word when I set out for my tutorial. My pupils were a tall, thin young man from South London, spectacled, confident, laconic, prematurely bald, a mover and shaker of the Students' Union, aggressively plebeian in his shabby jeans and zipped windcheater, and a languid Etonian, dressed with casual and expensive good taste,

190

sporting his black and pale blue tie, fluent and idle. They were chalk and cheese, and they detested one another. One, with his clever, nagging mind, his Socialist commitment, his lurking sense of grievance; the other with his future assured, Lloyds, a bank, a business, wherever his rich father put him. I sensed a mutual envy. Paul, the Etonian, would like to have been as bright as Ron. Ron, the scholar, though he would never admit it to himself, would like to have been as certain of his future as Paul.

We were talking about the flow of neo-classical ideas from Byzantium to the West, long before the fall of Constantinople in 1453, when the classical 'explosion', the Diaspora of scholars, the making of the Renaissance, was supposed to have taken place. Paul was very interested, since one could talk in terms not only of generalities but, as he preferred, of individuals; scholars from Constantinople actually known to have come to Italy in the early fifteenth century. Ron, who liked to think in terms of economic determinants, was less happy. Were he able to jump the Middle Ages, I thought to myself, hearing his South London whine, he would no doubt write a thesis on Usury and the Renaissance; the Money-Lender as Patron. To his Marxist vision, art and culture were mere bubbles on the stream, no more than symptoms. There had been ferocious arguments between the two of them when Paul had called him a Barbarian, a Philistine, while Ron had smiled his socially inferior, intellectually superior, smile.

I did not want to argue today; I was too preoccupied to hold the ring. But Ron was at his most polemical. 'Does it matter?' he said.

'Does *what* matter?' I asked him, knowing perfectly well what he meant.

'I mean, is it really important whether people in France started studying Greek and Latin authors in 1353 or 1453?'

'I think that's a pretentiously utilitarian argument,' said Paul.

'And I think yours is a romantic one,' said Ron.

'Well, Ron,' I said, 'does anything matter? Does history matter?'

Except as a means to an end; getting you to Oxford, getting a degree, then getting a job?

'It depends what *kind* of history,' said Ron. 'I think this is

191

anecdotal history. What matters is that the ideas *did* come, not *when* they came.'

'Even if it materially alters the received ideas of cause and effect?' I asked.

'Yet it doesn't, does it?' he insisted. 'We know what the cause was, we know what the effects were; all we're discussing is the date.'

'But in placing it *before* the Fall of Constantinople,' I said, 'we're surely achieving a new perception of the relation between East and West, and reducing the importance of the Fall.'

Ron stretched out his scuffed blue training shoes towards the fire, smiled his exasperating smile, and said, 'I still ask, does it *matter*?'

It was then that my telephone rang. I snatched up the receiver immediately. 'Tom?' asked a woman's voice, uncertainly. It was Annabel. I wished I could ask the two of them to leave the room, but it would have been still more embarrassing. 'Excuse me!' I said to them, then asked her, in a low voice, 'Are you all right?'

'Yes, yes, I'm all right. Enzo isn't, though. He nearly died. They had to operate on him. He's at the Westminster Hospital. We said it was a burglar.' At this, I was filled by a vast wave of relief.

'That's wonderful,' I said, before realising it was hardly the most felicitous word.

'No one's been told you were here,' she went on. 'Enzo was afraid they'd both be sent back. Guido's still here. Why did you do it?' She sounded tearful now.

'I can't explain now,' I said. 'I'm giving a tutorial, but I'll call you very soon. Thank you.' I put down the receiver and faced my pupils, again. They were grinning.

'You look happy, sir,' said Paul.

'Do I?' I answered. 'Just an optical illusion. Let's return to Constantinople.' But I *was* happier, and it was very hard to return to Constantinople, harder still to attend to Ron's perverse logic chopping. Distracted, I allowed the hour to degenerate into an argument between the two of them, in which what was said was substantially less important than what was felt. I scarcely listened to them, simply intervening now and then, to maintain the facsimile of attention.

That Enzo had nearly died did not, I found, concern me at all, save that, Enzo not being dead, I could not be charged with his murder. The tutorial at last over, with Paul and Ron still grinning at each other, and at me, I lunched at High Table, enjoyed a good claret, in which I silently drank to my lucky escape, and contrived to be polite to Cooper, who was talking to a morose classics don about a recent archaelogical find in Rome, near the Forum. Normally, it would have interested me, despite Cooper's gift for squeezing the juice out of almost any topic, but Annabel's call had left me still in a state of great excitement. Enzo had been stabbed by a burglar! No doubt the three of them had told the police that they had found him in the flat, chased him into the corridor, and there, Enzo had been stabbed. Consuela, the au pair girl, had not been at home, so could not contradict them. Rosie alone could tell them *I* had been there, but they were hardly likely to question her. The woman who had looked out of the flat and had seen me with the knife did not know me from Adam.

Now, knowing what I had learned about Gelli, I must be off to Italy to look for him, and in the meantime, must avoid reprisals. The gun was coming, and I wondered who would bring it. Lunch over, I went to the Bodleian, and worked again on Hawkwood. I knew that I would have to revise my whole book, yet I did not care. It was going to be a process of discovery, of myself, as much as of Hawkwood. It would march step by step with my investigation and that, too, was coming into clearer focus.

I could be certain now that Simonetta had been killed by neo-Fascists. I could be almost certain that Gelli, whoever he was, had sent them. What they had done to Simonetta was all of a piece with what they were. What they had done in Bologna station. What Enzo and Guido had done to Annabel, had tried to do to me, in her flat. Had Hawkwood ever hated anybody? I doubted it. Perhaps he had hated the French, when at first he fought for King Edward and the Black Prince. The rest was business. 'Those that I fight I do not hate, those that I guard I do not love.' But I had detested Enzo and Guido from the moment I walked into the pub. Their brutality in the flat had simply exacerbated it. Would I have hated the members of the Red Brigade, hated Della Martira and his group, had I found out that it was they who

193

had been responsible for murdering Simonetta? The question was academic, but somehow I felt I might not have done. The murder of Moro was as cruel and horrific as anything perpetrated by the neo-Fascists; perhaps if I had seen the Red Brigades at work as I had seen Enzo and Guido, I would have felt the same about them. As it was, it seemed to me that in their neo-Fascism, sadism and nihilism came first, merely sanctioned by the ideology. In the case of Della Martira and company, and probably that of the Red Brigades, it was the ideology that led to cold atrocity.

When I returned that evening to my cottage, an envelope lay on the mat, addressed to me in a large, firm, evidently Italian, hand. I opened it up. There was no note or letter, simply a ticket for the left luggage office at Oxford railway station. I felt, once again, the throbbing palpitation in my chest. I had a temptation to tear the ticket up and forget about it. What the hell would I do with a gun? But, scarcely a day ago, I might have asked myself, what the hell would I do with a knife? No one would ever find the knife, though; or no one could possibly connect it with me. Whereas if the police ever did come to the cottage on my trail and found the gun, what then? 'We have reason to believe that this firearm belongs to you, sir. May we see your permit?'

It was a phone call an hour or so later that decided me. 'Tom Cunningham?' said a Cockney voice, which seemed familiar to me. 'We're going to get you, you cunt. You're fucking lucky you ain't being done for murder.' Then the receiver went down, and the dialling tone buzzed in my ear. As I stood there, holding my own receiver, I realised that the voice was Ted's. Yes, I would collect the gun. Assuming that it was the gun.

It was. The package I was given the following day at Oxford station was rectangular, wrapped in brown paper, with no label, and nothing written on it. I took it from the clerk with a certain apprehension, as if in some mysterious way he might divine what it was, but he handed it to me without comment, and I drove home with it, feeling much as I had when I was carrying the knife on Westway.

Once in the cottage, I tore off the brown paper, and a wrapping of corrugated paper beneath that, to disclose a cardboard box, sealed with sticky tape. This I ripped off in turn, and there, in its bed of straw, lay the gun, a black Beretta automatic, obviously not new. Beside it were two clips of cartridges. I took out the gun, weighed it on my hand, then broke it open. There was already a cartridge clip inside. Closing the gun again, I put on the safety catch, and pointed the gun, aiming it at the mirror which hung above the fireplace. I wondered what would happen should I ever have to use it. I had not fired a gun for years, and then it had been a rifle, on the firing range in my school's army corps. Apparently it was far harder to hit people with a hand gun than it ever seemed on the movies; or was I thinking only of a revolver, which in real life people seemed to hold with both hands?

Perhaps I should take it out in the woods somewhere, to practise. Perhaps I should join a gun club, and practise there. Perhaps, perhaps. The gun might at any rate be useful if Ted and his friends appeared. The trouble was that they might appear when I was absent, smash the windows, pour petrol through the letter box, burn down the cottage, do any of the things that London Fascists so often did to Asians. But I would certainly keep the gun now. It was better than a knife, after all, and much better than an air pistol.

If only it had had a silencer, like the gun which had been fired at me outside the cottage! The Fascists might come, I might, with a single shot, even scare them away, but the report would echo all over the village. My neighbour, the retired doctor, would be round. 'I thought I heard a gun shot.'

'A shot? Good Heavens, no. Perhaps it was a car backfiring.'

Yes, one shot would surely put them to rout, but what would the consequences be? I found myself, perversely, wishing that Ted would ring to threaten me again, so that at least I could threaten him, in return. But he did not ring, nor did any other menacing Fascist. The only call I got, from anyone involved in the affair, was from Sindona, inside his New York gaol, from whatever phone it was he deviously contrived to use, evidently convinced that my phone would not be bugged, since the call came, this time, to my cottage.

'I've heard certain things,' he said. 'From certain visitors I've had. You should be careful. Knives are dangerous. It's easy to make enemies.' Who could have told him? But that was Italy, bad news spread like a forest fire.

'Such as Gelli?' I asked.

'Who told you he'd been here?' he snapped at me.

'Why, no one,' I said, surprised.

'There are names that should not be mentioned. Let me just say that you should be more careful. I'm astonished. I've always seen you as una persona seria, una persona per bene. A good, decent man.'

'Sometimes one's not allowed to be,' I said.

'You should be here. In New York. You could keep out of trouble. You'd be safe.' Like you're safe, I thought, wanting suddenly to laugh. 'And you could write my story at the same time. I'm allowed visitors. You know that.'

'Were they . . . Gelli's men?' I asked.

'What did I tell you! What did I say to you! *Ma*. In a sense, they were. In the way that they all are; all such people. He uses them when he has need of them, and discards them when he doesn't.'

'Is he still in New York?'

There was a pause. I could see the sly expression creeping over his face. 'He'll be back in Italy, soon. On no account mention he was here. To anyone.'

'I shan't. Where will he be, in Tuscany?'

'Perhaps. Perhaps in Rome. But not at the Excelsior. Not in his suite there. When will *you* be going?'

'Not till December, when term ends.'

'December. That's quite a good month. He likes to be in Italy for Christmas. To stay with his family. There's time, yet. I'll keep in touch with you. I'll tell you where to go, and what to do. They're still trying to extradite me, did you know that? I can't be at peace, not even in prison.' The old, shrill note of persecution had returned to his voice. 'Day after day, I have to waste my time and money, fighting it. You'd think it was enough for them that I was in gaol. After all I've done to save my country! But if I do come back, they'll regret it! I'll bring the whole house down!' I did not answer. His fury subsided. 'And afterwards,' he said, 'you should still come to New York. It takes no time to get here. You can visit me. I still don't live too badly. I've told you; I'll put you in the Pierre. You can fly Concorde. Sooner or later, the truth will have to be told!'

'You know I'd like to . . .' I said.

'No, no, you wouldn't like to, otherwise you'd have been here by now. *He* comes. He's the only one that's really loyal to me. Everyone else is ashamed to come and see a man in gaol. Even if he's unjustly in gaol! You're the same as the others. You believe all that shit about the Franklin Bank. About that rascal Ambrosoli. You think I'm just a fantasist!'

'On the contrary,' I said. 'Nothing could surprise me, now.'

'Let me give you advice. You're like me. A decent person. Don't let yourself get embroiled in squalid things. Things that should be left to ruffians. Delinquents. Criminals.'

As you left it to Arricò, I thought, thinking of Ambrosoli, dead in the street in Milan. No, no; Sindona would never spoil his own, delicate white hands, even though I knew he had threatened to 'smash the faces' of his foes, if he should meet them. That would be assigned to a delinquent, to a ruffian. 'I haven't got much choice,' I told him.

'Don't try to be a hero,' he said. 'Certain women aren't even worth protecting. But you won't be blamed. I'll see to it. I'll talk to the right people.'

'Thanks,' I said. 'It may be a little late, I'm afraid.'

'I'll talk to you again; before December. Before you go to Italy. But sooner or later, you must come to New York.'

I picked up the gun, wrapped it in rags, and took it down to the cellar, concealing it beneath a pile of logs. How far Sindona's writ ran, whether he'd communicate with Gelli, I did not know, but in the meantime, I intended to keep the gun handy.

I had another call at half past six the following morning, which woke me. I fumbled for the phone on my bedside table. Annabel's voice said, quick and tremulous, 'They're coming on Thursday night. For God's sake be ready. Please don't ring me!' Then she cut off.

It was Wednesday morning. The warning left me curiously unmoved. Indeed, if anything I was glad I could get it over, glad that at least they would not be coming when I wasn't there, breaking and burning, leaving a ravaged home for me to find.

I gave a couple of tutorials that morning, then I drove home to the cottage, went down to the cellar, took out the gun from beneath the log pile, and put it in my pocket. Then I drove out deeper into the country, looking for woods where Simonetta

197

and I had sometimes gone to picnic. The trees were mostly conifers, still giving shelter and cover in the midst of winter. Finding the woods I wanted, I wandered deeper and deeper into them, across the snapping twigs, between the boles of the pines and firs, meeting nobody, until at last I felt I was far enough in to be safe. Then I took six empty beer bottles I had brought with me, and carefully set them up on the trunk of a fallen tree. I walked twenty paces away, aimed the automatic, and fired at the farthest bottle on the right. I missed it. The ejected cartridge case flew through the air. At the noise, a crack rather than a report, which was comforting to me though in all conscience loud enough, there was a frantic fluttering, and pigeons rose into the air. I fired again. This time, the bottle shattered. More pigeons flapped into the sky. I fired once more, and hit the trunk beneath the second bottle from the right. That was enough. I did not want to aim to kill. If I did hit a car, that would surely be sufficient. Besides, I had so little ammunition.

I put the gun back into my pocket and, instead of retracing my steps, wandered deeper still into the woods until eventually I turned and, in a vast circle, sometimes losing my way, struggling through bracken, breathing in the sharp scent of the pines, I found my way at last back to the car.

Annabel had not said what time on Thursday night they might come, but I guessed it would be in the early hours, judged by what I'd read of their *modus operandi*. I was at home, anyway, by nine o'clock, taking up my place in the living room, reading, as seemed appropriate, my notes on Hawkwood, Hawkwood and the White Company, sitting just out of view by the window, with only the table lamp beside me lit. While I read and waited, never able for long to keep my eyes on the notes, tempted continually to look up and out at the empty road where they would have to arrive, I found myself studying Villani's description of Hawkwood's troops, and reflected that there were analogies between them, the ruffians of their time, and Ted and his National Front thugs. 'The English were all lusty young men,' Villani had written, 'born and brought up in the long wars between the French and English, warm, eager and practised in slaughter and rapine, for which they were always ready to draw their swords, with very little care for their personal safety, but in matters of discipline very obedient to their commanders.' Then the fascinating and oddly reassuring picture of them 'through a disorderly and over-bearing boldness', sprawling about their camp 'with so little caution, that a bold resolute body of men might in that state easily give them a shameful defeat'. With their love of fighting and violence, their perverted patriotism, what were the Teds of this world but a distorted mirror image of the young thugs who fought the French for no good reason but gain and greed, who surely despised the Italians for whom they fought, and on whom they preyed? Perhaps it would be easier, now, for me to understand them, too, and their excesses, their pillaging and massacring.

They would have been loyal to Hawkwood because they respected his leadership and, above all, his courage. Physical strength and courage were their ideal; just as they were for the young thugs of today. Save that in them, nationalism – still far in the future in Hawkwood's time – had turned brutal and sour; the easy, islander's contempt for foreigners which the English had shown for centuries had gone rancid.

And they came. It was after two in the morning, I was beginning to doze, had to take sharp hold of myself several times, when I heard, at last, what I had been expecting, the sound of a car driven slowly into our road. I switched off the light, pushed open the stiff little window, heart beating hard, and saw a black saloon drive cautiously towards the cottage, slower still as it approached, until at last it stopped, just outside the front gate, where it remained, stationary and silent.

I could make out two men in the front, two or possibly three in the back, of which the nearest to the window seemed to be Ted. I wondered if Enzo and Guido might be among them. Enzo, hardly; Guido, possibly, and Guido shot people. Very slowly, the two near-side doors opened. Ted, it was certainly he, though he wore a scarf across the lower part of his face, got out of the back, another man, in a dark anorak, heavy and tall, got out at the front. Each, in his right hand, was carrying what appeared to be a bottle. Molotov Cocktails, I thought, with alarm. There was no time to waste. Before they could get to the gate I fired, aiming deliberately at the side of the car. I did not want to hurt them, nor did I want to immobilise the car. There was the *crack!* which I had come to know in the woods, then the sound of the bullet hitting the metal door. The cartridge case spun out into the night.

Ted let out a cry, 'He's fucking firing at us!' then he and the driver leaped back into the car, the doors slammed, and with a roar and a screech, it was away up the road, vanishing round the corner at the far end, as I thrust my head out of the window, watching it go. My heart beat faster still, in the aftermath of action. I would have the doctor round, soon, I was sure of it. Meanwhile, I must hide the gun as quickly as possible. I had taken a risk, I knew, the risk of discovery and trouble with the police, the risk that, if Ted and his crew came back at all, it would be with guns of their own.

I rushed down into the cellar, and hid the gun where I had hidden it before. Scarcely had I come back upstairs again than my doorbell rang and there, indeed, was the doctor in his dressing-gown, sleepy and agitated, so that I suddenly wanted to laugh; there was a comic predictability about the scene. Each time a gun was fired, unexpectedly and inconceivably, there he promptly was. 'I heard a shot!' he cried. 'I'm absolutely sure. It seemed to come from here. Then a car. It tore right past my cottage. Are you all right? What happened?'

'I heard it, too,' I said, 'the car,' having long since decided the story I would tell him. 'I thought it was just the exhaust.'

'No, no! I'm sure it was a shot!'

'But who would shoot at me, or at the cottage?' I asked, innocently.

'You *must* have heard the shot!'

'I was asleep,' I said, 'whatever it was woke me up.'

'If it was a shot, there'd be a bullet.'

Yes, there would indeed, not to mention a cartridge case. That, too, had occurred to me. My hope was that the bullet had lodged in the car, and that if he or anyone else looked for it now, they would look for it close to the cottage, never guessing that I had fired it. The cartridge case was a hostage to fortune.

'Phone the police!' he said.

'You think I should?'

'Most certainly! Even if it wasn't a bullet, whoever it was can't have been up to any good. You've had intruders before.'

'I know,' I said. 'Perhaps you're right; I ought to phone the police.' I did. The doctor stayed with me until their car arrived; I poured us both a drink. I needed one myself; as my adrenalin subsided, I was beginning to tremble.

It was the same detective who had been before, and had been so sceptical of my responses, though the two constables he now had with him were unknown to me. There was a weariness about him which transcended sleeplessness, as if he were inured to the fact that I would procrastinate again. 'More trouble, sir?' he greeted me, when I opened the door.

'Well, I think so, yes,' I said.

'There was a gun shot!' cried the doctor from the hall, behind me.

'A *gun* shot?' the detective repeated.

'Well, it could have been,' I said.

'I'm *sure* it was!' said the doctor. 'I heard it from my house. A car arrived and stopped. There was a shot. Then the car went racing away.'

'So now you've had two intrusions, sir,' the detective said to me. 'One here, one in your rooms at college, and now somebody may have fired a shot at you; or at least at your home.'

'I couldn't say,' I answered. 'I was asleep. It woke me up. It could just have been a car backfiring.'

'Asleep?' he said, looking at me sceptically. I was fully dressed.

'I was reading,' I told him. 'I fell asleep.' No use telling him that I had got up and dressed; the doctor could quickly put paid to that one. Another look, this one more sceptical still. Any moment I would hear, 'I have reason to believe.'

'If there was a shot, then there'll have to a bullet somewhere,' the detective said, while I prayed it had indeed stayed in the car, that he would never find it, that above all he would not look for it now, so that if it still was about, as the cartridge case must be about, I could find both before he came again, in daylight.

'We'll come back later in the morning and have a look for it,' he said, to my colossal relief. 'Not much use hunting for it now. We'll be back about eight o'clock, if that's all right with you, sir. In the meantime, please see that you don't disturb anything in the garden, or walk on the path any more than you have to.'

'Of course not,' I said. It could not be in the garden, but the cartridge case would be.

'I must ask you what I asked you before, sir,' he said. 'Is there anyone who may possibly have a grudge against you? Anything in your possession which someone might want to steal? Some document? Some record or paper which might implicate them?'

'Why, no,' I said. 'As I told you the last time, it's all as mysterious to me as it is to you. As for this business of the shot and the car, well, I'm not denying that my neighbour here may be right. I simply have no knowledge of it. As I've explained to you, I was asleep.'

'So you said, sir.' Another narrow look. 'With respect, sir, if you want us to help you, you must be prepared to help us.'

'I'm afraid I don't quite understand you, officer,' I said, wide-eyed.

'I'm sure you do, sir.' The constables, in turn, looked askance at me. I assumed that the doctor was looking at me too. When the policemen had left, he tightened the cord of his dressing-gown and said, 'It *was* a shot, you know.'

'I have to take your word for it,' I said. 'If it was, perhaps they'll find the bullet when they return.'

'I know a shot when I hear one,' he said. 'I was in the war.'

'God knows what's going on,' I said.

'You're sure you've no idea who's been doing all this?'

'I can't begin to guess,' I answered.

He shook his head. 'Bewildering,' he said. 'I must be very frank with you. I find it most disconcerting. That's twice something has happened in this road.'

'I know,' I said, 'I'm very sorry.'

'If you *can* help the police . . .'

'Of course, of course,' I assured him, and saw him out with apologies and promises.

I was up at seven, looking in the garden, then the road, as surreptitiously as possible, ready to dart back into the house if anyone appeared. I found the cartridge case on the lawn, thank God. There was a chance I might have missed the bullet, but I did not think so. Then, though, there was the question of the gun itself. Should the police suddenly take it into their heads to revise their line of inquiry, to sense, at last, that it was I, not they – whoever they might be – who had fired the shot, I wanted to be safe. So I went back to the cellar, retrieved the Beretta, wrapped it carefully again in cloth, put it in a biscuit tin, and buried it in the back garden, beside a rose bush. They would surely not go as far as to look there, and after they had come and gone, I would take it somewhere else. Perhaps even to the left-luggage office where I had collected it.

When the police returned, there were four of them, the three who had come in the small hours, plus the detective who had come to my college room. Down on their hands and knees they went in the front garden, across the wet grass, along the garden path, but finding nothing, as they were bound to find nothing.

'You're quite sure you haven't thought of anyone it might have been, sir?' asked the detective who had previously been round that night. He was a lean, middle-aged man with blond, receding hair, and small, very pale blue eyes, set closely together. Doubting eyes, I thought, perfect for a policeman. Detective-Sergeant Smales. Let him doubt me.

'No, I haven't, I'm afraid,' I said.

'You go to Italy a lot, sir, don't you?'

'Why, yes, I do,' I said, and laughed. 'You're surely not suggesting it might be the Mafia?'

'You never know, sir,' he said. 'We have to cover every possibility.'

'That's rather a remote one, isn't it? What could the Mafia be looking for, in Oxford?'

'We don't know, sir,' he said. 'But maybe *you* might have some idea.'

I shook my head. 'It just seems quite incredible,' I said.

They stayed, searching, for an hour, asked me more questions, were clearly unsatisfied with my answers, left, went, asking questions in the village, came back, told me they were satisfied it had indeed been a shot, but when I again affected ignorance, got in their car and drove back to Oxford. 'We have reason not to believe.' For how could those good country coppers ever believe what had happened last night; and why? That it was I who had fired the shot, the National Front who had been in the car, an Italian Fascist whom I had knifed, the reason for their being there. That I was off, now, to Italy, in search of a bigger Fascist still, that my informants were an amorist turned terrorist and a convicted swindler who had slipped in and out of an American goal where he was serving twenty-five years.

That night, Della Martira phoned me. 'Did you get it?'

'Yes, thanks,' I said. 'And I used it.'

'You *used* it? Great! Did you hit anybody?'

'No,' I said. 'At least, I don't think so, but it scared them away. They came in the middle of the night; in a car.'

'Italians?'

'English Fascists. National Front.'

'Bravo! Bravissimo! Now, listen. I have a lead for you. A man you ought to see. Who can lead you to the man you *want* to see.'

'So this is a man *you* want me to see.'

'Sei maligno!' said Della Martira. 'You're malicious!'

'Who is he?' I asked. 'Where is he?'

'He's based in Milan, but often comes to Rome. It would probably be better for you to see him there.'

'Better for you, or better for me?'

'Ma che maligno! I'll tell you his name when I see you. He's a banker.'

'A friend of Sindona?'

'Well, not exactly a friend. I'll explain. Ring me at the number you have in Bologna, as soon as you know when you're coming.'

I said that I would, and wondered what he had in store for me this time, for what quarry he now wanted me as a decoy. A banker, an acquaintance of Sindona. Probably a substitute for Sindona, who could scarcely be kidnapped from his upstate New York prison; unless, of course, he was allowed again to come to Italy. I did not trust Della Martira, but then I trusted Sindona still less.

And it was Sindona who called me next; the following evening. 'Do you know when you arrive in Italy?'

'Not exactly,' I said. 'I shall probably leave about December 10. For wherever I can arrange to fly to.'

'Fly to Rome. I'll send you a ticket, if you need one.'

'Thank you,' I said. 'I think I'll be all right.'

'There's someone I want you to meet. Someone who can probably tell you where . . . a certain person may be.'

204

'You surely must know where he is, yourself. You seem to see him often enough.'

'Ah!' Again I could imagine the sly smile. 'But I'm just a poor prisoner. And our friend, the certain person, flies all over the world. When he goes to Italy, how can *I* be sure where he'll be?'

'What's the man's name?' I asked.

'Pazienza! I'll let you know when you get to Rome. I have a most important message which I want you to give him.'

I drew a bow at a venture. 'Would he be a banker?'

The voice grew sharp again in the way I well knew. 'How did you know? Who told you that?'

'No one,' I said. 'I guessed.'

'Ci sono conti da regolare!' he shouted, suddenly. 'There are accounts to be settled! Some people have no concept of gratitude! Some people too easily forget those who helped them! Those who then find themselves in trouble! Through no fault of their own!'

'I'll do what I can,' I told him, convinced by now this must be one and the same man.

'Listen,' he said. 'I'm going to say his name once, and only once; quickly. Calvi Roberto!' he said, so quickly, so softly, I could scarcely hear him. It was a name that meant little to me, though I associated it vaguely with financial complexities, a hint of scandal. 'I'll remember it,' I said.

'You must surely have heard it before.'

'I've a vague memory.'

'I thought you knew Italy.'

'I'm a mediaevalist,' I said.

'That's true. Will you be staying at your usual hotel, in Rome? The small one? The second-class one?'

'I expect so.'

'Eh, va bene. You'll let me know the exact time that you get to Rome. When you arrive at your hotel, you'll get a package. Within it, there'll be a letter to you, and another envelope, which you'll deliver to this man. You are on no account to open it yourself. When the man reads this letter, he will tell you what you want to know. He should then arrange to give another envelope to you. That will in turn be collected from you by someone who will telephone you at your hotel. Do you understand?'

205

'I do. But where must the letter be delivered by me?'
'At a hotel in Rome. You'll find that out when you arrive.
Ora basta! That's enough, now.' And the phone went down.

X

I arrived in Rome in the middle of December, at Ciampino
Airport, on a cheap flight, in the small hours of the morning. I
had had no intention of accepting Sindona's doubtful charity.
There were no buses into town at that time; I took a taxi. By
night, under a moon, the city when we reached it had an eerie
splendour. Ghosts seemed to be abroad in the shadows,
between the pillars, beneath the monuments. The cupolas
and campanili, the immense Roman walls, the pockmarked
bulk of the Colosseum, all seemed to have suffered a moon
change. It was as if the macabre essence of the city had
somehow been disclosed. Even the gigantic sweep of steps of
Santa Maria Maggiore seemed to be awaiting some dire
event, an assassination or a massacre. I thought of poisoned
Popes, stabbed Caesars, the Gracchi beaten to death by
murderous senators. What phantoms squeaked and gibbered
in the streets? What would happen to me, this time; would I
become another phantom, as I could so easily have done in
Piazza Vittorio?

I knew something about Calvi now, there had been time to
talk to Aldo, who had talked to Lucetti. Sindona indeed had
made Calvi; and had tried to break him. Sindona had taken
him up, finding him diligent and dim in his bank in Milan,
seducing him with dreams of grandeur, illusions of power and
glory, presenting him to the Vatican, whom he had seduced
already. Then, only two years ago – for who else could it have
been, who else would have known so much? – plastering the
walls of Milan with virulent posters, viciously detailed,
accusing Calvi of being a thief and a cheat, ripping his
reputation to shreds, extracting, it was believed, great sums
of hush money.

'But Calvi has friends,' said Aldo, on the telephone. 'He
made important friends. Bigger, even, than Sindona. And

they saved him. From investigation. They were after him, the Bank of Italy, they had him cold last year. But he escaped! Incredible! They put the chief investigators on the spot! Investigated *them* on trumped up charges. One of them even went to prison for six weeks. Imagine that! Mario Sarcinelli. One of the most important bankers in Italy!'

'Did Gelli do it?' I asked.

'Who knows? It could well have been. Poor Calvi. Now he's finished. If they'd left him alone, if he'd never met Sindona . . . I think he once used to be an honest man. Nothing but banking and his family. He fought on the Russian front; that was all the adventure he wanted. He knows he's done for now.'

Hanging, it seemed, by a thread, his Banco Ambrosiano hopelessly over-extended, ready to fall at any moment. No wonder Della Martira was so interested in him. No doubt Sindona wanted to screw more out of him.

Through the Piazza Barberini my taxi took me, where Neptune too looked ghostly and minatory under the moon, his shell less a cornucopia than a weapon. Down the narrow Via Sistina to my small hotel, where the sleepy clerk unlocked the glass door and welcomed me. 'Ben tornato, professore! There's a package for you.'

From Sindona, of course. It was a large, square, brown envelope. I carried it up in the tiny, claustrophobic lift and opened it in my small, cramped room on the top floor. My name was typed on a label stuck to the envelope, and inside it was a typed letter to myself on heavy, expensive cream paper, at the top of which was written, in elaborate blue scrolling, Michele Sindona, though not surprisingly, there was no address. There was also a bulky white envelope on which was typed, 'Egregio dottore Roberto Calvi'. My own letter, in which I was addressed as Lei, the formal usage, said:

Gentilissimo Professore, This letter should be awaiting you on arrival at your hotel. Enclosed is the communication which you should hand personally to the banker Roberto Calvi. On no account should it previously be opened by you or anyone else, or entrusted to any third party. You should ask dott. Calvi to open and read the communication in your presence, and to tell you immediately whether he intends

207

to comply with its contents. In the event that he does, he should within the following few days consign to you a package intended for myself. I myself or my representative will be in touch with you after your interview with Calvi.

The package should be given to my representative, who will identify himself to you. He will present you with a copy of *I Promessi Sposi* by Alessandro Manzoni. On no account should you entrust the package to anybody who does not first give you the book, which will be marked with a red cross on page 235. Dott. Calvi has been asked in the enclosed communication to assist you to make contact with the person whom you wish to see.

In the first instance, you should telephone the Excelsior Hotel, in Via Veneto, tomorrow morning, and ask for dott. Calvi, making it clear that you are calling him at the instance of dott. Sindona. Should there be any difficulty in gaining access to him, you should leave a message to the effect that dott. Sindona wishes him every success with Ehrenkreuz. I wish you a very pleasant and profitable sojourn in Rome, and hope to be personally in touch with you, soon.

Much of this, no doubt by intention, was obscure to me. I was exhausted. I put package and letter back in the original envelope, stuffed them under my mattress, and fell asleep. But scarcely had I done so than the phone beside my bed rang. It was Della Martira.

'Benvenuto a Roma. I must meet you as soon as possible.'

'I have someone else to meet first,' I said. 'I think you know who it is.'

'When are you meeting him?'

'I don't know; as soon as I can. I have to arrange it.'

'Well, you won't be able to see him till some time after breakfast. There's a bar in Via Sistina, the same side as your hotel. Just by Via Francesco Crespi. I'll be there at eight.'

I groaned. 'Oh, God,' I said, 'make it nine, will you?'

'Nine, then.'

Della Martira was already in the bar when I got there, his back to the street, his blond head bent over a copy of *La Repubblica*, a ham roll and a cappuccino on the counter before him. He was wearing his dark glasses. He made no response as I came in and sat down on his left-hand side, ordering a cappuccino for myself. Finally, without looking at me, he spoke. 'What has he asked you to do?'

'To deliver something,' I replied, in a low voice, looking straight ahead of me, as he did. 'To get something from him, in return.'

'That'll be money,' said Della Martira. 'He's done it once, he'll be trying it again. He got $500,000 out of him a couple of years ago. He'll hope to pull the same trick. It may not work. The fellow is desperate, but he's got better protection now.'

'And what do you want from him?' I asked.

'I can't tell you that here. I can tell you nothing, here. We'll tell you when you come and see us.'

'Is it going to be like the last time?' I enquired.

'I can't tell you that, either. Call me later today, after you've seen him; otherwise, I'll call *you*. Here is my number.' He took a piece of paper and a pen out of his pocket, wrote down a telephone number, and handed me the paper. Once again, I sensed an element of masquerade. In his conspiratorial demeanour, even in his deadly seriousness, he was still, somehow, playing a part. And because he was playing a part, I had a feeling, in the last analysis, that he was in danger. He had escaped in the Piazza Vittorio, but in a world of cold professionals, he remained a romantic amateur. Had he some wild plan to kill Calvi, as he had wanted to kill Sindona? Or had the others decided they wanted to kidnap Calvi, as they had wanted to kidnap Sindona? Calvi, from all one heard, was Sindona's proper successor in the extent of his fraud and the range of his connections, even if there was no suggestion that he had yet had anybody murdered.

'Mi raccomando!' Della Martira said. He got up from his stool, paid his bill at the cash desk, and walked out of the bar, without another word to me.

I knew the bar well. The public phones were situated at the side in a dark, remote corner. I went round there, phoned the Excelsior, and asked for Calvi. 'Who wants him?' asked a man's voice, when I had apparently got through to his room.

'Professor Tom Cunningham, from Oxford University. I've been asked to call him by Michele Sindona.' There was a pause, then the voice said, 'Momento.' A second, longer,

209

pause, then the voice of another man said, 'I'm Calvi. What do you want with me?'

'I've a letter for you,' I said. 'From Sindona.'

'You can leave it for me with the porter here.'

'It's essential that I deliver it personally.'

A second hiatus. I waited, wondering what would ensue. At length, Calvi said, 'Tomorrow then, at twelve o'clock. But it must be very brief.'

I hung up the phone with a feeling of satisfaction. I would see Calvi, but the day was now my own, I had time to recover, time even to go to the Vatican Library if I wished. And going to the Vatican assumed, now, an added dimension, for the trail led precisely there. Calvi, after all, was 'God's banker'; Aldo had dropped other hints. Calvi had been Sindona's protégé, and Sindona it was who had persuaded the Vatican to hitch up its skirts and dance the merry jig of international finance, high risk investments, high potential profits. 'The Italian Government decided to tax the hell out of them back in the late 1960s,' Aldo had said. 'They had to take chances. There's a great big American archbishop, a bodyguard, who's in it, too.'

I took a taxi to the Vatican Library where I pursued, again, the shade of Robert of Geneva, hoping I might shed light on Faenza since there, too, there had been Papal involvement. Hawkwood's forces, in the service of the Pope, had, as so often, gone unpaid. Whom were the Vatican paying now, and who was paying the Vatican? Back, as I was, in Rome, I had a strange sense of continuity, as of a seamless garment, woven across the centuries. I read, in the Library, of the Papal Legate, but found myself thinking of the Papal bodyguard, the American archbishop, a foreigner, as Robert of Geneva had been, a warrior cleric.

This time, I found it harder to resist the lure of analogy. However facile, it seemed somehow relevant. The past now, as I studied, kept invading the present, while the present threw light on the past. There was no escape for me now in history, not even a transient one. History repeats itself, I thought, the first time as tragedy, the second as farce. But no, Marx was quite wrong, at least so far as Italian history was concerned, whatever he may have thought he knew of Roman history. It repeated itself not once, not twice, but endlessly, and this in itself was its tragedy. It had its farcical elements as well, but they were not fundamental. Fascism was a farce, but it had left its curse on the country. The war in Cyrenaica was a farce, but it had led to the multiple cruelties of the Nazi occupation. Sindona's financial empire was a farce, but it had led to bankruptcy, death and misery; the ripples of it were with us still, and would be for years.

As I walked through the great sweep of St Peter's Square, overwhelmed as always by its marvellous panoply of colonnades, the sheer grandeur of its conception, a woman's voice called me, 'Tom! Professor'!' Looking round, I saw it was Teresa. She stood there smiling, wearing a blue and white ski jersey, a man's tweed cap pulled down at an angle on her head. It was clearly no coincidence, but I was glad to see her. We came towards each other, and I found myself kissing her. Her cheek was very cold. A winter sun lit up the great square and sparkled on the pillars, but it gave no heat. 'I'm really glad to see you!' she said.

'And I you,' I answered. 'I suppose you want to talk to me.'

'Yes,' she said. 'I've got a car. Come with me.' She took my arm affectionately, smiled up at me, and led me out of the square, through the streets, to the busy, down-to-earth Piazza del Risorgimento. There she had left her car, a battered little blue Fiat. The whole car seemed to shake and clatter as I shut my door. The back seat was strewn with a paraphernalia of books, newspapers, magazines, gloves, cigarette packets. 'Are we going to Trastevere?' I asked.

'No, no. We're not there any more.' She drove, recklessly and impatiently, out of Prati, far across the winter city, past the great white mass of the pyramid in Piazzale Ostiense, stopping at last outside an unexceptional, modern block of flats. As we drove, she asked me, 'Are you seeing Calvi today?'

'Tomorrow,' I said. 'Am I allowed to ask why you're so interested in him?'

She laughed. 'He's like Sindona. Everyone wants something from him. Even the ones who got plenty from him. They want more. He's completely crooked, did you know that? Almost as crooked as Sindona.'

'Wasn't he his protégé?'

'His protégé, and his victim. I hear Sindona's sent you a message for him.'

211

'Yes, he has. I've no idea what.'

'You mean you haven't looked? How reliable you are, you English!'

'Someone's got to be.'

'Well, Calvi isn't. Sindona isn't. They prey on honest people. But Sindona's worse. He corrupted Calvi.'

Getting out of the car, she unlocked the door of the flats, and we went up in the lift. It was quite small; we stood close together. She took off the green woollen glove on her right hand, reached out, and stroked my cheek. 'I really *am* glad to see you,' she said, and seeing again that sensual face, the mocking look in her dark eyes, I felt that same strong current of attraction.

We got out of the lift at the fifth floor, and she led the way some ten yards down a carpeted corridor, opened the door of a flat, and led the way inside. It was a total contrast to the dingy squat in Trastevere in which she and the others had been living. This place was altogether more comfortable and bourgeois, no mere pad for transients. It was pleasantly if unexceptionally furnished with an abundance of cane and straw; cane chairs, straw mats, open bookshelves, prints and watercolours on the walls, a few rugs spread on the floor of the living-room, which led out of the hall. She turned to face me, smiling again. 'There's no one here,' she said. 'We can make love, if you like,' and she kissed me.

'What a splendid idea,' I said.

She kissed me again, took my arm, and led me out of the living-room, into a small bedroom. The low, broad bed was covered with papers, books, and clothes, like the back seat of her car, which she swept haphazardly on to the floor while I took off my overcoat. Teresa pulled off her thick ski jersey, revealing her brown, slim shoulders and arms, the abundant black hair in her armpits, her small, rounded breasts. She kicked off her short, suede boots, unzipped her jeans, and began to draw them down her sturdy, compact thighs. I slipped my hand between them and started to stroke her; her pubic hair was unusually springy and thick. With urgent, impetuous fingers, she in turn unfastened my trousers, until she could grasp me and play with me.

Once together on the bed, she made love with a kind of frantic hunger, stroking, sucking, licking, caressing as if she

212

must take what she could while it was there to be taken; or while she was there to take it. She squatted over me, at last, to bring herself to climax, and she reached it very quickly. Her whole vigorous body went quiveringly tense, her eyes closed, her head jerked backwards, she gave a series of ecstatic cries. Slowly, gradually, her body relaxed, her eyes opened, and she lay down beside me, putting her arm around my shoulders, a rapturous smile on her face. 'Era tempo,' she said. 'It was high time.'

'It was,' I said, and kissed her mouth, yet even as I did so I felt like a cork bobbing on a stream, subjected only to one more event in a world of unreality, a chain of occurrences in which I had simply by chance become involved. Yes, I had wanted to make love to Teresa almost from the moment I met her in the restaurant; yes, I had enjoyed making love to her, and wanted to make love to her again, but it was as though it were all happening to somebody else. This kind of frantic coupling was, I felt sure, an essential part of Teresa's life, and that of all her fellow-revolutionaries, seizing what they could, where they might. From what I had heard, it had been a feature too of the Resistance movements in Europe during the war. It was nothing to do with my own world, or the life I had led until now, however exciting or enjoyable.

And nothing to do with *him*, I thought, in a moment of sudden, sheer incongruity, as Teresa began playfully to fondle me. Amidst all the sacking of cities, the rapes and abductions, there was never a word to be found about his carnal indulgence. An English wife, still tantalisingly obscure, an Italian wife from the court of Milan, who would cost him a fortune in jewellery; nothing more. Here, at least, there was no correspondence between Hawkwood's Italy and mine.

'What are you thinking of?' Teresa asked me, and with a start, I answered, 'Oh, nothing special.'

'Nothing special? You're not thinking of *me*? Ma che disgraziato! What a wretch!' and she grabbed my hair in mock rage, shaking my head. 'Che vergogna! How shameful!'

'I meant nothing *else* in particular,' I said, and she bent to kiss me, then let my head fall back on to the pillow. 'I'll forgive you, in that case,' she said.

'That's kind of you.'

She continued to lean over me, examining my face as

though it suddenly appeared strange. 'How odd you English are. So different from Italians. So detached.'

'But I'm an Italianised Englishman.'

'Oh, yes, but you're *still* different. You always will be.'

'Should I try to change?' I asked. 'I seem to have changed a lot, as it is.'

'Yes, you have; I can see you've changed. But not a lot. Only a little.'

' "In spite of all temptations . . ." ' I said, in English.

'What?'

'Just an old English song,' I said, and pulled her down to me again, joining her in her escape.

We lay a long while afterwards in each other's arms. This time I was thinking of nothing, only feeling full of a languorous sense of well-being which shut out the world, real or unreal. We were disturbed, at last, by the sound of the front door being opened, and I pulled out of her embrace, sitting bolt upright on the bed.

'Don't worry,' she said, 'It'll only be Sandro. I'll see he doesn't walk in. Sandro!' she called. 'Sono occupatissima! Vengo fra poco! I'm very busy. I'll come in soon.'

'Va bene, va bene, capisco,' he called back, in a jocular tone. 'All right, I understand!'

'There you are!' she said. 'Relax! Lie down!' and she put her arm around my neck, dragging me back beside her.

'Has he still got the gun?' I asked.

'Of course he has. We've all got guns. We sent *you* a gun. And you fired it, didn't you?'

'Yes, I did,' I said. 'I fired it at a car. There were Fascists inside. English Nazis. They'd come to attack my cottage. Or me.'

'And they drove away again?'

'Yes, thank God.'

'Che bello! And you knifed a Fascist too? An Italian one?'

'Yes.'

'Better still. He didn't die, though?'

'Fortunately not.'

'Fortunately? It would have been all for the best. There can't be too few Fascists. I killed a Fascist in Milan, last month.' She raised her right hand, as though she were aiming a gun. 'Bang! Just like that! Right in the head!'

214

'Seriously?'

'Oh, yes, quite seriously,' and she laughed. 'It's us or them, isn't it? He'd have done the same to me.'

'And Calvi?' I asked, as I'd been wanting to ask all afternoon.

'Will I shoot Calvi? No, what's the object? Everyone wants to shoot Calvi. He's like Sindona. If they don't want to shoot him now, they will as soon as the balloon goes up. When things catch up with him, as they're bound to.'

'Does Claudio want to shoot him?'

'Claudio wants to shoot everybody. He still has to prove himself.'

'As a revolutionary?'

'As a womaniser, as a revolutionary. What's the difference? He was never sure of himself before, however many women he screwed, and he'd never be sure of himself now, however many people he killed. But it's important to keep Calvi alive. Then he can talk; or we can make him talk. Then it could blow the whole conspiracy apart. The whole, filthy network. The Vatican, the government, the bankers, the Masons, the Mafia.'

'The Masons?' I said.

'Oh, yes, of course. The Masons.'

'I thought that was just Sindona. When he went to Sicily and faked his kidnapping. All that stuff about revolutionary Masons; I never believed it.'

'Sindona never told the truth. They're Masons, but they're not revolutionary.'

'So I'm to be a decoy, again.'

The light had failed. Beyond the windows, it was gloomy now, and in the gathering darkness of the room, with the comforting warmth of her body beside me, these were mere words, thrown into the air, without consequences or co-ordinates.

'One day or another, sooner or later,' she said, 'Calvi will run away. We want you to be able to find him for us.'

I wondered if she was telling me the truth. The conspiracy, meanwhile, seemed so vast, was assuming, all the time, such massive ramifications, that no conspiracy theory could truly do it justice. How much could I believe? How much could I *dis*believe? 'And the Mafia?' I asked. The Mafia, who killed without compunction, the Mafia, who used killing as a tool of the trade, the Mafia, who had been killing people for centuries before the Fascists, let alone the Red Brigades.

'Where there are drugs, there's the Mafia,' she said, propping herself on her elbow, taking a cigarette from a packet by the bed, and lighting it with a tubular lighter. 'Where there are crooked bankers, there is the Mafia. Where there's filth and greed and corruption, there is the Mafia.'

'The Mafia, the Vatican, the Masons, the government,' I said. 'Do you think you can beat all of *them*?'

She gave me another teasing caress. 'Si può limitare i dispiaceri,' she said. 'One can limit the damage.'

We got up, dressed, and went into the living-room. Sandro, wearing jeans, as he had been in Trastevere, sat reading the radical newspaper, *Lotta Operaia*, its titled blocked out in large red letters. He looked up at me with a faint, amused smile. 'Welcome back to Rome,' he said. I shook hands with him, slightly disconcerted, but Teresa was quite unembarrassed. Her jaunty Roman disinvoltura, the cool, dismissive scepticism which seemed to inform her every gesture and expression, except when she made love, were unchanged. If anything, she seemed to delight in the situation, smiling at me, squeezing my hand. 'He's here to see Roberto Calvi,' she told Sandro, flinging herself on a sofa. She was wearing, now, a short-sleeved green blouse; the ski jersey had been left in the bedroom. She had not brushed her hair which, dark, abundant and untidy, hung about her face, giving her the look of a mischievous child. 'Sindona's sent him. He's got a letter from Sindona to Calvi, and he hasn't even opened it! Ammazzalo che inglese! What a damned Englishman!'

'Gente seria,' said Sandro calmly, 'honest people.'

'Gente strana,' replied Teresa. 'Strange people.'

'To an Italian,' said Sandro, still perusing his newspaper, 'a sealed envelope is an irresistible challenge. Especially when it's addressed to somebody else.'

'I'm curious by profession,' I said. 'I'm an historian.'

'Curious, yes,' said Sandro. 'But disciplined. We can all guess what's in the letter anyway. Sindona will be trying to screw more money out of Calvi.'

'Does the word Ehrenkreuz mean anything to either of you?' I asked.

'Ehrenkreuz?' repeated Sandro. 'Not offhand. Why do you ask?'

'It means something to Calvi,' I said. 'Sindona told me, in a letter, that if I had any trouble in getting to see him, I should send a message wishing him success with Ehrenkreuz.'

'One of their dirty little secrets, no doubt,' said Sandro. 'I can probably find out. We've got people who have made quite a study of them. Both of them. But why are you prepared to do all this for Sindona?'

'To get to Gelli.' I said.

'Ah,' said Sandro, 'tutto spiegato. That explains everything. Except why you want to see Gelli.'

'I want to know who killed my wife. I think he may have been responsible.'

'If she was blown up on a train, poor thing,' said Teresa, 'he probably was.'

'You'll have a job with Gelli,' Sandro said. 'He's more powerful than the Presidente del Consiglio. More powerful than the Pope. That poor old Polish Pope, who doesn't know what day it is. Who's being taken for a ride by that American archbishop.'

'His bodyguard?' I asked.

'His gorilla. His banker. Che imbroglione! What an operator! It's no surprise he comes from Chicago. The poor old Pope doesn't know whether he's coming or going. And when anybody gets too close to it, out they go. Pouf! Like the last Pope!'

'Was that Gelli?' I asked.

Sandro laughed, and dropped his paper on the floor. 'Quite possible. Calvi hopes Gelli will save him; he already has, once.'

'But Gelli visits Sindona in prison,' I said.

'Sindona hopes he'll stop him being extradited. He's got twenty-five years over there, and he's already slipped out, once. He probably hopes they'll give him time off for good behaviour, eventually. But here, they'll do him for murder. For having Ambrosoli killed. That's thirty years inside, and he knows he'd never survive in an Italian prison.'

There was the sound of a key turning in the front door lock and Della Martira appeared, elegant as ever in his expensive leather jacket, still wearing dark glasses, full of an urgent, edgy restlessness. 'Ciao!' said Teresa, drawing out the word, sprawled on the sofa, giving him a curiously feline smile. He seemed to pick up her message immediately, for he darted me a swift, suspicious look. She now smiled at me, a very different smile. She clearly wanted him to know.

'Well, what have you fixed?' he snapped at me.

'I'm seeing him tomorrow,' I replied.

'When? Where? What time?'

'At the Excelsior. At noon.'

'Ma dai, Claudio!' called Teresa, in her thickest Roman accent. 'He'll see him tomorrow; isn't that good enough for you?'

Della Martira looked away from us both and muttered, 'That depends. That depends on what happens.'

'I don't know what will happen,' I responded. 'I only know what Sindona wants to happen. More or less.'

'And what's that?' asked Della Martira.

'Well, I think you know as well as I do. It must be money. Whatever it is, I'm meant to collect it within the next few days. Then someone will pick it up from me. Someone from Sindona.'

'Why should Calvi pay him?' Sandro asked. 'Now he's got Gelli on his side.'

'But so has Sindona,' I said.

'Masons,' said Sandro, 'all Masons.'

'I don't understand,' I said. 'I thought Gelli was a Fascist.'

'He is,' said Sandro. 'A total Fascist. The most fascist Fascist in Italy. A Fascist with Fascist friends all over the world. Germany, Uruguay, Argentina. But he's a Mason, as well. That's where he gets his power from. *He's* a Mason, Sindona's a Mason, Calvi's a Mason. The President of the Council is probably a Mason. The Pope would probably be a Mason; if he wasn't a Pole.'

'And the Mafia?' I asked.

'Who knows? Why shouldn't they be Masons too? One doesn't necessarily exclude the other. In Italy, nothing excludes anything, if there's money to be made. Everyone's got his snout in the trough. Provided he's a Mason or a Fascist or a mafioso.'

'Or the Pope's bodyguard,' said Teresa.

I felt myself plunging deeper and deeper into viscid waters,

218

waters where seaweed wound itself around my legs, trailed itself in slimy coils about my face. For the first time, I had a feeling of being utterly lost, confused beyond redemption.

'What are you thinking about?' Teresa asked me, sympathetically. Della Martira did not miss the tone of that, either.

'I'm just a little bewildered,' I said. 'Are you sure all this is true?'

Sandro shrugged his heavy shoulders. 'In Italy now, anything can be true. Provided it's corrupt enough.'

Della Martira was prowling like a beast in a cage. '*Aoh!*' Teresa assailed him, in her Roman voice. 'Sit down, Claudio, for God's sake!' Della Martira dropped petulantly into an armchair. 'But you haven't told us, Tom,' Teresa said, 'what happens if you *do* find Gelli? If he *was* to blame?'

'I don't know,' I replied, as always. I would know when I found him; I believed that with a growing, almost mystical, certainty. At the moment, he was still not real to me. Not real in the way Enzo and Guido had been real. Not real enough to kill even if I was aware, already, that Enzo and Guido were small fry, that it was he, Gelli, who used them and manipulated them. But he remained no more for the moment than an abstract concept, a kind of emblem of evil. I had no idea whether, when I met him, if I met him, I would hate him, as I had found myself hating Enzo and Guido, however much the more harmful he was. But all I heard now simply made him appear more remote. He seemed to have spun a web of corruption round the world. Would I find myself stabbing him, as I had stabbed Enzo, stunning him, as I had stunned Guido, shooting at him, as I had shot at the National Front's car?

'You'd knife him, wouldn't you, Tom?' Teresa broke into my thoughts, 'like you did that fascist pig in London!'

'I was forgetting that,' said Sandro, turning to regard me with a new interest. 'You did well. I'm surprised. I'd hardly have expected it from somebody like you.'

'Nor would I,' I told him. 'It was force of circumstances, I assure you.'

'Tell us, tell us!' urged Teresa, fairly bouncing on the sofa. 'Where did it happen? How did you do it?'

All three of them were looking at me closely now. It was

flattering, yet it made me feel a fraud, as if I were taking credit for something done by someone else. Sandro was quite right, it had been completely out of character, yet now I had done it, I knew I might be capable of doing it again. Not like them. Not casually. Not for an ideology. But under the brute pressure of events, of sudden rage.

'It was in a flat,' I said. 'Or just outside it. In London. Belgravia.'

'I know it, I know it,' Sandro said.

'We were in this woman's flat. The English woman who's been helping the Fascists. I was just leaving. I ran into Enzo and Guido as I came out into the street. Enzo pulled a knife and forced me back inside. Upstairs. Back into the flat. Then he and Guido started beating her up; Annabel. She had a little child; who heard her screaming. Who started beating on the door. So . . . There was a whisky bottle on the table. I managed to pick it up. I hit the one with the knife; Guido.'

'Che bello, che bello!' cried Teresa, her eyes alight.

'I got the knife,' I said. 'Then I more or less managed to turn the tables.'

'Bravo!' exclaimed Teresa, and Della Martira gave her a resentful glance. 'Then you knifed Enzo!' she said. 'How did you come to knife him?'

'I didn't mean to. I was trying to get rid of them both; kick them out of the flats. We were in the corridor, going towards the lift. Enzo tried to pull out his keys and hit me with them, so . . .'

'You stabbed him,' said Sandro. 'Perfectly logical.'

'It was a reaction.'

'A very sound one.'

'Let's drink!' cried Teresa. 'To Tom's reactions!' She jumped up, ran out of the room, and came back with a bottle of spumante and four glasses on a tray. Opening the bottle, pouring out the wine, she handed a glass to each of us in turn. Della Martira accepted his sullenly, but he did drink with the others when Teresa enthusiastically proposed the toast, 'To Tom! Don't stab Calvi, though,' she said to me, 'and please don't hit him with a bottle; not until we tell you to!'

'If he doesn't, someone else will,' Sandro said. 'That, or something worse.'

'He's living on borrowed time,' said Della Martira. 'He can

220

never meet all his debts. Billions and billions. He got away with it last year.'

'And how!' laughed Sandro.

'But it can't go on,' said Della Martira. 'The Bank of Italy will never give up now. They want revenge. Sarcinelli won't rest until he's put him inside; and not just for six weeks. For a lifetime. Gelli's saved him once. Even he can't swing it again. Calvi's finished. The Banco Ambrosiano is finished. I've heard he's buying up his own shares all over the world. Che porcheria!'

'The Vatican have helped him too,' Sandro added.

'Of course they have,' said Della Martira. 'Those "letters of comfort". He couldn't have conned people without them. God's banker! But the con's over. They'll drop him in the shit as well. That big gorilla. That American archbishop. He must be running scared too. He would have bought it, if they hadn't poisoned the last Pope.'

'Is that what they might do to Calvi?' I asked.

'Something like that,' said Sandro. 'Sooner or later. Sooner, now. If we can't get to him first.'

'Ma sei pazzo?' Della Martira asked him. 'Are you crazy?'

'Oh, I'd guessed as much,' I told him.

'Of course he had,' said Teresa. 'It's you who are crazy, Claudio, if you really thought he hadn't. He isn't stupid, you know, even if he is English!'

'Don't worry,' I reassured Della Martira, 'I shan't talk about it.'

'Of course he won't,' Teresa said. 'And don't forget he saved your life! *Aoh!*' And she gave her Roman cry.

'I've not forgotten,' said Della Martira morosely.

'I don't really understand what Calvi's been up to,' I said.

'No one does,' said Sandro. 'It's unspeakably complicated. By design. Sindona began it. Calvi carried it on. He bought a bank from Sindona; through the Banco Ambrosiano. They falsified the price, and split the difference. Then it grew and grew. The Vatican were in it up to the neck with their own bank. The Bank of Italy found out about it. Eventually they'll make him produce full accounts for the Banco Ambrosiano, then the shit will hit the fan. It'll be an even bigger crash than Sindona's; if Calvi's allowed to live that long.'

221

XI

At ten minutes to noon the next day, I was walking down the Via Veneto. With its garish cafés, their horrible, glassed-in pavement annexes, the jostle of tourists on its pavements, the gimcrack modernity which had obliterated a handsome part of Rome, it was a street that I had always detested, and today it was under the rain – a heavy, splashing Roman rain which had been drumming on my hotel terrace since the small hours and was doubtless set in for the day, filling the city with a scuttling infinity of black umbrellas. I had no umbrella myself, only a raincoat, and the rain soaked my hair, blew into my face, and trickled down my neck.

By the time I arrived at the railings which protected the Excelsior from the less privileged world, I was drenched and depressed. However spurious the pretensions of the place, however dubious the *bona fides* of the guests who stayed there, I had entered at a disadvantage. As I crossed the threshold, moved past the doorman into the ornate hall, I felt like a bedraggled intruder, an interloper, the cynosure of drier, richer, better dressed people. And Calvi had a suite. I should have guessed that.

A tall, suspicious, broad-shouldered man opened the outer door to me. I thought immediately of Sindona's 'heavy', though this man did not look like a Sicilian. He had cropped, greying hair, high cheekbones, and a high complexion. I wondered for a moment whether he would frisk me for a gun, though I had no gun. It was in its tin, buried in my garden. Even had I wanted to, I knew I could never get it through an airport. Yet almost perversely, I felt no sense of danger in Rome, even if, on the face of it, I was almost courting danger, going into the midst of danger, to the very country which was the source of the danger I had experienced in England.

The fact was, I acknowledged, that Italy, for all my long, intense acquaintance with it, was still 'abroad', a place where nothing could truly harm me – as indeed I had not yet been harmed – while England was home, and thus reality.

The gorilla did not frisk me. He regarded me for a few moments, after I had given him my name, looked with suspicion at the package in my hand, then finally turned his broad back on me and led the way across the ante-room to a closed door. On this he knocked, calling, 'È arrivato l'inglese.'

'Va bene!' responded a man's voice, which I recognised as Calvi's, from behind the door. The big man opened it, and stood aside for me. In the middle of the inner room, neutrally comfortable, with the anonymous opulence of a de luxe hotel, stood a large desk. Calvi sat behind it. He looked at me at once with beady suspicion, like a man who feels the world is full of enemies. He seemed almost the antithesis of Sindona, not a cunning, agile Sicilian but a plump, dour, heavy man who looked exactly what he was, or what he had been, a banker, dedicated to his work, his office and his ledgers – a banker rather than a financier, a man who might finance financiers but disapprove of their fantasies. Bald, soberly dressed in dark suit and tie, his great domed head, with its pale expanse, threw into relief a large, curiously ostentatious moustache, which seemed like a relic of his military days. It could even have been a soldier's face. Unlike Sindona's, it was difficult to think of it as a swindler's. His eyes, too, were utterly different from Sindona's flickering, darting, lizard's eyes. They were dark and melancholy; one could not conceive them being anything else, even when he was not under the kind of pressure that assailed him now.

I wondered whether to shake hands with him, and decided I should try. 'Good morning,' I said. 'I'm Professor Tom Cunningham.'

'I know, I know,' he said, with weary indifference, looking away from me now, as if I were simply the latest of his persecutors, keeping his right hand palm downward on the desk, so that I changed my mind about a handshake. 'You've brought me a package.' He looked at the envelope in my hand then upwards, in dismissal, at the bodyguard, who left the room with ponderous discretion, softly closing the door.

Calvi stretched out his hand, now, not to take mine, but for the envelope. I gave it to him, he nodded at me, laid it on the desk, and returned to looking at the papers in front of him. 'My thanks,' he said.

'I'm afraid I have to ask you to open it now,' I told him. 'In my presence.'

He looked up at me again, with guarded impersonality. 'Why should I do that?'

'It was Sindona's request.'

'And you always carry out his requests?'

'Occasionally,' I said.

'The requests of a man who is in an American prison. How can he even convey you his requests?'

'He seems to have access to a telephone,' I said.

He shrugged, picked up the envelope, and tore it open. Out of it he drew a thick letter, several pages long, and began to read it. He did not ask me to sit down. As he read, I watched his face. The expression of the sad, dark eyes did not change, but his mouth sometimes twitched, sometimes tightened, and once, reading the third page, he stopped, looking past me, up and out into space, as though he found it hard to go on. Finally his eyes returned to the letter, and he slowly finished it, laying the last page down on the desk and staring at it, silent, still, for several minutes. Then he glanced up at me and said, 'È un uomo bestiale.'

I could not disagree, but I waited for him to speak again. 'Are you aware of what he wants?' he asked, finally.

'No.'

'Really?' he said, regarding me again, now with puzzlement. 'But he says that I must give what he wants from me to *you*.'

'I know,' I said. 'He told me as much as that. I simply don't know what it is that he wants.'

Calvi sighed. 'Money,' he said. 'What else could he want but money? He's had half-a-million dollars from me. Now he wants another quarter-of-a-million. I'll have to think about it. I'll have to think about how to get it. As for the other thing . . . The thing he wants me to tell you. I presume you must know about that.'

'Yes, I do,' I said.

'Well, he isn't here. He isn't in his suite, here. And so far as I know, he isn't in Italy. He's probably in Montevideo. I could find out for you, I think, if you want me to.'

'Find out if he's in Montevideo?' I said. 'It doesn't really matter.'

'Why do you want him? If it's not presumptuous of me to ask.'

'My wife was killed,' I said. What was the object of dissembling now? 'She was blown up on a train. I think he may know something about it.'

'You think he was responsible?'

'I think he'd know who was responsible. If he wasn't responsible himself.' He nodded, glumly and ponderously. 'That explains something.'

'What?' I asked.

'Why a person like you, a person who seems decent, should be running errands for Sindona.'

'Well, that's why,' I said.

At last he invited me to sit down, and I did so, in a hard-backed chair, a few feet away from his desk. 'How did you meet him?' he asked.

'Here in Rome. In a restaurant.'

'When?'

'Last summer.'

'Last summer!' he repeated, giving me a suspicious, puzzled look. 'He went to prison in October, 1979. For twenty-five years. In New York State.'

'I know,' I said. 'That's where he is now. It wasn't where he was then. Don't ask me how or why. Perhaps your friend Gelli had something to do with that as well.'

'He does what he likes in that gaol,' Calvi muttered, almost to himself. 'America! It's worse than here! Gelli. The Mafia. Who knows? And now he's blackmailing me again.' He looked at me once more. 'He wants to destroy me,' he went on. 'But he's already destroyed me. As a man of honour. As a respected citizen. As a person of esteem. With his dirty tricks, his filthy posters; all over Milan! Do you know about that? Accusing me of things that *he* did! That I could never have conceived!'

I felt contaminated. For whatever reason, I had been doing Sindona's dirty work, and so far I had not even had the smallest benefit from it. I was not an inch closer to Gelli. And doing not only Sindona's dirty work, but also Della Martira and his group's. Work less dirty than Sindona's, certainly, but

225

something that was still quite alien to me. I had no quarrel with Calvi, whatever he might have done, no cause to spy on him, to lure him into traps. He seemed, in any case, to be blundering into them himself.

Looking at him now, one saw the parody of what he should have been, and no doubt used to be; a ponderous functionary, bent always over his books, devoid of geniality, a human calculator, sobrely weighing prospects and possibilities in the abstract. But Sindona, the arch tempter, choosing him for these very qualities, had found the weakness they concealed from the world, and now he was doomed, seduced by Sindona as such men, in their blinkered rectitude, would sometimes be seduced by a woman. Having sold his soul to Michele Sindona, he was mortgaging it to Licio Gelli.

'I need three days,' he said.

For my part, he could have three days, thirty days, for ever. But at this moment, I was Sindona's envoy, it was to me, or at least through me, that he was appealing, and willy nilly, I was being forced into playing a repugnant part.

'It's nothing to do with me,' I said. 'If you want me to tell him that, I will.'

He would consult Gelli, I was sure of that; wherever Gelli might be, ask Gelli to intercede for him. The actual raising of the money was probably no more than the half of it.

'Will you come back in three days?' he asked. 'At the same time? I'll tell you then.'

I hesitated. I did not want to come at all. I was feeling like some squalid debt collector. 'I suppose so,' I said, at last.

He rose, as I myself rose to go, extending his hand to me. 'Mi dispiace,' he said, 'I'm sorry.' Sorry about what, I wondered? About his inability to raise the money, his predicament, his fall from grace? I nodded as if I understood, but once past the staring gorilla, once outside the suite, wondered whether it was for me, perhaps, that he felt sorry.

I hurried through the marbled foyer, and back up the Via Veneto in the rain, anxious to be away from gimcrack, modern Rome, to escape for a while into the Villa Borghese. I would not wait for Sindona to call me, I thought, walking across the grass, beneath drenched evergreens. I would leave a message for him at the usual New York number, at once ambiguous and explanatory, then I would head for Padua, staying in Bologna on the way, though not, given my mood and mission, with my in-laws in Florence. I had had it in mind, in any case, to go to Padua if I could, if my pursuit of Gelli and my obligation to Sindona would allow me. Padua drew me and fascinated me, itself a Hawkwood city, now a city which, at one and the same time, could accommodate the supposed headquarters of the Red Brigades, and a thug like Barbuti, the neo-Fascist bomber. A city where, moreover, I could find the decent policeman I had learned of in Bologna, doing his job, no doubt, so far as his superiors and their superiors permitted him.

In Bologna I would see Aldo and Lucetti. I did not know how much I would tell Lucetti, who would leap on every succulent scrap of scandal, mayhem and intrigue, devouring it. I would rather, ideally, have Lucetti mediated through Aldo, but he could help me in Padua, I was sure.

I turned out to be right. We met, the three of us, in the same restaurant as before. Lucetti, providentially, was detained at his newspaper, which gave me nearly an hour alone with Aldo. From him I hid nothing. He listened to me with a mild astonishment, constantly shaking his head in disbelief, murmuring, 'But who would ever have believed it? Who could imagine it of *you*?'

'Not me,' I said. 'I can scarcely believe it even now. I still feel as if it's all been happening to somebody else.'

'It's dangerous, Tom,' he said, 'as I told you before. You could lose your life.'

'It's gone too far, Aldo,' I replied. 'It's a question of momentum now.'

'And where does the momentum take you?'

'I don't know. To Gelli, I suppose, eventually.'

'And then?'

I sighed. What could I tell him, or anyone else who asked the question? 'We'll see,' I said. 'I shall play it by ear.'

'I hope to God you never find him. That man's been killing people all his life. Killing them, or having them killed. Even Lucetti doesn't like to talk about him.'

'I'm aware of that,' I said.

In the chattering, clattering bustle of the restaurant, amidst the cornucopia of food that hung or lay about the place, it was hard to remember the stunned misery I had found there on the night of the bomb.

'No one's been caught,' said Lucetti when he arrived, full as always of conspiratorial glee, greeting me with expectant enthusiasm. 'Che vita movimentata che conduci! What a momentous life you're living! You must tell us everything!'

'I'd like *you* to tell me something,' I replied. 'Such as what you know about a Fascist called Barbuti, who's an expert in explosives, and teaches in Padua.'

Lucetti ordered ham and melon from the waiter, poured himself a large glass of wine, lowered his voice, and said, 'He's mad.'

'In what sense?' I asked, when he said nothing more.

'Mad. Just mad. A crazy Fascist. An intellectual. He teaches German literature to girls. In his early thirties. Thin, with glasses. Looks as if he wouldn't harm a fly. Hates Jews. Whenever a bomb goes off, they always interrogate him; sometimes put him inside. But never for very long.'

'Could he have bombed Bologna station?'

Lucetti took a long draught of wine, and refilled his glass, before answering. 'He could have done. Or the Italicus.'

'Or my wife's train.'

'It's possible,' he said, without looking at me.

'And if he did?' Aldo asked me. 'And he tells you that he did?'

'Then we'll see,' I said, for here, too, I had no plans at all. 'There's a policeman I want to find too. The one your friend in the questura here recommended to me. And I want to meet somebody from the Red Brigades.'

'But why?' asked Aldo. 'Aren't they extraneous? Wasn't it the Fascists who bombed Simonetta's train?'

'No doubt,' I said. 'But I think it was the Red Brigades who could have killed me in the Piazza Vittorio, who shot at me again at my cottage, who stole all my notes in the British Museum, and who broke into my college room. There are things I want to clear up. You can call it a desire for completeness, if you like. But if I'm in Padua, it's worth a try.'

Lucetti speared a large piece of ham on his fork, stuffed it into his mouth and, still chewing, summoned the waiter for more wine. 'Dreams,' he said. 'Illusions. If you want completeness, stick to history.'

'There's that too,' I said. 'Hawkwood fought for Padua. He won the Battle of Castagnaro for them; his greatest victory. I've been there often enough before to look at archives.'

'Then look at archives,' Lucetti said, 'that's my advice. If you must go looking for the Red Brigades, I can give you a name. Someone who knows someone who knows. Who might take you to one of the chiefs. You might even get on with them if you meet them. They're mostly university lecturers and professors.'

'That's another reason why I'd like to see them. Because I'm baffled by them.'

'You'd still be baffled by them,' Aldo said. '*I'm* baffled by them. One of them, one of the big ones, he's in hiding from the police, was here at the university with me. He specialised in Ancient History. Now he specialises in having people shot in the legs.'

'Ragion per cui. That's why,' said Lucetti.

'He's an idealist, I suppose,' said Aldo. 'It doesn't pay to be an idealist in Italy. You end up either becoming a cynic, or shooting people in the legs.'

'Would you call Gelli an idealist?' I asked.

At the sound of the name, Lucetti glanced anxiously around him, as though walls had ears, spies were everywhere. 'Attenzione!' he said.

I dropped my voice. 'Well, is he?'

More softly still, quite untypically, Lucetti replied, 'Who knows? Who knows how far he's used Fascism, and how far he believes in it? In the war, they were sceptical about him. Who knows what he really wants; whether it's a Fascist Italy again, or just power for himself.'

'And is Masonry a means to an end?' I asked. 'Or an end in itself?'

This time, Lucetti closed up completely; something that I had never seen. He turned all his attention to his plate, carefully cutting up his osso buco. Aldo caught my eye, and shook his head in warning. 'Cambiamo discorso,' he said, 'let's change the subject.'

'To what?' I asked, a little brusquely. 'To Calvi?'

With the mention of this name, Lucetti instantly looked up at me again, drawn despite himself. 'Calvi?' he said, as I had guessed he might. 'What about him?'

'I saw him today,' I said.

'Saw him? Where? In Rome?'

'Yes. At the Excelsior.'

'And what happened? What did he tell you?'

As well keep a pig from truffles. 'Nothing material,' I said. 'Sindona wants money from him. Calvi hasn't decided if he'll give it to him.'

'How much?' asked Aldo.

'A quarter-of-a-million dollars.'

'Menaggia!' exclaimed Lucetti. 'That's on top of the half-a-million he's had from him already. God knows where he'd get it from, this time. He owes money all over the world.'

'And the Vatican won't help him any more, apparently,' I said.

'I've heard that too,' said Lucetti. 'But you shouldn't get involved with it, it's blackmail.'

'Yes, I realise that,' I said.

'Blackmail,' Lucetti said, again, softly, as if he were thinking aloud, 'but he isn't the only one, he isn't the biggest.'

'What do you mean?' Aldo asked him, but it was Lucetti, this time, who shook his head and again fell silent, while Aldo gave me another meaningful look.

'I'm told Calvi's been buying up his own shares,' I said.

Once more, Lucetti rose to the bait. 'He's used banks all over Latin America – Peru, Panama, Nicaragua. The Bahamas, as well. All of them set up with help from the Vatican bank, the Institute for Religious Works. Help from the Archbishop. It couldn't last for ever. He's chasing his own tail.'

'Couldn't he catch it?' I asked. 'Now he's got Gelli?'

'Gelli's not God. He doesn't want the bank to crash. He's been too heavily involved in it, himself. He and . . . and the people in his group.'

I guessed what he meant.

'And the Mafia?' asked Aldo, quietly.

'And the Mafia,' Lucetti said, after another pause.

'Poor devil,' said Aldo. 'I wouldn't give much for his chances, when the crash comes.'

'You know he attended the banquet for your Queen, in Rome?' Lucetti asked me suddenly.

'Calvi?' I asked.

'No, no,' he said irritably, 'not Calvi.'

'I didn't know,' I said.

'Well, he did. He was there.' Lucetti's voice dropped lower still. 'Queens, ambassadors. He got $800,000 out of the American Ambassador in Rome. He and General Miceli. The head of the Secret Services. Before the elections; for anti-Communist propaganda.'

'And was that what they used it for?' I asked.

Lucetti shrugged. 'Who knows? Miceli's his friend. He was Sindona's friend.' His voice gradually grew louder, his eyes gleamed, as fascination overcame discretion and he warmed to the black romance of Gelli's exploits and his great acquaintance. 'He's a counsellor of the Argentine embassy in Rome as well; he got oil from Gaddafi for Argentina.'

On and on went the recitation of mystery, chicanery, deceit and betrayal. The war. The disappearance of the Yugoslav gold reserves. 'Thirteen hundred cases! Sixty tons of ingots! Two tons of old coins! Six million dollars! God knows how many diamonds! Whipped away under the Nazis' noses!' His short spell as a parachutist, ended by a broken arm. His sudden, strange appearance, grandly uniformed, as a German interpreter in the Republic of Salò; when he was known to speak no German. His still stranger liaison with a group of anarchists, with whom he had stormed a Nazi prison. His involvement, or non-involvement, with the murder of a Fascist Republican, when he swore he'd been shooting only at a couple of Germans. His post-war jobs as chauffeur to a Christian Democrat deputy, public relations man, bookseller, manufacturer of mattresses. Then – in a whisper, again – his vast assembling of documents and secrets. 'Ah caro professore! If you could study those documents, what history you'd be able to write!'

'And the Masonry?' I dared at last to ask, but not even in full flow would he be drawn on that.

'Lascia star,' he muttered, 'lascia star, let it be.'

Padua was not a city that I knew very well, but it was one that always heartened me. With its ancient churches, its sublime statuary, its cloisters, its fine old university, it still, when I reached it, seemed the last place on earth to find such murderous conspiracy, such political ferment, such unforgiving

231

hatreds. Yet Padua had been involved in an infinity of wars. Padua was intimately known to Hawkwood, had employed Hawkwood, had given him the chance to win his greatest battle. My previous visits had been made to consult the city archives, seeking his story, but those were in the days before the Red Brigades had given the city its new and dark association.

I arrived there early the following afternoon, and went to the small hotel not far from the station where I had usually stayed in the past. It seemed strange that I was not here, now, to study and admire, to wander about the glorious churches, tombs and statues, to gaze again at Donatello's bronze horseman, Gattamelata, wishing, as I always had, that there had been a Donatello to do as much for Hawkwood, to put him on horseback not as Uccello had so synthetically done, but as the sculptor had put Gattamelata. How much more might I have known about him had his face, too, been modelled from life, in such strength and symmetry! From my hours of looking at the statue, I had gleaned something of the old mercenary's combination of authority and humanity. Hawkwood, a hundred years earlier, must surely have looked a little like him. From such a statue, by such a sculptor, I might have divined more about what happened at Faenza and Cesena than from any archive.

I did not want to call either of the numbers Lucetti had given me from the hotel. In Padua, I could not be quite sure. I called both from a public kiosk, and got a response from neither. So I went to the questura and asked for the decent policeman, Pacione. I was not sure how much I should tell him, nor exactly what I wanted to ask him. I wanted to know something about Barbuti, I wanted some indication of who, in Padua, ran the Red Brigades, and whom ideally I should try to see. I did not want to speak too much about my own mission, and what I had formulated of my intentions.

Inspector Pacione was there, and he did not keep me waiting long. His bare little office reminded me of that of his friend, Inspector Roccomonte, in Bologna. He was a man in his late thirties, with a handsome, Nordic face, bright, watchful blue eyes, wiry, receding blond hair, a short, straight nose. 'I know about you,' he said.

'From your colleague?' I asked. 'Inspector Roccomonte?'

'Not just from him,' he said. 'You are becoming quite famous in Italy, Professor Cunningham. To tell you the truth, I'm a little surprised to find you here at all, let alone in Padua.'

'If you mean I'm in danger,' I said, 'I assure you I've been in danger in England.'

He did not look at me, but began to roll a pencil up and down his desk, smiling a close-lipped, mirthless smile. There was no need to speak. 'Here in Padua,' he said, at last, when I would not break the silence, 'we are in the front line. I don't know how well you know Italy.'

'Fairly well,' I said.

'But not Padua.'

'I've done research here.' I said.

He turned his vivid blue eyes on me again. 'What kind of research?'

'Historical research. I'm a mediaevalist.'

He gave an ironic grin which was almost a grimace. 'Things have changed,' he said. 'Here in Padua, Padua now, we have extremists of all kinds. I don't know why. We are an ancient city. An ancient university city, as you know. Universities have often bred radicals. They have often been the centre of unrest. But this is different, Professor Cunningham. I don't think you would understand. I believe you teach at Oxford. You see, it's not so much the students who are dissident here as the faculty. The professors. It's they who set the pace. They who stir things up. They who are preaching revolution. Violence. Murder.'

'The Red Brigades, of course,' I said.

'Do you know much about them?'

'Something.'

'They know about you,' he said, and this time stared long and hard into my face.

'I rather thought they did.'

'Certain things happened,' said the Inspector. 'Involving you. I'm not sure exactly what. A shot was fired in Rome, I believe. Apparently you saved somebody. Someone who wasn't supposed to be there. I think you know who I mean.'

'I think I do.'

'Then something happened in England. In Oxford, in London. Again, we're not quite sure. But we have heard.'

'You seem to know quite a lot,' I said.

He shrugged. 'It's our business to know. We collect a great deal of information. Our problem is to act on it.'

'I think I understand.'

Another look. 'Perhaps you do. But you clearly don't understand the risks you are running. Coming here. Where the Red Brigades are strongest. Is that why you did come, Professor Cunningham, by any chance?'

'Partly,' I said. 'There's someone else who interests me too. His name is Barbuti.'

Now his head positively jerked up, as though controlled by a wire. 'Mario Barbuti? What do you want with *him*?'

'I've just heard a lot about him.'

Now he picked up the pencil and began scribbling on a pad, no pattern, no picture, only a hatching and a shading. 'Il dramma di Padova,' he said, 'the fate of Padua is that it seems to attract terrorists. From Left and Right. From all over Italy. Barbuti makes bombs. We know he makes bombs. I've often interrogated him. I've had him in this office a dozen times. But it's hard to get proof. Certain people are, let's say, protected.'

'Yes, I know.'

'I'm not quite sure what you're about, Professor Cunningham,' he went on, 'why you should be in Padua. What you want. Why you're even in Italy at all. I know your wife has been killed. I'm very sorry about that. But I advise you to leave Padua. In fact I *ask* you to leave Padua; as soon as possible. It's not an order. I can't give you an order. But for your sake, for *our* sake, I am asking you to leave.'

'I won't be here long,' I said.

'You should leave today. Even tomorrow could be too late. In other words . . . If you stay here, you cannot expect us to protect you.'

'I don't,' I said. 'Any more than I expect it of the English police.'

I got up, thanked him, shook hands with him, and left. He gave a short, resigned movement of his blond head, and opened one of his files.

I walked through the narrow, mediaeval streets to the Piazza del Santo, to commune with the statue of Gattamelata and to think of Hawkwood. I needed to think of Hawkwood, who would have treated such a warning with disdain. So must I. I

234

could have died in Rome, in Oxford or in London; why should I not survive in Padua? The knowledge that Hawk-wood had fought and flourished here gave me, as had his memory on other occasions, a warm yet irrational comfort. As I studied the great bronze, as I yet again examined the strong, familiar face, I thought of Hawkwood riding, striding through the little streets, hero of Castagnaro, scourge of Verona, champion of Florence, giving Padua a last victory before Milan reached out to swallow it up.

As I turned away, finally, from the statue, deciding to call the two phone numbers again, a grey car stopped in the road almost opposite me. A dark-haired, well-built young man in an overcoat jumped out, and ran across the pavement to me. 'Are you Professor Cunningham, from England?'

'Yes,' I said.

'Then you must come with us. It's something important.'

Before I could reply, he had hold of my right arm, and was hustling me towards the car. My immediate instinct was to resist, at least to cry out, but he urged me, 'Non si preoccupi, non si preoccupi, don't worry!' and it was sufficient for me to hesitate. Next moment, a second young man, this one with red, wiry hair, had jumped out of the car, pulling me backwards with him, while the other one pushed, and I was wedged on the back seat between them, while the car accelerated away. The driver, I saw, was a fair-haired girl, wearing a green beret. Beside her was another young man, tall, with blond, wavy hair, wearing a camel-hair coat. Instinct, again, told me that they were not Fascists. They seemed tense and determined, but I sensed none of that malignity which characterised Enzo and Guido.

They did not threaten me with knife or gun, nor did they speak, until I spoke to them, the car by now having threaded its way through the old town, past the railway station, and out towards the periphery of the city. 'Who are you?' I asked.

'You'll find out,' said the young man who had first approached and seized me. He looked straight in front of him. I found myself less frightened than curious, hopeful, if anything, that this would give me a short cut to those I wished to meet, to what I needed to know.

'You're Red Brigades aren't you?' I asked.

'Pazienza,' said the red-haired man.

235

We were out in the country, now, travelling between midwinter fields of stricken olive trees and barren vines. I did not try to talk to them again; nor did they speak to one another. At length the girl, driving fast, turned off the main highway, on to a steep side road, where she drove between stone walls, till at last we reached an open, barred, wooden gate. Through this she turned, stopping before a rustic, two-storey house and a cluster of farm buildings. Hens picked and clucked about the yard. 'Andiamo!' said the dark man beside me. He opened the door of the car, and leaned back to grasp my arm.

'There's no need for that,' I said, jerking it away. For a moment, he seemed to wonder whether he should grab me again, then he stepped back, and allowed me to get out, the red-haired man close on my heels. The air was very cold and exhilaratingly fresh. The girl driver and the tall man got out of the front of the car. The girl herself was above middle height, dressed elegantly in a long, tight blue coat. The dark man led the way to the front door of the house, turning twice to make sure I was following him, then took the heavy, iron knocker of the door and banged it in a complicated tattoo. A moment or so passed, then the ponderous wooden door was slowly, creakingly opened, to reveal another young man, swarthy, tall and squarely built, with a boxer's broken nose, carrying a sawn-off shotgun in his hands. He looked at me, then at my escort, raising his eyebrows.

'Tutto bene, everything's fine,' the dark man reassured him, and he stood aside to let us pass.

'He's in there,' he said, nodding towards a door that led off the red-tiled hall. The dark man went to the door, knocked respectfully, and a man's voice from behind it called, 'Avanti!' The dark man opened the door, and stood aside to allow me in.

Before a log fire stood a middle-aged man of average height with rich, black, wavy hair, and a beard. He wore what looked like an English, brown sports jacket, blue slacks, and a silk scarf at his throat. He was smoking a small cheroot. His eyes were a deep brown, alert and intense. It was hard to imagine he would ever smile. 'Did he come willingly?' he asked.

'No trouble,' said the red-haired man.

The bearded man looked hard at me. He did not offer to shake hands. 'Professor Tom Cunningham,' he said, a statement, rather than a question. 'I, too, am a university professor. Or rather, I was. At present, I'm not in a position to attend the university.' And now he did smile, though it was scarcely more than a grimace, a wry, ironic twitch. With a gesture, he waved me towards a wickerwork armchair, a few feet away.

'Why have you come to Padua, Professor Cunningham?' he asked.

'Maybe to meet you,' I said. 'If you are who I think you are.'

'And who do you think I am?'

'One of the leaders of the Red Brigades,' I said.

'Assuming that's so, why would you want to meet me?'

'To have certain things explained.'

'Such as what?' he asked.

'Things that have puzzled me. Things that have happened in Rome. Things that happened in London, and in Oxford.'

'It's we who are puzzled, Professor,' the bearded man said. 'We want to know why you saved Sindona's life. We want to know why you still maintain contact with him. We want to know why you came to Rome to see Calvi on his behalf.'

'Well, I'm quite prepared to tell you,' I said. 'There was never any need to burgle my room in college, nor my cottage. There was no need to steal my notes in the British Museum, still less to shoot at me.'

'It was *you* who tried to shoot at *us*!' cried the bearded man, with sudden passion. 'Our man shot back in self-defence!'

'I had an air pistol!' I retorted.'

There was a pause. 'An air pistol?' the red-haired man repeated, sceptically.

'Then you were foolish,' said the bearded man. 'In the dark, a pistol is a pistol.'

'I suppose that's why I bought it,' I said.

'Why did you save Sindona?' he shouted at me, with renewed vehemence. 'Why did you want to protect such scum?'

Now that the question had been asked, I found it hard to answer. Why, indeed, had I protected him, unless it was a mere reflex action or, less laudably, I had hoped to preserve him for my own purposes? 'It was a natural reaction, I suppose,' I said, lamely. 'You come out of a hotel with someone you've been talking to, all at once you see someone else pointing a gun at him, your instinctive response is to warn him to get down.'

The bearded man strode forward, bent over me, and shouted into my face, 'But why were you with him in the first place? Why were you with him at all?'

His rage engendered in me neither fear nor anger, simply a desire to explain, after which we would have cleared the air, we would understand each other, I could ask the questions that I wanted to. To the bearded face so close to mine, so taut with impotent fury, I replied, 'I wanted his help'.

'Che schifo! How disgusting!' said the professor, contemptuously and, straightening up, he walked histrionically away, as though he could not bear to be near me. 'His help!' he repeated bitterly, his back now turned towards me. 'What help could you ever get from *that*? What comes from dirt but dirt? What comes from shit but shit? What you saved deserved to be destroyed! What you saved will go on spreading filth and corruption!'

'You don't understand!' I shouted, now consumed by rage myself.

'I understand!' he yelled back, rounding on me. 'You let him use you! You're still letting him use you! The way he's always used bourgeois people! When they thought they were using *him*!'

At this, I wholly lost control. 'My wife was killed, you bastard!' I shouted, and leaped up from my chair. At this, three of the younger men rushed at me, knocking me back into it, pinning me down there, while I lay panting, glaring with fury at the professor, who looked back at me with equal hostility.

'E come c'entra?' he asked me, 'how does that come into it?'

In my anger, I heaved and wriggled in the chair, almost pulled my right arm free, but was then pulled back again. 'She was blown up,' I said, 'on a train. I want to know who did it. Sindona was a means of finding out.'

Some of the anger seemed to subside in the professor. 'And has he told you?' he asked. 'Have you found out?'

238

'Not yet,' I said, 'but I think I'm on the way.'

'Thanks to him?'

'Partly thanks to him.'

He gave me another of his brief, bitter smiles. 'I doubt it,' he said. 'Sindona promises; he doesn't deliver. In gaol or out of gaol. Let him go,' he told the three men, and they released me. 'I had heard about your wife,' he said. 'And in London I know you knifed a Fascist.'

'Yes, that's true,' I said. 'In self-defence.'

'The important thing is that you did it. What does Sindona want from Calvi?'

'Two hundred and fifty thousand dollars,' I said.

'He'll get what he always gives everybody else; a promise. Calvi has no money. He hasn't had any for years. Whatever he gets, he has to use to pay off a debt, and that just creates another debt. But how would going to Calvi help *you*?'

'It might lead me to Gelli,' I said.

Once again, the impact of the name was instant and stunning. The professor fell silent, and though I could not see the faces of the other four, all standing behind me, there was a palpable tension in the air.

'Why Gelli?' asked the professor at last.

'Because I'm sure he knows. Because he may well be responsible, himself.'

'What isn't he responsible for?' asked the girl, speaking for the first time. She had an engagingly deep voice, with a Northern inflection.

'And did Calvi tell you where to find Gelli?' asked the professor.

'Probably in Uruguay,' I replied.

'He may well stay there,' said the professor. 'It can't go on for ever. Even in Italy.'

'The Masonry?' I asked him.

'You know about it?'

'Something.'

'No one knows everything; except for Gelli. It's too vast. Too unthinkable. Even for here. Though when it all comes out, which it must and it will, then nothing will seem unthinkable.' Anger began to rise in him again; his voice grew louder, he spoke faster, the expression in his eyes became implacable. 'Then they'll see that we've been right! Right in everything we've said! They'll see that our way is the only way! That things have gone too far for any kind of compromise or accommodation! That to build, we must first destroy! Knock down the whole dirty, stinking structure! Annihilate all the filthy rats that come scuttling out of it! From top to bottom; but especially at the top! The corrupt politicians. The corrupt judges. The corrupt police. The corrupt Secret Service. All of them, everyone! Make a bonfire of the lot! Do to them all what we did to Moro!'

When he had finished, he was out of breath, panting, his chest heaving. He seemed quite unaware of me, now; his eyes seemed fixed on some invisible Grail. From behind me, I heard the red-haired man mutter, 'You're right,' and the others followed him. 'You're right, you're right!'

'Did you hear?' the bearded man asked, lowering his gaze, turning it back to me, again. 'What hope is there for the young? What hope is there in this so-called democracy? Everywhere they look, they see cynicism and chicanery. Everywhere. In the courts, in the government, in the Vatican! They see corruption rewarded! They see a man like Gelli more powerful than anyone in Italy! A Fascist! A fixer! He calls it Masonry! Macchè massoneria! Masonry be damned! That's just a name; like Mafia. A name for conspiracy. A name for modern Italy. If they didn't all get together under one flag, it would be another.'

'I supppose it would,' I said, thinking of the world he would build, which in the end would be no better, merely harsher, crueller, the terrible swift sword succeeded, in time, by a new kind of conspiracy and corruption.

'You're an historian,' he said, as though it was a crime.

'Yes,' I said.

'Well, *I'm* an historian too. At least, I used to be. Of modern European history. What a fraud! What a farce! Just one more way of endorsing the Establishment; telling lies about the past! Even Marxist historians; they're still worse, because their training should tell them that they're doing something futile! That every day they spend in universities is a day lost to revolution; a day spent supporting the swindle!'

'Bravo!' said the girl.

'You, too,' the professor rebuked me. 'You're an accessory. Even in England. Even where things are better. But

240

only quantitatively. It's still capitalism. There's still corruption. Even if you haven't got the Mafia and the Masons and the Church.'

'That's a very Marxist reading of history,' I said, 'and of historians.'

'But you *are* an accessory!' he told me. 'You even saved Sindona!'

'We must agree to differ,' I said. There was no possible dialogue.

'There's another thing,' said the professor. 'You've been associating with the Lotta Permanente group, in Rome. Claudio Della Martira was with you in the Piazza Vittorio, the night that you saved Sindona.'

'You shot at him as well,' I said.

'There was some confusion. It was his own fault, for being there. What was he doing?'

'I've no idea,' I said, 'I've never asked him. Just observing, I think.'

'Lotta Permanente planned to kidnap Sindona,' said the professor, 'the way we kidnapped Moro. But they're amateurs. They'd undoubtedly have bungled it. Groups like Lotta Permanente hinder the revolutionary struggle. Objectively, they can be said to be working for the opposition.'

'*They* certainly don't think so,' I said.

'What they think is unimportant. The thinking of all these little groups is essentially romantic. You are still in contact with them, in Rome; we know that. Do they have any plans for Calvi?'

'They haven't told me,' I said. 'I know they're watching him.'

'I would advise you to have no more to do with them. You are only putting yourself in danger. There are powerful forces at work in Italy which I don't think you could possibly comprehend.'

'I think I comprehend them better than you think,' I said.

'In that case, I need not explain to you why you should give up your links with Lotta Permanente immediately.'

'Thanks for your advice,' I said. 'I have one question for you.'

'What is it?'

'While I'm in Padua, can you help me to find Mario Barbuti?'

'Barbuti,' said the dark young man, wryly. 'That isn't very difficult. He doesn't hide himself. He knows he's not in any danger.'

'Precisely,' said the professor. 'Why do you want to find him? Do you suspect him of blowing up the train your wife died on?'

'Yes, I do.'

'It's quite feasible,' the professor said.

'There's no problem finding him,' the red-haired man said. 'He teaches in the girls' liceo, not far from where we picked you up. And he eats in the student mensa.'

'Scum,' cried the professor. 'Fascist shit.'

'He's a maniac,' the dark man said. 'We've watched him often enough. He usually leaves, most days, about half past five. Or you can find him at lunchtime in the student *mensa.*'

'My thanks,' I said. 'And now, if you're agreeable, I should like to go.'

'All right, all right,' said the professor, irritable and distracted. 'We've nothing more to say to you. Certain things have been explained. Tell nobody you've been here. No one you've met me. No one at all, you understand?'

'I understand.'

'Not that they'd find us here,' he continued. 'We leave as soon as you're gone. Drive him back, Franca,' he told the girl. 'Only you. Take a different route.'

'Goodbye, then,' I said. I made no effort to shake hands with him. I did not want to. I did not loathe him, as I had the Fascists, but I found him in his arid self-righteousness, his vengeful idealism, profoundly antipathetic.

On the drive back into Padua, Franca was unexpectedly friendly. I sat beside her as we sped through the darkening countryside. Her driving, with its pace and impetuosity, reminded me of Teresa's. Indeed she herself, though so different in build, colouring and accent, reminded me a little of Teresa, with her suggestive, frequent smile, with a manner that verged on flirtatious. More poignantly, her easy, humorous self-possession made me think of Simonetta, though her complexion was higher and more Nordic. 'Are

242

you really a Professor of History at Oxford?' she asked. 'How splendid!'

'Splendid?' I said. 'I thought your group condemned it as counter-revolutionary.'

'Oh, yes!' she said. 'In the long run. The final analysis. But it must still be a marvellous life: in Oxford. I studied history here, in Padua, with the professor. I'm still nominally at the university, but as you can imagine, I don't go there very much. It's sad about your wife. What was she doing in Italy?'

'She was Italian,' I said. 'A Florentine.'

'What a shame. How terrible. Barbuti could well have done it. They're always using him for vile things like that. They may even have used him in Bologna. He was interrogated, I know. But they're all protected, these people. There are even rascals in the Secret Service who want to blame us for it. Fabricating evidence; just as they did when the bank was blown up in Piazza Fontana.'

'Yes, I know about that.'

'The professor's right about Claudio Della Martira; he *is* an amateur. You should keep away from him. From all that lot.' She laughed. 'In fondo, è papagallo. He's a "parrot" at heart.'

'You know him?' I asked.

'Yes, I do. Bello, ma cretino. Handsome, but an idiot.' I glanced at her. Her eyes were shining, as though at some endearing memory. 'I hope he doesn't get himself killed,' she said. 'He's playing games. It's just a new obsession.'

'What does Barbuti look like?' I asked her.

'Fair. Thin. Not very tall. You'd never take him for what he is.'

'So I've heard.'

She turned to look at me, to my alarm, as the car careered on. 'What will you say when you see him? What will you ask him? "Was it you who blew up my wife?"'

'I suppose so,' I replied. 'Eventually.'

'Here!' she said suddenly, 'Take this,' and, reaching into the pocket of her elegant blue coat, only her left hand, now, on the wheel, she pulled out a small automatic pistol, with a mother of pearl handle. A 'woman's gun'.

'Have it!' she said, thrusting it at me, as I hesitated.

'I couldn't possibly.'

'Take it, take it!' she said, impatiently, thrusting it at me,

243

again. 'I've got others, if I want them. You're going to need it!'

The car swerved across the narrow country road, and partly in my wish to restore her hand to the wheel, I complied, taking the little gun, thanking her, putting it in the pocket of my jacket.

'I'll drop you by his school,' she said. 'You can wait for him, there. He should be out quite soon. Ask the porter to tell you which he is.'

We were on the outskirts of the city, now, then back in the city itself.

'Do you like Padua?' she asked me, as if talking to a tourist.

'Very much,' I answered, inadequately.

Passing through its streets and squares, by its churches and porticoes, I was assailed by a strange sense of ambiguity; as if a great museum had come suddenly to malignant life. The walls, the cupolas, the colonnades, the statues, for so long no more than glorious mementoes of a lost past, had given birth to a new and virulent Padua. It must, I thought, have been somewhat the same in Nuremberg, when the Nazis came to power. The mediaeval relic made modern, but in the most negative and poisonous sense.

'Here we are,' she said, at last, stopping the car. 'I'm Franca, by the way.'

'Yes, I know,' I said.

'I hope I see you again. I wish you luck. That gun's quite good, at close range. There's a full clip in it.' She leaned across, kissed me on the cheek, and I climbed out of the car. With a wave, she drove off again, and went quickly round a corner.

XII

It was almost half past five. Girls were emerging from the school, laughing, chattering, linking arms, full of a joyful, exuberant life which made the narrow orthodoxy of the professor and his like seem alien and remote. Yet it was not. When these pretty, vital girls, with their long, loose hair, their glowing eyes, had gone on to the university, had fallen, perhaps, under the malign spell of others like the professor, they themselves might be among the next generation of terrorists. The thought seemed at once absurd and repugnant. Equally absurd was my own position. Again, I was a cork on the water, having my life lived for me. I had found the Red Brigades without even trying; now, it seemed, I was about to be pushed into meeting Barbuti, with no plan, no preparation, prey to a situation I had not created, a gun in my pocket again, the immediate future an enigma.

But I approached the porter, in his lodge, as Franca had suggested. I asked him to point out Barbuti to me, and he, at least, seemed to find the request quite normal, saying, 'He should be out quite soon. I'll tell you when he comes.'

I hovered uneasily outside the lodge, as the pretty, lively girls swept down the stairs and past me, books beneath their arms, some giving me, as they passed, quick, questioning glances.

'There he is!' the porter exclaimed. And there, indeed, he was, much as I had imagined him, a pale, lean, blond young man in his middle thirties, wearing spectacles, dressed in a long fawn raincoat which seemed to have been made for someone taller, carrying a briefcase, pattering quickly through a crowd in which, ordinarily, he would not have drawn my attention.

I asked him, 'Dr Barbuti?' and he turned toward me with a violent start, quite excessive in the circumstances, had I not known who and what he was.

'What do you want?' he asked, apprehensively. His voice was surprisingly deep. Behind the rimless glasses, his eyes were blue and very pale, strangely devoid of expression.

'I'm an English professor; from Oxford. I wanted to talk to you.'

'To me? Why to me? About what?'

'Italian politics,' I said, frantically improvising. 'The beliefs of the young.'

He stared at me, with intense suspicion. It was hard to look back into the pale eyes. 'How do you know about me?'

For a moment, my mind went blank, then, all at once inspired, I told him, 'Annabel Carlton.'

For a moment, he continued to stare into my face, unrelenting. It was a risk. If he knew of Annabel, he might

245

well know Enzo and Guido; if he knew them, he might know what had happened to them, and put two and two together. 'She had Italian friends,' I said. 'Friends from the Far Right. She looks after them, in London.'

At last, his lean face relaxed. 'I think I've heard of her,' he said. 'She's helped some friends of mine. But who are you, exactly?'

'My name is Cooper,' I told him, on another impulse. 'I specialise in modern Italian history, especially on the growth of Fascism.' Conquering reluctance, I extended my hand. There was an hiatus, then he took it. His fingers were limp and cold. I felt contaminated.

'Can we have a drink?' I asked him. 'A coffee?'

He hesitated, again, then he said, 'A coffee, yes. But not for long.'

We walked in silence out of the building, through the continuing, bright, stream of girls, some of whom saluted him, though he barely returned their greetings, with a slight, morose elevation of the head. Out in the mediaeval streets, he took long, quick strides, rhythmically swinging his brief-case, paying me no attention, until at last he stopped in front of a small, unadorned bar.

'We can go here, if you like,' he said flatly. We sat down in a corner at an iron table on blue-painted iron chairs which shrieked across the floor. Two men were drinking coffee at the bar.

'Buona sera, professore,' the man behind the bar greeted Barbuti. 'What can I get you?' He ordered an espresso, I asked for a grappa. He didn't drink, he said. I found it easy to believe. There was a kind of bleak, Robespierrean asceticism about him. In other circumstances, I reflected, looking at him, he might even have been a monk. An Inquisition monk.

'Well then,' he said.

'What interests me,' I began, 'is how Fascism has changed. How it differs, for example, from Fascism as it was till 1944; from neo-Fascism as it was, in the years that followed the war.'

He answered gravely, without looking at me. 'At bottom,' he said, 'Fascism has remained philosophically the same. It has obviously had to adapt itself to changing realities. To the technological advance in Western society. To the new

246

realities of political power. To the alteration in Communist strategies. To the different role played in Italy by the Catholic Church. To the modified nature of the Jewish conspiracy.'

He was a very different animal from Enzo and Guido, but, in his more cerebral way, just as repugnant. I could quite imagine him killing people, blowing up people, not for the sadistic gratification, but out of a cold, perverted sense of necessity.

'At the end of the war,' he said, 'Fascism was momentarily demoralised. It had been betrayed by Communists and self-seekers in Italy. It had lost its great leader. Its exponents were being murdered, imprisoned, exiled and persecuted. Most Italian politicians and left-wing intellectuals, most of the corrupt Press, most of the Western so-called democracies, had written it off.' He pushed his coffee cup across the iron table with a clatter, leaned back in his chair with an expression of deep satisfaction, and said, 'But they were all wrong.'

'Quite evidently,' I forced myself to say, but he seemed not to hear. His face continued to reflect the same self-satisfaction, the same apparent sense of vindication. 'It took more than twenty years,' he continued. 'Twenty years for the youth of Italy to begin believing again. Twenty years for the propaganda of the Church and the Jews and the Communists to lose its hold. To be discredited. To be shown up for what it is. Lies!' he cried, in a new, harsh, angry voice, which caused the two men sitting at the bar to turn round. 'A filthy, vile attempt to distort the truth, and turn Italy away from her destiny! The old men couldn't turn the tide. They kept Fascism alive, but that was the most they could do. We lost a whole generation; to the soft life, to the corrupt life. But then the young began to see what was happening; how Italy had been sold out and betrayed. They saw how the greatness it achieved under the Duce had been lost. They saw how Communism had been allowed to creep its way into every corner. They saw how the Christian Democrats, the Church and the Jews were buying and selling Italy. And they rebelled! They began to fight back! Just as the squadristi had fought, after the First World War! And they will conquer, as the squadristi did! They, too, will march on Rome, when the time comes!'

247

He did not trouble to lower his voice. One of the men at the bar slipped off his stool, and walked quickly out. The proprietor, assiduously cleaning glasses, gave no overt sign that he had even heard.

'That's fascinating,' I said. 'I've never thought of it like that. That Fascism jumped a generation.'

As though emerging from a kind of trance, he turned his cold, pallid gaze back to me. 'It's only the beginning,' he said. 'There's much to be done. Sacrifices to be made. By people, and of people. Sacrifice by those who fight to restore Fascism. Sacrifice of those who get in the way. Intentionally or innocently. It makes no difference, objectively.'

None, I thought, none, and wanted to smash my fist into his cold face. 'Carne, carne!' Once again, I found the words surging up in me, violent and primitive. How easily he might have killed her; my wife! How negligible a thing it would have been to him! I looked away, hoping I could conceal my growing rage, wondering whether I could see my plan through, could stomach what he said.

Neither of us spoke, for a while. Finally I recovered control of myself, and turned back towards him, though I avoided looking at his face, asking him if he would like another coffee.

'All right,' he said flatly. I ordered another grappa for myself, which I drank off at once, gaining a little relief from its raw, immediate impact. I must ask him something, I realised, to get him talking again, and I said, 'How long do you think it will take to succeed?'

'When it happens,' he replied, 'it will happen very quickly. Like the March on Rome. It all depends on the ground being prepared. That's what we are doing now. One or two attempts have been planned, but they were premature, and they aborted. Those who planned them belonged to the older Fascism, or they were not true Fascists at all. It is the new Fascism which will triumph. But I couldn't tell you exactly when. Nobody can.'

'Perhaps we could have dinner,' I said. 'Perhaps we could go on with this.' It was the next move in a plan I had almost formulated, though in its final outline, it was vague. Stay with him, dine with him, if I could bear it, then go back with him either to wherever he lived, for preference, or to my own hotel room. There, I would at last drop disguise, and ask him

248

what I wanted to know. This, however, was the second delicate moment in my converse with him. Less crucial than the first; after all, if I could not keep him with me now, there might be other opportunities, where in the first instance, to lose him might have been to lose him for good.

There was, as I had anticipated, a hesitation. Then he said, in the same flat, graceless way, 'All right,' and stood up. He led me through a dark network of little alleys to a small, rudimentary trattoria. There was blue and white chequered oilcloth on the solid, unvarnished, rectangular wooden tables. The one at which we sat down was still scattered with breadcrumbs, crumpled paper napkins, rivulets of spilt wine. Though it was still quite early in the evening, the room was already almost full of men in overalls, boiler suits, donkey jackets, loudly talking and arguing, with hardly a woman to be seen. Barbuti seemed popular there; several of the men looked up to greet him deferentially as we came in, and the proprietor, a large, bald man with heavy forearms and a crooked scar across his forehead, came over, smiling, to shake hands with him. 'Buona sera, professore, come andiamo?'

Barbuti nodded, as if acknowledging the greeting, rather than returning it. I found it hard to eat at all though, unlike Barbuti, I ordered a quartino of red wine. It was rough and unpalatable. He ate a large portion of spaghetti al sugo, the red and white mound consumed with a zeal that belied his slender looks. To my relief, he did not talk as he ate, attacking his food with a distracted concentration. I ordered a steak, but regretted it when it arrived; it was meagre and stringy. Barbuti's second course was duck; again, he did not speak at all as he ate.

I racked my brains to think of how I could start him talking again, for the momentum must be re-created, we – or he – must still be speaking as we finished our meal, just as we had in the bar. It was only when the coffee came that conversation began again. He had spoken merely to the waiter, and once to a young man with long, black hair swept carefully back, wearing a red anorak, who came quickly and furtively into the trattoria, bent to whisper in Barbuti's ear, received a whispered response, and hurried out again, exchanging greetings with the big proprietor as he went. I felt uneasy in

249

the place; there was something inimical about it, a curious, throbbing undercurrent of menace. From the gestures around me, the belligerent tone of the voices, I had the impression of a lurking violence. It was a place where Enzo and Guido would have been at home. There was no outward or visible sign of Fascism, no photographs, flags or insignia, but the feel of it was unmistakable.

In so disturbing an atmosphere, it grew harder than ever to address Barbuti. When finally I did so, it was to say, 'But if the Fascists take power, can they *hold* power?'

This was more of a challenge than I had meant it to be, and as his bleak eyes turned on me, I wondered whether it would offend him. But he said, 'There would obviously be difficulties. The Jewish lobby in the United States. The Communists here, who might always get support from Russia. But if we could hold firm only for a few months, I believe our revolution would spread. We'd have support from South America immediately. And things would move again in Germany. They've had enough of democracy. They've had enough of Red terrorism. When they saw what was happening in Italy, they would follow our example, just as they did between the wars.'

'So you think that terrorism is counter-productive?' It was a question I could not resist, though I hoped that in this form, it was camouflaged.

'The Left uses violence as an end in itself,' he answered. 'We use violence as a means to an end.'

'To destabilise the State?' I asked.

'Precisely. Left-wing violence may achieve the same effect, which serves our purpose; just as it did in the 1920s, when we had to respond to the terrorism of the Left. Because when the State is eventually destroyed, it will fall again not to the Left, but to us.'

'Then the Left are playing your game.'

'Effectively. It was the same in Weimar Germany. Fascism knows that violence is necessary. Fascism knows that violence can purify. Fascism knows that violence is an essential arm of the State. It must express the virility of the State. But controlled, creative violence is one thing; anarchy is another.'

As he expounded his perverse logic, I felt anger beginning to consume me again, and struggled once more to suppress it.

250

Later, I told myself, later. 'Aren't you going to require a leader?' I asked. 'Another Mussolini?'

At the sound of the name, heads turned to us from nearby tables. Barbuti seemed to ponder the question for a while, before he said, 'That was another epoch. There will never be anyone like that again. Great men are the product of their own, historical time, although they change their time. But because he existed, because he gave us an example, it's less important now to have such a man. His example will always be with us. His memory will always inspire us. No one could take his place; but no one needs to.'

'Is there no one who wants to?' I asked disingenuously.

'We have someone who might show the way. Someone who's capable. Someone with great connections.'

Indeed you have, I thought. Someone who orders bombings. Someone who engineers frauds and swindles. 'But not another Duce?' I said.

'How can there ever be another Duce?'

I ordered more coffee for each of us. The moment was very near. In a grotesque, parodic way, it was like an attempted seduction. At length I said, 'There's so much else I'd like to ask you. Details I'd like to fill in. Points that I'd like you to clarify. I know it's getting late; but I have to go back to Rome tomorrow.'

What would he say? The hiatus was infinite. With careful nonchalance, I asked the waiter for the bill and seeing this, the proprietor came over to us; had we enjoyed the meal? Oh, yes, I said, of course we had. Barbuti gave him merely a brief double nod. Then the bill had been brought, the proprietor had gone, and Barbuti said, with morose indifference, 'My apartment's just round the corner.'

His apartment was very small, two floors up in an old and dank palazzo. On the front door, there was an arsenal of locks and bolts; with a bunch of keys as big as a gaoler's, Barbuti went through a protracted ritual of small detonations; no lock was turned less than twice; there were bolts which seemed to give out an endless series of metallic discords before at last they had been shot and yet another key was produced. The door itself, I saw, was seamed and scarred from what must have been numerous attempts to break it open. Clearly it had happened so often, and was expected to happen so often again, that he had given up any attempt to restore its appearance. Mauled, gouged, chopped and battered, it bore its wounds like some weathered old warrior.

At last it was open, and we were in what was clearly but one room, though a dark green curtain divided it across the middle. It was a small shrine to Fascism. Photographs, posters, mementoes were everywhere, in suffocating abundance. Photographs, above all, of the Duce, in fez, in military helmet, the massive chin always arrogantly tilted; in black shirt and boots, in pristine, all white uniforms; inspecting troops, shaking hands with Hitler, orating from balconies. There were posters, from the Fascist years, lurid and bombastic, conveying in their strident vulgarity the very spirit of the regime. There were other photographs of Hitler, a photograph of the Nazi troops jackbooting through the Arc de Triomphe. There were red, white and black swastika flags, SS daggers, an axe surrounded by the *fasces*. In a crowded bookcase which ran along the wall to the left of the door, *Mein Kampf* was sandwiched between *The Magic Mountain* and *The Sorrows of Young Werther*. Stacked in the far right-hand corner, I noticed what seemed to be coils of wire and cable, a large, transparent, plastic bag which contained what looked like lengths of white plasticine. It was here in this malign sanctuary that, appropriately, he made his bombs.

Yet his hatred, from what I had heard, was curiously compartmentalised; it did not seem to overflow into his teaching. Among those lively, good-looking girls, he was apparently a patient and conscientious teacher, though I wondered if he ever made a joke, if he ever laughed with them, if he was ever attracted to any of them. No, I could not conceive it. He was a monk indeed, a Savonarola perhaps, who would scourge and scarify, and turn away from all delights of the flesh; yet he would willingly destroy flesh.

He took off his long, strangely sinister, raincoat, put it on a hanger, and hung it carefully behind the door. He held out his hand mutely for my own coat, which, when I gave it to him, he hung from the same hook as his own. With all its putrid memorabilia, I realised that the little room was far from untidy. Indeed, its limited space was used with meticulous economy. Looking at him, I was reminded suddenly, with a frisson, of Himmler, whose cold, inhuman face, whose chilling eyes behind their spectacles, whose peaked deaths-head cap and immaculate black uniforms, had something of the same, aseptic tidiness, the same fastidiousness.

He sat down on a hard, upright chair beside a small table, on which lay several piles of books and a large diagram, drawn in green ink, of what appeared to be an electrical circuit. When he saw me glance at it, he spilled a couple of books on top of it, from one of the piles, then carefully re-aligned them. He did not ask me to sit down, but I did so, on a box-sofa which clearly doubled as a bed. 'I must tell you something,' he said relieving me, at last, of the need to start him talking again. 'I'm not a great lover of the English. The English have always been our enemies.'

'Always?' I questioned.

'Throughout this century. Our enemies in Africa. Then our enemies in Europe. They are still our enemies, but now there's no need for them to show it. If Fascism returned to power, we would see it again.'

I did not try to contradict him. It was only a matter, now, of waiting for the moment. I let my right hand fall, imperceptibly, to my pocket, and there, I felt the gun.

'Not quite in the same way, perhaps,' he said. 'Britain has no Empire now, and she will never get it back again. She hasn't the same interests in the Mediterranean. But when she sees Italy becoming strong, trying to expand, to fulfil her destiny, then you can be sure she'll try to impede her again.'

'And what is Italy's destiny?' I asked.

His eyes filled with the visionary light one had seen on film, in photographs, in Himmler's eyes, when he was with his beloved Führer, when he was inspecting or addressing his cherished SS. 'To be great!' he cried. 'Great as she was under the Duce! Great as she still would be, if she hadn't been betrayed! Great as Rome was, in the days of the Empire! A country purified of all racial trash! Of gypsies and Jews and perverts! Of slimy priests and crooked Sicilians!'

'An Italy that stops short at Rome?' I asked.

The visionary gleam disappeared from his eyes, the tension went out of his body, and he turned to look at me stonily. 'The true force of modern Italy has always been in the north,' he said. 'Rome was corrupted by a thousand years of the Papacy. Mussolini renewed it. It can be renewed again.'

253

It was now that I asked him, 'You make bombs, don't you?'

This time, the light in his eye was one of suspicion and hostility. 'Who told you that?' he demanded, looking at the table in front of him, where the diagram lay, then to the corner, and the mysterious plastic bag.

'Your Fascist comrades in London,' I said.

'*Who?*' he snapped. '*When?*'

'What does it matter?' I replied. 'It's true, isn't it?'

My change of tone had plainly taken him aback. For the first time, I saw him disconcerted, the icy self-sufficiency breached. 'What if it is true?' he said. 'What affair is it of yours?'

'Just that you might be able to help me,' I said, 'to clarify something for me.'

'What? Clarify what?' He seemed ready, at any moment, to spring out of his chair; to flee, or to attack me, or to snatch up some weapon. I was not sure. Meanwhile, I slid my hand into my jacket pocket.

'There was a train blown up,' I said.

'What train? What are you talking of? I don't know anything about it! If you mean the Italicus, I had nothing to do with it! I was interrogated! I was persecuted! They never proved a thing against me!'

'No, it wasn't the Italicus,' I said.

'You've deceived me!' he cried. 'You've tricked your way in here! You're not interested in Fascism! You don't care about our philosophy! You don't care about our struggle!' The tone in his voice was that of a petulant and disappointed child. 'Get out of here!' he shouted at me. 'You're a liar! You're a cheat! You're probably a spy!'

'No, I'm not a spy,' I told him, 'but there's a few things I want to ask you about.'

He began to start up from his chair, but as he did so, I pulled the gun out of my pocket, and pointed it at his heart. 'Sit down,' I said. It was a moment that gave me an enormous pleasure. All the detestation that I felt for him, all the horror he aroused in me, were given sudden, joyful release. He sat back again, staring at me with a mixture of fury and astonishment. He did not speak. I had the gun, and with the gun I could make him talk, though I knew that somehow or other, by whatever coercive means, I would have done so, anyway. Should it turn out, as I suspected, that he had bombed Simonetta's train, I was uncertain what I'd do; knew only that I would do it in the moment, on the impulse that possessed me. Kill him, wound him, spare him; I was a cork on the water again, even when I might seem most clearly in control. I would know what I must do only when I had to do it.

The rage must have been apparent in my face, for in his own face I noticed now a trace of fear. 'The train was blown up last year,' I said. 'On 4 March. At exactly 11.46 in the morning, travelling north from Florence, nine and a half kilometres short of Bologna. My wife was on that train, and she died.'

As I spoke, as he heard the details, an odd expression of relief, almost a smile, passed across his face, and in that instant, I sensed he had not done it.

'Then it wasn't me,' he said.

'You've blown up trains,' I said, still pointing the gun at him. 'Why shouldn't it have been you?'

'It wasn't!' he cried, and his voice rose. 'It wasn't! It couldn't possibly have been!'

'*Why* not?' I shouted at him. '*Why* shouldn't it have been?' and I thrust the gun towards him.

'Because I was in prison!' he said. 'I was in Rome! I was in Regina Coeli!'

When he said that, I felt a surge of disappointment. I realised that I wanted to kill him, that I wanted an excuse to shoot him. His repellent face seemed to hang like a moon in front of me, to the exclusion of anything and everything else; its expression of relief, even satisfaction, was more enraging to me than even the cold venom I had seen in it before. I heard the words, 'Carne, carne!' in my head again, and tried to banish them. I must not shoot him. I must not kill him. Yet I was longing to kill him.

'Prove it!' I said. 'Go on, prove it, you bastard!'

'Yes!' he said eagerly. 'Yes, I can! I've got a newspaper! I'll find it for you!' and he began to get up, saw the gun still pointing at him, and frantically sat down again. 'I have it!' he said, speaking in a quick, tremulous, ingratiating voice. 'It's in the next room! I'll fetch it!'

'I'll come with you,' I said, and stood up, motioning, with the gun, for him to stand up, too. I wondered for a moment if he might leap at me, and, keeping my finger tightly round the trigger, half hoped that he would, but he simply, if nervously, rose in his turn and turned his back on me, though not his head, and sidled across the room, looking at me, till he reached the dark green curtain. 'Pull it right back,' I told him. He complied, revealing a space in which clothes hung from a rail on the far wall, a small, old fashioned, iron porcellino stove stood in the left-hand corner next to a couple of green filing cabinets, while half-open doors on either side disclosed a minuscule bathroom with basin, lavatory and shower on the left, a still smaller kitchen with a sink and electric cooker on the right.

'It's in there,' he said, gesturing towards one of the filing cabinets.

'Open the drawer, then stand back,' I commanded. 'If you try anything, I'll shoot you.'

'I won't!' he said, 'I won't, I promise you!'

'Then do it,' I said, waving the gun.

He pulled open the upper drawer, then fairly jumped away from the cabinet. I came round to the other side of it and looked in; it seemed to be full of coloured folders. I saw no kind of weapon. 'Which folder is it?' I asked.

'The blue one.'

I waved him away from the cabinet, took out the blue folder with my left hand, and passed it across to him. 'Find it for me,' I said. With shaking fingers, he opened the folder, pulled out a page from a newspaper, which he held towards me, and pointed at it with an oscillating finger.

'There!' he said.

I took the paper from him with my left hand. 'Turn your back to me,' I told him, 'and clasp your hands behind your head.' He hesitated, manifestly frightened. 'Go on,' I said, 'I shan't shoot you, if you behave yourself.' At this, he obeyed. Holding up the page, which came from the Roman newspaper, *Il Tempo*, I saw that its date was 20 March, 1980. A small news item on the Cronaca di Roma page had been marked in blue. 'The neo-Fascists Aldo Cucci, 26, Mario Barbuti, 34, and Domenico Pizzolini, 30, were released from Regina Coeli prison yesterday,' it read, 'after three weeks' investigation by the examining magistrate, Dr Mauro Invernizzi, pursuing his inquiries into the unexploded bomb found last month in the left luggage office in Stazione Tiburtino.'

'Turn round,' I ordered, and let the newspaper fall to the floor.

'You see?' he said, dropping his hands from his head, turning to face me again, his expression now that of a condemned man who has been vindicated. 'I was in gaol! You see? I couldn't have done it!' It was almost as though he had gained a victory over me. He gave out a subdued sense of triumph.

'Who did it, then?'

'I don't know,' he said, in a pantomime of innocence. 'I've no idea.'

'Of course you have. You Fascists did it; it's your filthy speciality. *Tell me!*' And I found myself shouting at him, in my anger, my frustration, my intense desire to know. As he cowered in front of me, I took a step forward and pressed the barrel of the revolver against his forehead. 'Tell me! Who was it? *Tell* me!'

'I can't, I can't!' he shrieked back. 'I just don't know!'

'You must do! You all know one another, you dirty, murdering Fascists! Tell me, or I'll kill you!'

'You'll have to kill me, then! I'd tell you if I could! I wasn't in on it! I was in prison! You've seen for yourself! It could have been any one of twenty!'

On that impregnably cold, Nordic face there were now pearls of sweat. Sweat ran in a little stream from his left temple, beneath his glasses, over his cheekbone, down to the sharp promontory of his chin. I did not know whether I believed him, I knew only that I was not going to shoot him, and I felt a sudden, great reaction, one of weariness and anticlimax. I was condemned to go on.

'Give me your keys,' I said, as I watched him, not in hatred now but in disgust and contempt. 'Throw them on the floor.' I pointed the gun at his face. He took out the great bunch of keys, and dropped it on the floor. 'Now lie down,' I told him. 'Face downwards, with your hands by your sides. Looking away from me.' Again, he complied. I bent down, and picked up the keys. 'You've been lucky,' I said. 'If you *had* killed my wife, God knows what I'd have done. You don't deserve to live. It sickened me to listen to you. Fascism is dead. It will

257

never rule this country again. All it can do is what *you* do, and people like you. Kill and maim innocent people.' He neither spoke nor stirred. 'As for your Duce, he was a clown. Un buffone. A big bladder of wind. More corrupt than any Pope. He brought out the worst in Italy, not the best.'

The body twitched on the floor, then was still again. If I were to take a revenge, perhaps this was the best that I could have. 'He was a thug and a bully and a fraud,' I said. 'He didn't make Italy great, he made her pitiful. He nearly ruined her. He left a curse on the country. You are part of it. What makes you people any different from the Red Brigades? You both murder people for your stupid perverted ideologies. You both do vicious, brutal things, and pretend you're doing it to save Italy. But Italy *has* been saved. It's been saved from swine like you. Swine like Mussolini.'

As he lay there, I felt a great desire not to shoot him but to kick him, as an ultimate sign of my contempt. I drew back my right foot, knowing that I would not do it. Then I turned and walked quickly out of the flat, through the front door, wondering if he would try to follow me, with some weapon of his own.

Shutting the scarred door, I looked at the great bunch of keys and wondered, for one helpless moment, which would fit the plethora of different locks. One long, mortice key would surely fit the lowest keyhole. It did, and I turned it. Then, with a Yale key, I found another lock, and turned that too; once, twice, three times. That should be enough.

I ran down the stairs and made my way out of the building and through the streets, until I found myself in a piazza I knew, then made my way back to the hotel. I dropped the keys in the street.

XIII

Calvi received me, on my second visit, with a kind of melancholy resignation. 'I'm very sorry,' he said, 'you must tell Dr Sindona that I'm unable to pay him. At this moment, I can't pay him anything.'

'Very well,' I said. It was nothing, after all, to do with me, and to be cast again as a debt collector, a bilked one at that, embarrassed me.

Calvi's face, today, was that of a sad, old dog. Whatever he might have done, it was hard not to feel sorry for him. 'This is a difficult time for me,' he said. 'I have many obligations. In a few months, things may have changed. I hope so. In that case, perhaps, I can pay him some of what he wants. If this doesn't satisfy him . . .' He gave a heavy hopeless shrug. 'He will have to do what he thinks best. I shall have to run that risk.'

'Very well,' I said, and we sat staring at each other. There was a pathos about him, an air of muted appeal, not so much to help him as to forgive him, to understand him, to see him as he had been, rather than what he was.

On an impulse, I found myself asking him, 'Are you a Mason?'

The question made him start out of his silence. 'Why do you ask me? What has it got to do with anything? Are *you* a Mason?'

I had a further impulse to say yes, but I shook my head. I was sick of masquerade. 'You are,' I said, 'and Licio Gelli is.' He looked at me in silence, this time almost reproachfully, till eventually he asked, 'Did Sindona tell you that?'

Now I did lie. 'Yes,' I said. There was another pause. This time he dropped his gaze, as if he had been caught out in something shameful. I found myself watching his moustache, with a kind of fascination. It seemed more than ever irrelevant, a flamboyant gesture in the void, something belonging to a brief, more dashing past, which could never be revived. Looking up again, he said, 'Ha un significato relativo. Its significance is relative. A means of mutual co-operation. Of getting help, when help is needed. When other people may refuse help.'

'Like the Vatican?' I asked.

His gaze grew sadder than ever. 'You're evidently well informed,' he said. 'It's not a plot. It's not a conspiracy. They say some people have been blackmailed into joining. By certain other people. Not me. Not in the least. I needed help, and I was offered help. That's all it is.'

'I see,' I said, and wondered if his spoon was long enough.

259

'I'd have preferred to meet you in other circumstances,' he said.

'Perhaps we shall.'

'I hope so. I hope so. Lei mi sembra una persona per bene. Anch'io in fondo sono una persona per bene. You seem like a decent person to me, and so am I, at bottom.'

'I'm sure you are,' I said. And still would be, perhaps, but for meeting Sindona.

'But there are certain people,' he said, 'certain people in the world, who corrupt what they touch. Corrupt whoever they meet. I don't think I need to explain myself.'

Did he mean Sindona? Did he mean Gelli? Did he mean both of them? Had he hired Satan to drive out Mephistopheles? I simply nodded.

'As for Licio Gelli,' he said, 'I can tell you he is in South America. Either in Montevideo or Buenos Aires, I'm not sure. He moves between the two. He has many friends and interests in both.'

'Will he be back?'

The eyes became opaque. 'I don't know. It's hard to say.'

'Thanks,' I said, and stood up.

'I'm sorry I couldn't do more,' he said, standing up in his turn. 'The next time, perhaps.'

Then I had left his room, left his suite, gone past the gorilla who, even had he frisked me on the way in, would have found nothing. My gun was locked in my suitcase, back in my hotel room. When I heard from Sindona, or his minion, I would tell him that Calvi couldn't pay. Once more, I walked out of the hotel, up the Via Veneto, as fast as I could, as though I were escaping. The day was bright and cold, the sky a pure and cloudless blue, against which towers, cupolas and trees stood out with crystalline immediacy. The city's beauty was irresistibly seductive, even to those as wary of it as I was. Its spell today was absolute, however treacherous.

I was expected by Teresa at three o'clock, in the apartment. 'I should be alone,' she had said casually, 'but if I'm not, it makes no difference. How are you? How was Padua? Did you find any Fascists?'

'Oh, yes,' I said, 'I found the Red Brigades as well. Or rather, they found me.'

'Ma pensa! Just think! Then you'll tell me all about it!'

260

'Yes, everything.'

Before I lunched, in the Via della Croce, picking my way through the exuberant, guitar-strumming young who, even in winter, thronged the Spanish Steps, I went back to my hotel in the Via Sistina and, for no conscious reason, took the little automatic out of my case, and put it in my pocket. Then, lunch over, I rode across Rome in a taxi, enjoying again the glories of the light. In Piazzale Ostiense the pyramid, too, was resplendent in the sun, with a massive, austere elegance.

I pressed the bell push of Teresa and Della Martira's flat, and heard the buzzer sound. There was no answering buzz; the front door stayed closed. I buzzed again. Still there was no reply. I looked at my watch. Eight minutes past three. Perhaps she had gone out, and had not yet come back. Ten more minutes passed. I buzzed a couple of times more. Then an elderly woman in a black coat and hat came up to the front door and opened it with a key. I walked in behind her and followed her to the lift saying, in vague extenuation, to assuage any fears, 'My friends . . . they expected me at three.'

She stayed in a corner of the lift, watching me uneasily, but I got out of it before she reached her floor. I hurried down the corridor with a sudden, growing feeling of apprehension which became unbearable, a small explosion in my stomach, when I found that the front door of their apartment was ajar. I stopped, pulled my automatic out of my pocket, and cautiously shoved the door still farther open with my foot, then stood listening. No sound came from the apartment. I peered round the front door. The door of the living-room was closed. Then, looking down, I saw with horror that a flow of blood had seeped under the door, running about a foot on to the dark brown tiles of the hallway.

I stepped across the threshold, seized the handle of the living-room door with my left hand, flung it open, then stood instantly back, out of sight of anybody in the room. There was no sound or movement. Cautiously, I took a step forward, the gun extended, then another, till I could see into the room. The blood came from Sandro's body. It lay a few yards from the door, on its back, his eyes and mouth open, as if in frozen astonishment. Blood ran out of the mouth, blood was still running from at least three wounds in his body; he had been shot both in the chest and the stomach. The blood had seeped

261

through his thick, blue jersey, flowed sluggishly across the tiles of the floor, and under the bottom of the door.

Beyond him, on the sofa, lay Della Martira, his body contorted, right leg raised, right arm flung out, as though, when he had been shot, he had been trying to leap off the couch. A bullet had gone through his forehead, just below the line of his blond, abundant, wavy hair. From the bullet hole, a line of blood moved in a slow rivulet down his handsome face, beneath the habitual dark glasses. Blood had smeared the gold chain and medallion that he wore around his neck, had reached his expensive, blue silk shirt, but had not touched his leather jacket, which hung open, unbuttoned. There was nothing to be done for either of them; both were quite manifestly dead.

But where was Teresa? Had she escaped? I prayed she had escaped. I looked desperately around the room, behind the sofa, behind armchairs; there was no sign of her. I ran out of the living-room, past Sandro's body, down the corridor to her own room, where, again, the door was shut. In my frantic anxiety, I took no precautions, simply twisting the door handle, bursting into the room, hoping, hoping to find it empty.

But she was there. There, face down, on the floor, the back of her head blown off, leaving a mess of blood and pulp and brains so horrifying that I wanted to vomit, had to look away, went to the window, opening it, to breathe in the cold air for a few minutes, until at length the spasm had passed. Even then, I stayed at the window, fearful of looking at the grotesque sight again. Perhaps she had run from them, towards the window, in a pitiful attempt to find help, to cry out in fear and anguish to the street below.

I had to look at her. It was my duty to look at her. The last tribute, however futile, that I could pay her. Finally, I did look, turning very slowly, seeing the body, the poor, mangled head, closing my eyes, opening them again, finding them now full of tears.

The gun was still in my hand. I put it back in my pocket. Had they, the three of them, tried to use their guns? If they had, it had obviously been too late, and since there was no sign of them, whoever killed them had probably taken the guns away. They'd been professionals, obviously. Fascists.

Mafiosi. Hired hit men. Professionals, where poor Della Martira, as they all seemed to say, had been an amateur. Perhaps it was he who had exposed them to their cruel deaths, he who had somehow blundered, letting the killers in, giving them their chance. Who'd ever know? Yet for the others, too, it had seemed a kind of game, however lethal. It was dangerous to stay, I knew, but I forced myself to go on looking at Teresa. In death, she seemed pitifully small, like a stricken child. She was wearing blue jeans, and a purple woollen shirt which had ridden up her back, disclosing the dark, firm flesh. I wanted to turn her over, to look one last time at her strange, ironic face, but it seemed like a further violation. I walked slowly out of the room, turning for a final look, feeling, as I went, as if I were somehow betraying her.

I walked past the door of the living-room without entering it again, then, half-alarmed, half-ashamed, realised I had turned its door handle, and the other's, too. I took out my handkerchief and wiped the handle of the living-room door, then went back to Teresa's room and wiped its door handle as well. I walked to the still open door of the apartment and peered out carefully into the corridor. There was no one. I slipped out, leaving the door of the flat ajar, as I had found it. I did not want to use the lift; it was bad enough having shared the lift with the old woman in the first place.

Where were the stairs? I tiptoed down the corridor, past the lift, and found the stone staircase behind a door on the right. I ran down it, still on my toes, as fast and as quietly as possible, reminded as I ran of the night at Annabel's. There was nobody, when I emerged, in the small vestibule, no one in the street outside. I tried not to run as I went quickly round a corner, then, in a large detour, made my way back to Piazzale Ostiense. I did not take a bus from there; I continued to walk, until at last I reached a Metro, which took me back into the centre of Rome. The day was still cold and beautiful, but it held no allure for me now. I knew I must leave Rome, and leave it soon, but not too soon, for that, too, could be risky. I wondered, as I walked, if I should phone the police, and changed my mind about it half-a-dozen times. To phone them, or even a newspaper, in an accent they might identify as foreign, could at once start speculation; which could lead, eventually, to me. And this is Italy, I thought, not England;

however fast the police got there, what could they find? Whom could they hope to catch? And whom would they even want to catch? I must leave Rome, I thought, but not Italy; but if I stayed in Italy, it should be somewhere where I did not have to register, or leave my passport. With my in-laws, perhaps, though I would not like to use them in this way. Even with Aldo. Besides, it was another five days before my excursion flight was due; though that was unimportant.

Then all such marginal thoughts were swept away by the memory, the enormity, of what I had just seen. They were images, I knew, which would stay with me for the rest of my life, would swim into my head when it was least prepared, would plague and torment me in the night, hover before me when I woke, lurk somewhere beneath the surface of my mind, never to be exorcised. Never before had I seen a body so brutally violated. Yet in a strange way, I was shocked, rather than surprised. It had been coming. It had been in the wind, on the cards, the dreadful corollary to all that had been happening to me. More, had I been asked to guess a victim, I would probably have named Della Martira, who had the mark of nascent disaster on him; a role player in a world of murderous authenticity.

Did that apply to me, I thought, with sudden alarm? Was I equipped to move and survive in such a living nightmare? Was I not an amateur, blundering about among deadly professionals, escaping through luck, rather than courage or resource?

When I reached my hotel, like a refuge, the large, dark, jocular porter was on duty behind the desk. 'A lot of messages for you,' he said, 'from America, too,' and he thrust a handful of paper slips at me. I took them from him, with a hand that trembled, mumbled my thanks, and went up in the lift, fumbling through them. Five of the messages asked me to phone Sindona's contact number in New York. The others were from someone unknown to me, calling himself Rocco; Sindona's henchman, no doubt. I reached my room, slammed the door shut, locked it, lay down on the bed, and shook. I wanted to weep. I felt very cold, though the heating was on, and I had not taken off my overcoat. I was still trembling when the telephone rang, and a man's voice which I did not know, deep and southern, said, 'Professore, buona sera. I'd

264

like to meet you, in case you have news for me, and our mutual friends.'

'I have no news for you,' I replied, 'none at all.'

'None?' said the voice, disbelievingly. 'You haven't seen our other friend?'

'Yes, I saw him this morning. His answer is no. At least for the moment; no. He cannot do what he has been asked to do.'

'We must meet,' said the man. 'It seems to me essential we should talk about this. My people will be very concerned.'

'No doubt they will,' I answered, 'but there's nothing to discuss. And I can't see you, at the moment. For various . . . reasons. I have your number. I'll call you if things change.'

'I'm sorry, but this is vitally important. Before you leave Rome, I must see you. How long will you be here?'

'I can't say,' I said, 'it depends on a lot of different things. I'll call you, I'll call you,' and I put the phone down. Then I picked it up again. 'I don't want any more calls,' I told the porter. 'Not till further notice.'

Amidst the sensations of shock and nausea and grief was another; one of guilt. In some way I could not identify, I felt I had let the three dead people down, was in some obscure sense responsible for their murder. Yet what could I have done? Convey to them my feeling they were in peril? Warn them that if they persisted in their plans, they might be killed? What reasons could I have given but the merest intuition? They would have derided me. Most sharply of all, I felt that I had let down Teresa. I had made love to her; I could and should have done more to persuade her.

More than ever, I felt utterly alone; I could not share my misery with anybody. Certainly not with my parents-in-law, if I alighted on them. There, I would have to dissimulate, go through the ritual motions, hope they would attribute my melancholy, again, to Simonetta's death. In my despair, I thought, as I had done before, of Hawkwood, who took carnage for granted, who walked among mutilation and the wounded with compassion at best, indifference at the worst. 'Carne, carne!' The words, now, took on a macabre and fearful resonance. I had, indeed, seen flesh, shattered flesh, mangled flesh, dead flesh. How could I ever get inured to that? What consolation could it be to think that a man, if exposed often enough to butchery, would take it, in the end, for granted? And yet, perversely, I did derive a kind of consolation, if only to think that he had been through such things so long before, l'inglese italianato, a fellow Englishman; had been through so much more and so much worse, quantitatively at least, emerging in the end with a kind of rough dignity. Perhaps there was, after all, a *modus vivendi* to be reached.

They had been killed because of Calvi; I was quite sure of that. Killed because, in their ingenuous zeal, they had been planning to kidnap him. It had leaked out, of course; and they were dead. Big predators gobbled up the smaller ones. Had Calvi known of this, even while I was talking to him this morning, when it could actually, simultaneously, have been going on? Perhaps he had, yet, unlike Sindona, it was not something for which I could think him responsible. Unlike Sindona, in the murder of Ambrosoli, he would not personally have engineered it. It would have been Gelli, I was almost sure, or a Gelli surrogate.

Then I began to wonder and to worry. When the bodies had been found, when the investigation began, how soon would it be before I was traced as the foreigner in the lift? The old woman would talk. I did not look Italian, nor entirely sound it. I had been to the flat before; somebody may have seen me then. And since there were no secrets in Rome, or did not seem to be, someone no doubt, some police informer, would know I had frequented Della Martira, as the Red Brigades knew. Again: if the police even cared.

I should have shut the apartment door, I thought, and wondered why I ever left it open; on a ludicrous impulse, perhaps, to leave everything as I had found it. But why should anyone expect the door to be open? And seeing it open, how much more likely it was that the bodies would be found.

I looked at my watch; it was almost time for the television news. I went below, in the claustrophobic lift; there were three more messages waiting for me, two from the mysterious Rocco and one from Sindona's contact number. 'They're very insistent,' said the hotel porter, raising his eyebrows at me.

The television set stood in a corner of the tiny ante-room, off the narrow hall. It flickered and burbled, unattended. I turned it to the correct channel, and watched the news when it came on. No mention of the murders; but there would be

266

other bulletins to come. Was I obliged to watch them all? I went back to the hotel porter. 'I'm leaving Rome tomorrow morning,' I said.

He glanced at the register. 'Va bene, professore. You were going to stay another four nights. Are you going back to England?'

'I don't know,' I said.

He gave me a quizzical look, but said nothing. It was at this moment that a large, broad shouldered man with wavy black hair and a full moustache came hurrying through the glass front door, into the foyer.

'Buona sera! Cerco il professor inglese Cunningham,' he told the porter. 'I'm looking for the English professor Cunningham.'

Before I could stop him, the porter had indicated me with his head. The man turned to me in delight, gripping my hand. 'Molto lieto! Sono Rocco!' but I had guessed who he was. 'If you can give me ten minutes. Or would you have dinner with me?'

'No, I can't,' I said. My impulse was to shove him out through the door, but I conquered it, suggesting, 'We could go in the television room.'

He looked at it, and hesitated. Then he said, reluctantly, 'All right, then.' We sat down on a sofa. He did not take off his opulent cashmere coat, but he did, after a quick, uneasy look around, stand up again, go to the television set, and turn up the volume. He was a quintessential southerner, I thought, effusive, ebullient, obtuse. 'I had to come to you,' he said. 'It's very urgent.'

'Well, I've nothing to tell you,' I replied impatiently. 'Calvi won't pay, and that's that.'

He looked warily around him. 'It's better not to name certain names. Did he say why?'

'He said he hadn't got it, but he might have it later.'

'Disgraziato!' said Rocco. 'Of course he's got it. What's a quarter-million dollars to him, with what he's stolen? Doesn't he know what'll happen to him if he doesn't pay?'

For the first time, I noticed that he was carrying, incongruously, a red-bound copy of *I Promessi Sposi*, and wondered whether he had ever previously heard of it, let alone read it. 'He probably does,' I said, 'but that was his answer.'

'You're quite certain?'

'*Yes!* Go and see him yourself, if you don't believe me!'

'Pazienza, pazienza!' he replied, but I had no more patience with Sindona's squalid extortions. I got up; Rocco, too, hastily rose. 'If there's anything else, will I be able to get you here?'

'No, you won't,' I said. 'I'm leaving.'

'Leaving!' he said, taken aback. 'I was told you'd be staying several more days.'

'Well, I've changed my mind, I'm going. Probably back to England,' I lied, anticipating his question. He looked displeased.

'Have you told our friends in New York?' he asked.

'Our friends in New York State?' I said. 'No, I haven't. Tell him yourself, if you want to. I've done what I promised him I'd do.'

With the same air of surprise he nodded and extended his large hand. 'Molto lieto,' he said formally, though he did not look in the least happy. I took his hand without enthusiasm. His very shoulders, as his cashmere coat passed through the glass front door, reflected his displeasure.

I went upstairs and telephoned my in-laws. The General answered, clearly surprised, if pleased, to hear me, more surprised still when I suggested that I might come to stay, though with characteristic punctilio, there was only a fractional hesitation before he said, 'Ottimo, ottimo, that will be splendid'. I wondered whether his wife would think it splendid, but she would accept it, I knew, with a facsimile of good grace. While I was there, I would go up to Bologna; would see Aldo but not Lucetti, because Lucetti would probe, Lucetti might guess, Lucetti did not keep confidences. I knew Della Martira, I had been in Rome, Della Martira was dead, I had left Rome. Ergo, I must surely know something. By tomorrow, surely, the news would be out, the search would be on.

Would I tell Aldo? It was possible. I had a desperate urge to share the pain and the burden with somebody, and I could trust Aldo completely. In Florence, I could plunge into the records; at the National Library, at the Uffizi, I could resume the comfort of my communion with Hawkwood, losing, or trying to lose, myself again in the turmoil of his age, pursuing

268

the *ignis fatuus* of what he had really done at Faenza and Cesena. I need never despair, never abandon the search; there was always another archive to explore, always a letter to be found from some minor member of the Signoria, a memorandum drawn up by or for a prelate, even, the ultimate reward, a letter sent by Hawkwood himself.

At two in the morning, Sindona rang and woke me. I had forgotten to tell the night porter I wanted no calls. 'Why didn't you ring me? Why didn't you let me know all this yourself? Why does my man in Rome have to ring *you*?'

'I was asleep,' I told him curtly, too weary and sickened to dissimulate.

'Asleep? I wish *I* could sleep! You know where I sleep? I sleep in a cell! On a bed like stone! I, who was used to living in the finest luxury!'

'He won't pay,' I said. 'That's all there is to it; he says he can't and he won't.'

'Then he'll pay in other ways!' shouted Sindona, careless in his rage, it seemed, of whoever might overhear him.

'You must do what you think best,' I told him. 'I'm sorry; there's nothing more *I* can do for you. I'm leaving Rome tomorrow. And now, if you'll allow me, I'm going back to sleep.'

XIV

I took an early train to Florence, bought half-a-dozen newspapers at Stazione Termini and opened one of them, tremulously, when I sat down in my compartment. It was on the front page. STRAGE NELL'OMBRA DEL PIRAMIDE. UCCISI CON COLPI DI PISTOLA TRE ULTRAS. 'Carnage in the shadow of the Pyramid. Three extremists, killed with pistol shots.' There were dreadful photographs of all three corpses, which brought back the scenes to me so clearly that I had to put the paper down, close my eyes, and try to clear the fearful images from my mind. Opening my eyes again, I put a hand over the photographs, and tried to read the text. The bodies, it appeared, had been discovered that evening by a neighbour, suspicious that the door of the apartment had been left open so long. There! I thought. Had I shut the door, who knows when the murders would have been discovered? The neighbour, a Signora Anconetani, had at once called the police. All the victims were described.

Sandro, it appeared, was a pregiudicato, who had been in prison for terrorist offences. He was from Fano, on the Adriatic, and had once studied engineering. He was twenty-eight. Della Martira was thirty, and had worked as a journalist. Teresa was only twenty-three. I found tears starting to my eyes. There were, at the moment, no suspects, though the police believed the crime had been committed by another extremist faction; though whether from the Right or from the 'Extra Parliamentary' Left, where they themselves belonged, was not yet clear. No message of any kind had been left, no claims of responsibility had yet been made.

In Florence, which I reached with an instant feeling of relief, even of escape, the General was pleased to see me; Laura, his wife, was plainly suspicious. Why had I suddenly decided to stay with them? The question was implicit in certain swift glances, certain brief silences. I could not really blame her.

Before dinner, when the butler, in his striped blue jacket, served martinis, the General pointed out the story of the murders in *La Nazione*. 'Poverino,' he said, 'poor fellow. He was a Florentine. Della Martira. I knew his father a little. He was a lawyer. A very decent man. He couldn't understand his son; why he suddenly got these strange ideas into his head. He wasn't a student any more. He didn't come from a poor family. He had a decent job.'

'Poveri genitori,' said my mother-in-law, 'his poor parents.' I made no response but an anodyne nod.

They put me in the room which had once been Simonetta's, and still contained her pictures, an ancient, pigtailed doll, books she had read as a child, a poignant scattering of ornaments and souvenirs. Her presence, there, seemed achingly real to me, the loss of her unbearably bitter. Was that why her mother had put me in this room? With a subtle malice posing as solicitude? I could not bear to be in the room, where even the peculiar sweet scent of my wife seemed to hang in the air. The evocation of her, vulnerable and young, made me think of the dreams of adolescence; and the brutal way that all her dreams had been aborted. Sometimes, I felt that she was there with me, and then I would wonder if she'd have approved what I was doing, or would simply have dismissed it, in the way she had, as a piece of silly self-indulgence, the pursuit of some macho fantasy. She had never approved of revenge; yet my quest had not begun as revenge, only as an attempt at discovery, at lifting the weight of bewilderment and pain.

'But look what's happened,' I could hear her beautiful, low, beguiling voice say. 'You've stabbed people. You've hit people. You've threatened people. You've made love to women as if I'd never existed. You've been running errands for a blackmailing crook. You could be in danger of your life. What's all that got to do with me?'

Everything and nothing, I thought. These are things that have happened, just as *your* death happened. Horrible, inhuman things that spring out of what Italy's become. Or what it always was. Don't blame me for what's happened to me. Don't blame me for trying to assuage my pain.

'So you're here again to follow your condottiere,' said the General, at the dinner table, 'the one whose name I can never pronounce.'

'Call him Giovanni Acuto, than,' I told him, as I had before. 'The Florentines always did.'

'Can you really expect to find anything new, after all this time? I mean, anything old that's new?'

'One lives in hope,' I said. 'Documents get lost. Records get ignored, or dispersed. Or forgotten in some palace or castle.'

'And that's how you justify yourselves, you historians. By discovering something new about the old. Like an explorer in reverse.'

'I wouldn't know how to justify myself,' I said. Less than ever now. 'But there's slightly more to it than that. It's not just discovery for its own sake, as far as I'm concerned; or discovery for kudos. I want to understand the man.'

'How can you hope to? He died six hundred years ago. It's quite a different mentality. I don't suppose *I'd* understand him, and I'm a soldier. A general like he was; or rather, not like he was. But what is it you want to understand?'

'A paradox,' I said. 'A decent man; or what appears to be a decent man. Whose troops take part in two appalling massacres.'

The General laughed. 'Other times!' he said. 'In those days, massacres were commonplace. In every city that got stormed. It was the fashion. That was a mercenary's perquisite. His bonus. That's how their generals paid them; especially when their employers didn't. You think your man was very different, because he was an Englishman? After all, he fought in Italy for years. We had plenty of time to corrupt him!'

'Oh, yes,' I said, 'l'inglese italianato. That was what they called him, as you probably know.'

'Precisely! More Catholic than the Pope! And with English troops, right? I'll tell you something about troops abroad. I've commanded them myself, in Africa. Morals disappear. They're like beasts let loose. And they don't regard the native inhabitants as fellow humans. I believe it was the same in Viet Nam. Didn't the American soldiers call the Vietnamese gooks? They weren't fully human; so what you did to them didn't matter.'

'But did *you* allow it?' I asked him. 'Did *you* encourage them?'

'I stopped them when I could. It's not always easy. Men get drunk. Men taste blood. Men run amok. Especially mercenaries. Your Giovanni Acuto probably couldn't have stopped them, if he'd wanted to.'

'According to report,' I said, 'he may even have encouraged them. First in Faenza, then in Cesena. He was carrying out orders himself.'

'There you are, then, that was his excuse! He didn't initiate it, he did what he was told. He was a mercenary. He followed instructions, from whoever paid him.'

'Or failed to pay him,' I said.

'Whoever employed him, then. You're too sentimental, Tom! It takes a soldier to understand another soldier. And to forgive him.'

'Perhaps.'

His wife looked at me and said, 'You've got a gun in your room.'

I looked back at her with a start. 'A gun?' I said.

272

'You left your case unlocked. The maid was unpacking it, this afternoon. Why have you got a gun, Tom?'

'What kind of gun?' the General asked me, with interest.

'Oh, it's just a little automatic,' I said.

'But it's a real gun, isn't it?' my mother-in-law asked. 'A gun that fires bullets. A gun that can kill people.'

How characteristic of her, I thought, that she should wait till she could achieve the maximum impact; springing her discovery not only on me but on her husband. 'I've had threats,' I said, not looking at her. 'My room in Oxford was burgled; and an intruder broke into my cottage, in the middle of the night.'

'Dio buono!' said my mother-in-law. 'But why bring the gun with you to Italy?'

'Because I think they come from Italy. The people who threatened me. The people who did these things.'

'You brought the gun to Italy?' the General asked, regarding me significantly. 'You didn't get it here? It isn't easy to bring guns through airports nowadays; unless you came by boat and train.'

'I flew,' I said. 'As a matter of fact, I got the gun here. Someone gave it to me. A friend. But I'm afraid I can't tell you who.'

The General continued to stare at me, clearly unsatisfied. 'Guns are dangerous,' he said, 'to people who aren't used to using them. And I can't believe that you are. Guns not only kill; they can get you killed.'

'I'm well aware of it.'

'May I see the gun? Where is it now, Laura?'

'Still in his case,' his wife replied. 'Tina left it where she found it. She was very frightened.'

'I'm sorry,' I said.

'Have you used it?' the General asked me.

'If you mean have I ever fired it, no,' I said.

'Have you ever fired a gun at anybody?'

I hesitated. Should I tell him? Of the shot I had fired into the Nazis' car, outside my cottage? And, telling him of that, explaining why they were there, what I had done to Guido and to Enzo, why I had been forced to do it, all leading back, inexorably, to the death of his daughter. It was something that I could not face. Gazing down at the table, I merely shook my head.

273

'I think you'd better leave the gun with me,' the General said. 'You'd be safer without it.'

Perhaps, perhaps not, I thought. If Barbuti and his friends, or even the unknown brutes who had killed Teresa, Della Martira and Sandro came after me, I'd like to have the means to defend myself.

'I'll think about it, if I may.'

'It's illegal, in any case, if you haven't got a permit,' the General told me, 'and I don't suppose you have.'

'No, I haven't.'

When his wife had gone to bed, the General poured cognac, and we sat in armchairs on either side of the fire. He smoked a cheroot. 'Ho l'impressione che hai sofferto molto,' he said. 'I have the impression you've suffered a lot.'

'Haven't we all suffered?' I asked, uneasily.

'Of course we have, of course we have. All of us who loved her so much. But in you, I've noticed a great change. I think this gun is part of it. I don't know how. I don't know why. But I know it has something to do with Simonetta being dead.'

'Indirectly, perhaps.'

'Indirectly, yes, that goes without saying. Now, I want to tell you something. As one who loved her, in his different way, as much as you did. In a father's way. We can't bring her back. We must accept that; however horribly she died, however arbitrary it was. You must decide to live. Sooner or later. Whatever you have in your mind, whatever you're trying to do, I don't intend to ask you what it is, I beg you to give up. The best way to get even is to live. To live on. To remember her, and love her memory. Don't let them destroy you, as they destroyed her.'

I sighed. 'You may be right,' I said.

'Explore the past, not the present. At least there's no danger in the past.'

But I knew there was no such dichotomy.

I took the gun with me next day to Bologna; not because I thought I might need it, but because I had nowhere to hide it, and was reluctant to surrender it to the General. I left early, though I saw him at breakfast, where he made no mention of it.

Leaving Bologna station, I had the customary frisson of dread, found myself again, for a moment of terrible illusion,

274

among the noise and the dust and the rubble and the agony, remembered, as I came out into the forecourt, how the taxis had been crushed and smashed beneath the masonry.

Aldo was in his office at the University, rising from behind his desk to greet me with his heartening, healing affability. The room had nothing in common with my own, in Oxford. It was modern and functional, crowded with gadgets; a word processor, a small computer with its screen, a tape recorder. There were shelves and shelves of books in meticulous order, neat stacks of historical journals, the inevitable wan, complaisant female postulant fluttering about the room, diligently submissive, painfully self-effacing, waiting, in an eternal limbo, for possible promotion in the hierarchy. She looked at me with nervous goodwill, offered a tentative, limp hand, and hurried out of the office.

'E allora,' said Aldo, sitting down again, and motioning me to do so, 'poor Della Martira is dead. It's surely something to do with that.'

'It is,' I answered.

The morning's papers still gave many columns to the murders, but had nothing of substance to add. The commissioner in charge of the case had been interviewed at length, but said virtually nothing. There were still no suspects, still no indication whether the killings had been carried out by Right or Left. Della Martira was described as a volatile and impetuous personality, drawn to extremist causes by an irresistible romanticism.

'Do you know something about it?' Aldo asked me.

'I found the bodies.'

He looked at me, and whistled. '*You* did? Before this woman?'

'Yes. The door was open. I walked in. Sandro and Della Martira were in the living-room. Teresa . . .' I found it hard to say this. 'And Teresa was in her bedroom.'

Aldo shook his head in dismay. 'Then you left,' he said.

'What else was there to do? I couldn't help them. Nothing could be done for them.'

'I'm not blaming you, Tom. Che brutta esperienza! What a horrible experience! Did anybody see you?'

'An old woman in the lift. She let me in when she arrived at the front door. I couldn't get an answer; obviously.'

275

He was silent for a while, then he asked, 'Why did it happen?'

'They were planning to kidnap Calvi.'

Aldo looked at me sharply. 'Davvero? Really? They must have been crazy. With Gelli protecting him. They surely knew about that.'

'That wouldn't have stopped Della Martira,' I said. 'If anything, it would have been an incentive. Two birds with one stone. One of them the biggest bird of all. "An irresistible romanticism." That paper's not entirely wrong.'

Aldo looked at me with an affectionate sympathy. 'It's hit you hard, hasn't it?'

I could only nod, unable to return his gaze, feeling near to tears again, not trusting myself to speak. 'Don't tell Lucetti anything,' I said at last.

'Of course I won't,' he promised.

'I'll go back to England, soon,' I told him. 'I didn't want to leave right away. It might have looked bad. The old woman must have talked to them; told them I got out on that floor, even if nothing's been mentioned in the papers, yet.'

'Well, she's your alibi. The police must know from their pathologists that the killing had been done before you arrived.'

'I suppose so,' I said. 'Do you think I should go to them now?'

He considered it. 'You're better off returning to England. There's a lot of things the police might want to know which you wouldn't want to tell them; and they might not believe you anyway. What were you doing at the apartment? How did you know the three dead people? You could be in front of the investigating magistrate for weeks.'

'You're right. I'll go home. But there's one other thing.'

'What's that?'

'I'd been making love to her,' I said. 'Teresa. That's why I was there.'

Again he looked at me with compassion. 'I did warn you,' he said. 'Not to get involved in all this. Not to get mixed up in our imbroglios.'

'Well, I am mixed up in them,' I said, and told him now about Barbuti, told him about the Red Brigades, the professor who had harangued me in Padua – 'Professor Muro,' he

276

said, 'it's bound to be him' – while he shook his head in wonder and concern. 'Leave,' he said, at last. 'For God's sake leave Italy. Leave and don't come back for years. Till all this is over. Till it's all been forgotten.'

'Oh, no,' I said, 'I have to come back. There's Gelli, yet. There's Gelli, now. I *have* to find him. I *have* to talk to him.'

He reached out and grasped my hand. 'For *my* sake!' he said. 'Forget it! Stay in England! You've escaped; by a miracle. But you can't escape indefinitely. You've seen what happens. You see what these people do to one another. Without thought. Without pity or compunction. Why do you think *you* can survive?'

'Aldo,' I said, 'I don't care. It doesn't worry me whether I survive. Don't you understand that?'

'No, I don't,' he said. 'I don't want to. That's how *they* talk. That's how *they* think. That's nihilism. The neo-Fascists. The Red Brigades. Poor Della Martira. People who want to die don't care about life; their own or other people's. Is that how you really want to be?'

'It's not what I want,' I said, 'it is what has happened to me.'

A strange thought occurred to me as I sat in the train, on my way back to Florence. That what had happened to me might also have happened to Hawkwood. That Hawkwood, too, had somehow lost his first wife, his English wife. That Hawkwood, the brave soldier in France, might have degenerated into the butcher of Faenza and Cesena not because he became italianato, but because, he, too, was courting death, and cared nothing for life; his own or other people's. As Emilia turned into Tuscany, as fields gave place to terraced hills, I rebuked myself for such baseless speculation, such morbid solipsism.

Yet the notion would not go away. It grew inexorably in my mind, putting out shoots and branches in implacable profusion. One knew nothing of his first wife, save that she had probably been English, had borne him two sons and perhaps a daughter, was meant to have accompanied him to Pisa. And then: what? Heaven knows I had laboured, as others must have done before me: looked in the British Museum Library; seen what there was to see in Sible Hedingham, where his tomb had supposedly been carved with two stone wives;

277

looked in the Public Record Office, in the Uffizi and the Biblioteca Nazionale; looked in the Pisan archives. There was no trace of her; nor any of the postulated daughter, save a gnomic reference, here and there, to a certain Fiorentina. I had given up the search, not least because I wanted to learn more about Cesena and Faenza, but perhaps there was nothing more to learn, except by indirection. If I looked harder for the wife, I might find, not exculpation, but at least a kind of resolution. In the couple of days in Florence that remained to me, I would dig in the Uffizi, at the Biblioteca Nazionale, and I would be digging for *her*, whoever she was, discovering, if I could, how she died and where, knowing only that it must be before 1377, the year he married Donnina, the daughter of Bernabò Visconti.

He was a faithful man, by all accounts – or lack of accounts – in an age of licence, of libidinous condottieri who sired bastards in abundance. He had stayed with his second wife, married off his daughters, uxorious, it seemed, until the day he died.

Had his first wife gone down with the plague? His daughter, too, if there was one? Had they been snatched and slaughtered by his enemies? Held for ransom, then perished in captivity? I was filled with an intense excitement, increasingly sure that this was not self-indulgence, mere identification, but a leap into rich new territory.

'You haven't given me the gun,' said the General, with muted reproof, when I got back to San Domenico. We were alone, again, in front of the fire, though standing, now, each with a drink in his hand.

'I've got rid of it,' I said, a little too quickly.

He looked at me with a nascent smile, as if to say that though he did not believe me, he would not be insistent. My mother-in-law's attitude, by contrast, was resentful. She spoke to me only when she had to, with a cold politeness which seemed, I thought, to amuse her husband. For the most part, she turned towards me her beautiful and elegant profile, which reminded me so painfully of her daughter's; except that Simonetta's profile was informed with a humour and intelligence absent from her mother's. I was in disgrace. I had brought a gun into her home. I had stayed elsewhere on almost all my other visits to Florence since Simonetta died;

278

now, when I finally and unexpectedly did invite myself, I had a dangerous weapon in my case.

Outside the villa, away from the Signora's hostility and the poignancy of Simonetta's room, Florence soothed and revived me. The very contrast with Rome, the very difference in its size and its beauties, were a solace. The perennially changing light, giving new definition, all the time, to the panoply of domes and campanili, the sombre regiments of cypresses that ringed the city, the mountains that appeared and disappeared through cloud, the khaki swirl of the river, enchanted me, as they had always done.

Only a scattering of winter tourists wandered the Piazza della Signoria, as I wandered it myself, on my way to the Uffizi, admiring yet again the petrified violence of the statues beneath the loggia and around the square, doubly affected by the soaring, rough elegance of the Palazzo Vecchio, where I had married.

If her name was Fiorentina, I thought, as I had thought before, she must have been born in Florence, or while Hawkwood was serving Florence. No English girl born in England would have been christened Fiorentina. Unless – theories, endlessly chased by counter-theories – she had been re-named when he came to Italy, or her name, like his, had been corrupted. I felt suddenly happier in the Uffizi, though day by day, I found nothing. But I was travelling hopefully now and, in travelling, in pursuing the quest, could lighten the impact of what had happened in these last days.

I looked at each morning's papers. The story of the murders was featured in them all, each day, but without the same sensational projection. The police commissioner continued to speak, but to say nothing. Only on the third day after the discovery was there a mention of a mysterious straniero, probably a German, who had entered the building with a woman tenant, and got out on the floor where the three 'extremists' had lived; and died. Asked about this, the commissioner had replied that the most strenuous attempts were being made to trace the man. My stomach contracted as I read this, till I reflected that if it had taken so long for my visit to come to light, they could not seriously want to find me. Perhaps because, as Aldo had said, they knew I could not have been the murderer; perhaps because, so long as I remained at large, I could be used to divert attention from the real killers. One way or the other, it seemed like a reprieve.

When I left Florence for Rome, the General drove me down to the station in his Alfa Romeo; it was an early train, and a good excuse for the Signora to remain in bed. Her smile, as she grudgingly offered me her cheek the previous night, had been the most fleeting of formalities.

'Ti vedo un po' meglio,' the General said, as we drove down the narrow exquisite, steep hill. 'Un po' più tranquillo. You seem better, to me; a little calmer.'

'Yes, I am. I think it's happened to me here.'

'With us? Or in Florence?'

'Both.'

The General laughed. 'English diplomacy. Don't take too much notice of Laura. She's in a strange state, still; it's understandable. When the gun was discovered, it upset her.'

'Yes, I'm sorry,' I said.

We did not speak again till we had reached the station. There he helped me take my case out of the boot, shook hands with me, looked warmly at me, and said, 'Tom: give up the gun. You don't need a gun. I've told you that. You're not a soldier, and you're not a gangster.'

We kissed each other on both cheeks, and I left for my train. He had moved me, but he could not persuade me. The gun was in my pocket. I would check it, suitably concealed, in Rome.

XV

'If you go now,' Sindona said, 'if you go right away, he will see you.'

'I'm teaching,' I replied, 'I have obligations.'

It was midnight; he had phoned me in my cottage; the first time I had heard from him since I was so brusque with him, in Rome. Now it was early March; I had lectures to give, tutorials to hold, my monograph to write, not an hour to spare in the day. I had been left in peace till now, thank God; no night-time visitations, no telephoned threats, no burglaries.

I flew to Pisa the next day. To my shame, I told the college that my mother-in-law was ill. I was as reluctant to do it as I was reluctant to travel; what certainty had I that Gelli would even be there, let alone that he would see me? How could Sindona, in a New York State prison, be so sure? It was expensive as well as inconvenient, yet the thought that I might miss my chance, the possibility that I might never be given it again, forced me to go. I would not stay in San Domenico. The pressures and tensions were enough as it was, without contending with my mother-in-law's frosty, tacit reproach. I would be in Florence, in Tuscany, for as short a time as possible. Gelli's villa was at Castiglion Fibocchi, near Arezzo. I had its telephone number to ring; I would be told when I could come; or so Sindona said. I would see Gelli; then I .would fly home. But when I saw him . . . It was this, more even than the uncertainty of whether I would do so at all, which consumed me.

What would he tell me? How would I react to it? What would I then want to do? My gun was in Rome, but there seemed little point in getting it. A man like that, who had been endlessly alert for forty years now, would surround himself with every possible protection. With a gun in my pocket, I would never get past his gates, let alone be received by him.

All the way down to London by train, all the way by aeroplane to Pisa, I rehearsed, almost feverishly, what might happen and how I would approach him. He was no Enzo, no Barbuti. There was no sticking a knife in his ribs, or a gun at his head, and persuading him to talk. He would tell me what he wanted to tell me, and he might not tell me the truth. How would I know? Yes, I had her train blown up. No, I didn't have it blown up. Or yes, I had it blown up, but of course I regret it greatly, there was nothing personal in it, if only I had known . . .

As the moment of meeting approached, it concentrated the mind wonderfully, making me realise how vague and unformulated my notions were about it, and about him. And, by extension, how vague they were about myself, and what I would do. I had proceeded with an almost mystical assumption that finding him, seeing him, would somehow be enough in itself; a resolution; that – as I had told Aldo and the rest – I would know what to do when it happened. But if I knew what to do, would I be able to do it? Not there and then, if it was anything violent; for I had found, now, this unexpected violence in myself. Had Barbuti said yes, it was me, yes, I blew up that train, I killed your wife, I don't care, would I have shot him, in that hideous apartment of his? With the rage he engendered in me, it had surely been possible; a rage which had left me almost disappointed, when he had proved it could not have been he.

That rage, potentially so murderous, would surely fill me again, if Gelli admitted his responsibility. And then? Then, with no gun or knife, only my bare hands, with armed men sure to be guarding him, what could I do; save fight down my rage, and wait? Wait for how long? I was not a Sicilian or a Sardinian, bound to vendetta. To this extent at least, the General was right. If vengeance obsessed me, it would destroy me. I did not care if I died, with Simonetta dead; but to live for nothing but revenge was worse than death.

I knew myself better now, knew a primitive side of me I had never been aware of, which could and had consumed me. That was the difference between my situation now, and what it had been when Aldo first warned me. L'inglese italianato. They had been there, the violence and the rage, and Italy had brought them out in me. At the same time, I retained the feeling that, when I met Gelli – if I met Gelli – something would be revealed to me. I did not know what. Something which would explain to me *why* Simonetta had died, why people should kill in this brutal, random way, why Italy should be a prey to them. It was about Italy, in particular, that he would tell me something, something which I did not yet understand, something which would reconcile me with a country I was steadily ceasing to love, a country which seemed, after so long, to be revealing its true essence to me, as I had had to confront my own.

Every trail, after all, seemed still to lead to Gelli. Each Fascist outrage seemed to have its origin in him. He had espoused Sindona, he had befriended Calvi, he might have murdered a Pope. And there was much more besides, revealed to me so far only in hints and glimpses, as though a curtain were being periodically, tantalisingly, pulled aside for transient moments. What I had seen and heard so far was only the tip of the conspiracy, I was sure, a conspiracy so massive and pervasive that it could barely be imagined. That, too, was something which I felt would be revealed to me, and in its turn would tell me about Italy.

I did not even know what Gelli looked like, had heard him only vaguely described, but he held for me a kind of putrescent fascination. There seemed a Luciferan quality about his life; a shameless, immoral odyssey, in which there was no place for anything but self-interest, in which blackmail, murder, robbery were simply means to an end. I was aware of the hideous attraction of pure evil; or at least, pure amorality. There seemed an awful sweep and scope to his life, a bold living out of what, in other people, would remain but half acknowledged fantasies. Hannah Arendt had written of the banality of evil, speaking about Eichmann, the repugnant little functionary, a Barbuti-figure, surely, with his pale-skinned, Nordic face, his spectacles, his dehumanised aspect. But Gelli did not seem banal. His, by contrast, was the flamboyance of evil, the romance of evil. What, ultimately, could he want? Did he see himself as a new Mussolini, a Fascist dictator, joining hands across the sea with the vicious generals of Buenos Aires and Montevideo? Or was it all no more than a diabolic game, played for its own sake as much as for profit, out of a Iago-like malignity, in which Fascism, Masonry, the Mafia were simply convenient disguises?

And then, beyond Italy, like seemed to call to like, brute to brute, Fascist to Fascist. The heritage of Fascism lived on in the world like a persisting poison.

Oh, but I wanted to meet him! So preoccupied was I that I did not even notice when the plane began its descent into Pisa, the Alitalia hostess leaning across with a discreet smile to tell me I should fasten my belt.

To be back in Florence this time gave me, as I emerged from the station in Piazza Santa Maria Novella, no release. It was raining, the light was grey and lowering, the taxi ride through the familiar, much loved streets to my hotel in the Via Porta Rossa did nothing to cheer me. A feeling of dread and expectancy consumed me, pulsing in my solar plexus. Once in my hotel room, I called the number of Gelli's Villa at Castiglion Fibocchi.

A woman answered. 'Signor Gelli, please,' I said. 'My name is Tom Cunningham. He's expecting me to call him. I have an appointment with him.'

'*Who?*' asked the voice. I spelled out my name, and there was a pause, then the woman said, 'Momento.' Sweat trickled out of my armpits as I waited. I felt as though I were hanging helplessly, endlessly in space. I listened intently for the sound of footsteps, and at last I heard them; then the phone was picked up again, and the woman said, 'Il Signor Gelli non c'è. Signor Gelli isn't here.'

'Isn't there now?' I asked, in desperation. 'Or isn't there at all? When will he be back?'

'I don't know,' the woman said.

'But is he at home at the moment? Is he staying at his villa?' Another hiatus. 'I've come specially to see him,' I said. 'From England. I've just arrived; I'm in Florence. He said he'd see me. Dr Sindona told me he would. At least let me know; is he in Italy?'

'Yes,' said the woman, 'he's in Italy,' filling me at once with a vast and disproportionate relief.

'Then what should I do?' I asked. 'When should I call him again?'

Still another pause, then: 'You can call him this evening'.

I flung myself back on the bed, feeling drained. He was in Italy at least. Whether he was at the villa, whether he would ultimately see me, were other matters. It would fit in well with his persona, from what I knew of it, to keep me waiting, facendo anticamera, as they said in Italy, dangling in suspense, giving up hope, till finally he agreed to see me. Perhaps I should simply hire a car and drive out to the villa, calling his bluff, if bluff it were.

In the event, I managed to restrain myself till early evening, filling the long, bleak, rain sodden afternoon first with a protracted lunch in Nandino's busy little trattoria in the corner of Piazza del Carmine, where I was greeted with a cordiality I found it hard to reciprocate. The two little rooms, although it was after half past two, were still full of eating, chattering people. Usually, I enjoyed the true Florentine atmosphere, the aspirated Cs, the chanted rhythms of the speech, enjoyed the sight, before and afterwards, of the massive, craggy walls of Santa Maria Del Carmine, but today

I was distracted. Was he there? Would he see me? The questions chased one another round my mind.

When I had eaten, there were still hours to fill. I wandered about the streets and squares in the rain, blind for once to their beauties, visited an exhibition of Michelangelo's drawings in the Palazzo Medici, but even their sublime mastery of contour and detail could not comfort me. I was waiting for six o'clock, six o'clock was the limit I had given myself, then I would phone and, if he still was not there, phone again, till it was too late to try, and then, after God knows what kind of night, I would start trying again in the morning.

I was back in the hotel at five. I drank a couple of cognacs in the bar, and the warmth of them gave me a fleeting relief. At quarter to six, I was back in my room; at six, with the same, burgeoning feeling of dread, I picked up the telephone, and called the villa in Castiglion Fibocchi. For what seemed an unendurably long time, the phone peeped at me, unanswered. At last, it was picked up, and this time it was the voice of a man that answered. Was it he? 'Signor Gelli?' I said.

'Non c'è,' said the voice, 'he isn't here,' and despair invaded me again.

'Will he be there later?'

'I don't know.'

'Then he *might* be? I'm Tom Cunningham,' I said, 'the Englishman. I rang before. I've an appointment to see him. Fixed by Dr Sindona.'

'Well, he isn't here.'

'Shall I ring later this evening?'

'He won't be here.'

'Then tomorrow? Will he be there tomorrow?'

'I don't know.'

'I'll ring tomorrow, then.' I said. 'Will you tell him I called? Tom Cunningham?'

He would not be there tomorrow; I was sure of that now. I wondered if there had ever been a chance that he would be there at all, and began to curse Sindona, who had sent me here, as much as Gelli, who might be playing games with me. More time to kill. I dined in the hotel, feeling too demoralised to go out to a restaurant, looking up the planes to England at the porter's desk, wondering how long to give it, how many more abortive phone calls, before calling it quits and flying home. After dinner, I turned on the television set in my room and watched a Western film, bizarrely dubbed into Italian, an inane quiz programme, endless new bulletins. I went on watching till every channel had closed down, then lay sleepless in bed, wondering not how I would react when I at last saw Gelli, but whether I would see him at all.

At eight the following morning, I went down to breakfast. I restrained myself till nine, then telephoned the villa again. This time, there was no answer at all. I tried twice more, still without reply. At half past nine it was the same; and at ten o'clock. I would hire a car, I thought, and drive there. It was at least a positive policy, however futile. I would try again at noon, lunch in Florence if I failed, then drive out to Castiglion Fibocchi.

Again, I wandered the city, looking now into favourite churches, into Orsanmichele, walking on to Santa Croce, making phone calls every half-an-hour or so from whatever cafe or bar I happened to be passing, always without an answer. Finally, I went back to my hotel room, and turned on the television.

Flicking from channel to channel, I found the news bulletin; and there was a face, confronting me from the screen, a face I had never seen before, yet somehow found relevant and familiar; that of a grey-haired man, eyes curiously hard and implacable behind his spectacles, the mouth, despite a full underlip, clenched and retentive. I wondered, vaguely, who it was, then heard all at once the name 'Gelli', and was instantly alive, staring compulsively at the screen, listening intensely to the words, seeing pictures of a villa – at Castiglion Fibocchi, I now heard – of men, clearly plain clothes policemen, carrying cases of what seemed to be documents out of the villa, and loading them into cars. My excitement was such that I could hardly take in the words that were being spoken: '. . . boxes of documents . . . thought to be a Masonic Lodge known as P.2 . . . some of the most respected and influential names in Italy . . . Gelli the Grand Master . . . no trace of him at present, though an active search is in progress . . . the implications said to be immense . . . after long and patient investigations by the police . . .'

The item concluded with one of the loaded cars being

driven out of the gates of the villa. I leaned back in my archair, my eyes closed, overwhelmed by myriad emotions. I was too late. Perhaps Gelli, or Sindona, knew I was going to be too late, and had brought me here simply out of malice. Of course no one would catch Gelli; I was sure of that. They wouldn't want to.

He would probably be out of Italy by now, if he had even been here at all, on his way back to South America, where the generals and his other fellow-Fascists would look after him. I wondered about the size of the scandal. It would, indeed, be immense, I was sure of it. Great men would be named, great reputations would crumble to dust. Robes and furred gowns would no longer hide all. I wondered how and why it should suddenly come to light; or, in my now developed cynicism, why it had been decided to bring it to light.

For my own part, I was deeply dejected. Gelli could hardly come back to Italy now, except, perhaps, on the kind of sporadic, clandestine visits made by Sindona. What hope had I left of ever seeing him, unless I could somehow track him down in South America? And how could I afford to go there, on what might well be another wild goose chase? The last, great, central piece in the malignant jigsaw would elude me for ever.

Lost in my gloom, I thought at last of Aldo and Lucetti in Bologna, and it was Lucetti I phoned, convinced that he would know more than most people about it; and be gleefully glad to tell me.

So he was. 'Carissimo mio!' he cried, from his newspaper office. 'Hai visto che casino? You've seen what a whorehouse it is? Didn't I tell you? That it was something big, something colossal? Everyone's in it, right the way up to the heads of government! It'll bring the government down, you'll see! Policemen, publishers, judges, Secret Services, Army officers! Industrialists! He's dragged them all into it! If they go on trial, who'll be left to try them? I'm surprised there's even anybody to arrest them! Your friend Calvi's in it, of course. He won't have Gelli to protect him now. That's the end of him.'

'And Sindona?' I asked.

'Oh, probably. But Sindona doesn't matter any more. Either he'll fend them off and stay in his American gaol for twenty-five years, or they'll get him back here and finish him in prison.'

'What will happen?'

'What ever happens here? It'll be settled all'italiana. There'll be a tremendous scandal. Resignations all over the place. There'll be a Parliamentary Commission, which will sit for ever. Then gradually the dust will settle, and we'll go on very much as before. Cosa vuoi? What do you want?'

'And Gelli?'

'Oh, Gelli isn't finished. He knows too much about too many people. I know he's gone off with the most incriminating documents of all, so there'll be plenty of people happy to let him stay in South America. Where he has dozens of friends.'

'I was meant to see him,' I said. 'That's why I'm here. Sindona had arranged it; or he said he had.'

'Perhaps Sindona knew what was about to happen, and wanted you to see Gelli while you could. One of Sindona's people gave him away, it seems; someone who was helping him when he was in Sicily. The police were interrogating him, and the whole thing came out. P.2. Propaganda 2. That's what he was running all these years, from the Excelsior, in Rome. They say he had something on everyone in Italy; everyone in public life. They either joined, or else.'

'Was he trying to take over the government?'

'Who knows? He would have liked to. There was a right-wing plot somewhere in the background. There have been two or three abortive coups already. Come up to Bologna: I believe Aldo has something that he wants to show you.'

'About Gelli?' I asked.

'No, no. About that mercenary you're studying. Whose name I can't pronounce.'

'Hawkwood? Giovanni Acuto?'

'That's right! Some damned document: he says you'll be delighted. A colleague found it, I believe; a friend of his. If you're in Florence, come up here tomorrow and have lunch. In the usual restaurant. I'll call Aldo.'

At almost any other time, I would have been greatly excited. It might, it seemed, be the very kind of document I had been praying for, and if Aldo was so pleased, it must surely be important. By my disappointment and depression now were such that it came as no more than a palliative. I would go up to Bologna tomorrow, obviously, but without the buoyant hope which would otherwise have filled me.

For the rest of the day, I listened endlessly to the radio, endlessly watched news bulletins on television. Each time, I learned a little more. Each time, there were hints of further ramifications, further horrors. Gelli's career was rehearsed and discovered, much of it being familiar to me; the obscure origins, the Fascist preferment, the Yugoslav gold, the constant, cunning change of sides, roles and allegiances in the chaotic years after Italy's surrender, the bookshop he so bizarrely ran, the powerful friends he made – clips and photographs of the sturdy, grey-haired man side by side with princes and potentates – the rumours of a Mafia connection. How strange, I thought, that the Masons, blamed for so long as conspirators, should have been infiltrated by and used by one of the arch-conspirators of his era. For use them he plainly had. He was a Fascist first, a Mason, manifestly second.

What a superb launching pad it must have given him, one seemingly untainted by Fascism, one from which he was so perfectly placed to play on the guilt and to exploit the greed of almost every powerful figure in Italy. He had, according to Lucetti, taken the most scabrous documents with him, but those he had left, those piles and cases of them, would clearly tell a tale to keep Italy buzzing for months, a Parliamentary Commission at work for years. Not for the first time, I found my repulsion leavened, however reluctantly, by a kind of fascination.

Again, the frisson of Bologna station; again, the horrifying memory of the crushed taxi cabs. In the restaurant, there were three people waiting for me, Aldo, Lucetti, and a large, plump, jolly man with dark, receding hair and massive shoulders, who spoke Italian with a slight German accent. 'This is Professor Hans Russmann,' said Aldo. 'He's from Alto Adige, and pretends to be Italian.'

'I'm also a mediaevalist,' said Professor Russmann, taking my hand in his great plump paw. 'I know your work well, and I admire it. And I think I have discovered something that will interest you; about your English mercenary.' His exuberance, his geniality, began to bring me out of my melancholy, and to evoke an answering enthusiasm, buried till now beneath my disappointment as though under volcanic ash.

Aldo poured wine into my glass. 'È una vera scoperta,' he assured me, 'it's a real discovery.'

'Shall I show him now?' asked Russmann, with a teasing smile.

'Let him eat first,' said Aldo. 'He'll be too excited, otherwise.'

'I'll be too excited if I *don't* see it!' I said.

At this Russmann shrugged his large shoulders, picked up a briefcase, and drew out of it the photostat of a manuscript, which he handed to me, continuing to smile at me like a benevolent father waiting to see his son enjoy a present. 'I came upon it by chance,' he said. 'In the papers of a completely forgotten Bolognese treasurer; I'm an economic historian, you see.'

I examined the photostat. It was a letter, written in Italian, in that tormenting, trompe l'oeil script of the time, which it had taken me so long to master, by Coluccio Salutati, who I knew had become State Chancellor of Florence in 1376. Dated 1377 – the fateful year of Hawkwood's depredations in Faenza and Cesena – it was addressed to Roberto Morello, evidently a member of the ruling council of Bologna. After the customary courtesies and formalities, Salutati – and here I felt a pounding in my chest – wrote of the English knight, Giovanni Acuto.

'You are wise to have taken the measures that you did. He is greatly solicitous, for he has never forgotten the death from plague of his wife and of his daughter, when they were held for ransom by the Pisans.'

The words danced before my eyes. I scarcely dared to look at them again, in case I had imagined them or found that, in some magical way, they had disappeared. I was aware of Aldo, Lucetti and Professor Russmann looking at me, smiling at me. I blinked, and looked again at the letter. These were indeed the words, and, reading them again, I felt a triumphant sense of vindication. I was right! It was true! His wife and daughter had died a wretched death, struck down by the plague when in captivity. Used, no doubt, as a surety of Hawkwood's 'good' behaviour.

I read the rest of the letter. It made no further mention of Hawkwood, dealing subsequently with that most Florentine of topics, monetary matters; a proposed loan, it appeared, from Florence to Bologna.

For a minute or so, I could not speak. I sat there, hearing the voices of my three companions, but not distinguishing the words. There was no way I could answer them, even had I wanted to. I wondered when the deaths had taken place, whether the Pisans had taken Hawkwood's wife and daughter hostage when he was fighting for them or against them, in those early years in Tuscany when he was perpetually changing masters. I must go again to Pisa and scour through the archives, hoping there might be something I had missed – for I had read so much – a document that would give me a date. How significant, though, did the date I knew now become! 1377: Faenza and Cesena. Could the ransoming of his sons have regenerated the fearful memories of what had happened to his wife and daughter, exacerbated the bitterness and lurking desperation within him, eroding his natural repugnance from such orders to destroy?

With difficulty, I managed at last to focus on my three companions. All of them were smiling at me with an affectionate amusement. 'Are you back again?' asked Lucetti.

'Didn't I tell you, Tom?' asked Aldo.

I gripped Professor Russmann's big hand: 'How can I thank you?'

'But you have!' he said. 'Just to see your face! I know how it feels. We're like scientists, making a great discovery. The whole world seems to stand still.'

'I can't believe it! It's everything that I suspected, everything that I'd been thinking, but given up hope of ever proving.'

'No, no,' said Russmann, 'we must never give up hope. A historian is never beaten.'

'It's incredible.'

'In Italy, everything's incredible!' cried Lucetti. 'The past's incredible, the present's even more incredible.' He wanted to speak of Gelli, it was understandable, though I myself, having at first been unable to think of Hawkwood for thoughts of Gelli, now could not think of Gelli with my mind so full of

Hawkwood. Thus a conversation which would have transfixed me only ten minutes earlier now largely passed over my head, apprehended only in snatches. Famous names were named, secret service generals were bruited, the imminent resignation of the President of the Council was mentioned. For form's sake, I tried to assume an expression of interest, looking into Lucetti's face as he spoke, but was aware chiefly of the face itself, of the mouth endlessly moving, the chin thrust forward, the eyes dark and aglow. 'Che schifo!' Aldo kept saying, 'Che schifo!' but Professor Russmann seemed largely amused, directing a smile at me from time to time as though he, like myself, were somehow extraneous to such squalor.

I had read the newspapers that morning, anyway, on the way to Bologna, and had already supped full of horrors. It was as though some huge stone had been lifted up, and a thousand, thousand slimy things were crawling out from under it. The Church apart – and did I not know of the bodyguard-archbishop? – there seemed no section of official life that was not tainted by the scandal. In their Gadarene rush for power and wealth, in their quaking fear of sins exposed, these bastions of the Italian Establishment had fallen over one another to join P.2, and to profit.

I could not wait, now, to get to Pisa, though first I must return to Oxford, and see out the rest of the term. In my euphoria, I did not worry, for the moment, about Gelli. Of my two quests, one seemed all but resolved. In my own mind at least, Hawkwood, if not exonerated, was at last explained. His wife had died, his daughter had died, and the feeling had gone out of him. He had not slain the nun in Faenza, I was sure of it, he had sent a thousand women out of Cesena, his sins had surely been those of omission. Thou shalt not kill but needst not strive . . .

And one day, I thought – as I flew back the next afternoon, from Pisa itself, conquering the temptation to stay – I might still find Gelli. I read about him, again, on the flight to London. More skullduggery had been exhumed. More black adventures. More famous names had been dragged through the mire. The government was clearly going to fall. There was word of the Mafia, talk of the South American connection, of Gelli's friendship with Juan Perón. How safe he would be in

South America, how snug on his farm in Uruguay, how welcome to the cruel thugs of Buenos Aires! Yet my sudden, half-miraculous, discovery had made me an optimist. I had bought off, after all, a longer shot than finding Gelli. Mere money, if I could only get enough of it, could probably take me to him. It could never have taken me back six hundred years to find what I had found; or what had been found for me. I had the photostat in the inside pocket of my jacket. I took it out and perused it, reading it and re-reading it, holding it like a talisman.

XVI

In the year to come I would badly need that talisman. Like a soldier back from a savage war – I had to try to settle again into the quiet, peaceful rhythm of what passed for civilised life; quieter still in Oxford, where the colleges had known for centuries how to domesticate the pressures and passions of the world outside, winnow and desiccate the outrages of history. As Cooper did. As even Collings did, though he did it so innocently, without blood-lust or sadism. His roistering narratives were completely free from the pornography of violence.

Returning to Oxford, seeing them so often during term, Cooper on my staircase or at High Table, Collings at his house, or at meetings of groups and committees, I found each in his own way naïve and vexing. Both spoke to me, in those first days, about Gelli and the P.2 scandal. Collings revelled in it. 'Good God, the whole country's just one great jungle! You can't blame a fellow like Gelli. He just sees his chance, and makes the most of it.'

We were walking down St Aldate's, between great walls that seemed to enclose a parenthesis in time. A March wind whipped Collings' broad, pink face, and blew confusion through his thick, grey hair. He spoke of Gelli as he might of one of his historical figures; there was no blood, no broken bones, no suffering or misery. In my more intimate knowledge, I saw him as a great, exuberant child.

'He's killed people,' I said. 'He had many people murdered.'

'Yes, yes, yes, of course he did!' said Collings, as though this were the most peripheral of details. 'He's an adventurer. He's unprincipled. Adventurers are.'

'He has trains blown up,' I said. He was about to deprecate this, as well, then gave me a quick look, remembering.

'I'm not going to defend him,' he said but, implicitly, he did.

Cooper, by contrast, was diminishing him. It was the Master who raised the subject, during dinner at the High Table. 'You've just come back from Italy, haven't you, Cunningham? What do you make of this P.2 business?'

How hard to answer! To answer briefly and dispassionately, to conceal rather than declare my own, passionate interest. 'It doesn't surprise me,' was what I actually said.

'No? You knew about it, did you? You expected it? I must say it astonished *me*. What about you, Cooper? You're the great expert on Fascism, and the fellow's meant to be a Fascist, isn't he?'

Cooper was not astonished by anything; the mechanism of his mind protected him from shocks of any kind. 'Yes, he *is* a Fascist,' he said, pressing his long, thin fingers together.

'*And* a Mason,' said the Master.

'Yes, a Mason too.'

How comfortably we sat at our beautiful table in the beautiful, panelled dining-hall, with its portraits of former masters, dead prelates, extinct statesmen hanging on the walls. How comfortably we issued our opinions.

'I don't think he is politically significant,' Cooper pursued. 'There was nothing ultimately serious about the conspiracy, I suspect, despite all the talk about a right-wing coup.'

'It was serious enough,' I said. 'It killed people, and it ruined people. It turned Italian public life into a cesspit.'

'I mean *politically* serious,' said Cooper, 'in terms of its ultimate consequences. It seems to me to have been informed principally by self-interest, rather than by political ambition. The historical moment is hardly propitious to Fascism; even in Italy.'

He was right in a way, but at the same time utterly wrong, because he would always get everything wrong, however correct his conclusions. There were a thousand things I could have said to him, but I said none of them, reluctant to disclose myself before him, them, people who lived outside the grubby torments of the modern world.

'Would you agree with that analysis, Cunningham?' the Master asked me.

'Broadly,' I said, 'though Fascism seems to be doing quite well in South America,' then took refuge in my port and Stilton.

In something of the same way, I could not bring myself to tell Collings about my discovery in Bologna. I kept the precious photostat in a locked drawer of my desk, careless now of burglars, taking it out at times to see and savour, referred to it when I was working on my monograph, but otherwise kept it hidden and secret. It was unfair of me, perhaps, not to show it to Collings, not even to tell him about it; after all, he was as interested in Hawkwood as I was, but just as I felt he was ignorant of modern Italy, of Gelli and the horrid reality he stood for, so I could not share with him anything of such private consequence, whose resonance had changed not only my perception of Hawkwood, but my perception of myself. My monograph compelled me more than ever, but the academic life was a trial to me now. I had been posed, implicitly, too many questions about myself and my profession, not only by the professor in Padua with his Marxist claptrap, his twisted notions of 'objective reality', but by everything that had been happening to me. I was not above the conflict, like Cooper, nor beyond it, like Collings; I was inescapably part of the conflict.

Indeed, as I walked the quads and cloisters, forced myself through my tutorials and lectures, saw in my unguarded moments the horrible images of death in that apartment, my impatience grew to unbearable proportions. Half-ashamed, I realised that I missed the infernal rhythm of the past months, however horrific they had sometimes been. When my clever pupils asked me clever questions, when I stood on some dais talking about mediaeval money or the demographic impact of the plague, I was aware of taking part in a charade. I found myself, however unwillingly, even wanting Sindona to call again, and wondering what was happening to Calvi.

He was doomed, now, I was certain of it, and I felt a little sorry for him. Robbing Peter desperately to pay Paul, deserted by the Chicagoan archbishop, robbed too of the bulwark of Gelli, whose exposure had exposed him, what could he do but follow Sindona into gaol, flee as Gelli had fled, or put an end to himself? I thought of him, sitting in melancholy gloom behind his desk in his suite at the Excelsior, like a large, hunted animal. At least he had not paid Sindona again.

I did not know whether I would stay at Oxford, now. I did not think I could ever truly settle down in what had been my routine. I did not want to turn one day into Collings, or degenerate into Cooper. History was a means to a comfortable and painless life, studying other people's pain, history as a means of making a living: it was ungrateful to me now. I had found a rationale in history, but it was special and personal, probably unique. I did understand Hawkwood, I was beginning to understand myself, yet I doubted the value of what I had been doing at Oxford, or would do in years to come.

The 'real' world, for what it was worth, tugged and nagged at me. There were moments, even, when I felt a perverse nostalgia for the time when Ted and his Fascist thugs were threatening and assailing me, felt tempted actually to pick up a phone and call Annabel, at least to find out what had become of her, and of her vicious friends. In the event, though, it was Annabel who called me, one morning at my cottage. I recognised the breathless modulation of her voice at once, with a guilty flicker of satisfaction. 'Tom? It's Annabel! Do you remember me? I've been trying and trying to get hold of you, but you never seem to be there.'

'I've been in Italy,' I said.

'Oh! Lucky old you! Was it exciting? There's been so much going on.'

'Yes,' I said, slowly. 'Yes, I suppose you could say it was exciting.'

'It must have been! All that stuff about Gelli and P.2. I think he was behind it all, you know. Enzo and Guido have been just going round in circles. Their money's been cut off. They simply don't know where they are.'

'I'm sorry to hear that,' I said.

'You're so sarcastic. Enzo's still not really better. He seems to have shrunk. I know you didn't really mean it.' Didn't I? I thought. 'I believe he almost realises that himself now. The you-know-what, their friends in England, they're still helping them. They're both living down in Brighton at the moment, but of course those people haven't got the same resources.'

'I don't suppose so,' I said.

There was a silence. 'I'd love to see you, Tom,' she told me. 'When you come to London. Or I could come to Oxford, if you wanted.'

'Well, that might be a good idea,' I replied. 'Why don't I think about it? How's your little girl?'

'Oh, she's getting better now. She couldn't sleep for weeks. She'd wake up screaming every night. With nightmares . . . It was awful, wasn't it?'

'Horrible,' I said.

'Enzo apologised. So did Guido. They bought her things, you know. They both went to Harrods and spent a fortune. But it was very difficult for her to understand.'

'I imagine so.'

'You don't think much of me, do you?' she asked.

'Oh, God, Annabel,' I said, 'don't ask me to make moral judgements. Not on you, anyway. You know what I think of Enzo and Guido.'

'Yes, I do. Perhaps you're right. But don't you ever fall in love with the wrong people?'

She was pitiful and ludicrous, but the thought of her still, to my embarrassment, excited me.

'I'll call you,' I said.

'You will? You will, won't you?'

I put down the phone, sensually aroused, morally revolted. I should have nothing more to do with her, of course, but the temptation was there. Then I thought of that appalling evening, her bruised and tearful face, the cries of her little daughter as she beat against the door, and I shuddered. I did not think I could go back there again. 'I'd come and see you in Oxford . . .'

A further temptation was to call Sindona, but I resisted that too, though I longed to know more than I could glean from the Italian newspapers of what was happening to Calvi. As for Gelli, they attributed a phrase to him, just four words, which gave me some small insight. 'Sono un po Cagliostro. I'm a bit of a Cagliostro.'

So he was, I reflected; or seemed to be. But then so, surely, was Sindona. Cagliostro, two hundred years ago, had been a parvenu, jumped up, like Sindona, from a poor Sicilian family. Like Gelli, he had exploited Masonry, in his case 'Occult Masonry', whatever that may have been; but hadn't Sindona postulated something that he called 'revolutionary Masonry', whatever that was? Cagliostro had duped and swindled and cheated his way into high society, marrying a countess, posing as an alchemist, coming to grief, at last, in France, over the scandal of the Queen's diamond necklace. Then it had been the Bastille in Paris, the San Leo prison in Rome, to which he was condemned for life on a conviction of heresy, after first being sentenced to death. He had died in the prison.

Sindona had finished in prison, but Gelli, so far, had avoided it. Did he believe he would end in one, eventually? I did not think so, did not even think he expected prison at all. Un po Cagliostro. Just a little; not wholly. Cagliostro had peddled the elixir of youth; Gelli peddled the elixirs of wealth and power. Cagliostro had dealt in filtres and potions, Gelli dealt in blackmail and promises. Un po Cagliostro. There was no evidence I knew of that Cagliostro had had innocent people slaughtered, that Cagliostro had been interested in political power, besides the wealth that he achieved in such abundance: and lost entirely. High society had received and trusted him, as the Italian Establishment had received and probably trusted Gelli. Trusted him, at least, to make them richer than they were, and not to give away the secrets that he held over them.

Sindona telephoned me at last; at dead of night, inevitably, waking me again. 'You see what's happened to Calvi now?' he asked, with a gloating satisfaction.

'What?' I said, though I could guess.

'Haven't you heard? Haven't you read about it? He's on trial. They found his name on the P.2 list, of course, and enough evidence to put him in gaol for ever.'

'Poor fellow,' I could not stop myself saying.

'Poor fellow!' Sindona repeated scornfully. 'He's got what he deserved. He forgot his friends. He betrayed the people he owed everything to.'

'Did he?' I asked.

He ignored the nuances of my question. 'Gelli's sorry,' he

298

said. 'He's told me to apologise to you. He really did mean to see you. He didn't think they'd close in quite so quickly. He'll be back in Europe sooner or later, he says, and then he will see you; maybe even in London.'

'That's very kind of him.'

'Oh, he's a decent man. He keeps his word. Look at them all scuttling round, now he's gone! All the people who thought that they could use him. All the people who tried to use *me*.'

'He's in Uruguay then, or Argentina.'

'Who knows? He's not in Italy, that's certain. He's not in Europe. He might be here; in the United States. They'll never find him.'

'No, I don't suppose they will,' I said.

'You sound a bit down. Don't worry. You'll see him, sooner or later. Pazienza! I'll call you again!'

However detestable I found the man, however squalid his exultation, I still felt a sense of great relief. There was light, of a sort, at the end of the tunnel. It was the first time, too, if Sindona was to be believed, that Gelli had acknowledged my existence directly, let alone my desire to see him.

Next morning, unable to buy the day's Italian papers yet in Oxford, I telephoned Lucetti, in Bologna.

'Calvi?' he said. 'He's been arrested. He's in gaol in Milan, with several of his friends. They found all that stuff on him in Gelli's villa. Now they're going to charge him with foreign exchange fraud. That's only the beginning of it. It'll all come out, now. All the swindling that's gone on in the Banco Ambrosiano. They must be shaking in their shoes at the Vatican: God's banker! They'll need God's protection now, the archbishop and the I.O.R. "God's Vatican bank!"'

I got the Italian papers the next morning as I always did now, and there it all was. Calvi was to be prosecuted in Milan, where the Banco Ambrosiano had its seat. For currency offences, as Sindona had said, and as Sindona, better than anybody, knew; for it was he who had been behind it. Also, there was immensely worse to come. He had still to be charged with his peculations and his frauds, his desperate manipulation of funds, his world-wide finagling, in the Banco Ambrosiano, whose mighty, massive walls must soon crumble at a blast, like the walls of Jericho.

Walls, walls. The walls that were closing in, inexorably, on Calvi. The walls on which Sindona had stuck the viciously accusing posters, nearly four years ago, to give the game away. I wondered how Calvi was feeling now, between other walls; those of his prison cell. He would not be as resilient as Sindona, I was sure of that – or as Cagliostro for that matter. Sindona, in any case, was probably half glad to be where he was, within the walls of an American prison, where he was relatively safe, rather than those of an Italian gaol, where he would be a target. He must always, from his earliest, upstart days, have envisaged prison as a risk, a possibility, whereas for Calvi, the son of a bank clerk, brought up in a tradition of dull, dedicated service and financial rectitude, however far it may have been perverted, prison must seem the ultimate disgrace. His cover may have been 'blown' by the posters of 1977, but then, and in the hard years that ensued, there must always have been hope; hope personified by Gelli, of whom he was supposed to have said, 'He had the reputation of being a very important man. He gathered people around himself, and he succeeded in gathering me for the sense of protection he gave, through membership of the P.2 lodge.'

How wonderfully comforting it must have been when Sarcinelli, the biter bit, the pursuer pursued, was gaoled himself, as he seemed to be moving in for the kill! How joyful Sarcinelli must be now, with the quarry caught!

'The best thing Calvi can do,' said Lucetti, when I telephoned him next, 'is appeal when they convict him, which they're bound to do, get out on bail, before they charge him with the rest, then disappear. This is nothing, compared with what's coming. He knows he's on his own, poor devil. I hear that he appealed to the archbishop and was told it was his problem, not the Vatican's. He isn't God's banker, any more; he's Gelli's!'

The trial took place with extraordinary speed, in a country where defendants could languish endlessly in gaol, waiting to come to court. Term had been over for several weeks; I had gone through the annual purgatory of marking examination papers, attending vivas to decide the borderline cases, but never had I done so with less enthusiasm, so uncertain of the value of what they had done, and what I was doing. The thought that careers, even lives, could hang in the balance as the consequence of these papers seemed at once absurd and alarming. As I ploughed my way through one after another, read the naïve or precocious views on the strategic errors of the Third Crusade, the economic significance of the city-state in mediaeval Italy, I had a growing sense of futility and despair. What depressed me was the idea of history being studied in the void, taught, for the most part, by a cloistered, privileged intelligentsia who had seen nothing and done little in their lives, to those whose lives were barely beginning.

I read the judgements, sometimes glib, sometimes second-hand, sometimes ingeniously perceptive, all founded on nothing but book learning, the fruit of libraries, classrooms, lecture halls. I had been just as guilty myself as both student and teacher; airing my callow views on soldiers, statesmen, courtesans, then handing the word down, meretriciously, to those who followed me. How facile I had been, as undergraduate and don, how disproportionately I had been rewarded!

I saw myself reflected, now, in the clever candidates who were up for a First, as we vivaed them, asking our tricky, logic-chopping questions, rather than in the poor, beleaguered creatures struggling to avoid a Third, as my colleagues swooped on them like wolves. 'That may have been what you *meant*, but it was not what you *said*.'

A First, a Second, a Third: what did it ultimately matter? We were only playing games, making patterns and parables out of dead people's lives. A First might get you into the Foreign Office, a Third might not stop you making a fortune in the City. Neither had anything to do with the truth; any more than had the sophistries of my fellow dons. I found myself looking at them, more than at the candidates, seeing the glint in the eye of those who obviously enjoyed hounding their quarry, the more sombre look, opaque behind spectacles, of more sombre dons, the ill-restrained eagerness of the young enthusiasts, burning to ask their questions. What did any of them really know?

A small, bright girl, on the fringe of a First, had written in her paper on the role of the mercenary in mediaeval Italy, quoting Muratori's description of them as 'fierce locusts', and Gregorovius' view that 'the sole reason they did not establish lordship in Italy was because the leaders lacked the political idea and the adventurers the bonds of nationality.'

301

'But Hawkwood's men had the bonds of nationality,' I said. 'Would you say he lacked the political idea?'

She looked at me, as quick and alert as a squirrel. 'I don't think he had any ideas except to make himself rich,' she said.

'But he died poor. Or relatively poor. Getting Florence to commute his taxes. Hocking his wife's jewellery.'

She looked at me with a subdued amusement, clearly suspecting me of an idée fixe, one of those daft old dons whose obsession must be humoured. So she did not answer me; she merely, and demurely, bowed her head.

How much I could have told her! How tempted I was to do so, for a moment, but I was silent, too.

By the time Calvi came to trial, it was high summer, and I was in Pisa, living in a pensione which was always full, at this time of year, with plump and raucous Germans. I laboured through the State archives, hoping to find what I had never found there before, some document alluding to the ransom of Hawkwood's wife and child, their deaths in captivity, but in three days of looking I found nothing that I had not seen before, and left for Florence, pursuing the possibility that Salutati's papers might throw up another letter, one, perhaps, from the Bolognese, Robert Morello, but there was none.

I stayed in the Via Porta Rossa, and went out once to see my in-laws, in San Domenico. The Signora had forgiven me by now for my gun. The General was as genial as ever. 'You seem better,' he said, strolling along his olive slopes, across the road, below the villa.

'Yes,' I replied, 'yes, I feel a bit better.' Of course I feel better. I'm not on the run. I've not just seen three corpses; seen my girlfriend, with the back of her head blown off. The crime has been ascribed to 'i soliti ignoti', as was predictable. Oh, yes, I feel better; or nothing like as bad.

The General wore an open-necked, long-sleeved white shirt, out of which tufts of black hair sprouted from his sturdy chest. There was a white, broad-brimmed hat on his head. He laughed, happy in the sunshine, and he squeezed my arm. 'The more time that passes, the better you'll feel. Ti giuro. I swear to you.' I smiled, as best I could, and nodded. I did not want to disappoint him.

Once again I went up to Bologna, for a lunch with Aldo, Lucetti and Professor Russmann. The trial, predictably, was fascinating Lucetti, though to myself it seemed, for all its scandals, no more than the prelude to something much greater, while the photographs of Calvi, now pinched and worn, were saddening, whatever he might have done.

'Sindona's been feeding them with evidence from New York,' Lucetti said avidly. 'That's the word. No one knows more than he does about the whole *casino*; after all, it was he who planned it.'

'What will Calvi get?' I enquired.

'A colossal fine, probably,' Lucetti answered, 'and not too long in gaol. That'll come later; after the next trial. He's already tried to kill himself, you know. He slashed his wrists.'

'Poverino,' said Aldo. 'Will the Vatican escape, as usual?'

'They're doing their best. I heard he gave his wife and daughter papers that involved them. They had them in the car, after seeing him in prison, and an I.O.R. man's son tried to snatch them. Signora Calvi sat on them!'

'Bella roba,' Aldo said.

'Oh, there's much, much more to come,' said Lucetti cheerfully. 'We'll have the verdict and the sentence in a couple of days; and that will just be the beginning.'

They came on my final day in Florence. Calvi and his associates were found guilty. He was gaoled for four years, and fined an astronomical seven million pounds. He appealed, and was at once released from prison. It would be a year or so, one read, before the appeal came to court. Meanwhile, no doubt, he would be charged with his crimes at the Banco Ambrosiano, and might or might not disappear, as Lucetti had predicted. There was no sign that Gelli could help him now. He was certainly in South America. From time to time, there were sightings of him, even interviews, which I read with compulsive attention. They were strange affairs; a compound of threat, allusion and apologia, though without the pervasive whine of self-pity that ran through all Sindona's monologues. 'Sono un po Cagliostro.'

When the date of Calvi's appeal was announced, it was for June, the following year. Between now and then, things could surely do nothing but get worse for him, though, inexplicably, he was reappointed President of the Bank. The walls were closing in, even if they were not, for the moment, prison walls. His wife may have sat, so loyally and so swiftly, on those documents, but whatever they were, they could hardly save him.

As the months went by, as summer modulated into autumn, as autumn in turn became an Oxford winter, I gleaned odd pieces of information, some from Lucetti, some from the newspapers, some from occasional, crowing phone calls from Sindona. The Vatican might help Calvi after all, Lucetti told me from Bologna, one chilly autumn day, as I sat before the fire in my college room. 'It's his last chance,' he said. 'But they've issued these letters of comfort for a whole lot of his crooked companies. Manic is one of the biggest, in Luxemburg. Then there's United Trading, which they're meant to make more direct use of; that's set up in Panama, with subsidiaries in Liechtenstein.'

'What for?' I asked.

'To keep the money going round and round. Some of it for Calvi. Some of it for the Vatican. From United Trading. They don't even attempt to account for a lot of that. Calvi uses his to buy his own shares and keep the price up. It can't last, but it might just last a little longer, now the I.O.R. have done this. They've got interests in both companies; they may even control them, for all I know. Nobody's sure.'

'It makes my head spin,' I said. There seemed no rhyme or reason. The Banco Ambrosiano's board was joined by none other than Benedetti, President and saviour of Olivetti, the most brilliant of the new entrepreneurs; a precious seal of approval. Within a couple of months he had gone, in a blaze of recrimination. The head spun again.

It was Sindona who spoke to me first of Flavio Carboni. 'Ma vede che gente! Altro che Gelli!' he said, over the transatlantic phone. 'Look at the people he's in with, now! Nothing like Gelli! This Carboni: a cheap little operator! A Sardinian! Amico della malavita! Friend of the underworld!' This, spoken from his own prison, but there was no semblance of irony. I asked Lucetti about Carboni, to be told much the same. 'Un sardo. Piccolo mascalzone. Molte donne, molte macchine. A Sardinian, a little rogue. Lots of women and cars.' And he added, 'Pure un'aereo. Even an aeroplane. Very useful for escaping. He's a property speculator. Poor Calvi! He must be desperate, now.'

Down, down, down; from plausible villains to transparent ones. But then, who was morally lower than Sindona?

'They say he's changed,' Lucetti told me. 'Non fa più pezzo grosso; è diventato molto nervoso. He doesn't play the big shot any more; he's got very edgy. Carboni's frightening him. He's told him they're out to kill him: not to trust his bodyguards. Not to sleep at home. To watch where he goes.'

Calvi himself was reported, in one of the Italian newspapers I bought, to have said that he was really frightened. It was a question of having to survive 'in a climate that was becoming like a religious war. The atmosphere favours every kind of barbarism.' Where would he run? Where could he hide? Gelli's word went round the world. Something horrible would happen, I was sure of it, and while I waited for it to happen, while I read dire stories of the Bank of Italy's continuing investigation of Calvi's own corrupt bank, I continued to dangle in the void. A religious war, he had said. What kind of religious war? Was it a religious war because it involved the Vatican? It was a strange phrase. So I waited for Gelli, as one might wait for Godot, waited for whatever was going to become of Calvi.

It was none of my business, yet my brief involvement, my meeting with him, had left me hooked, despite myself. He was, after all, a major piece of the great jigsaw, leading in one direction to Sindona, in another to Gelli. Instinctively, I felt I was not free of him, or it.

I weakened, and when Annabel next phoned to ask if she could visit me in Oxford, I agreed. There was more to it, though, than just a physical urge. In some obscure way, I felt the need to see her; she was part of it, and *it* was what dominated my days, so that those who knew nothing of it, however likeable and sympathetic, were less acceptable than anyone who was initiated.

She was dressed as modishly and elegantly as ever; a fur coat, a mink wrap, blue tights against the cold, a pale blue Angora jersey. In the cold, crisp air, her flawless, well cared for skin radiated good health, as did her perfect, white, carnivorous teeth. She was half-an-hour late when she drove her Mercedes at flamboyant speed into the little road and stopped, with equally unnecessary panache, outside the cottage.

'Darling!' she cried, flinging her arms round me as I opened the door, kissing me on the lips, putting her cold cheek against mine. 'What an absolutely gorgeous place! How lucky you are!'

'It's better in the summer,' I said, 'when the blossom's out, and the flowers are growing in the garden.'

'Oh, but I love it, anyway! It's so marvellously picturesque! Is it very old?'

'Early nineteenth century, I think.'

'How super!'

I helped her wriggle out of her fur coat, whereupon she turned round to kiss me again, her tongue in my mouth this time, laying to rest my burgeoning feelings of irritation, guilt and self-disgust, the thought that she was vapid and mindless. We were quickly in bed, a bed no other woman had been in since Simonetta died, and Annabel made love as if in a frantic anxiety to please, stroking and sucking, 'Do you like that? Do you like that?' seeming at once voracious and pathetic.

'You're so good,' she said, panting, as she lay beside me, on her back, her carefully cut and tinted hair spread across the pillow.

'No, it's you,' I made myself say.

'Is it? Is it really?' and she turned her head to kiss me. I felt myself wishing intensely she would go, and feeling bad about that, as well. As though she could sense my mood, she said, 'We've split up, you know; Enzo and I.'

'I'm glad to hear it,' I said.

'He didn't kill your wife. I'm sure he didn't, Tom. Neither Enzo nor Guido.'

'No, I don't think they did,' I said. 'But I've no doubt they would have done, if they'd been told to. They wouldn't have thought twice about it.'

'I still think you're awfully hard on them. I know they were horrible that night. But it was jealousy. Enzo admitted it. He couldn't bear to think that you and I had been making love.'

'So he wanted to see us do it again,' I said.

'Don't!' she pleaded. 'Please don't talk like that, Tom!' and she ducked under the covers, taking me again in her mouth, as though it were an act of expiation.

Later we drove into Oxford and, at her wish, walked around the colleges.

'Oh, I adore it here, I always have! I'd love to live here. How I envy you. It makes London seem so cheap and tawdry. All of us rushing around like idiots all day, with nothing really to show for it.'

'Don't be deceived,' I said, as we strolled. It was dusk, the street lights were on and, under a light mist besides, the college buildings took on a kind of Gothic enchantment, shapes softened and mysterious.

She seized my arm. 'You mustn't spoil it for me! I like to think of you being enormously serious and dedicated, with students sitting at your feet, and hanging on your every word.'

'You'd be very disappointed.'

'I'd love to come to one of your lectures. Could I? Do you think I ever could? Do you think I ever could?'

'If you wanted to be bored to extinction.'

'I'd not be bored! I know I'd be fascinated; especially when it was about Italy. I wish I could come here and be a student. But I was always too stupid.'

Three girls in huge white woollen jerseys came cycling past in a phalanx, calling to one another in the loud, confident, high voices of the public schools. 'I'd love to be them,' said Annabel.

'It's all a bit unreal.'

'But that's what's so lovely! That's what I like so much about it! You're away from all the horrors and the pressures! You've got time to think about things.'

'It has its own pressures,' I remarked, as we walked past Magdalen.

'Where would you live if you could, then? Italy?'

'I'm not too sure,' I said. 'I used to think so.'

'Then your wife was killed. You poor thing! It must hurt you every time you go back there.'

Yes, it did, which was why I had to go there and to keep going there, but what could I tell her of that? Italy heals, I suddenly remembered the Master fluting. Italy heals, Italy destroys. Whatever I wanted was to be found only in Italy, I knew; whatever surcease, whatever deliverance. Oxford had become now, doubly parenthetic.

Annabel would want to stay the night, I knew, but I knew, too, that I had had enough of her, that I could never sustain the mask, the courtesies, so long. I would tell her something, but whatever it was, she would not believe it. She was used to being treated badly, and it depressed me that I would join the long line of those who had done so. Besides, she had helped me, even saved me, that night they came to burn down my house, whatever her motives may have been.

It was Saturday evening, a bad day to make an excuse about the morning; a lecture to give, a meeting to attend. I would have to think carefully. Meanwhile, I took her to dinner in a small Italian restaurant I knew, and grew uneasy as she became more and more affectionate towards me during the meal, her large, beautiful, stupid blue eyes smiling continuously into mine. I did not say much to her, and her expression changed gradually to one of sympathy and understanding; I must be thinking of my wife. She squeezed my hand several times, she pushed her booted foot hard against mine, beneath the table.

'I'd love to ask you to stay,' I said, when coffee came.

'But you don't want me,' she said, and her face seemed to disintegrate, in sudden misery.

'No, no, not at all,' I said rapidly. 'It's been wonderful to see you, marvellous to be with you. I have to get up very early tomorrow, that's all; I've a pupil to see.'

'Don't worry,' she replied, 'I know how tiresome I can be.'

'Annabel,' I told her, 'you'll have to bear with me. A lot of strange things have been happening. It's nothing to do with you. Really. Nothing at all.' It was partially true. At all events, it seemed to cheer her a little. She looked less wretched.

'I wish you'd let me try to make you happy,' she said, and pressed her thigh against mine.

'You do,' I answered. 'You *have* made me happy. It was wonderful. One day, I hope I'll come out of all this.' And you are part of all this. I brought you up here because you are, but now you *are* here, I cannot bear the sight of you. I cannot stand the memories you bring back to me; your brutal friends, the suffering of your little daughter. I cannot stand myself for having gone to bed with you.

When we left the restaurant, she drove me back to the cottage. I was afraid that when we got there, she would try to stay the night. Stopping the car outside the cottage, she turned to smile at me, as if to say that I could change my mind

308

if I wanted to, but if I didn't, she would not complain. I leaned over, kissed her briefly on the lips, and climbed out of the car. She sat there, still smiling at me understandingly, through the window, then, with a wave, I trotted down the path to the cottage. The car stood where it was for several minutes, after I had let myself in. Then, at last, she started it up, and, with relief, I heard her drive away. I did not want to see her again.

XVII

The year turned, spring came, the Falklands War began. Sindona called me, to jeer. 'Che cretini, voi inglesi! What cretins you English are! Not only did two of your biggest banks lend money to Calvi, but you know where a lot of it's gone?'

'I've no idea,' I said.

'To Argentina: that's where! To buy missiles to use against your ships! Gelli fixes it; the money comes from Calvi. If you lose the war, you can blame yourselves!'

Could it be true, I wondered? Yes, of course it could. Where Gelli was concerned, anything frightful could be true; his conspiracy lapped the edges of the world. Our ships were being sunk, our sailors blown up, our soldiers burned to death, because Calvi stole money which he gave to Gelli, and Gelli gave it to his Argentine protectors. I felt less sorry for Calvi, now; whatever the panic that had made him do this. As for Gelli, favours no doubt necessitated favours. Give me refuge, and I shall arm you. Una mano lava l'altra. That people would die, people might be burned, was of no more consequence to him than what happened at Bologna Station; or to Simonetta's train.

'Calvi's finished,' said Sindona. 'His accounts are open to inspection now; did you see that? The Stock Exchange has forced him to quote the shares of the Banco Ambrosiano, so it'll all come out. The Bank of Italy are still asking questions. If he'd stood by me, it never would have happened. Un presuntuoso! He's presumptuous! If I hadn't picked him out, he'd have still been nobody!' And happier for that, I thought.

309

'*I* discovered him! *I* saw what he could do! He was internationally minded; but he needed somebody to guide him. At bottom, he's just a functionary.'

'And Gelli?' I asked.

'He hasn't forgotten you. Sta sicuro. You can be sure of that. When the time comes, when the moment is propitious, he still means to see you.'

And so I hung on in limbo. I was not even able to complete my book on Hawkwood. Salutati's letter had been a godsend, a revelation on Hawkwood and his life. I had recast much of my manuscript accordingly, I could well publish it as it was, and shed new, unsuspected, light on him. But I could not bring myself to do so. The book was incomplete because my whole investigation remained incomplete, and in some way I felt, but still could not articulate, I knew it would not be complete till I had seen Gelli.

I went to Pisa and Florence again at Easter, looked again at the archives in Bologna, but could find nothing more, nothing to expand and corroborate Salutati's priceless letter. It was not that, though; or not that, alone. I needed Gelli. And while I stayed in limbo, I was aware of my own inadequacy. I was living a half-life, tutoring dully, lecturing mechanically, cutting myself off from social contacts, not even going to High Table to dine. People ceased, gradually, to invite me to their parties and dinners, and I could not blame them. They made allowances for me, I could tell; I must still, clearly, be in a state of mourning. But if that were true, it was only part of the truth.

Summer, and examination Finals, came round again. On the last day of May, Lucetti phoned me from Bologna. 'The moment of truth has arrived. The Bank of Italy has written to Calvi, insisting that he account for foreign loans made by the Banco Ambrosiano.'

'Then the game's up,' I said.

'Inevitably. And on June 21, his appeal is due. Finita la commedia.'

Wondering what next, I was less fit than ever to assess examination papers, let alone to serve on viva committees. On these, I was sometimes appalled to hear myself; I had become a parody of the worst, most bullying, inquisitorial dons, snapping my questions at scared candidates, scorning their answers. From the looks they gave me and their attitudes towards me afterwards, I could tell what my colleagues thought, but once the vivas began, there was nothing I could do to stop myself. The only form of restitution I could make was, to their surprise, to urge for clemency and generosity in our assessment, when I myself had probably done more than anyone to spoil the examinee's chances.

A week after Lucetti called, he phoned me again. This time, Calvi had met his board of directors – the board he had once, by all accounts, intimidated and addressed as if it were a silent, captive audience. Now, the worms had turned.

'He told them he couldn't possibly let them or the Bank of Italy know where all the money had gone; it would be a breach of the international banking laws. But this time, they wouldn't have it. They've voted against him, ten to four. Even shooting Rosone didn't keep them in line.' In April, a gunman had shot Rosone, the Bank's vice-president, in the legs, then had been shot himself, that very day. 'He's nowhere to go now; at least in Italy.'

It was another nocturnal call from Sindona that told me Calvi had absconded. 'He's disappeared, the imbecile,' he said. 'Where does he think he can hide? Carboni probably fixed it; he'll have taken him for a fortune, and he'll never be able to deliver. Carboni's small time. The only way Calvi will disappear is into a hole in the ground. I'll find out soon enough where he is. So will anyone who wants to find him.'

It was what Lucetti, and indeed I myself, had been expecting. Calvi's face, with its dark, melancholy eyes beneath the balding dome and above the slightly ludicrous moustache, looked at me from a score of photographs, in the Italian newspapers I bought each day. Seen thus, it looked the face of a henpecked husband in some French farce. There was no menace or authority in it; yet he had been feared and respected in his time. I wondered where he had gone. To South America? Only if he were still working with Gelli, rather than fleeing from Gelli. The Middle East? A stronger possibility. Italian financial villains had been known to flee there.

Then Calvi phoned me. The surprise was so great that at first it stunned me. 'Who?' I asked, recovering, 'who?'

'Calvi,' said the voice, reproachfully. 'Roberto Calvi. I'm

in London.' Now I heard it again, it *was* his voice, but I remained confused. London. Why ever should he be in London? It was ten o'clock at night; I was in the sitting-room of my cottage, making a desultory attempt to read an academic journal.

'I have to see you,' he said. 'It's immensely important. Soon. As soon as possible.'

'Where are you?' I asked.

'You must tell nobody, you understand? No one at all.'

'Very well,' I said.

He then spoke two words in English, neither of which I could understand. I asked him to repeat them; again, they were quite unintelligible. Finally, he spelled them for me. Chelsea Cloisters. Then, laboriously, he spelled out the address, Sloane Avenue, and gave me the number of the flat, 881. 'Tomorrow morning,' he said. 'Can you come at eleven o'clock tomorrow morning?'

'No,' I said, 'but I could come tomorrow afternoon.'

We agreed that I should be there at two o'clock.

'Knock four times and say it's Tommaso.'

Putting the phone down, I felt the familiar tension in my stomach. I was off again; the hiatus, thank God, was over. I was sure that something mightily significant was about to take place. Calvi was on the run, he was in London, he wanted my help. It did not occur to me that I should turn him in, that he was, after all, skipping bail, a convicted criminal in flight. Nor was I drawn to go by any great desire to help him in his plight. It was rather that I felt it might help *me*.

I knew Sloane Avenue only vaguely, remembering it as a narrow road which began, under some other name, at South Kensington Station, running south until it reached the King's Road, a fat, jolly, rubber tyred Michelin Man grinning from his white tiled building, at the north-west corner. I recalled, too, that there were 1930-ish blocks of what looked like bachelor flats, on both sides.

Chelsea Cloisters, on the right, was one of those. What could Calvi possibly be doing in such a place, I wondered, except hiding? Outside, it was presentable enough, with its brick walls interpolated with white facings, its eight paned windows, its canopied front door, its large entrance hall. Once up in the lift, once across the worn carpet and through

312

the battered swing door of the eighth floor, one found delapidation and despair. The place was redolent of loneliness. The uncovered wires and cables that twined above the narrow, carpeted corridor like a profusion of snakes emphasised the impression of negligence and despair. The corridor, with its pale grey walls and darker grey doors, was that of a bleak institution, where alcoholics and compulsive gamblers came to eke out their declining years. The solitary decorations were brass ashtrays, fixed to the walls, as if to encourage the denizens not to set the place alight. I walked on till I found, on my right, the numbers 881 on a door's brass plate. I knocked four times, and called, as he had asked me to, 'Sono Tommaso.' From within, I heard his voice call, 'Momento!'

I heard his footsteps shuffle to the door, a double lock was turned, then it was fractionally opened. The dark eye peering through the crack was recognisably Calvi's. Seeing it was I, he opened the door wider, to admit me. 'Questo è un postaccio,' he greeted me. 'This is a disgusting place.'

It was certainly bleak. Across a tiny vestibule, he led me into a small living-room, furnished with the sterile indifference of a second-rate hotel. There was a sofa, a wooden table, a few hard-backed chairs, an ugly armchair of functional design, and a bed which crowded the room, and seemed to have been brought in from the adjacent bedroom, through whose half-open door I could descry another bed.

Calvi had shaved off his moustache; it was the first thing I noticed. Without it, his face looked curiously naked and defenceless; less comical, now, than vulnerable. He had lost weight, though he was still plump and stocky, but the comedian's eyes looked tired, there were more lines on the face than when I had seen it last, in Rome.

'You're surprised to find me somewhere like this,' he said, sitting down ponderously on the sofa.

'Well, yes,' I replied.

'I, too, am surprised; it's an insult,' he said, and his voice shook. 'I told them to find me a decent place. Not a big hotel. Not somewhere where I would be known. Just a decent, comfortable place. Money was no problem. London's large. It's full of good apartments. And this is what they found me! *This!*' And his voice rose. The telephone rang, and he picked it up. 'Si? Si? E va bene! Mi telefona ancora; ogni venti minuti! Ha capito? Phone me again every twenty minutes! Understand?' Putting down the phone, he said, 'Un mascalzone! A rascal! A smuggler. He brought me here, from Austria. He got me out of Italy. In the back of his wretched little fishing boat. His cigarette smuggling boat. Crouched like a criminal. Me! Can you imagine? That's what I've come down to! That's how I left Italy for Yugoslavia! Like a thief! Like a fugitive! To Yugoslavia from Muggia: a little fishing village that I'd never heard of!'

It was hard to respond. Looking about the ugly room, I noticed two cases: an open suitcase which seemed to contain a plethora of pills and potions, and a black briefcase. 'My medicines,' said Calvi, noticing the direction of my gaze. 'And my secrets. They both go everywhere with me. My secrets are my only protection. They'd kill me for my secrets, but without them, they'd kill me even quicker. They want to do it here. I'm sure of it. I don't believe in certain people. I don't believe in this escape. I chose London; nobody would ever think of me in London. But he's put me in here. Why would he put me here? He and this crook, Vittor? Because it suits them. Because it's like a warren. People can go in and out with no one noticing. That's why. I'm sure that's why.'

His plump hand shook. He stood up, came over to the case, reached into it, and took out a carton of pills, which I saw were marked as Valium. There were syringes in the case, too, and a bottle of pills marked Paracetemol; but these were only the peak of the pyramid. 'Permesso,' he said. He lumbered across the room to a minuscule kitchen, set virtually in a cupboard, and I heard the hiss of water as he turned on a tap. He emerged with a glass of water in his hand, used it to swallow a couple of pills, then put the carton back into the bag.

'They killed my secretary today,' he said. 'My poor Teresa. That's to scare me. That's to warn me. They're saying she threw herself off the fourth floor balcony at the Bank; and left a note condemning me for what I'd done. That's incredible. She was always loyal to me. Either they forged the note, or made her write it. Then they killed her. These are dreadful times, Professor. Cruel times.'

'I know,' I said.

'But you're an honest man. A decent man. I could tell that, even when you came to see me on behalf of Sindona. You were embarrassed, I could see.'

'That's true.'

'Ecco! It was because you wanted Gelli, wasn't it?'

'I still do,' I said.

He took a bottle of Scotch out of his case, and poured me a drink; then the telephone rang again. Picking it up, he went through the same, clipped conversation. 'That's Vittor,' he said. 'I've told him to keep ringing me. He thinks it's as a precaution. But I want to know where he is. To make sure that he's not on his way here. That he doesn't see you here. He, or the other one.'

'Carboni?' I asked.

He gave me a swift, alarmed look. 'How did you know?'

'I've heard,' I said.

He continued to stare at me, as if debating whether to continue, till he told me, 'I need help. When you're in desperate trouble, when you've been betrayed and abandoned, when you're fighting for your life, yes, your life, you can't always be discriminating. Do you understand me?'

'Yes, I think so,' I said, tempted to ask: then how about Sindona? And Gelli?

'Quello li non sarà una persona colta, ma in questo momento, è utile. That man may not be a cultivated person, but at this moment, he's useful to me. He's arranged things. Getting me to Yugoslavia. To Klagenfurt. Now here; I flew here. To Gatwick, with Vittor. This smuggler. Now Carboni's here too. At the Hilton Hotel, with two women.' The broad, rubbery face contorted with disdain, making it more than ever a comedian's. 'He can't travel without girls, he can't move without a girl.'

I realised that, by a bizarre irony, Calvi had had to turn to someone who was the antithesis of all he stood for; good form, sobriety, the outward and visible show of rectitude. Carboni's sin, clearly, was that he did not pretend to be other than he was, just as this flat offended Calvi with its shabby sterility, its lack of comfort and camouflage.

'I saw him yesterday in the Park,' he said, 'near his hotel,' and he began to vibrate with indignation at the memory. 'I told him, this is an insult, this is intolerable! This is not a fit

315

place for a man of my standing. "Then what *is* a fit place?" he asked. "The *Uragano*? The back of a motor launch that smuggles coffee?" I promise you, I could have slapped him one! Then he said he was sorry about this place. He'd look for another. He'd get me one today; but he hasn't. You can see he hasn't! And I don't trust him!' His whole, plump body seemed to subside, to be filled with fear. 'I don't trust him,' he said again, in a whisper. 'I don't trust either of them. That's why I rang you. That's why I want you to help me. To give me shelter. In Oxford. Just for a day or two.'

Now, when he looked at me, his eyes seemed that of a sad old dog, mutely pleading. 'Non sono poveraccio,' he said, 'I'm not a poor devil.' He got up from his chair, went to the open black bag, and pulled out of it a thick green wad of dollars. 'I would not be ungrateful.'

'I don't want money,' I said impatiently.

'No,' he replied, deflated again, dropping the dollars back into the bag. 'That was wrong of me. Lei è una persona per bene. You're a decent person. I apologise. But I'm asking you a favour, I realise that. You've every right to refuse.'

'I shan't refuse,' I said. 'You can stay with me in Oxford, if you like.'

I was careless of consequences. Once again, the script seemed pre-ordained. The lines had been written for me. Now his fear gave way to a consuming relief, one could almost see it flooding through him as the crumpled body grew straight and erect. He reached out and grasped my hand, in almost pitiful gratitude. 'I'll not forget! I shall never forget! It may be for only a day . . .'

'I can drive you back now if you like,' I said.

'No! Not now. I have to be careful. The best time's tonight. They're going out tonight. They and those two Austrian girls Carboni's brought with him. They'll be gone for an hour or two. Can you do it then?'

'I suppose so,' I said. 'I'm not quite sure how I shall spend the time.'

'I'll give you money!' he said eagerly. 'Go to a hotel! Hire a room!'

'No, no,' I said, 'don't worry. I shall think of something.'

I drove to the British Museum and worked in the Reading Room until it closed, at eight o'clock. It was the proper place to be, the place where, reading and thinking about Hawk-wood, I would gradually grow calmer. I did not know whether Calvi was really in danger in London, or whether it was just his paranoid fantasy, whether Carboni was a friend to him, or a treacherous enemy. Many people must have wanted him to die. If he had fled, it must mean that he was a threat to them, a force outside their control – unless he was indeed on his way to Gelli – carrying documents that could damn them, the contents of that minatory black case. So to keep him alive, to keep him at large, might even be a moral duty, above and beyond the human one.

There were many questions I must ask him, when I got him to Oxford. For the moment, I found myself reading again the letter Saint Catherine of Siena sent – or rather, in her illiteracy, caused to be sent – beseeching Hawkwood to change his ways:

> I pray you sweetly for the sake of Jesus Christ that since God and our Holy Father too have decreed for us to go against the infidels, you, who so delight in wars and battles, should no longer fight against Christians, because that is an offence against God, but go and oppose the Turks, for it is a great scandal that we who are Christians should persecute one another. So from being the servant and soldier of the Devil, you should become a manly and true knight.

There was no record I had ever been able to find of Hawkwood's reply, though remembering his famous answer to the monks who wished him peace, it was not difficult to imagine what it might have been. The servant of the Devil? Il diavolo incarnato? No, he was neither. He was not even irreligious; he had lived and died a Christian, of a kind, as any Crusader was a Christian. But by then, there were no more Crusades; if you wanted glory, it was to be won in France, and after the glory came money, and after the money came Italy. Besides, by the time the prolific little saint had written to him, his wife and daughter would be dead. A futile appeal.

When the Reading Room closed, I was quite serene again. I sat in the pub in Great Russell Street, drinking a couple of whiskies, then went to a nearby restaurant, where I found it hard to eat. My excitement was growing once again. I wanted

317

to be on the move, to get back to those gloomy flats, so appropriate a symbol of Calvi's plight, to snatch him away from there, bring him to Oxford, and set him free as a bird. Though God knew how long he would fly.

I arrived at Chelsea Cloisters ten minutes early, and parked the Volvo on the other side of the street, outside the grim, brown, lowering walls of the old Harrods furniture depository. My heart was beating very quickly. I wished that I had brought my Beretta. Calvi, it was true, projected his own, dread situation on to the world, but there was evil in the air. Carboni, Vittor, and whoever they might have here at their beck and call, lurked in the shadows of the mind; and then, there was Gelli.

At one minute to eleven I got out of the car, sweating, glad to be briefly in the cool night, crossed the road, and went up the steps, under the canopy, into the entrance hall of Chelsea Cloisters. The porter, behind his desk, was talking to an elderly, grey-haired man with beetroot face and brass-buttoned blue blazer, who spoke in a loud, slurred, over-emphatic drinker's voice. I muttered, 'Eight-eight-one,' as I went past them both to the lift. Down the bleak corridor, beneath the proliferation of cables I went, knocking four times on the grey door of Calvi's flat, calling, 'Sono Tommaso!'

The door was opened at once. Calvi was standing there in his dark, formal, banker's suit, the black briefcase in his hand. 'Andiamo subito!' he said. 'Let's go immediately!' His agitation was almost pitiful. He went ahead of me down the corridor, scurrying along with the awkward motion of a man unused to haste. The lift was still there, and as we descended in it, he stood clutching his briefcase against his chest with both hands, as if at any moment he expected someone to get in and snatch it from him. But the lift had a clear passage to the ground floor, and in the foyer there was only the porter talking still to the red-faced man, both glancing at us with perfunctory interest, as we walked to the front door.

'Where's your car?' Calvi asked me urgently, as we went down the steps. I pointed across the street at it. He looked furtively and fearfully up and down Sloane Avenue, waited till a couple of cars had driven past, then crossed, with me at his side. 'Ah, a Volvo,' he said, as if this were some kind of reassurance, climbing ponderously into the front passenger seat.

I made a U-turn and headed north-west towards the A40, turning up the broad, handsome sweep of Queen's Gate, westwards past Hyde Park and Kensington Gardens, trees ghostly in the dark, down Kensington High Street, north up Church Street, and down Holland Park Avenue to the vast roundabout, and the motorway. All this time, Calvi was turning constantly to look out of the back window, speaking not a word. His tension communicated itself to me, and began to irritate me.

'There's nothing following us,' I said. 'I'll see if there is, I'll look in the mirror.'

'If there is you must stop,' he said, 'and go back to the flats. I can't run any risk. I'm in danger all the time. But *they* think I'm still in the flat. They didn't even know I was going out, let alone where I was going. How will you get to Oxford?'

'On the motorway,' I said, 'the way I always do.'

'Is it safe? Will there be much other traffic on it? Maybe we should take another route.'

'At least it won't take long,' I said, 'less than an hour; it's far quicker than the older route. If we see anything, I can always come off it.'

'It may be too late.'

I sighed: 'It's up to you, But at this time of night, I don't suppose there'll be a great deal of traffic on the A40 either.'

There was very little indeed on the motorway. Still, Calvi turned constantly to watch whatever was following us. I drove in the fast lane, at a steady seventy. We were passing beneath the great, gouged chalk walls, some seventeen miles out of Oxford, when I was aware of a large, white car suddenly gaining on us, tearing up behind us, in the fast lane.

'Attenzione, attenzione!' Calvi cried. My stomach contracted. The car, I could now see, was an Alfa Romeo. There was no way that I could leave it behind, no exit that was near, no visible gap in the central reservation. 'Sono loro, sono loro!' Calvi cried. 'It's them! It's them!' but I knew very well that it was.

The Alfa Romeo was hard on our tail now; it began hooting, and flashing its headlamps off and on. I was not going to stop, nor was I going to move over, fearing the risk of being run into the hard shoulder. If the worst came to the worst, I might always try to break through the central reservation. I did not try to go any faster; it would serve no purpose.

Frustrated, the Alfa Romeo now pulled out and passed me – I made out four or five dark, seemingly masked, men inside it – and drove deliberately in front of me, slowing its speed, weaving about in the road. Suddenly it stopped dead, and I only just avoided it, tugging the stearing wheel round, to swerve into the centre lane. Instantly, and before I could get back into the fast lane, the Alfa had started again, crowding me, forcing me towards the inside lane, and the hard shoulder. Unless I wanted a collision, there was nothing I could do but move inwards. I began to sound my horn, hoping at least to attract the attention of whatever cars might pass us, so that they might notice something, remember something, perhaps even call the police from one of the emergency phones.

A clutch of cars came suddenly down on us, hooting in their turn, as the Alfa forced me still farther across the road, then came a huge container lorry which I thought for a moment would hit us, but with a protesting blast of the horn, it managed to swing in time across the centre lane, and miss us. The Alfa was so close now that I could see that the man nearest to me, in the front passenger seat, was wearing a Balaclava helmet. I wished fervently that I had my gun. I was on the hard shoulder now, aware that Calvi was yelling in fear and panic, but unable to distinguish any words. I was aware too, that he was frantically trying to undo his seat belt. Then I stopped the car, just before it hit the grass bank, feeling as impotent and vulnerable as in a nightmare. Calvi, snatching his briefcase from the back seat, tried to throw his door open, but there wasn't the space; it jammed when it had moved barely a foot, and he could not possibly squeeze through it. He gave a great cry of frustration and alarm; then the men were out of the Alfa, and upon us. My own door was wrenched open, and the man in the Balaclava helmet struck me across the face, shouting abuse at me in a thick Southern Italian accent. 'Cazzone! Figlio di puttana! Perchè ci rompono i coglioni?'

I wondered if I were going to be shot dead, if they were

320

going to kill both of us; there was a murderous rage in his voice. Now another man, with dark, wavy hair and a scarf tied across the lower part of his face, a revolver in his hand, pulled him aside, and put the gun against my head, shouting, 'Fuori, fuori! Out of it!' I tried to push down the catch of my seat belt, but my fingers had lost all their strength.

'*You* do it!' the second man shouted to the first, who released the belt, then seized my arm, dragging me out on to the road. Lying there, I saw the two of them lean across the front seat of the Volvo to seize Calvi, who kicked out at them, clutching his precious briefcase. They shouted abuse at him, but a third man, also with a scarf across his face, a peaked cap pulled down low on his forehead, and dark glasses over his eyes, came up behind them and ordered, again in a Southern accent, 'Don't mark him! See that you don't mark him!'

As I lay in the road, watching them drag Calvi, struggling, out of the car, uncertain of what they would now do to me, I found myself curiously calm, as though all my alarm had been in the waiting. I was no more afraid to die than I had been at any time since Simonetta died; it was Calvi I felt sorry for, as they hauled and mauled him like a captured beast, shouting insults at him, 'Bastard! Traitor! You know what happens to people who betray us!' wrenching the black briefcase out of his hands as he shouted, 'No, no, no!' like a great, cosmic protest against his fate. Again he kicked out, but the third man dodged him, seizing his leg, still another leaped out of the Alfa, he too in a Balaclava and with a revolver in his hand, and he thrust the barrel close to Calvi's face. 'Do you want to die here?' he shouted. 'If you want to die here, we can see to it for you!' and at last Calvi subsided, ceasing to struggle, ceasing to shout, allowing himself to be pushed and pulled into the back seat of the Alfa Romeo. The first man with the revolver bent over me, pointing it at my head, and I wondered, as though I were looking on at the scene from a distance, whether he would pull the trigger. I was still in my bizarre, almost euphoric, state of detachment.

'Go on, get up!' the man said. 'Get back into your car!' Then he wasn't going to shoot me; at least for the moment. Life and energy began to flow back into my body, but the strength had gone out of my legs. I tried to stand up, but instantly fell back again.

321

'Alzati, stronzo! Get up, you turd!' the man with the revolver shouted at me.

Again, I tried. Again, to my frustration and embarrassment, I fell back. The man with the gun and the fourth man each grabbed an arm and dragged me to my feet. 'You're going to drive, you understand?' the man with the gun snarled at me. 'You're going to follow us!' I looked across at the other car where poor Calvi now sat, in the back seat, between two of the men, his mouth gagged, his bald head bowed, in the posture of an animal resigned to slaughter. I tried to speak, but my mouth betrayed me as my legs had done and at first, no words would come. 'Where?' I managed at last to say. 'Where?'

'Never mind where,' said the man with the revolver, pushing me towards the half open driver's door of my Volvo. 'Just follow our car, that's enough.'

I managed to slide through the door, and into the driver's seat. The man with the revolver got into the back, pushing the muzzle against the nape of my neck. 'Do up your seat belt!' I complied; it seemed like another reprieve. At least they were not going to shoot me yet, to shoot me here. I felt sure they were going to kill Calvi, and I sensed that he felt it too. That they did not want to have a mark on him showed the cold concern of the butcher, anxious not to damage the goods, rather than the humanitarian. The men were mafiosi, I felt sure of it; from their appearance, from their accents, from the restrained ferocity, the controlled brutality, with which they behaved; as though part of their very professionalism was to work up a hatred for their victims. The chilling self-righteousness of the Red Brigades, the callous savagery of the neo-Fascists, were something qualitatively different.

There were three men in the Alfa Romeo, now, with Calvi, one each side of him, and one in the driver's seat. The driver pulled the Alfa Romeo further up on the hard shoulder, leaving me room to move, and stopped some twenty yards on. 'Draw up behind him,' said the man with the revolver. I obeyed him, and the fifth man came trotting up beside us, pulled open the passenger door beside me, and climbed in. He was smaller than the others, a hollow-cheeked weasel of a man, with a cap, a Southerner's full black moustache, a blue

322

overcoat with the collar turned up to obscure his face. 'Let's go, let's get it done with!' he said.

The Alfa Romeo started up again; Calvi's large, bald head seemed to have sunk even farther. 'Follow it, and see you don't lose it!' said the man with the revolver, jabbing it again into my neck. 'We're going back to London, we'll turn off at the next exit. Be ready.'

The Alfa Romeo drove off into the slow lane, reaching about fifty miles an hour. The two men in my car starting talking to one another in what I recognised as a Sicilian dialect; I could not understand everything they said, least of all the slang and the nicknames, but the callous, cruel tone of it was clear enough. Their conversation was not only in dialect, but deliberately allusive. No name was mentioned, not even Calvi's, though the contempt in their voices when they spoke of 'that one' or 'him' made it plain enough whom they were referring to.

'What about the bricks?' the man with the revolver asked, when we had gone a mile or so.

'We'll find them there,' the weasel answered, 'there's plenty of them, down by the river.'

'Why should there be bricks down there?'

'We went there early this morning, when it was low tide,' said the weasel. 'There's bricks and stones; they're building something, there. That's why they've got the scaffolding too.'

'As long as you're sure. We've got to have the bricks. He's told us so. The Chief.'

Gelli? I wondered.

'Never mind the bricks,' said the weasel. 'Just as long as we've got the rope.'

'Don't worry about that,' said the man with the gun. 'That's in the boot.'

Poor devil. Did they mean to hang him?

We reached an exit from the motorway, and the Alfa Romeo turned. 'You turn too!' said the man behind me, and prodded me with his revolver, again. I followed the Alfa Romeo down the slip road, under the motorway, back east along the road which runs parallel to it, then on to the motorway, again. The Alfa Romeo remained steadily in the inside lane, now doing about sixty miles an hour, moving into the centre lane only on the scattered occasions when it overtook a slow-moving car. There were no lights on this part of the motorway; the headlamps of the cars cut bright channels into the dark. Each time the Alfa Romeo overtook a car, the man behind me gave me a prod in the neck or between the shoulders, to make sure I followed it.

'We've got the briefcase, anyway,' said the weasel. 'He'll be pleased about that. Did you see the money that son of a whore had in his pockets? A fortune!'

'Don't take any of it!' the man behind me warned. 'You know what we've been told.'

'As long as there's room for the bricks!' the weasel replied, and they both laughed.

The bricks. The rope. They were certainly going to kill him, and I supposed they were going to kill *me*. Again, as I drove on into the night, I felt strangely alienated, almost fatalistic.

'Oh!' the weasel addressed me suddenly, as we now came under the hideous orange glare of the last section of the motorway. 'Are you frightened?' I shrugged, and did not answer. They both laughed again.

'Of course you're frightened,' said the man behind me, giving me yet another jab with the gun. 'The other one's probably shat himself by now.'

'That wouldn't look good,' said the weasel. 'We were told that we mustn't leave a mark on him,' and they laughed once more.

It would have been easy to lose the white Alfa now, as we came closer to town and the traffic increased; possible, perhaps, even to stop, once we were off the motorway and had cars around us, to leap out of the car and to run for my life. But if I tried, the man behind the wheel would shoot me, I was quite sure of that, even if it meant the car crashing. Besides, I would lose vital moments unlocking my seat belt, which imprisoned me. There was no bluff to call. I was as helpless as the wretched Calvi.

We had now left the motorway, and were at the great, green roundabout which led straight on towards Western Avenue, or, to the right, along the Uxbridge Road. There was nothing coming; the Alfa Romeo drove straight across the roundabout and I followed.

On, on, losing the Alfa once at traffic lights, to the fury of the man with the gun, catching it up again as it dawdled in the slow lane, awaiting me, on now past the ribbon development of West London suburbia. 'Che schifo, questa strada, what a filthy road,' said the man with the gun. 'How glad I shall be to get home.'

'That bastard should have stayed at home,' said the man with the gun.

'I wish he had,' said the weasel. 'All this theatre. Ropes and bricks. We could be seen. It's a risk.'

'It's what he wants,' said the man with the gun.

'It's a pity,' said the weasel. 'We could have done it all there; the usual way. We could have dumped him along the road. No one would have known.'

I wondered whether I could crash the car. But then, as I entered the flyover at the end of the Westway, passing under the battery of the signs, following the one indicating Westminster and Brighton, it seemed no better than a double risk. Perhaps, at the very end, when we arrived at wherever we were going to, an opportunity might come; or the choice between certain death and the risk of death would become so plain that I would have nothing to lose. I still felt curiously calm. To have lived for so long now and at times so intimately with violence seemed to have had its effect. I could never be as cruel and as violent, as callously brutal, as these men. But they did not frighten me; and that was what my shrug was meant to say.

The white Alfa Romeo turned sharply right as we approached the motorway's roundabout, then left, heading south towards the Holland Park Avenue roundabout, turning east there, then south again down to Kensington High Street, where we turned, and headed into town. I wondered if we were on our way back to Chelsea Cloisters and the squalors of 881, but the Alfa, running along beside the two parks, the Albert Hall, the banal ugliness of the Albert Memorial, did not turn down Queens Gate, nor did it turn down Sloane Street. Instead, it roared down into the tiled womb of the underpass, beneath Hyde Park Corner, along a deserted Piccadilly, south down the Haymarket, and into the Strand.

The men talked very little now. There was a tension in their silence which suggested that something was about to happen, but what, and where, in the very heart of London? The Alfa made the detour round Aldwych, then down again, by the sleeping neo-Gothic of the Law Courts, on down Fleet Street, passing the shiny, black glass bulk of the Express building, moving into the outside lane, and stopping at the traffic lights at the bottom.

It was at this moment that Calvi suddenly tried to turn round and look at me, but before I could see his face, the expression in his eyes, the man beside him, who had taken off his Balaclava, reached out and wrenched his head back again. 'What does the bastard want?' the weasel muttered. On my left, I became aware of the serene grey shape of the dome of St Paul's, delicately illuminated by floodlight, making my plight, the horrors of what was happening, what was plainly about to happen, seem the more unreal.

The lights changed. The Alfa turned south off Ludgate Hill, working its way back towards New Bridge Street.

'Have you got it ready?' asked the man with the gun.

'Everything's in order,' the weasel answered.

Now the Alfa turned left, along the river, towards Blackfriars Bridge. Across the dark water, the night was lit up by a great, glass office building, sitting above the bank like a giant conservatory. The Alfa drove on to the bridge, and stopped by the kerb, halfway along.

'Drive on!' snapped the man with the gun. 'We'll tell you when to stop!'

I pulled out past the Alfa Romeo, and drove to the end of the bridge.

'Take the next left,' said the man behind me. I turned off the main road into a side street, took a right turn at his behest, and bore right at the end of that short street. The gun was pressed into the back of my neck, again. I was aware that beside me, the weasel was taking something metallic out of the inside pocket of his jacket; glancing down, I saw that it was a syringe. So they were not going to shoot me, but what *were* they going to to do me? For one blinding moment, I thought that I would crash the car, had actually begun to turn the wheel, then, just as suddenly, I decided that I would gamble. There was a vestigial chance they did not mean to kill me.

'Stop here!' ordered the man behind me.

I drew up by the kerb. My mouth was dry, my heart was throbbing. The weasel lifted the syringe, its needle pointing upwards, and squinted at it like a malign nurse. Then, as though from very far away, I heard the man with the gun: 'When you wake up, you'll find your friend under the bridge.' Then quite unexpectedly, I felt a sharp pain, as the weasel jabbed my thigh with the needle of the syringe, a further, searing pain as its liquid flowed into me; then sudden oblivion.

When I woke up, it was light. My head ached, my mouth was dry again. I had no notion where I was, till I looked out of the car window at the sombre, narrow street, and I remembered. My God, I was alive! I was still alive! I looked at my watch; it was twelve minutes past five. Where was Calvi? What had happened to Calvi? Then I remembered the last words of the man with the gun: 'You'll find your friend under the bridge,' and at once I tried to move out of my seat, only for the seat belt, still fastened, to cut across my stomach and restrain me.

I undid it, and got out of the door. The air was cool, and as I stood on the pavement I swayed, feeling sick and giddy. I stood still for a few moments, breathing deeply, then turned and walked up the street, making my way back to the bridge, walking as fast as my condition allowed me, wondering with dread what I would find beneath the bridge.

Now I was on the main road, walking up towards the bridge, while the sparse, early morning traffic passed over it. There were no boats to be seen on the placid water, which glinted and sparkled under a gentle sun; just a black hulk, a dredger perhaps, moored like a rock in the middle of the river. I was on the bridge now, walking past its handsome iron cross-hatching of blue and white, past the stone benches, set back from the pavement, on towards the steps which led down to the walkway beneath, still not daring to look over the edge. When, at last I did look, I could see nothing, and had a moment's hope. Then I went down the stone staircase to the riverside, past the fat, brown pair of marble columns and the great white balustrades, while the cars that went by in the underpass below set up a roaring cacophony.

And now, looking over the parapet, I saw him. They had hanged him. He hung pitifully from a length of yellow rope, tied at the outer joint of two poles of scaffolding, his bald head bowed, his arms hanging limp at his sides, like a giant rag doll. From the top of the parapet, a narrow ladder led down behind the scaffolding grid, to the river. He was dead, there was no doubt about that, but I had to pay him the final respect of making sure. I climbed over the parapet, went down the ladder with my back to the river, hopped on to a little bridge of planks at the foot of the scaffolding, then made my way carefully across a horizontal scaffold pole, till I had reached the hanging body.

The eyes were still open. Strangely, there was less suffering in the face than dignity, as though in death he had found a vanished self-respect, a new peace. The pockets of his now crumpled dark suit bulged, and there was another bulge at the front of his trousers. Reaching forward, I delicately touched them. It felt as though I were touching bricks and stones, and all at once I recalled the conversation in the car. Why the bricks? I wondered, why here? But for the moment, the shock of what I had found obliterated thought.

I stood looking at him for a minute or so, I reached out and touched him again, in a futile gesture of compassion, then I made my way back across the scaffolding pole, back along the planks, back up the narrow ladder, and over the parapet. Then up the stone steps, and on to the bridge itself. I felt sick. The politic thing to do was clearly to absent myself as quickly as I could, but instead I walked to the stone benches and sat down with my back to the parapet, looking across the road, across the bridge, half aware of the traffic, the occasional pedestrians who passed, the increasing strength of the sun as it played on the river.

I would not go to the police, I knew, any more than I had gone to them in Rome, when I had found the three bodies in the flat. There was nothing the police could do; just as in Rome. They would never find the murderers, even if I described what I had managed to see and hear of them. They would be back in Italy today, would disappear in Italy, be protected in Italy; by the very people, the powerful people, who had wanted Calvi dead.

I felt a great pity for him. But it was a private matter, something to be kept to myself, not out of any fear, for they had not frightened me, but because I still felt it was my business, my affair, something to be seen through to an end that had not yet been reached.

I stood up at last, and made my way slowly south, across the bridge. Bricks, I thought, why bricks, till suddenly I had it. Bricks meant Masons; an image of Masons. And Blackfriars, black hoods; that probably meant Masons too. Gelli, no doubt; the cruel symbolism, the brutal irony, seemed indelibly to bear his stamp. Calvi had been killed not only as a punishment, but as a warning. To me among others, I thought, as I turned off the main road, making for my car. Gelli had spared me, Gelli had warned me. Climbing back into my car, sitting there for perhaps half-an-hour, while the street became steadily busier with cars and people, I wondered where Calvi might have gone, had he been spared, why he had come to London at all, or whether Gelli had lured him to London, so that he could play on him this last, horrific jest.

XVIII

To drive back to Oxford was to resume, hideously, the events of the night. When I drove between the chalk bluffs, the memory was especially fresh and horrible, so that it seemed an invisible barrier was set across the road, through which I would be unable to pass. I moved into the slow lane and shut my eyes a moment as I drove through; then I was clear. I was still on the road, I heard myself let out a deep sigh, then my body shivered.

On the car radio, I heard Calvi's death reported in the news. The body had been found by a clerk, an hour or so after I had found it. Financier who had jumped bail. Hanging beneath Blackfriars Bridge. Due to lodge an appeal. Other charges expected. Secretary's suicide. Just voted out by the directors of his bank. Investigation by City of London police. Coroner's inquest.

The investigation would find nothing. The inquest would discover nothing. How could they hope to? Carboni and Vittori would be gone by now. Besides, what business was it of ours, of London, of England? These were Italian matters, settled now in the Italian way. A swindler had met his end. The Mafia would be evoked. There would be talk of Masonry,

P.2., the Vatican. Then the dust would settle, and the mystery would remain. As it would remain with me; and even I had not seen Calvi hanged, could not be sure how it happened, whether they had manhandled him over the parapet, walked him down the ladder, across the planks, along the scaffolding pole, before putting the rope around his neck and pushing him free; or whether, in their sadistic ingenuity, they had made him do this himself, pointed their guns at him, till he put on the rope, and jumped. Oh, yes, there had been Mafia as well as Masonry in it.

Sindona called me at home that night, with such gloating satisfaction that I could scarcely bear to hear him. 'Che bella fine! What a beautiful end! And all his own fault; all his own doing!'

'Do you think so?' I asked.

'Of course it was! He forgot who he was! He forgot his obligations! What did he think he was doing? Where did he think he was going? The whole world wasn't big enough! Did he really believe he could run away, and blackmail people?'

As he had been blackmailed, I thought. 'He was desperate,' I said.

'Of course he was. He'd overreached himself. He had no friends. But I'm *your* friend. You saved me; now I've saved *you!*'

Should I thank him? Should I believe him? 'That's kind of you,' I said.

'Kind? Yes, of course it was kind! You were extremely rash. Why help a man like that? Why get involved with him? He'd only pull you down with him. I spoke up for you. "He's an honest man," I said. "But he's English. There's things he doesn't understand, that's all."'

'Well, thank you.'

'Now we're even. As for the one you want to meet, he'll be in Europe soon, and then he'll see you. Probably in Italy. I'll tell you when.'

I thanked him again. Perhaps he had indeed saved my life, as he insisted, but I didn't want to talk to him.

The following day, it was Lucetti who rang me. 'Vengo! Vengo a Londra! Per l'inchiesta! I'm coming to London for the inquest!' He sounded as if he were coming for a royal wedding, or for Wimbledon. 'Come with me! I'll get you a Press pass, as my assistant! Our sister paper's got a correspondent there, but I've persuaded them to send me as well! He was murdered, of course. The whole of Italy knows that. And probably the whole of Italy wanted to do it!'

'I'll see you in London next week, then,' I told him.

In fact, it would be more than a month before he came. The inquest, called for the following Friday, merely provided for the identification of Calvi's body by his brother, before being adjourned, so that the City of London police might 'thoroughly investigate'. They could thoroughly investigate for a month, a year or a decade, I thought, without emerging with the ghost of a solution. Meanwhile I read the Italian papers day by day as the speculation ran wild, the cries of murder grew stronger and louder, the Vatican bank was impugned, the bodyguard Archbishop Marcinkus was named, Sindona was mentioned, the Exocet deal was uncovered. No one in Italy, least of all Calvi's family, seemed to give the least credence to the idea of suicide, but a week before the resumed inquest was due, the City police were reported to believe in it.

I drove down to London early on the morning of the inquest. I had come to terms with the M40 by now, could drive between the gouged chalk with scarcely a shudder. The Coroner's Court stood – or lurked – in the heart of the City, in a narrow street named Milton Court, not far from Moorgate, overlooked by a functional, strangely anachronistic, modern building, all stone stairways and glassed-in walkways, up and along which one went, a floor above street level, following unlikely signs in red and white which pointed one through the maze. Not that one needed them, this day. The narrow corridor seemed to be full of a mass of chattering Italians, bringing a noisy, uninhibited vignette of Italian life to this unlikely English backwater.

Among them, chattering more volubly than anyone, was Lucetti, who broke away from the group as soon as he saw me, a large smile on his face, his hands raised in greeting. He wrung my own hand, kissed me on both cheeks, and cried, 'Now the English court will tell us the truth! Now the English will solve our mystery for us!'

'You never know,' I answered, knowing all too well.

The court, when we had passed through a door into a little outer office, then gone through yet another, to discover it, was small, compact, bright and modern, with not a whiff of Dickens, not a touch of Serjeant Buzfuz. There were benches of highly polished pine, a minuscule witness box, a dais on which the Coroner's own seat was raised. Above that, again, was the shield of the City of London, St George's red cross on its white background, a small red dagger – the dagger that purportedly killed Wat Tyler in 1381 – in the upper left segment, a lion and unicorn alert on either side. The Press benches, on the right-hand side of the court, were quickly overrun by exuberant Italians, laughing, arguing, calling to one another, while the more sobre English reporters bestowed themselves as best they could. The jurors, six men and three women, came uneasily into the court, to sit on their benches at the left-hand side. I did not envy them.

'Dicono che son' degli ingenui, i tuoi poliziotti,' Lucetti told me, as we sat down together. 'They say your police are ingenuous. They think it's suicide.'

'What does it matter?' I responded. 'Your police won't catch them either. It's "i soliti ignoti", the usual unknowns,' and those near to us laughed.

To watch the inquest, to listen to the evidence, was to attend a kind of drama, loosely but ingeniously based on a true tale of which one had cognisance. The coroner was a large, middle-aged man, with dark hair, beginning marginally to go grey. He presided with a comfortable authority, rather like an experienced Prime Minister, I thought, from whom secrets have been kept by his Cabinet. A young clerk from the *Express*, whose black palace we had driven past that night, described how he had found the corpse. He had glimpsed a head beneath the bridge, had looked more closely, then, to his horror, had seen the head was attached to a suspended body, dangling just above the river. There was the diligent Detective Inspector Tarbun, of the City of London Police, plunged into an affair whose terms of reference, vast and obscure, must seem utterly remote to him. There was the eminent pathologist, Keith Simpson. There was the eminent solicitor, David Napley, bald, lean and dark hued, representing, with a proper scepticism, the interests of the Calvi family. Inquiries, he said, had not revealed any reason why Calvi

332

should travel to London to take his life. Nor would they ever, I thought.

Keith Simpson, with a quiet, distinguished certainty, said there was no evidence that Calvi had been drugged or manhandled in the hours before death. 'My conclusion is that death was due, without question in my mind, to asphyxiation by hanging, that evidence of drowsiness was entirely lacking and that there was no evidence to suggest that hanging was other than self-suspension.'

Which could be true, I thought, as the Italian journalists rustled and buzzed around me, as Lucetti dug me in the ribs and raised his eyebrows in a parody of incredulity. Tarbun, the earnest policeman, provoked the Italians' derision still more. 'Unless some further evidence is placed before me at some future date, there is virtually nothing further I can do to cause my officers to work on any other aspect of this case at all.'

Quite fair, I thought, completely fair, in all the circumstances. There was no evidence, he said, to suggest Calvi had been drugged and taken unconscious to the scaffolding. Quite true, I thought; but then, why should there be? As for my own evidence, what ought I to do with it? Stand up, histrionically, in court, as in some American television show, and cry that *I* had evidence, *I* had been with Calvi when he had been kidnapped, *I* had driven behind his car, all the way to Blackfriars Bridge, while they talked about the rope and bricks?

MYSTERY DON SHOCKS INQUEST

I could imagine the headlines in the tabloid Press. Did I owe it to Calvi, or to Calvi's family, two of whom, a brother and brother-in-law, now sat, sombre and disoriented, in the court? After all, to have killed himself was a confession of guilt, an act of total despair. For him to have been killed, however horribly, left them at least with the illusion that he might have cleared himself, wriggled miraculously off the hook, winning both the appeal and the still more oppressive case that was to follow. For the thrust of the proceedings, quite clearly, as hour succeeded hour, testimony followed testimony, was towards a verdict of suicide. The pathologist believed in it. The policemen believed in it. You could tell

333

that the coroner, however judicially impartial he might be, believed in the police.

To speak up would surely be to condemn myself to death – Calvi's own death had been a warning to me, as well – but it was still not that which stopped me, still rather my conviction that I was doomed to fight my own battles, work out my own salvation. This inquest was no more than a charade, was nothing, finally, to do with me. What it revealed, now, was a strange sub-world I had not known of. Vittor was not there, nor was Carboni; their statements were read out in court in policemen's prose, which if anything made them sound the more arcane. Calvi's flight from Italy to London had been a strange progression; to Trieste, first, then to the village of Muggia, next to Yugoslavia in Vittor's boat, from there to Klagenfurt by car, by private plane to Gatwick, Calvi arriving with his own passport clumsily doctored.

Carboni's movements, before and after Calvi's death, had been odd in the extreme; but so had Vittor's. He had returned to Chelsea Cloisters at one in the morning, he said, having spent a couple of hours with Carboni and the two dis-appointed girls from Klagenfurt, who had thought Carboni would show them a better time. He had arrived at the flats, inexplicably, not only without a key, but without his docu-ments, which he claimed to have left in his suitcase. The porter, not surprisingly, had taken much persuasion before he would let him in. When at last he relented, there was no Calvi to be seen in 881, but the television set was still switched on, displaying a blank screen. Yet Vittor, accord-ing to his testimony, did nothing, did not even try to ring Carboni. He simply went to bed, got up at eight the next morning, and quit the country, flying from Heathrow to Klagenfurt.

As for Carboni, he had been frequenting not only the two disillusioned sisters from Klagenfurt but a family called Morris, from West London; a husband who worked in the housing department of the Borough of Hounslow, an Italian wife, a daughter called Ondina; hardly the customary ac-quaintance of so flamboyant a wheeler-dealer. They had all, supposedly, met on an Italian holiday. It was Ondina whom Carboni took with him to Chelsea Cloisters, on the Friday morning, when he could get no answer to his phone calls,

Ondina who left a strangely enigmatic note for Vittor: 'Dear Silvano, I've looked for you all day but haven't managed to find you. Get in contact immediately with L. Vito. (signed) O. Dina.'

It was Ondina – or O. Dina – with whom Carboni, next morning, flew whimsically from Gatwick Airport to Edinburgh; thence to Switzerland, where he was arrested. The testimonies shrieked aloud of evasion, suppression, equivocation, ambiguity; the Italians stirred and muttered on their benches, but neither policemen nor coroner seemed moved.

At lunch, I took Lucetti and his colleagues to a chophouse which I knew, in the City. 'Bello! Caratteristico!' he exclaimed. 'This is more like the real London! This is more like Dickens! Now I need only the fog!'

He made mock of the inquest, was full, as always, of a plethora of theories, was convinced as ever that it had been murder. 'Carboni and Vittor! Both crooks! They're both inside now! They got out of the way, and left Calvi to it. Then Vittor couldn't get out quick enough. Carboni is in P.2. Calvi was mad to trust him.'

We returned to the court, in modern, modernistic, London. The jury retired. 'Poor, simple Englishmen,' Lucetti said, as we sat waiting, with a few of his colleagues, in a pub nearby. 'What can they know? What can they decide?'

'They'll decide on suicide,' said one of the other journalists, a quiet, dark, cadaverous Venetian with long, lank black hair. 'Like good, simple Englishmen. It's what the police want. It's what the pathologist says. It's what the coroner seems to believe. What difference does it make? He's dead. Everybody knows he's been murdered, and almost everybody knows who did it.'

'There's insurance,' said a third journalist, Lucetti's colleague, a slender, bright-eyed, dark young man, with a short black beard.

'Ah, yes, there's that,' said the Venetian. 'Yes, suicide would knock that on the head, it's true; if it exists. Assuming there was anybody mad enough to insure him.'

Word passed back and forth from the court. The jury was still out: still out. 'Una giornata massacrante,' said Lucetti, 'a killing day.'

'And they've been told not to bring in an open verdict,' said his young colleague. 'What other verdict is possible?'

'Unlawful killing,' I told him, 'but they'll never give that.'

'They won't stay out much longer,' the Venetian said, caustically. 'The English like their weekend.'

At last the call came, and we trailed again up the stone steps, down the glassed-in walkway, through the odd antechamber, into the pristine court. The jury made their way in, looking wearily perplexed, and sat down on their benches. The coroner asked them formally for their verdict. The foreman stood up, and announced that it was suicide: 'He killed himself.' There was a majority of six to three.

'At least there are three English who haven't been fooled,' Lucetti whispered.

It was now that the coroner spoke again. If his summing-up had been a touch surprising, his *obiter dicta* were completely unexpected. First, he expressed his condolences to the Calvi family. Next, he eulogised the police, extolled the dedication of Barry Tarbun and his assistant John White. 'I do this deliberately,' he declared, 'because I am aware of comments reported in the Press about two weeks ago, allegedly made by a judicial colleague in Rome, in which it is alleged that he said there was no co-operation from the CID in this country and there was a cover-up by the CID. Unfortunately, all of us who find ourselves in high office are known to suffer from an obnoxious disease known as verbal diarrhoea. I can only believe that he was affected by such an acute attack that he made these remarks.'

'Sica, he means Sica,' whispered the Italians.

Coming out of the court, they were as astounded by the *obiter dicta* as by the verdict. 'But what did Sica say?' demanded Lucetti. 'Nothing like that, which I've ever seen. No criticism of that kind.'

He was speaking, I knew, of the Roman judge, Domenico Sica, engaged in the investigation: and I myself had been surprised, I myself was unaware of such words.

'It won't finish here,' said the Venetian, drily. 'The Calvis won't stand for this. They're bound to lodge an appeal.'

'Another appeal!' Lucetti said, and everybody laughed.

We went to an Italian restaurant in Soho for a noisy, convivial dinner, at which Lucetti was in his element, ribald and irreverent, savaging the inquest, ridiculing the jury's verdict. 'Ma che atleta, questo Calvi!' he cried. 'What an athlete, this Calvi! An Olympic triple jumper! Sixty-one years old, un grassoccio, a fat man, and he could leap over the bridge, fill his pockets with bricks, dance across the scaffolding, and hang himself!'

They all laughed, but I did not laugh with them. I had seen the hanging body. I had driven behind Calvi to Blackfriars.

In the weeks that followed, I thought a great deal about my own position and the ethics of it, somewhat consoled by the fact that the Italian Press had greeted the verdict so scornfully, that the Italian investigation into the death was continuing, that the Calvi family's lawyers were working to re-open the case. It was already plain, surely, that the verdict should have been an open one; the jury themselves had sharply disagreed.

Meanwhile, the calls that came from Sindona – who telephoned also to deride the verdict – suggested that Gelli's arrival was coming closer, and with each such call, my sense of anticipation grew. Un po Cagliostro. The more I thought about it, the more I thought about him, still less did the analogy seem relevant. A swindler, a trickster, a parvenu; he was all those things, which Cagliostro himself had been. But he was a warrior, too, a man who was ready to kill. Cagliostro had never been that, nor, for all the vertiginous social climbing, did his activities ever have the fearful range of Gelli's.

It was in thinking of Hawkwood that I began to gain more sense of Gelli. Moving from Hawkwood to thoughts of his Italian contemporaries, his fellow condottieri, and those who had followed them. Thoughts of the Malatestas and the Sforzas. Thoughts of those condottieri who, unlike the foreigners disdained by Gregorovius, had wanted more than money and the short-term advantage, and had gone for, and gained, political power. Through Hawkwood, I had come to understand myself better; through myself, in my unsought adventures, I had come to understand more of Hawkwood, but l'inglese italianato was still an Englishman, still, in the last analysis, a thought ingenuous, however sporadically ruthless, not ruthless enough, however avid for money, not avid enough for power.

337

And if Gelli was an upstart, if Gelli had risen from obscurity, then so had many of the great condottieri. Carmagnola had been a peasant. Gattamelata was a baker's son. The Sforzas were rough, illiterate farmers from the Romagna.

It was late in August that Sindona told me to be ready. 'I can't tell you what precise date. I can't tell you what exact place. Your best policy will be to go to Milan, maybe sometime next month, and wait there till you're contacted.'

'Are you *sure*?' I asked. 'You know what happened the last time. I really don't want to go through that, again. It's simply demoralising.'

'It wasn't his fault!' Sindona said. 'I've explained that to you. He didn't know when they were going to raid his villa. He's coming to Europe. He has important business there. He *has* to come. And while he's there, he's promised he will see you. He always keeps his word.'

Or makes good his threats, I thought. And so I was back in limbo, waiting for the call, wondering whether the call, when it came, would be any more productive than it had been the last time, wondering, on other, less frequent, occasions, mostly alone at night or in the early morning, what I had wondered so often before: how I would react, if I met him. For there was still only one question that I wanted answered: 'Why did you have my wife killed?' and in the nature of things, what answer could I hope for?

'I had no notion. It was unfortunate. It was quite fortuitous. It could have been anybody.' Which was precisely it; precisely the viciousness of it. That it could indeed have been anybody, it *had* to be 'anybody', the very randomness of it was its essence. At such moments, I sometimes heard in my head John Hawkwood's old battle cry of 'Carne, carne!' and longed for a bloody revenge. Then I would try to calm myself, to pursue comforting analogies. A bomber pilot, high above the city, might pull the lever to release his bombs, with no thought of whom they might destroy. Yet Gelli's bombs, the neo-Fascist bombs, had the innocent, the anonymous, the uninvolved, as their chosen targets. No, no, I would remind myself, whatever happens when I see him can happen only as a direct, chemical consequence of our meeting, as inexorably and as inevitably as when neutrons bombard an atom. It would resolve, too, I felt sure, the ambivalence of my feelings

338

about Italy, an ambivalence which had begun when Simonetta died, which had left me aware of what I had always disliked, rather than what I had loved, had left me unable to reconcile savagery with beauty, treachery with humanity, fanaticism with sensibility. To the fundamentally romantic, idealised picture of Italy had succeeded one of an Italy hard, brutal and devious, the sentimentality of the streets no more than a veneer over corruption and cruelty.

It was, untypically, on a warm September morning that Sindona called me again. I was sitting outside the cottage in my small garden, full of the flowers Simonetta had loved so much, many of which she had planted herself. There was clematis, there were exotic red and voluptuously overblown white roses, there were pale banks of hydrangeas, there were the tall, country garden regiments of sunflowers. 'Next week,' he said. 'Milan. I'll tell you when to go, and where to stay.'

The day before I was due to fly to Milan, alerted by Sindona, Lucetti telephoned me. 'They've got Gelli!' he said. The words astounded me. 'Who's got him? Where?'

'In Switzerland. We've just heard the news. He turned up in Geneva. Imagine it! Disguised; his hair dyed black, with a moustache. An Argentine passport. He walked into a bank; tried to withdraw over a hundred million dollars. Money that Calvi had left there, obviously. They got suspicious, and they had him arrested. Now he's in gaol. They'll try and extradite him to Italy; but they may not try too hard!'

'I see,' I said, dejectedly.

'What's wrong? You sound as if you're disappointed.'

'No, no,' I said, 'it's a surprise, that's all. I thought he was in South America.'

'Everyone did. But now he's in Switzerland. Plenty of people in Italy must be praying he never comes back. He knows a great deal more than Calvi. Do you still want to see him?'

'Yes, I do.'

'Well, if you hurry up, maybe you can visit him in prison, before he skips!'

I put down the phone with a feeling of dismay. The sole consolation was that this time, at least, I had not gone to Italy, to consume my substance in waiting.

Sindona's inevitable call came that night. 'I have bad news,' he said.

'I think I know what it is,' I told him. 'He's in gaol. In Switzerland. I heard from Italy.'

'That's true,' Sindona said. 'That's true, for the moment. But he won't stay there. They can never keep him. Not even there, a top security gaol, from what I'm told. Bars are not strong enough. Walls are not thick enough. And when he's out again – he'll see you.'

'Thanks,' I said laconically.

'Coraggio! He'll be out before you know it. Long before they can bring him back to Italy. He ran a risk. It was a lot of money. But Switzerland's not Italy. Wait and see!'

But for how long? Gelli was still not out of gaol by the following March, when the Calvi family's appeal against the inquest's verdict came to the High Court. Could he hope to escape from the Champ Dollon which seemed, by all accounts, a modern equivalent of the Château d'If, with its electronic gadgets, its floodlights, its watchtowers, its warders peering night and day out of glass booths? On the other hand, he had not yet been extradited to Italy, any more than had Sindona. Lucetti and Sindona might be proved right.

From a distorted sense of duty, or perhaps simply out of the depths of my aimless frustration, I drove down to the High Court to attend the Calvis' appeal. I was to be in the public gallery this time. Walking through the long, severe stone galleries of the courts, I came upon the Venetian journalist, on his way to the Press seats. 'They'll win,' he said indifferently, 'the case will be re-opened; and who cares? What difference will it make? They'll have another inquest. This time they'll bring in an open verdict; which they should have done before: and we'll be no closer to finding out what happened.'

The scene here in the High Court, more grand and formal than the Coroner's court, with all its polished pine, seemed farther away than ever from what had happened nearby that night, under the bridge. Here, there were judges in robes and full bottomed wigs, counsel in wigs and black gowns; a ceremony deeply and quintessentially English, to deal with an affair which was deeply and quintessentially Italian; an impossible marriage.

The Calvis, now, had a calm, comfortable QC who made

340

devastating sport of the coroner's summing-up. He was wrong, he said, to have accepted a statement from Carboni, when he was known to be a potential suspect. The movements of Calvi and Vittor on the night of the death were crucial; they should not have been presented to the jury as unchallengeable statements. 'The jury,' he said, 'listened to evidence from thirty-five witnesses for almost twice as long as a jury in a Crown Court has to listen to evidence.'

And I remembered how that summer day had dragged on and on into the gentle dusk of evening, how the jury had wearied and wilted on their benches. The coroner's phrases, in his summing-up, were exhumed, and held up quizzically for inspection. 'With any luck, we should be away from here quite soon.' Words which, at the time, had seemed to represent the view of everybody, after so many vexing hours, but here, in the cold light of court, took on a new significance.

'These were unfortunate words,' said the QC, 'and quite contrary to the current climate of thinking on how one should deal with a jury.' More words were held up to the light. An open verdict had been described as 'a super open door to scuttle through'. As a matter of logic, it was the only door through which the jury should have gone. There was talk of 'misplaced levity'.

Another QC spoke up for Carboni, who was on the run. The inquest had not been conducted with unseemly haste. Calvi had had a motive for self-destruction. Signor Carboni had not come for fear that he might be arrested, because of the help that he had given Calvi.

As the cultivated voices wove their skilful arguments, I felt that I was in no place to judge them. Like historians, theirs was a discipline that distorted, that wrenched action and passion out of context, into a safe and sterile moratorium, where words took the place of deeds. Whatever was discovered, whatever was decided, it would never really be the truth.

I did not return to London, and the High Court, the following day; I was sure there would be another inquest, now. And so it proved. It was set for June, almost a year after the first, a year after Calvi's death, and in the same, strange corner of the City; the Coroner's Court.

The coroner was, of course, a different one this time.

Carman, the QC who had mauled the original coroner, was representing the Calvis again, but this time, the immediate family was there: Signora Calvi herself, who had married him when he was young, diligent and obscure, her large, dark eyes full of woe, her fragile body looking as if it had been hollowed out by grief; her daughter Anna; and her son, the balding young Carlo. Vittor was to come; just released from gaol, his passport restored to him. Carboni, accused now of the attempted murder of Rossone, the vice-president of Calvi's bank, would stay in prison, but two of his pert young mistresses were to appear, an Italian and an Austrian, to explain why Carboni had placed fortunes in their Swiss bank accounts.

This time the jury were taken down to the river, where they descended the steps, looked over the parapet, and saw where Calvi had died. There would plainly be none of the 'unseemly haste' which Carman had excoriated in the High Court. The case, the 'show', as one felt moved to call it, would run for a whole fortnight now; while Lucetti and his fellow journalists sauntered, chattered, preened, debated and enjoyed themselves, and while I sat among them again day by day, feeling pity for the widow, while the police were made to seem so many coppers in a Harlequinade. 'It was treated as a normal suicide from the word go,' said one of them. A policewoman was reported to have said, 'The most unfortunate thing is that this Signor Calvi decided to kill himself or get himself killed under one of *our* bridges.' Much sport was made of this, but had she not seized the heart of the matter? What *was* it to do with London? Why *did* he come to London?

The dogged new coroner, in his confusion, once called Roberto Calvi to the witness box, rather than his son. 'Bello, bello!' muttered Lucetti. 'And if he *did* come?'

The Calvis' QC was as formidable as ever. He asked a policeman whether the death, with all its bricks and rocks, 'may have had a ritual significance of humiliation,' and the policeman said that he had thought of it. He asked Professor Simpson, the pathologist, whether it might have been easier for criminals to have taken Calvi down the river by boat (I'd never heard them mention a boat) rather than for so obese a man to have performed such feats with a pocketful of bricks.

342

Professor Simpson agreed that it would have been easier, 'as a matter of common sense'. He asked Professor Simpson to consider ethyl chloride, and curare-like drugs which relaxed the muscles. Professor Simpson gave serious consideration to them both.

Signora Calvi, under her great cloud of blonde hair, came into the witness box, and said some devastating things. Her husband had been threatening to name names. They were the names of important people in the Vatican. He had talked to the Pope himself about $1.4 billion which the Vatican Bank owed his own.

'Are you aware,' asked her counsel, 'that there are two very senior officials of the Vatican Bank whom the Italian authorities wished to charge with criminal bankruptcy?' At this, Lucetti dug me in the ribs, and pointed like a gun dog. Yes, she was, said Signora Calvi; the two wings of the Vatican, IOR and Opus Dei, were fighting one another.

'Did your husband tell you what he was planning to do about the appeal?'

'He wanted to make a deal, and if that didn't succeed, he wanted to go back to Italy to name names at his appeal.'

'Cretino,' Lucetti whispered in my ear. I shook my head in sorrow, thinking of how the man had doomed himself.

'My husband never stole anything,' said Signora Calvi, at which Lucetti elbowed me again, as he did once more when the Signora said that her husband's life insurance policy would, if he had not committed suicide, have been worth £1,750,000 to her. 'It is so painful to do this. I do this for my husband, not for the money.'

Drama upon drama. Next day we had Vittor, the small-time smuggler, freed from gaol, devoid of English, pitifully out of his depth. He was a man of trust, un uomo di fiducia, like Carboni. Why, he had not even been paid for what he'd done, though it was understood he would 'get something for it'. £4,400, Lucetti whispered to me. Young and pale, dark and good-looking, Vittor answered questions uneasily, in his north-east Italian. The Calvis' counsel called him a liar. He had invented a telephone call which Calvi was supposed to have made to his board of directors at the Banco Ambrosiano, at the very moment they were dismissing him.

'Are you lying about the conversation of the board meeting

343

of Banco Ambrosiano?' counsel asked him, and through his interpreter Vittor answered, 'Why should I tell lies?'

'To protect Carboni and yourself.'

And if he did not tell lies, what was his own, quite unprotected, life worth?

I found it harder and harder to join in the noisy euphoria of the Italian Press. It was a game to them, it was an increasing burden to me, yet still I somehow felt the duty and the urge to attend, each day.

But why had Vittor done nothing, that night, when he returned to an empty flat? Why, after sleeping soundly through the night, did he bolt for the airport? 'It occurs to me, and probably to this court,' said the coroner, 'that you made a very rapid departure.'

This time the coroner's summing-up seemed unexceptionable, an open verdict as probable as a verdict of suicide had been before. Again, I found myself in the nearby pub with Lucetti and his companions. 'Beata lei,' he said, 'lucky her. She'll collect all that insurance money now.'

It was three-and-a-half hours before the jury delivered their verdict; time in which the journalists gossiped, yawned, drank, speculated and periodically went off to phone their papers.

'Caro Tom,' said Lucetti, 'we Italians must apologise for the intrusion of our corrupt world into your simple, uncomplicated country. Next time we have a crooked banker on the run, we'll make sure that he goes to Spain or Germany.'

I tried to smile, but I still felt oppressed by it all, the dreadful resonance of the case, the fearful memories.

When the jury did come back, they returned their expected open verdict.

'Finita la commedia,' said Lucetti.

'Iniziata la commedia,' replied the Venetian. 'The play has just begun.'

And Gelli escaped. On an August morning. From the Château d'If. From the Champ Dollon, with its unclimbable outer fence, its twenty-two-foot wall, its arsenal of alarms, its multiplicity of gadgets, its watchtowers, its warders and its floodlights. Lucetti was on the phone to me; so was Sindona.

'You've seen?' Lucetti cried. 'Didn't I tell you that they'd never keep him? They allowed him visitors; did you know that? Secret servicemen came disguised as consular officials! Members of P.2 came. They let him take exercise on the roof: imagine that! He had messages sent him in Latin! It's amazing he even stayed in there as long as ten months! Those stupid Swiss; they were warned by the Italian police. They were even given names, the people who were planning to spring him! Now they're saying just one warder got him out! What a joke!'

My reaction was first of surprise, then of relief. However selfishly, I could not but be glad. Now I might see him. It had become, once again, a possibility.

'There you are!' Sindona told me. 'They couldn't keep him for long! He'll disappear for a while, as he did before. Then I'm certain he'll arrange to see you.'

'That's good,' I said, wondering, suddenly and perversely, why *I* could not have been among those streams of visitors, only to think, as soon as I put down the phone, that this would not be Gelli's way. He dealt in symbol, image, gesture, Masonic robes, bricks under Blackfriars Bridge. He would never have received me in gaol.

XIX

He received me in a catacomb. The Catacomb of Santa Cecilia, on the narrow, beautiful Via Appia Antica, so close to Rome, yet still so rustic. Sindona, who had called Rome a city of catacombs had told me to go to Rome. 'He'll be there,' he said.

It was December. The term had just ended. Oxford was dank and dull. I had been helping to interview college candidates, choosing bright scholarship boys, listening to their pert, precocious answers, wondering yet again about what they were doing, what I was doing, what any historians could usefully do. As I listened to them, as I questioned them, I was no better than any accessory to the hoax.

I still had my gun in Rome. In some curious, comforting way, it reconciled me to going. With my gun, I could always defend myself. With my gun, I could kill Gelli, for I knew I

345

might want to kill him. My gun was not at Stazione Termini any more; it was in an orange, plastic safe deposit box, which my little hotel in the Via Sistina kept almost casually locked up in a steel cupboard. Yes, they had said, a little puzzled by the request, they would keep my deposit box for me when I was not staying there, if I wished. They knew I would be back.

'Will he come this time?' I had asked Sindona. 'Are you sure he'll come? Are you sure they won't catch him if he tried to come? They've caught him once.'

'They won't catch him again, I can swear to you. But that's for you to decide, caro mio. It's a risk *you* have to run, as well as him. If you don't see him now, I couldn't tell you when he'll be back again.'

There was no option but to take the risk. And, if I failed, to go on taking the risk. Flying to Rome, I did not feel the tremendous apprehension I had felt when flying to Pisa. The sickening anticlimax there, the grinding suspense and the final disappointment, had made me cautious and pessimistic. Like some disillusioned but persistent lover, I must respond for ever to the call, however hopelessly.

I had no telephone number to ring this time, I must wait for a call, which made it worse. But the call came to the hotel, the very first evening I was there. It was a man's voice, a Roman accent. 'Ten o'clock tomorrow morning. The catacomb of Santa Cecilia. Join the German party. When the guide tells you you've reached the tombs of 150 AD, at the bottom of a steep staircase, go down to the steps on your right. No police unless you want to be shot.'

'I don't speak German!' I protested, but he had rung off. The tension, the excitement, returned, as great as they had been when I came to Tuscany and thought I would see Gelli in his villa. It was hard to fill the intervening hours, hard to eat, in my usual restaurant off the Via della Croce, hard to return the pleasantries of the agreeable waiters, hard even to think, to rehearse, for the thousandth time, now I seemed to have come so close, what I might say or do.

The question was still the mandatory one, 'Why did you kill my wife?' but there was an infinity of other questions that I wanted to ask him. I wondered what the symbolism of this catacomb might be, what significance I should read into it, what implicit warning it contained for me. Did it portend some kind of martyr's death? Would there, quite soon, be an inquest on *me*, a mysterious corpse, found in a catacomb, apparently dead from natural causes, police or no police, but in circumstances that suggested ritual murder? To kill him, if I could, seemed itself a symbolic act; with one shot to rid Italy, the world, of such a source of evil, at whose disappearance a whole, horrible conspiracy would surely vanish too.

Perhaps that was what I should do; find him and shoot him, forgetting all thoughts of deliverance, of a mystical resolution. If shoot him I could. For surely he might expect that, surely he would come prepared, even escorted. Someone else, presumably, would be there to shoot me, if I brought the police. He must have spent most of his life escaping traps, avoiding ambushes. What hope had I got, then, the merest amateur, whose escapes and successes had come through brief, black outbursts of irrational rage, rather than any kind of calculation?

Though it was early December, the next morning, as on my last winter visit to Rome, was freakishly fine, with that sun which makes sporadic, whimsical appearances out of season. The light was crystalline, the sky a translucent blue, but faintly flecked with cloud. I took a taxi to the catacomb, and as it drove along the Via della Mura Latina, I was lost to everything but the walls, the overhanging trees, the castellation, the cypresses and the umbrella pines, the perfect swellings of stone. The sight was a strangely purifying, pacifying one; it seemed to reconcile me in some way to the Italy I had discovered and would find now, *in excelsis*, down in the catacomb; an Italy that belonged underground, out of the light, though not in holy places.

The Via Appia Antica itself, with its own walls and trees, its narrow charm, sustained my sense of joy. When I came to the catacomb, walked down the sunlit path to the area above the tombs, I was purged of all anxiety, ready even to accept the modern, sentimental image of the saint, with the vase of daisies set before it. I looked at the Christ from ottocento, the smiling face of Saint Urbino, the unsmiling countenances of Byzantines. My gun was in my pocket, but I felt no need for it, now. I did not want to kill Gelli, not, at any rate, for the moment, not unless he provoked and enraged me.

Though the tourist season would not begin again till Spring,

347

there was still a number of people waiting to be taken below. A crackling loudspeaker called each group in turn; the English-speaking group, the French, the Italians. I looked at my watch. It was a quarter-to-ten. There were about half-a-dozen German speakers, mostly sleek, elderly men with brushed back silver hair, blue eyes, and those almost aggressively healthy complexions, their sturdy wives, a couple of blond, restless children in their teens. Now my stomach began to undulate. Our guide came to us; a small, bald, professorial Italian. The loudspeaker announced our descent. The Germans looked curiously at me as I joined them; one or two nodded, and I nodded back, hoping I would understand the guide, at least when he spoke of 150 AD. But he was Italian, I consoled myself; I could choose the right moment to ask him.

He led us, chatting amiably in German, down the steps to the catacomb. Whoever might shoot me, it would surely not be he. Steps, steps, steps. I had been up and down so many steps. I thought of the steps that led down from Blackfriars Bridge. Down, down to the lower level, to the parapet over which I had leaned to see Calvi's poor, plump body hanging from the scaffolding. Or the stone steps to the City Coroner's Court where, in that one, interminable day, an exhausted jury had stumbled to its strange decision, and where another jury, only weeks ago, had decided that they had been wrong.

The guide was continuing to talk, in German; I could follow words and phrases here and there. I had been in catacombs before, but never this one. There was more light here, electric lights, set in the walls, than in others I remembered from my distant schooldays, when we had even carried candles, and feared to be left behind, doomed for ever to wander the labyrinthine passages. Shelves after stone shelves, holding tomb after stone tomb. The guides talked, the Germans listened with Teutonic diligence. We turned corners, passed grilles, went on and on beneath the rough rock walls. It would have been hard to concentrate on what was said, even had I understood German. I would meet him, now, I was going to see him at last. My excitement grew intolerably, filling my stomach, making my heart beat frantically fast.

I heard it now, I was sure, a hundred and fifty, as we reached the steep staircase, going God knows where, as I saw,

348

to my right, the stairs that led dauntingly down. I fell behind the group, waited till it had followed the guide dutifully around a corner, then began to descend the stairs. Yet another flight of stairs. At the bottom I saw nobody, and felt a strange, sharp mingling of disappointment and relief. Then a voice spoke behind me, in Italian. 'Drop the gun.'

I looked quickly round. Behind me on the steps stood a heavily built man in a light grey suit. He wore dark glasses and seemed to have dark, curly hair, a black beard. He had his hand in the right-hand pocket of his jacket, as if he himself were aiming a gun at me. It was he! I was sure of it!

'Take it out and drop it behind you,' he said, in a voice in which I could now detect a Tuscan cadence. 'Then take five paces forward.'

I took out the little automatic, and let it fall behind me, as he had ordered. It did not worry me. I had been in no immediate mood to shoot him.

'I'm not Barbuti!' he said. 'Walk forward.' I took five steps, and stopped. Behind me, I heard him grunt, as he stooped to pick up the gun. 'You can turn now,' he said, and I did. He was disguised again, of course. The curly, dark hair must surely be a wig. The dark glasses hid his eyes. But the full, intransigent mouth, the sturdy build, were unmistakable.

'Why here?' I asked. It was not what I had planned to ask, and I was surprised to hear myself saying it.

'I thought it would appeal to you,' he said. 'As an historian. The beginning of the end of barbarism. The birth of Christianity. And now, of the new Fascism. È una santa simpatica. And a likable saint. The patron of music. I'm a lover of music. Besides, a catacomb is not a place where people would be looking for me. Another reason why I use them.'

There was a kind of mocking authority about his demeanour. He was smiling as he spoke. He had put my little gun in his pocket; he still had not shown his own. 'Were you going to shoot me?' he asked. 'Many people have tried.'

'I don't know,' I said.

'You think I killed your wife?'

'Well, didn't you?' I asked, with sudden bitterness.

He looked at me in silence for a while, with the same, lurking amusement. 'I don't think so,' he said. 'There was no

349

intention. No consciousness of it. Some of my people were blowing up trains at the time; that's all.'

'On your instructions.'

'Only generically. There *were* specific occasions. The important ones.'

'Like the Italicus? Like Bologna Station?'

'As I said, the important ones.'

'*Why!*' I shouted at him, and in the hollowed space, the cry seemed to swell and grow into a great, echoing vibration.

He put his finger to his lips, still smiling. 'You're an historian,' he said. 'Sindona told me. He said you know a lot about Italy.' His tone and his expression changed. 'You know *nothing* about Italy! Nothing at all! You know the surface of Italy! The foreigner's Italy! But I'll tell you about Italy! You know the most important thing about Italy?' I shook my head. '*It doesn't change!* It never will! It's the same! It's always been the same! Under the surface! Under all the economic miracles! The pretence at democracy! Under that dirty dolce vita and the filthy Communism and the stinking corruption of the Church! Italians respect what they've always respected! Strength! A leader!'

'Condottieri,' I said, at which he paused.

'If you like,' he conceded. 'You write about them, don't you? You see: I know that, as well. I always know about people. I know everything there is to know about people. That's my business. That's my secret. To know what they don't want me to know. So that they'll do what I want them to do. Condottieri. All right, call us condottieri. People Italians can look up to. Strong people. Decisive people. Ruthless people. Mussolini was a condottiere. People who lead. People who succeed: and they're always admired. It's what Italy admires. It's what Italy *wants*.'

'Does it want *you*?' I asked.

Again, he was taken fractionally aback. 'It wanted me,' he said. 'It still wants me; and it still fears me. It knows I shall be back. I frighten it, and because I frighten it, it respects me.'

'Like a capo mafioso,' I said.

He stepped forward, raised his hand, and for a moment, I thought he was going to strike me. 'You're an Englishman,' he said, letting his arm fall. 'You don't know the difference. A mafioso can never be a condottiere. He's a Sicilian. He comes

350

from a primitive culture. He's not a real Italian. He belongs to the world of crime.'

'Blowing up Bologna Station,' I said. 'Wasn't that a crime?'

'*No!*' he shouted at me, stepping forward, again, thrusting his face up against mine, like that of an enraged bull. 'You're English! You're a liberal! You'll never understand! How could it be a crime when the purpose is noble?'

'Like another Fascist state?' I asked, and he took out his gun, now, an automatic pistol, on which I recognised a silencer.

'What if I shot you?' he said.

'I don't care,' I told him, and he looked at me.

'No, I don't believe you do,' he said at last. 'You're a strange man. You've done things that surprised me. You've stabbed people. You've struck people down. You've threatened to kill them with a gun. I knew English like you in the war. Officers. Mild-looking men. You'd never believe them capable of what they did.'

'You did quite a few things in the war yourself.'

'I was a soldier. I was a Fascist. I believe I did my duty.'

'As in Yugoslavia.'

At this, he smiled again. 'You're well informed. Era un bel colpo. It was a great coup. The kind of coup Italians admire.'

'And Calvi's coup? Would they have admired that, if he could finally have brought it off? And Sindona?'

'Calvi was a clerk,' he said scornfully. 'Un impiegato. What he did, he did in comfort, in offices, with pens and ledgers. Sindona is a swindler.'

'Un po Cagliostro?'

He smiled again. 'Just an ordinary swindler. He'll come to no harm if he stays in prison, in America.'

'Otherwise you'd have him murdered, like Calvi.'

'You were lucky that I didn't have you killed as well. What were you doing with him? Why try to save a parasite like that? He'd sworn an oath. He knew what would happen to him if he broke it.'

He was hateful, beyond doubt, and yet I could not hate him, any more than I could hate the Italy he had revealed to me. He had evaded my question, but at the same time, he had answered it. If he had not decreed Simonetta's death, it could still not have happened without him.

'Turn round,' he said. He still had the gun in his hand. I obeyed, wondering, in a detached, dissociated way, what frightful thing was going to happen to me now, as I had when I was in my car, driving back towards London, with a revolver pointed at my head, or when the weasel took out the syringe. I had told him the truth, I did not care. I was reconciled to death.

He hit me; a dreadful agonising blow, at which my whole head seemed to burst with pain. Then oblivion.

When I woke, I was sprawled in the passage of the catacomb, at the bottom of the stairs, and Gelli of course had gone. I was alive. I was still alive. My head throbbed appallingly. I put my fingers to the back of my skull, and felt a huge swelling. I was in no hurry to leave the catacomb. Reclining again, I looked up at the stone roof and thought perhaps that the symbolism was more apt than he knew. Out of these depths, out of this dark maze, had come something which, for a time at least, had had its splendour and, in whatever form, had flourished and endured.

Gelli was right; his Italy was real and paramount, a lurid reality, for ever there beneath the surface, like a gigantic pit. But it was not the only Italy. I stood up. I would climb out of the catacomb. I would make my way, again, down the Appia Antica, past the sunlit turrets, the walls and trees of the Via della Mura Latina, and there, for just a little while, I would forget him again. There, in the moment, as the Master had once flutingly said, I would find an Italy that healed.